"A del[ight]... eccentric and colorful cha[racters]... [an]imals or spirits. Dixie Lyle will entertain the reader page after page."
—Leann Sweeney, *New York Times* bestselling author of the Cats in Trouble mysteries

"A clever new series that deftly blends cozy mystery with the paranormal, and that is sure to please readers of both genres . . . *A Taste Fur Murder* is original and witty, with a twisting plot that contains more than a few 'shocks'."
—Ali Brandon, author of the Black Cat Bookshop mysteries

"An enjoyable read for cozy fans."   —*RT Book Reviews*

To Die Fur

"Blends pet cemeteries, animal spirits, and a cast of zany human characters . . . those who read paranormal mysteries will enjoy."   —*RT Book Reviews*

Marked Fur Murder

"The sort of wild and wacky mystery that could only come from the pen of Dixie Lyle . . . I think you'll enjoy the ride."   —*The Bookwyrm's Hoard*

A Deadly Tail

"It's a witty, zany story whose delightful animals are vastly entertaining."   —*Kirkus Reviews*

ST. MARTIN'S PAPERBACKS TITLES BY DIXIE LYLE

A Taste Fur Murder
To Die Fur
Marked Fur Murder
A Deadly Tail
Purrfectly Dead

PURRFECTLY
dead

DIXIE LYLE

St. Martin's Paperbacks

This is a work of fiction. All of the characters, organizations, and events portrayed in this novel are either products of the author's imagination or are used fictitiously.

First published in the United States by St. Martin's Paperbacks, an imprint of St. Martin's Publishing Group.

PURRFECTLY DEAD

For information, address St. Martin's Publishing Group, 120 Broadway, New York, NY 10271.

www.stmartins.com

ISBN: 978-1-250-07844-5

Our books may be purchased in bulk for promotional, educational, or business use. Please contact your local bookseller or the Macmillan Corporate and Premium Sales Department at 1-800-221-7945, ext. 5442, or by email at MacmillanSpecialMarkets@macmillan.com.

Printed in the United States of America

St. Martin's Paperbacks edition published 2021

10 9 8 7 6 5 4 3 2 1

This book is dedicated to all those who stood by me through the past few years, which have been the hardest of my life—my agent, my editor, my friends and family, and of course, all my fans, who've waited patiently while I dealt with a wide variety of trials and tribulations. I hope my words bring you a little happiness, because that can be hard to come by these days.

—DL

Chapter One

I've seen our dinner guests wind up in handcuffs before, but never until after dessert. We have standards, you know.

"I always knew this day would come," sighed Oscar. Oscar is the son of Zelda Zoransky, whom everyone calls ZZ. She's also my boss.

"We all did, Oscar," I said cheerfully. "We just figured it would be you wearing these bracelets. I'm too smart to get caught."

Oscar took a sip of his drink. "And yet, you have been. The next thing you know, Mother will have you as an exhibit in her zoo."

"Just a second," ZZ said, frowning in concentration as she worked on my handcuffs. "I've almost got it . . ."

ZZ's dinner parties are legendary. They're the centerpiece of what she dubbed her *salons*, an invitation-only gathering on her estate. An eclectic mix of the famous, the brilliant, and the interesting show up on our doorstep to enjoy a few days of ZZ's generous hospitality, and the only payment she demands is that her guests attend the nightly dinners. The food is decadent, the bar is open, and the conversation is lively.

Me? I'm Foxtrot Lancaster. It's my job to coordinate all this, which is even trickier than it sounds. I forgot to mention ZZ's large menagerie of (formerly) homeless exotic animals, her many, ever-changing hobbies, and the extremely large animal cemetery that abuts the estate. You'd think the last one would be the easiest; I mean, how much work can overseeing a bunch of grave sites be? Make sure someone mows the grass and nobody knocks over the tombstones and you're done, right?

Not so much.

But right at the moment, I wasn't thinking about the graveyard. I was thinking about the handcuffs around my wrists and how long it would take ZZ to get them off. Also, the soup smelled amazing, and I really wanted to have some before it got cold.

"You're doing fine, ZZ," said the woman sitting to my right. The improbably named Maxine Danger smiled; the slinky cocktail dress she wore matched her hair and lips, all three as red as the bell on a fire alarm. ZZ's current obsession was lock-picking, which explained both Maxine's presence and my predicament: Ms. Danger was a professional escape artist. ZZ's attempt to free me, using only a bobby pin, from the handcuffs I wore was being supervised by someone who could perform that particular trick blindfolded and hanging upside down—and no doubt had.

"Almost, almost . . . no. Damn it," said ZZ. She wore a black-and-white gown that suggested a tuxedo, though she'd opted not to cover her orange curls with a top hat; she knew where the line between homage and parody was, even if she frequently ignored it.

"I am sure you can do it," said Hironobu Masuda. "This Smith and Wesson model is the most commonly used type." Masuda gave her an encouraging nod; while he wasn't wearing a top hat either, his tuxedo was old-school enough to justify one. He could even have added white gloves and a walking stick and gotten away with it.

"Easy for you to say," muttered ZZ. "You design the damn things."

"Anybody mind if I go ahead and have my soup?" asked Amos Clay. He was a husky man in his fifties with the reddish complexion of an outdoorsman and bristly white hair. His dark-gray suit looked like it was as uncomfortable being worn as he was wearing it. "I'm starving."

"Don't mind me," I said. "Leave me a little bread and water, that's all I ask. And maybe a rat, if you can spare one."

Clay nodded and started to eat. Despite his rough looks and demeanor, he was a scientist—a forensic scientist who worked for the Fish and Wildlife Service helping crack down on the illegal animal parts trade.

"Those will be obsolete before too long," said Esko Karvenin. He spoke in a careful Southern drawl, every word clearly enunciated. "Flex cuffs are becoming more and more common." Karvenin was tall and thin, with a beaky nose and a fringe of gray hair around his birdlike skull. A roundish tuft of gray beard sprouted from the end of his chin like an errant dandelion puffball. His suit coat was a brilliant green etched with thin, neon-blue lines.

"Strips of disposable, injection-molded nylon?" said Masuda. His offended tone suggested that even saying the words had contaminated his mouth. "Never. Such things can be defeated with a sharp knife or a common cigarette lighter. They cannot even be double locked, which leads to overtightening."

"Definitely a problem," said Keene. "In fact, I much prefer the padded kind. Prevents chafing." Keene was our semiresident musician, a British rock star who liked the estate so much, he was practically a fixture. His tux wasn't as elegant as Masuda's, but Keene claimed it had once belonged to Harry Houdini and that he'd paid an extravagant amount for it on eBay.

Karvenin shook his head. "What y'all are talking about are the originals, which were really no more than ordinary cable ties. The technology has come a long, long way since those humble beginnings—they even have versions that use a key. And fireproofing them is hardly difficult."

"Or necessary," said Summer Coyne. She was Maxine's assistant, a short blonde in a short, black skirt, with a dazzling smile and huge eyes. "I can show you how to get out of a pair of those in about thirty seconds. *Without* using a lighter, a bobby pin, or a knife."

"Got it!" declared ZZ triumphantly. The cuffs popped open, and I was free. I picked up my soup spoon gratefully and took a mouthful before ZZ decided to demonstrate anything else.

"Well done," said Maxine. "You're a fast learner, ZZ."

"With her attention span, she has to be," said Oscar. "Summer, would you care to share *your* method with us?"

"For removing cable tie cuffs? Sure," said Summer. "First, you have to be reasonably limber."

"That leaves out my son," said ZZ. "The only thing flexible about him is his ethics."

"Touché," said Oscar with a smile, raising his glass in a salute. In his spotless, white dinner jacket, he looked like he could be toasting the launching of a yacht instead of a soup course.

"Well, the limber part only matters if your hands are cuffed behind your back," said Summer. "You need to pass your hands under your bottom and then pull your legs through so your hands are in front. Let's just assume we've already done that part, and I'll demonstrate the rest. Of course, for that, I'll need a cable tie. Maxine? Do you have one handy?"

Maxine pretended to pat down invisible pockets in her

skintight dress. "No, I don't think I do . . . but I'm pretty sure I saw one in Oscar's soup."

Oscar frowned, dipped his spoon into his soup and lifted a strip of bright-yellow plastic tied in a loop out of the bowl. "Ah," he said. "Well, at least it isn't a fly."

Maxine took it from him and wiped it off with her napkin.

"Perfect," said Summer. She held her hands out before her, fists clenched and thumbs facing up. "Maxine, if you would?"

Maxine looped the plastic around Summer's wrists, threaded the end through the locking mechanism, and pulled it taut.

"Good," said Summer. "Now, this is a heavy-duty tie, rated to a hundred and seventy-five pounds. Pretty strong, right? But I'm going to show you how to *break* it using nothing but leverage and your own muscles.

"Now, cable ties work on a very simple system. The strip has little plastic teeth along its length, and when the strip is threaded through the locking mechanism, a tiny plastic tab lets those teeth go one way and only one way. Pull the other way, the tab jams against the teeth. That's why they can be tightened but not loosened."

"But *you* can loosen them?" asked Amos Clay.

"Nope. In fact, I'm going to do something counter-intuitive—I'm going to tighten them. But first—" Summer held up her wrists. "As you can see, Maxine attached them with the locking mechanism facing down. The first thing we want to do is reverse that so the lock is on top. The easiest way is to use your teeth, like so." She bit down on the strap and tugged, gradually making the loop rotate until the lock was centered on top of her wrists.

"Now, I make sure the tie is as tight as possible." She grabbed the end of the strip with her teeth and pulled, tightening the loop until it dug into the skin of her wrists.

"And here's the final step. You raise your hands high and bring them down onto your stomach as sharply as possible. At the same time, flare your elbows to the sides and flex your back muscles like you're trying to touch your shoulder blades together. It may not work the first time, but keep trying; no cable tie is tough enough to resist for long."

She demonstrated. It took her only two tries before the locking mechanism broke and she was free. She stood and took a little bow as we all applauded.

In the middle of the applause, the look on Summer's face changed. She went from a big, beaming smile—she had the kind of smile that took up half her face—to a look of surprise, to a flash of panic.

Then she fell over.

We all leaped from our chairs. "I'm okay, I'm okay," Summer said from the floor. "But can someone help me with *these*?"

She stuck two high-heeled feet up in the air, resting her calves against the edge of the table. Her legs were bound from ankle to knee with at least twenty bright-yellow cable ties.

"Well, well, well," said Karvenin. "You do throw the most interesting soirees, Ms. Zoransky. Are you planning on producing a pterodactyl after dessert?"

Maxine shook her head sadly. "Summer, Summer, Summer. How many times have I told you, never show up to one of ZZ's dinner parties unless you're prepared . . . ?" She reached and plucked a flower from the centerpiece, and suddenly it was a pair of wire cutters. She used it to clip apart the cable ties, one by one.

"Outstanding," said Keene, chuckling. "What are you going to do for an encore? Should I be checking my underwear for the abrupt appearance of a chainsaw and several lobsters?"

Maxine smiled coolly at him. "From what I've heard,

that's just another Saturday night for you. But in any case, I wouldn't impose that sort of cruelty on a lobster; not exactly in the spirit of the event, is it?"

The event she was talking about wasn't the dinner—it was the upcoming fundraiser for ZZ's charitable foundation. While there were many causes ZZ championed, the one nearest and dearest to her heart was the rescue of exotic animals from a variety of sources: roadside attractions with appalling conditions, private citizens who could no longer care for their unusual pets, bankrupt zoos or circuses. ZZ's foundation did its best to find new homes for these animals, and when that wasn't possible, she took in the orphans herself. The Zoransky menagerie was quite extensive, with residents that ranged from large creatures like hippos to tiny ones like lizards, and they had their own vet to look after them.

"True, very true," Keene replied. "And since I've already agreed to perform at said soiree, I think I'm entitled to know what sort of act I'm expected to follow. What do you have planned in that devious but oh-so-stylish noggin? Give us a preview."

"A preview is precisely what I have in mind," said Maxine. "I like to test out escapes in front of a small audience before I perform them on stage, and this seems like the perfect venue. So, you unfortunate victims—I'm sorry, I meant to say lucky volunteers—get to see my latest escape before anyone else does. If everything goes well, I'll be officially debuting it to the public at the charity gala."

"And if it doesn't," said Summer, "you're all invited to the funeral. There'll be a buffet!"

"How dangerous is this escape in terms of bodily damage?" asked Karvenin. "Or, to put it another way—in the unfortunate instance of catastrophic failure, will an open casket become out of the question?"

"Never mind that," said Oscar. "What's truly important is whether or not an open bar is out of the question. The answer is always no."

"Well then," said Keene. "That all sounds very intriguing and thrilling while still remaining completely vague. Can we convince you to part with a few details? A preview of the preview, so to speak?"

Maxine nodded. "I think I can do that. Mister Masuda here is an expert locksmith; I've commissioned him to make a special lock, with only a single key in existence. The whereabouts of that key are unknown to me; Mister Masuda will produce it shortly before the escape itself. It will be used to lock the trap, and then the key will be sealed into a block of solid, transparent plastic that will remain in plain sight. The trap will be airtight; I'll have to escape before my air runs out."

"Sounds frightfully dangerous," said Keene.

"Especially to my paycheck," said Summer. "If the boss doesn't make it, I'm unemployed. Say, where do you keep the fire axes around here, anyway?"

"Which reminds me," I said. "I had the delivery men put your equipment in the ballroom—it came while you were in the pool. I double-checked everything against the manifest, but none of it's been unpacked; if you need any tools, like crowbars or utility knives—"

I stopped myself. "What am I saying? You just turned a rhododendron into a pair of wire cutters. We'll probably wind up borrowing tools from you."

Maxine took a sip of red wine. "Thank you, Foxtrot. Summer and I will go over the crates first thing in the morning—until then, I plan to enjoy myself. Tonight we celebrate life; when the Grim Reaper's in your rearview mirror, there's only one possible response."

Summer and Maxine raised their glasses in unison.

"*Go faster!*" they chorused, and we all lifted our own drinks and joined them in the toast.

But no matter how fast you go, the Reaper always catches up.

After dinner, I took my dog around the grounds for a walk. It was a warm spring night, the air rich with the smells of plant life waking and stretching. My pooch is an Australian cattle dog, which means he looks like someone smushed the bottom half of a golden retriever with the top half of a black-and-white border collie. He has one blue eye and one brown eye, he's very smart, and his name is Whiskey.

Also, he's a telepathic shape-shifting ghost.

. . .

Still with me?

It's okay if you're not. Some people are all right with the kooky boss and the eccentric guests and the on-site zoo, but as soon as I mention the large, animal graveyard, they start edging toward the door. That's fine, too; not everyone has my high weirdness threshold, and even those that do find that talking animals are where they draw a line in the sandbox.

Not that Whiskey actually talks; that'd be ridiculous. Dogs' mouths aren't shaped right for human speech—though I have heard some eerily accurate howling along to pop songs—so Whiskey communicates with me mind-to-mind, which is *so* much easier to believe that I almost never tell people.

And he's dead. I already mentioned that, right? Being dead, he's made of ectoplasm, which looks and feels normal and totally isn't. He can alter it to look like any dog breed, big or small, which makes sense since it's actually a supernatural material that doesn't have to follow the laws of physics—

Damn. Lost another one.

But *you're* still here, so I guess I'll keep going. Where was I?

Right. Walking my ghost dog.

[You know,] Whiskey's deep, cultured voice said inside my head, [I worry about you talking to yourself, sometimes.]

"I wasn't talking to myself, I was thinking to myself. Or, as it's sometimes known, *thinking*."

[It sounded suspiciously like a conversation, to me.]

"Oh, was I braincasting again? Sorry." Occasionally I thought a little too loudly, and Whiskey picked it up. "Sometimes the only way I can make sense of a situation is to pretend to explain it to somebody that doesn't know what's going on. A nonexistent sympathetic ear, sort of."

He glanced up at me with a worried look. [*I'm* a sympathetic ear.]

"Yeah, but my make-believe listener has two advantages you don't: one, they never interrupt with any concerns of their own; and two, they have no knowledge of the situation. This imaginary ignorance forces me to describe all the relevant details of an ongoing situation in a clear and concise manner, which often leads me to a better understanding of the situation myself. It's so useful, I'm thinking of writing a book."

A second voice, raspier and more casual, spoke up in my head: <*Writing a book sounds like a great idea. It'll give me more lap time.*>

That voice was Tango. She used to be my cat, back in her sixth incarnation, but now she lives here, on the Zoransky estate. She doesn't really belong to anyone—cats never do—but my boyfriend, Ben, is the one that feeds her. She's reincarnated, not dead, and communicates the same way

Whiskey does. Well, the same way but with a lot more snark in it. She's retained her appearance from when she was my childhood pet, a gorgeous, black-and-white tuxedo cat with an almost question mark on her forehead.

She came strolling out of the moonlit shadows like she owned them and joined us on our walk. *<Hang on, Toots. Sounds like you've been doing this talking-to-the-not-there thing for a while, right?>*

"Mostly since you two showed up. Up until then, I felt like my life was more self-explanatory." I stopped to let Whiskey sniff at some bushes. He might be a spirit, but he's still a dog.

<Right. And this fictional person you've been talking to, it's still the same one? Not a new one every time?>

I frowned. "I hadn't really thought about it. I guess it's the same one . . ."

Whiskey was really intent on that bush. Tango sat down and started to groom, which is her default activity for just about any situation. *<So do you explain the same thing over and over? Tell them things that, by this point, they should already know?>*

"Um. Sometimes?"

<Why? Do they have amnesia or something?>

"Of course not. Why would they have amnesia?"

<How would I know? You're the one that made them up.>

[Tango. Quit tormenting Foxtrot.]

Tango gave her head an elegant, feline shake. *<I'm the one being tormented here. You think you're the only person that hears her braincasting? I swear, if I have to listen to one more explanation of who we are and what we can do, I'm gonna hack up a hair ball. Let's see her narrate that.>*

"But—if I repeat myself sometimes, it's because—okay, actually I sometimes imagine I'm explaining this to, like, a *group* of people—"

Whiskey finished his inspection of the foliage and trotted over. [It's not important, Foxtrot. *Is* it, Tango?]

Tango stopped her grooming and looked up innocently. <*Nah. Just making conversation, is all.*>

"And sometimes one of them leaves, because things have gotten too strange or maybe they have to go to the bathroom, I don't know—"

And that's when my phone buzzed. Not unusual, except that particular buzz was the default setting for any number I didn't recognize. Again, not unusual—except I'm a little obsessive, so I've assigned different ringtones for different area codes, too. I may not always know who's calling, yet at the very least, I can tell where they're calling from.

But not this time.

I dug out my phone and looked at the screen. UN-KNOWN CALLER was all it said. I may not have every area code in the world logged, but I do have every continent and most of the countries. Where was this guy calling from, the moon?

I hesitated then hit ANSWER.

"Hello?"

The voice on the other end was smooth, male, and of indeterminate age. "Hello, Foxtrot. My name is Lockley Hades. Do you know who I am?"

I did, in fact. Lockley Hades was a well-known stage magician and illusionist, one who'd been waging a very public feud with Maxine Danger for the past year. They traded insults on Twitter, tried to outdo each other on stage, even threatened to reveal the other's methods. I was half convinced it was all one big publicity stunt—they were performers that specialized in fooling their audience, after all—but only half. When I jokingly asked Maxine when Hades was going to join her on tour, she'd given me a very, very cold look and said, "When I can pull his ashes out of a hat." I didn't bring up the subject again.

"Mr. Hades," I said. "I know who you are. How can I help you?"

"By listening to me very carefully and then considering my words with just as much attention. I'm a very careful man, Foxtrot; like you, I do my research. So I know how clever and resourceful and open-minded you are, which is why you're getting this call as opposed to your lover, Ben."

You know that horrible feeling you get in the pit of your stomach when someone gives you really bad news? Or that shiver you get when something really, really creeps you out? How about both together?

Sure you do—especially if you're a woman. The stalker vibe. Being in the crosshairs for no other reason than existing.

That's a bad feeling, but women have been experiencing it literally forever and have evolved ways to deal—none of them effective enough, unfortunately, but at least we can still function. If, you know, we don't get murdered.

Work as a professional assistant to famous people long enough, though, and you'll experience something even worse: realizing that the attention of said stalker is focused not on you but someone you care about. Someone you're supposed to keep safe.

Okay, maybe that's more a bodyguard's job than a personal assistant's, but I have an overinflated sense of responsibility, a nonstop work ethic, delusions of grandeur, and just a touch of martyr syndrome. So, when I get that shivery, sinking feeling from a potential lurker/obsessive/serial killer, I immediately go into full red-alert mode.

"I don't think I'm the one you need to speak to," I said

calmly. "You want Shondra, our security director. She's smarter than I am, more determined, and *extremely* good at her job. Really, she makes me look like an amateur."

"Yes, she's very talented. But she's not dating a Thunderbird, is she?"

And that's when the bad feeling in my gut leapt straight up my spine and hit the base of my skull, like one of those old-timey strongman tests where you hit a scale with a big wooden mallet and it sends a little metal striker up to ring a bell.

[Foxtrot, what's wrong?] Whiskey asked.

<*Yeah, what's going on, Toots?*>

I held up a hand for quiet. Both of my partners could tell something was seriously ungood, but I couldn't stop to explain until I understood it myself.

"Yes," said Hades. "I know that Ben Montain, Zelda Zoransky's personal chef and your paramour, is descended from a Cowichan tribe that intermarried with a race of supernatural, weather-controlling bird people. I know his sister, Anna, was one, too, and so is Teresa Firstcharger, the woman currently training him in his abilities."

There goes the rest of my audience, I thought to myself. *And I haven't even gotten to the electric elephant that lives in the haunted animal graveyard yet.* "You seem to know a lot. Are you calling to brag, blackmail, or just waste my time?"

"None of the above. I'm calling to warn you. Powerful beings have powerful enemies, as I'm sure you know. Thunderbirds are no exception."

I knew exactly what he meant. The Thunderbirds' ancient foes were a serpentine race called the Unktehila, predatory shape-shifters that were able to hypnotize their prey via a mystic gem embedded in their skulls. The Thunderbirds had driven the snakes into the depths of the ocean, and the Unktehila had never forgotten or forgiven.

"Let's say I know what you're talking about," I said. "What are you calling to warn me about? Are the Unktehila on their way?"

"On their way?" He chuckled. "They've already arrived. One of them calls herself Maxine Danger."

I allowed myself a moment of hope. *Right, sure, your biggest rival is also a mind-controlling, shape-changing underwater snake. Wow, when you name-call, you really go all out, don't you?*

But he knew about Ben, and Teresa, and Anna. He knew about the Unktehila. And, in fact, I'd been expecting something like this for a while; Eli had warned me the Unktehila had returned.

"If that's true," I replied, "why the warning? What's your part in all this?"

"My part in this will become clear soon enough. And the reason I'm calling to warn you is simple: there's going to be a war."

Chapter Two

A war.

A *supernatural* war.

A war where one side tossed around tornadoes, blizzards, and thunderstorms, and the other could take on anyone's appearance and control minds. Sort of like Vietnam, if you replaced the guys in helicopters with multiple clones of Thor and the Viet Cong with the cast of *Invasion of the Body Snatchers*. And threw in some hypnosis, just for fun.

The Vietnam conflict hadn't gone so well for the guys in the helicopters. Even without the evil-Jedi mind tricks.

"So," I said to my phone, "why are you telling me? Is this a declaration of hostilities? If you want me to choose sides, I'm pretty much already committed."

"No, Foxtrot. I don't want this war to happen any more than you do."

"Okay. I guess that opinion qualifies you as A, not insane, and B, a potential ally. Tell me more."

"I will, but for a more productive discussion, we're going to need more than just words. Skype would be better. I'll contact you tomorrow, and we can continue this face-to-face."

He didn't ask for my username, but anyone that could pull that hidden-area-code trick probably didn't need to. I wouldn't be terribly surprised if he pulled my social security number from his belly button—though I doubted that was why he wanted to see my face. "Hold on. If Maxine is an Unktehila, I'm going to need more than just a warning. Is Ben in danger? Is Teresa? Why is Maxine here?"

"Tomorrow." He ended the call.

I put my phone away. Both Whiskey and Tango were staring at me with worried eyes. I took a deep breath then relayed what I'd just been told.

When I was done, there was a moment of silence. Tango was the first to respond. <*I'm not afraid of snakes. Let 'em come.*>

[*That's* your response? We've just been informed of a potential battle between two immensely powerful supernatural forces—with us in the middle—and the most vital information you have to offer is your own lack of common sense?]

<*Not lack of common sense. Lack of* fear. *As in, scared, not being.*>

"Yes, Tango, we get it. You're completely over your fear of snakes. Now, can we—"

<*Over? That sounds as if there was once something to be* over, *which there was not. Ever.*>

Whiskey growled in exasperation. [Fine. If we postulate that you are not now, nor have you ever been, frightened in any degree by any sort of reptile that has ever existed, including but not limited to dinosaurs, mythical nine-headed monsters of the Underworld, and world-devouring Ouroboros serpents or ninja turtles, *then* can we move on to a productive discussion of our options vis-à-vis surviving the approaching apocalypse?]

Tango sniffed in a disapproving way. <*Yeah, as soon*

*as you calm down. We have important things to talk
about, so stop making such a fuss.>*

Whiskey shot her a look sharp enough to shave with.
[Indeed,] he growled.

I'm a multitasker. I get things done at the same time
as I'm doing other things, and the process works like
this: thing one is important, thing two is *very* important,
thing three is something I do all the time, and thing four
doesn't matter much at all. I start doing thing three immediately because I can do it without thinking, and I start
thinking about thing two. If any of the things can be done
simultaneously with thing three, I do that, and at the first
possible opportunity, I tackle thing two, since I've had
time to plan a course of action. While doing these things,
there are always gaps, little moments when I have to wait
for something to happen—a phone to ring, a file to load,
a fuse to burn down—and during these gaps, I work on
thing one if possible and thing four if not. Got it?

Thing two, at the moment, was the impending war.
Thing three was listening to the verbal sparring between
my two partners, which I could pretty much tune out by
now from being so used to it. In fact, while they traded
insults, I was actually thinking hard about good old thing
the second.

"We need to talk to Eli," I said.

[I agree,] Whiskey said.

*<You just had to go ahead and blurt that out, didn't
you?>*

[You have a different opinion? What a shock.]

It was Tango's turn to glare at him. *<No, I think Eli
needs to know, too. But since you said it first, I'm forced
to . . . agree with you.>*

[How tragic.]

"This can't wait," I said, already hurrying down the
path. Whiskey and Tango trotted to catch up with me.

"Only . . ." I stopped abruptly, and so did my partners. "Something smells."

[*Everything* smells, Foxtrot. Well, almost everything.]

I smiled. "Good point, doggy. But what I mean is that the phone call I just got—and what we learned from it—has a decidedly peculiar aroma. When someone drops a piece of information right in your lap like this, they always have an agenda. They're pushing a button and expecting a response. A *predictable* response."

[Such as immediately rushing off to inform your superior of your news?]

"Exactly. Eli's hard to pin down sometimes, but he always shows up when I really need to talk to him. Maybe this is a way to draw him out in the open."

[In which case it's the *last* thing we should be doing.]

<*But the Unktehila are master manipulators. They know we'd figure that out, so they actually told us this to ensure that we* wouldn't *go to Eli.*>

I held one hand up in the air and the other to my forehead. "Stop. This is how it starts—don't you remember what happened last time? The paranoia, the second-guessing each other, the mistrust?"

[You're describing a cat's natural behavior.]

<*Yeah. What's your point?*>

"We've got to be smart about this. We talk to Eli, but not directly; Whiskey, you get a message to him via afterlife channels then come right back. We should have code words to ID each other that we only use telepathically—I don't think the Unktehila can read private thoughts."

I switched to thought mode myself. *My word will be, um,* whirligig.

<*Um* whirligig *it is. Mine will be* Tangotangotangoqueen-oftheuniverse.>

[Mine shall be *a total lack of surprise.*]

<*That's more than one word.*>

[How observant of you. Are those blinders custom-made, or do you buy them in bulk?]

"Whiskey, Tango, and I'll talk to Ben. Come back as soon as you can, and meet us in the kitchen. Go!"

Whiskey didn't even bother with a parting shot—when there's a job to do, he's all business. He took off into the darkness.

<*I hate to be the pessimist of our group, but the phrase "divide and conquer" might also apply right about now. I'd never admit it to Whiskbroom, but you just sent our muscle sprinting for the horizon.*>

"Whiskey can take care of himself. In a fight between him and another shape-shifter, my money's on the one who faced down an electric elephant. Which is him."

<*Sure, but if I were the bad guy, right about now is when I'd go all monstery and eat you.*>

I put my hands on my hips. "Well? I'm waiting." She puffed herself up like a Halloween cat, but I wasn't falling for it. "Nice try. Come on, let's go talk to Ben."

She deflated and trotted along behind me, muttering, <*Ooooooh, so confident. Maybe I'm just lulling you into a false sense of security, how about that? I could* still *be a monster . . .* >

I bit my lip and refrained from answering.

Unfortunately—as is often the case in my job—I didn't quite make it.

When I first became a professional assistant, I thought the right approach to problem-solving was the linear one: define the problem, find the solution, launch yourself like a missile at the point where they intersect. But in real life, that rarely works; too many variables pop up along your trajectory, forcing you to veer and slow and ricochet before you can get to where you need to be. It's more like billiards than football, and more like ping-pong than billiards. In fact, playing ping-pong with two paddles and thirteen balls is probably the analogy I should have used in the first place, but I did get there eventually.

See what I just did?

So my methodology these days tends to be more reactive and bouncy than arrow-straight touchdown passes, and I'm comfortable with that. On my way to warn my boyfriend about an impending threat? Check. Able to deal with possible interruptions/distractions/obstacles? Also check.

Expecting possible threat to *be* one of said interrupting distractional obstacles? Check just bounced.

"Foxtrot!" said Maxine Danger. She still wore that stunning, shimmery red dress, but despite that, she'd managed to appear out of nowhere. Well, not nowhere, exactly—she was about to enter the garden just as Tango and I were leaving it. Which meant she was blocking the path, and I couldn't really go forward unless I pushed past her or dived sideways into a rosebush. Not optimal.

"I was hoping we'd have a moment alone," she said, smiling. "In fact, I came out here looking for you. Got a minute?"

"Of course," I said. *Got a minute?* is a question I answer so often in the affirmative—whether it's true or not—that my response is practically Pavlovian. "What can I do for you?"

Tango's reaction was less welcoming. Her back went up, and she hissed like a wounded tire. *<Run, Foxtrot! I'll hold her off!>*

Calm down, kitty. Let's see what she has to say, first.

Maxine glanced at Tango, but the look on her face was more sad than surprised. "Yeah, I'm afraid most animals don't really like me. Cats, dogs . . . and certain large birds. Did you know I spent most of yesterday trying to make friends with your ostrich? I finally got him to come near me, but that was largely through bribery—his keeper let me feed him. Did you know an ostrich will eat practically anything? According to Carol, they've found everything from car keys to old socks in their stomachs. You'd think I'd have more appeal than that, but apparently not."

I resisted the urge to take a step backward. "Really? I'm sure they wouldn't feel that way if they knew all you were doing to help them."

"I'd like to think so, but I doubt it. It's an instinctual thing."

That sounded dangerously close to the kind of admission a killer makes just prior to adding another victim. "What did you want to talk to me about?"

She hesitated then squared her shoulders. "I know your boyfriend, Ben Montain, is a Thunderbird. As is Teresa Firstcharger. Don't ask me how I know that, but I do. And I'm not here to expose them or anything like that. I'm here with a message."

A message. I hate messages. Memos are good, notes are fine, emails and texts are my bread and butter, but messages? Messages are *fraught*. Messages are the kind of thing sent by Mafia bosses and evil dictators and serial killers. Messages are to communication what Darth Vader was to parenting.

"Which is?" I asked, preparing to run for my life.

"He's in danger. So is Firstcharger. An ancient enemy of theirs is about to declare war—"

I held up a hand. "Hang on."

This was not, I assumed, the usual reaction she got to apocalyptic pronouncements. She not only stopped talking, she looked baffled.

"War between the Thunderbirds and the Unktehila, right?" I asked.

"What? Yes, but how—"

"It's my job to know. Here's the part where you drop

a few cryptic, ominous hints before vanishing into the shadows, right? Then we do this dance where you seem to be on my side but have a dark secret you can't confide in me until later, and then it turns out you're actually . . . what?"

She was quick to recover. "Late to the party, apparently. I take it the very capable Ms. Firstcharger informed you? That means things are much, much worse than I expected."

"Teresa didn't tell me a thing. And so far, neither have you."

She considered this then nodded. "Okay, cards on the table time. I'm an Unktehila myself. Would you like proof, or will you take my word for it?"

<Don't trust her, Toots.>

Maxine looked at Tango. "I don't expect her to, Miss Cat." So she could hear Tango—somehow I wasn't surprised. "But if she doesn't at least listen to me, many people are going to die."

"Let's say I believe you," I said, before Tango got her claws out. "Why are you telling me this? Is this a warning or an opening shot?"

"It's an attempt to stop the damn thing before it starts. I'm not your enemy, and I don't want a war. Do you?"

"That depends. Not a big fan of armed conflict in general, but some wars are worth fighting. From what I've heard, your people pretty much brought what happened down on themselves."

"That may be. But it was a long time ago, and it didn't happen to me—it happened to my ancestors. Mine and your boyfriend's."

So she was like Ben? Not so much a flat-out mythical being as descended from one? If true, that could make a huge difference. "Ben's family tree has its share of bird's nests, but that's not all it holds—there's a lot of Cowichan in there, too. Are you saying the same thing happened with the Unktehila?"

"Yes. Not so hard to believe, is it? Both races are shape-changers, and we both had our reasons to stay hidden. The Unktehila intermarried with the human race long ago, and we've kept to ourselves ever since—just like the Thunderbirds."

That didn't exactly jibe with the story I'd been told, but I didn't think now was the time to bring that up. "Until recently."

"Yes. Something's changed. It's waking up power that's slept in our genes for generations, and that power is not going unnoticed. Plans are being made, alliances formed. The same kind of thing that always happens when power is unleashed." She smiled. "I guess that was the myste-rious, cryptic part of the conversation. I'd go into more detail, but I forgot to bring the suitcase with my charts and graphs."

Not that she'd share those, even if they did exist. War was 10 percent battle and 90 percent politics, and the most effective weapon in either was information. I didn't ex-pect her to start throwing ammunition at me until she had to—I was just glad we were exchanging words instead of blows. I'm not much for knockdown, bare-knuckle brawl-ing, but that's okay; you can do more damage with your wits than your fists.

This wasn't a battle, though, not yet. It was an ex-change of information, and she'd already given up a fairly important piece—admittedly, one I already knew, but if we were going to build any sort of trust, I needed to give her something in return.

"Okay," I said. "Here's why I found your big reveal to be less than earth-shattering news. Your pal Lockley Hades just called me and told me pretty much exactly the same thing—including outing you as not one hundred percent human."

Her eyebrows went up, and then her expression darkened. "Hades? That . . . that . . . I should have known. Listen, you can't trust him. The only reason he told you was so he could poison you against me. He must have figured out that I was here and what I planned to do."

"And why would he do that, exactly?"

"Because," she said, her voice intent, "Hades is an Unktehila as well. One that very much *wants* the same war I'm trying to prevent . . ."

"Um," I said, trying to keep the panic out of my voice. "Quick question. Can you and Thunderbirds sense each other? Recognize each other on sight regardless of the shape you're in?"

"What? No. Unktehila can't even sense each other— we're really good at staying hidden. I wouldn't have even known Hades was another Unk if he hadn't told me himself—"

"Good. Now shut up and turn around."

Teresa Firstcharger was striding toward us in the moonlight.

Her First Nations heritage showed through much stronger than Ben's; her skin was duskier, her hair long and black and straight. She was tall and statuesque, with cheekbones like razors and the kind of dazzling white smile that makes dentists swoon. She was also smart, ambitious, and tough, with the political ruthlessness that made for a natural leader.

Oh, and she could boss around anything from a dust devil to a hurricane like it were a trained poodle.

Thunderbirds had a matriarchal society; she wasn't just Ben's teacher, she was a five-star general to his foot soldier. One of the scariest women I'd ever met in my life, she felt the same way about the Unktehila that I felt about marshmallows: they're better when burnt to a crisp.

"Tango, don't say a word," I hissed, and then it was time for introductions. Hereditary enemy, meet ancient foe. I'm sure you two have a *lot* to talk about . . .

"Teresa, hi!" I said brightly. "I didn't even know you were, uh, in town. This is—"

"Maxine, hello," said Teresa warmly. "How are you?"

"Getting ready for a new tour," Maxine said. "Yourself?"

Teresa made a dismissive gesture. "Oh, I'm keeping busy; fundraising, political networking, the usual. That's why I'm here, actually—ZZ wants to see if I can beat the drums for this charity benefit you're performing at. See if I can move a few tickets in my circles." .

I looked from Teresa to Maxine and back again. "You know each other?"

"We met at a charity event, years back," said Maxine. "We keep in touch." The look she gave me was unreadable.

Much like a snake's.

"Well," I said, "isn't this . . . serendipitous. I wish ZZ had told me, I would have had a room ready for you."

Teresa smiled at me. "Oh, I can perch just about any-where. I wasn't planning on staying, but if you have space, I wouldn't mind. Your chef *is* superb."

"Yes, he is," I said and smiled right back. I had some jealousy issues when she first started training Ben in his Thunderbird abilities, but I was over it now. Mostly.

"You can stay in the east wing," I said. "The same room you had last time, if that's all right?"

"Either wing is fine with me—but just for one night. I have some urgent business over the next few days, and I need to be mobile." Okay, now she was just playing around. I hoped Maxine wouldn't start making snake jokes—if an apocalyptic war erupted over some ill-timed puns, I knew who'd get the blame.

"I'll talk to you later, Foxtrot," said Maxine. "And I guess I'll see you at breakfast, Teresa."

"I'll be there," said Teresa. "Early bird catches the Belgian waffle, as they say."

Maxine strutted away, which is really the only way you can walk in a dress and heels like that. When she was gone, Teresa's smile became a lot more businesslike. "We need to talk."

Boy, do we. "About what, Teresa?"

"Ben. I may need him to travel with me for a while."

I frowned. "I don't understand. Is this more training? And if it is, why can't you just do it in Thunderspace?" Thunderspace was the Thunderbirds' home dimension, a place that's mostly sky. Time passes at a different rate there, so Ben and Teresa can cram an entire day's worth of training into a few minutes of their mundane schedule.

"It's not training. Ben and I aren't the only Thunderbirds in the world, and the Thunderbird Council has decided it's time we started doing some outreach with the others."

"Oh? You know where they are?" I hadn't known they even had a council.

"Many of them, yes. Most aren't aware of their abilities or heritage. Better that they're told what they are by others of their own kind."

"The way you told Ben?" I still wasn't too happy about how she handled that, but it had turned out all right in the end.

She shook her head, her long, black hair shimmering in the moonlight. "No. That was simply about establishing who was in charge. With two of us standing together, that will already be implied; what we need to do now is offer support and inclusion."

That made sense. Ben had been pretty freaked when he discovered he could control the weather, and a panicking Thunderbird could cause major damage without meaning to. Finding out they weren't alone would go a long way toward calming down a fledgling storm-herder.

Of course, this being Teresa, there was more to it than that. Every tribe needs a leader, and she was determined to be that leader. Which would probably make her the single most powerful individual in the world—unless some equally powerful force rose up to oppose her.

<Can I talk now?> an irritated feline voice asked inside my skull. *<Or would you prefer I just shut up permanently?>*

"Sorry, kitty," I said. "You know, I think Ben got some fresh catnip today. Maybe you should check."

<Yeah, sure. Maybe that truckload of rubber mice finally showed up, too. Or that crate of dog repellant.>

And then she sat down and started cleaning herself, which was her not-too-subtle way of showing disdain.

"Anyway," continued Teresa, "this is far more important than his cooking duties. I'm telling you so you can prepare an appropriate excuse for ZZ. Wouldn't want Ben to lose his job, would we?"

I wasn't convinced she meant the last part; an unemployed Ben would probably fit into her plans a lot better than one tied to a routine. "You're assuming Ben's going," I said. "He may feel differently."

"That's the other reason I told you before him. He's more likely to agree if you do."

"Um." I'm rarely at a loss for words, but suddenly I couldn't find a noun, verb, or adjective to something my something. What was the best thing to do here? Send Ben and Teresa away from the sudden surge in the local Unktehila population, or tell her what was going on and hope she didn't rain lightning bolts down on the estate?

She took my hesitation the wrong way. "Really, Foxtrot? You're a smart woman—I thought you'd see how vital this is, not just to me or to Ben, but to everyone."

I shook my head. "It's not that simple. I have to talk to Ben first—"

"You're not, though. You're talking to me." Her tone was cool, but there was no mistaking the anger hiding beneath it.

"Look, in principle, I agree. If Thunderbirds are starting to pop up, they're going to need someone to talk to. But that could be dangerous, for more than the obvious reasons."

"Enlighten me."

I took a deep breath. "The Unktehila. You said they might be coming back, too."

Her eyes narrowed. "That's still a possibility, yes. But you showed me I'd misinterpreted the vision I had."

"I know, but Eli thinks the Unktehila are still a potential threat." That much I could admit without giving anything away; the white crow had warned me a while ago about the possibility.

"I see. Strange how this suddenly concerns you."

Uh-oh. Teresa was sharp. Did she suspect?

"I'm sure it has nothing to do with the fact that I want to take your boyfriend away with me," Teresa said. "No, you're simply worried about his safety. Well, think about this: he's far safer with me than he is with you. Two Thunderbirds are considerably more powerful than one and a secretary."

I grinned. If you want to bait me, best bring your A game; I've been called far worse. "Hey, I'm not *just* a secretary; I moonlight as a security guard, too."

"Talk to Ben, Foxtrot. Or I will—and I'll make sure to tell him how resistant you are to his leaving."

And with that, she turned and strode away. I wondered if I could get Consuela to short-sheet her bed.

<She's going to be one angry bird when she finds out,> Tango remarked.

"Finds out what? That I didn't tell her she's sharing a roof with one of her ancient enemies, that a war is brewing, or that said enemy is posing as an old friend she's going to be chatting to over eggs Benny tomorrow morning?"

<*Doesn't matter. Whichever one you go with first, you probably won't live long enough to get to the other two.*>

"Thanks for seeing the positive side, Tango. I needed that."

<*Anytime. Should we kill her in her sleep?*>

"Let me think about it . . ."

Chapter Three

After my chat with Teresa, I headed straight for the kitchen, where I knew I'd find Ben. An earthquake, a flood, a plague of frogs, and falling meteorite all failed to materialize in my way, so I figured I was doing pretty well. I did have a telepathic cat with me, though, which (somewhat) made up for the lack of natural disasters.

<Seriously, we should kill Maxine Danger in her sleep.>

I veered away from the front door and went around the side of the house instead—less chance of being intercepted and distracted. "No killing houseguests, kitty. Bad for our reputation."

<Oh, please. People die all the time, especially here. How many corpses have we piled up so far? I'm amazed anyone still comes.>

"See, that's the kind of attitude that makes my job difficult." Around the corner, down the side.

<As opposed to the giant snakes, ghost sharks, weather-controlling bird folk, and varied assassins?>

"Those aren't difficulties. They're opportunities to hone my people skills."

Past the pool and cabana, around another corner, and

there's the back door that leads to the kitchen. Almost there . . .

<All right, we'll do it your way. Spoilsport.>

Ben was in there, cleaning up in his kitchen whites. He stopped what he was doing when he heard me, gave me a dazzling smile, strolled over, and kissed me. A very enthusiastic kiss, which normally I'd enjoy but right now was more of a distraction. Oh well, better than a spontaneous house fire.

Mmmmm. Much better, actually.

"So," he said at last, "how can I help you, Ms. Foxtrot? Here for a little extra dessert?"

"I wish. No, this is more of a two-kiss sort of visit."

"If you insist."

Mmm-hmmm. . . .

When—finally—I reluctantly pulled myself away, he sighed and looked into my eyes. "By two-kiss visit, you mean you need the extra sugar to cut the taste of what you're about to tell me. Right?"

"You are such a chef. And a terrific kisser. And absolutely right."

"Tell me."

"Maxine Danger is an Unktehila and so is her biggest rival Lockley Hades, and both of them are trying to convince me they're on my side in preventing the coming war with the Thunderbirds and that the other one is evil."

He stared at me. He blinked. I waited.

<I think you broke him,> Tango said, looking up from her food bowl. *<Great. Now I'm going to have to train a new one.>*

"No, no, I can handle this," Ben said. "My weirdness tolerance has gone way, way up since we started dating. Wait, that doesn't sound right."

"It's okay. Keep going."

He frowned. "Two Unktehila. Is the other one here, too?"

"No, I talked to him on the phone. He called me."

"Does Teresa know?"

"Not yet—but she's *here*. Not only that, Maxine knows you and Teresa are Thunderbirds, Teresa has no idea what Maxine is, and she and Maxine know each other socially. I sent Whiskey to tell Eli—he should be back any minute."

Ben stepped back from me, looked away, and rubbed his chin. "They both say they're on our side, huh? Damn snakes—can't do anything without getting all twisty about it."

"That's . . . one way to look at it."

He looked back at me and saw the concerned expression on my face. "I know, I know. You just told me that a supernatural, shape-changing snake person is right here, right now, and that's my first reaction? Not shock, not horror, not anger or fear? The big, bad bogeyman finally shows up, and I'm . . . what? Mildly irritated? Kind of annoyed?"

"I was going to say *miffed*. With maybe some disdain on top."

He threw his hands up. "I can't help it. It's strange for me, too, but I sort of feel like you just told me we have mice. I'm a little creeped out, a little upset, a little resentful. I thought I'd be all bloodlust and fury if I ever met one, but it turns out what I mostly feel is contempt—which actually bothers me a lot more."

<As well you should be. Mice are delicious.>

I ignored that. "Instinct is a funny thing. It kicks in the strongest when survival is at stake, but it doesn't always tell us to do the right thing or even the safest thing. Yours seem to be telling you . . . what?"

"The racist thing," said Ben. "That's how it seems. As if the Unktehila aren't just my enemy, they're a lesser species." He shook his head. "And that's leaving a pretty godawful taste in my mouth, Trot. Honest hatred is one thing, but this? It's not right."

I came over to him, took his hand. "There are some ugly things buried in our genes. You got an extra helping of an ages-old conflict between very different species; you can't blame yourself for that."

<Sure he can,> said Tango, looking up and licking the last of her snack from her lips. <Human beings are great at that. They can blame themselves for just about anything.>

"But I'm not a human being," Ben said. "Not completely. Maybe that's the problem."

Tango flicked one of her ears in an irritated way. <Nope. We're all meat, no matter whether it's covered in plain skin, feathers, scales, or fur. Meat gets hungry, meat gets thirsty, meat gets sleepy—we don't have a choice about that. But love and hate and everything in between? That we have a say in. We may have to shout down our instincts, but we can do that. I've seen cats adopt squirrels, pigs fall in love with elephants, prey become best friend with predator. Hell, I've even learned to tolerate the occasional canine.>

Then she started grooming. Tango doesn't make that many speeches, but when she does, she never lets them get in the way of the important things.

Ben raised his eyebrows. "Shouting down our instincts, huh? That may be the best definition of civilization I've ever heard—though it reminds of me of something else. Something about better angels?"

<Oh, sure, take the angels' side. You feathered types all flock together.>

Right then I heard Whiskey's deep voice in my head: [Foxtrot. I've alerted Eli, and he wants to talk to us immediately.]

I could tell Ben had heard his voice, too. "All right, just let me get this apron off—"

[Not you, Ben. Just Foxtrot, Tango, and I.]

Ben had already untied the apron, but he stopped short of pulling it off. "Oh. It's like that, huh?"

[I'm sorry. I'm sure you'll be fully informed once we've discussed matters—]

Ben slowly tied the apron back into place. "It's all right. Politics, right? Diplomacy. After that mess with the big cat gods, I should have expected this. Guess I'm just used to being a neutral party as opposed to part of a faction."

I felt awful leaving him there, but I had to. He saw my expression and grinned. "It's okay, Trot. Go do your job. I don't think hostilities are about to break out; I'm in no mood for a fight, and if they were going to Pearl Harbor us, they'd have done it already. Uh—you're sure Teresa doesn't know about this, right?"

"Absolutely. Though Maxine seems to know about Teresa—and you—which is all kinds of worrisome."

"Then you better get going before she finds out. Teresa talks about the Unks the way a podiatrist talks about foot fungus."

I opened the back door. Tango darted past me and right up to Whiskey, who was patiently sitting and waiting for us. With no hesitation at all, she smacked him right across the muzzle.

Whiskey sprang backward—Australian cattle dogs have a lot of spring in them—landed on all fours in a crouch, and snarled, [What was *that* for?]

<*Failing to follow protocol. What's the* password, *doofus*?>

He growled then said, [A complete lack of surprise.]

She sauntered past him casually. <*Funny, you looked pretty surprised to me. Next time you won't forget.*>

It was still a warm spring night, but the air seemed to hold a little more chill to it than it had a few minutes ago; this likely had less to do with the fact that I was approaching a graveyard and more to do with what was on my mind.

A large, spectral shark swam past at eye level when we walked through the gate—Two-Notch on her endless, restless orbit of the perimeter. To my right, a flock of brilliantly colored parrots and parakeets clustered on the arms of a large, stone cross marking the grave of a German shepherd, their bright feathers giving off as much phantom illumination as a neon sign. To my left, a pack of ghostly wiener dogs glowing a soft bronze wriggled across the path, and I stopped rather than just walking through them. While I was waiting, the spirit of a Russian circus bear named Piotr rode past on a unicycle, wearing his usual pink tutu and juggling three balls. Or were those hedgehogs?

Anyway, just another night at the Great Crossroads.

(Yes, I'll explain all this later. But I've already thrown too much at you already, and if I stop to elaborate now, you'll mutter something about buying popcorn, leave your seat, and never come back.)

Eli was waiting for us at Davy's grave.

Davy was the first animal to be buried in the Zoransky pet cemetery (note correct spelling), but far from the last; there were currently over fifty thousand actual bodies interred here and at least that many souls passing through every day on their way from one afterlife to another. Whoops, that came perilously close to an explanation.

Eli is—or appears to be, anyway—a white crow. I should probably say the ghost of a white crow, since he's just as invisible to the public as the rest of the animals, but somehow that doesn't seem right.

Eli perched on the marker for Davy's grave, and he paced back and forth while bobbing his head up and down. I'd seen other birds do that when they were agitated, but never Eli.

"Foxtrot!" he croaked when he saw us. "Finally! We have *much* to discuss."

"Yes." I stopped in front of the headstone. "How bad is this, on a scale from one to apocalypse? It's pretty bad, right?"

Eli stopped his pacing and stared at me with bright bird eyes. "It's . . . worrisome. Possibly bad, possibly *very* bad, perhaps maybe even good."

"Perhaps maybe? Well, as long as you're sure."

"I *am* sure. Sure that this is a highly unstable situation with far too many unknowns. You're going to have to proceed with extreme caution."

"I figured." I crossed my arms against a sudden cold breeze. "What, exactly, am I supposed to proceed with?"

"Talk to Maxine Danger. Talk to Lockley Hades. Do your best to ascertain which of them is telling the truth, and how much of it. Report back to me."

It was odd, how formal Eli's speech patterns became when he was upset; usually, his style was less refined, more vernacular. Almost as if he were just playing a part most of the time and his real persona only showed through when he was under stress.

"Okay," I said. "That's more or less what I was planning on doing anyway. But any information you might be able to impart would be a big, big help."

Eli looked down and gave his head a slow shake, making it look like he was scanning the rough granite of the headstone for bugs. "It's not always possible, or even preferable, to be well informed, Foxtrot. I know that's hard to believe, but it's true."

"I believe you," I said. "If someone were going to tell me, for instance, the exact moment I was going to drop dead, I don't think I'd want to know."

<Yes you would.>

[Oh, absolutely. She'd have a seating plan for the funeral done before the sun set.]

I scowled at my partners. "That is absolutely not true. Well, maybe a little. Okay, it's true but not relevant in this case."

[Do you think there'll be a buffet? I do hope there'll be a buffet.]

<You're a dog. To you, the world's a buffet.>

"Regardless," said Eli, "I can't tell you much. But I can say this: I'm not the only source of knowledge available."

Right. Just wouldn't be a conversation with Eli unless he threw a few mysterious hints at me. "You really put the *crypt* in cryptic, you know that? I don't mind being kept in the dark, but these random flashes of illumination are extremely annoying."

Eli hunched his wings in what might have been an avian attempt at a shrug. "Learning is about more than raw data, Foxtrot. How you learn something and who you learn it from can be just as important as the knowledge itself."

"Profound. Google should use that as their new slogan. Can you at least point me in the direction of said source?"

"Oh, he'll find you. But I can give you his name: Grandfather Serpent."

<Hold on. Serpent? Is that some kind of nickname due to his snakelike appearance or habits? Is he really skinny? Does he gulp his food down without chewing?>

"He's a ghost, Tango, like the other animals here. Well, not quite the same."

<Oh. Well, ghost snakes don't bother me. I mean, I'm not bothered by any kind of snake, ghost or not.>

[Of course you aren't.]

"I'm afraid that's all I can tell you for now," said Eli. "Except . . ."

He cocked his head to one side and studied me.

"Except what?"

"Be careful, Foxtrot. Be very, very careful." And with that, he took wing and flapped away.

I'm used to Eli being mysterious. I'm used to him being ominous. What I'm not used to is him being worried . . . and he definitely sounded worried.

"Okay," I said. "Regardless of what Eli just told us, I'm not in the mood to wait around—especially not for someone whose name is pretty much a synonym for *old* and *slow*. Let's go find us a snake."

So we roamed around the Great Crossroads, looking for the ghost named Grandfather Serpent.

This would be a good time to quickly explain exactly what the Great Crossroads is. It's where all the different animal afterlives—well, those animals that were pets, anyway—intersect with the human one. It's sometimes known as the Rainbow Bridge (google it and ignore anything that comes up in Norse), a way for beloved animal companions and their people to reunite after death. Animal spirits use certain graves as portals to enter the Great Crossroads, then hop, trot, slither, swim, or flap their way to a grave with a bronze urn on it; these urns contain cremated human remains, the only way state law will allow a nonanimal body to be interred here. Those graves are doorways to the human afterlife (don't ask me which one; I've never been, and Eli won't say) and let the dearly departed cross over for a visit. The choice is strictly up to the animal spirit, which seems fair to me; after all, we humans were the ones making most of the choices on this side of the grave.

So, there you have it. Thunderbirds, animal spirits, ectoplasmic dogs, telepathic cats, shape-shifting snakes. Everything else from this point on is pretty much mundane. Yup.

We found Grandfather Serpent over by the south fence talking to the electric elephant.

No, no, the electric elephant wasn't a robot. Topsy was a prowler (like Two-Notch), a roaming animal spirit drawn to the Great Crossroads by all the mystic activity. When I first met Topsy, she couldn't even speak the same common tongue all the dead share—and they don't really belong anywhere. They're too domesticated to make their way to a wild afterlife (yes, those exist, too) and didn't bond closely enough with humans while they were alive to use the Great Crossroads the way the other spirits do. Often, they come from zoos or circuses or aquariums, and not the well-run ones.

Topsy was electrocuted—over a hundred years ago—for killing her sadistic handler. Apparently this was what she was discussing with the large snake wrapped around her trunk.

Topsy had a somewhat unusual appearance. Most animal spirits look as if they're illuminated from within, bright colors shining and darker shades glowing, but not the electric elephant. She looked as if she were made of living shadow, a solid-black pachyderm with the chains that shackled her when she was executed still dangling from her body. Electricity arced and crackled over the darkness like a thunderstorm bleeding lightning; overall, not a welcoming sight.

None of which seemed to bother the large, reddish snake wrapped around her trunk. "So," the snake said, "nobody's ever told you about Thomas Edison?" He had a slight Punjabi accent—the snake, not Edison.

When Topsy replied, her voice was a slow, deep bass; living elephants communicate in frequencies too low for us to hear. {NO.}

"I can't believe it. The man does that to you, becomes a famous historical figure, and nobody even lets you know. I think you should look him up. He owes you an apology, that is what *I* think." The voltage crawling over Topsy's body didn't seem to bother the snake at all.

"Excuse me," I said politely. "Are you—"

"Yes, yes, just a moment, please," the snake said. "I'm imparting some very important information to my new friend, here. She was killed by Thomas Edison, you know."

"I did, actually." That was no distortion of the facts, either. Edison wasn't responsible for Topsy's electrocution in some sort of abstract way; he was the one who actually threw the switch, or at least gave the order. Edison was locked in battle with Nikola Tesla at the time, in something called the War of the Currents—Tesla was promoting alternating current, Edison direct current, and Edison was fighting dirty. In order to show how dangerous his opponent's version of electricity was, Edison used it to publicly kill Topsy. He also filmed it and showed the film around the country.

He still lost. Modern civilization wound up being powered by AC, with DC relegated to batteries. Tesla won the War of the Currents, but lost the publicity battle. Edison may have been a jerk, but he understood politics; he was the one who became rich and famous, and Tesla—undoubtedly the more brilliant of the two—died penniless.

Edison was dead now, too, of course. I wondered how he'd feel about having an angry, deceased elephant pay him a visit. I bet Tesla would enjoy it, anyway.

"So," Grandfather Serpent (if this was actually him) said, "This Edison person. Here's what I think you should do. I can talk to some people—I have connections—and we can arrange a meeting. I'm sure he's very sorry for what he did and would welcome the chance to make amends."

{I WILL CONSIDER IT.}

The snake chuckled. "Very good. And now, I believe this young woman would like to speak with me."

The snake slithered off Topsy's appendage as if it were a tree branch and dropped to the ground. Topsy waved a greeting at me with her trunk then turned and silently lumbered away.

"Greetings," said the snake. He seemed a little larger than he had a minute ago, but maybe it was just by comparison to what he'd been wrapped around. He quickly arranged himself into a pile of coils with his head sticking out of the center. "I am Grandfather Serpent. And you are?"

"Foxtrot," I said. "And these are my partners, Whiskey and Tango."

[Hello,] said Whiskey.

<*Hey*,> said Tango.

The snake nodded at each of us in turn. "Yes, and hello and hey to you as well. This is a lovely place you have here, just lovely."

"Uh, thanks. I'm not really in charge of the upkeep, but I'll pass it along."

"Very good, yes." The snake stared at me calmly but didn't say anything else.

"So," I said. I wasn't really sure how to start. "You're a snake."

"Very observant." He sounded more pleased than sarcastic.

"I may need some advice about matters serpentine."

Grandfather Serpent chuckled again. It was a dry sound, but not as sibilant as I expected. "One should always be wary concerning advice. It is frequently sharper than it appears and often grasped by the wrong end."

<*Which you probably know a lot about, right?*> Tango said. <*So what's your deal? Are you a biter, a squeezer, or a spitter?*>

"I am more of a talker than anything. If you need something bitten, squeezed, or spit upon, you will have to ask someone else."

"I'm something of a talker, myself," I said. "And what I'd like to talk about right now is the Unkhetila. What do you know about them?"

Grandfather Serpent stared at me. His tongue tasted the air, flickering like the wings of an insect. "Everything," he said. "They are my children, after all."

Chapter Four

[So,] said Whiskey. [You are some sort of . . . snake deity?]

Grandfather Serpent smiled. You wouldn't think a snake could do that, but he managed. "No, not at all," he said. "I am simply very old. The Unktehila are my descendants; as such, I feel a certain amount of responsibility toward them."

That answered a question I didn't really want to ask, because it meant that at some point human beings and not-human beings had become a lot more than friends. Since that also pretty much described my current relationship, you'd think I'd be more accepting—but, you know, snakes.

Moving on.

"Okay," I said. "So you're the progenitor of the Unktehila race. What, exactly, is their deal? Revenge? World domination? Unlimited gobbling rights to anything made of meat?"

<Never mind what they want. How do we kill them?>

Ah. My sweet, loving cat. Morals of a serial killer, tact of a sledgehammer.

Grandfather Serpent extended his head a little closer to

Tango. "It's very simple. You need only one thing, which most cats have in abundance."

<What is it? Ferocity? Intelligence? Cuteness?>

"Patience. Wait long enough and death will claim them for you. As it does all living things."

Whiskey snorted. [How profound. But not exactly valuable strategic information.]

"Information," said the snake, "is not valuable in and of itself. It's what you do with it that determines its worth—as well as your own. Consider this, and you will see its truth." And with that, he slithered into a hole in the ground that I hadn't previously noticed.

"Wait!" I called out. "That's—we need more! Come back!"

"I will return," I heard him say just as his tail was vanishing into the hole, "when you have . . . *digested* my advice."

And then he was gone.

There didn't seem to be a lot else we could do, so Whiskey and I drove home while Tango returned to the mansion. We decided to regroup in the morning, assuming war didn't break out during the night.

When we pulled into the mansion's driveway in the morning, everything seemed to still be in one piece; I sent a cheerful, telepathic "good morning and umwhirligig!" into the ether and waited for a response.

<Now him,> came the cautious reply.

[Why should I have to go first?]

<You're not, you're going second. Why so reluctant? Got something to hide?>

[You've turned completely paranoid overnight. My response remains a total lack of surprise.]

<And I remain Tangotangotangoqueenoftheuniverse.>

I sighed as I dug my keys out of my pocket and walked

up to the door. "And we're going to be doing this every time?"

<As long as it takes, Toots.>

I unlocked the front door, let Whiskey in, and followed him upstairs to my office. Tango was already there, curled up on the sofa in the exact spot Whiskey liked to sprawl. This was not a coincidence.

It was a big sofa, though, so there was plenty of room for both of them. I hung up my coat, sat down, and checked my email, then went downstairs to say hi to Ben and see how breakfast was going. Both my companions came with me, which was a little unusual; I guess we were all feeling a bit skittish.

Breakfast that morning was omelets, which Ben was making to order; Maxine Danger and her assistant, Summer, were just digging in. "Those look delicious," I said.

"Chorizo sausage and oyster mushroom," said Maxine, pausing with a forkful in midair.

"Too, too good," said Summer, her mouth full. "I'm gonna gain like twenny poundf. Shcuze me."

"Well, enjoy," I said. "You two are early risers."

"Not as early as Teresa," said Maxine. "She's already out for a morning run. That woman's always in motion."

I met her eyes and nodded. "True. I just try to stay out of her way."

Maxine didn't reply, just stuck her omelet-loaded fork into her mouth—then swallowed the whole mouthful without chewing.

I blinked. She smiled. I left and took my partners with me.

<Okay, that was creepy,> Tango said once we were in the kitchen. *<I mean, chewing's overrated in general, but did you see her throat bulge?>*

[Oh, I don't know. Who hasn't gulped their food down once or twice when in a hurry?]

<Once or twice? You could replace a dog's muzzle with a wet vac and he wouldn't even notice.>

Ben was hard at work, cracking eggs into a large, steel bowl. "Morning, crew," he said. "I see nobody got eaten overnight. I'm doing my best to stave off the hunger pangs of any snakelike beings currently sitting in the dining room."

I gave him a quick kiss on the lips. "Morning to you, too. How's it feel, cooking for the enemy? Is it weird? It must be weird."

Ben made a face. "It's fine. And we're not enemies; we're just on opposite sides of a very old dispute that really has nothing to do with either of us. The fact that she's willing to eat my cooking after revealing herself is a good sign, don't you think? Shows some trust."

<That's a really good point. You should—>

Ben and I both said it at the same time: *"No poison."*

<You two are terrible *at strategy.>*

[Yes, they are. If they had an ounce of sense, they'd have slipped some cyanide in your food bowl a long time ago.]

Ben gave me an odd look I couldn't quite read. "Ah, Trot—"

"Yes?"

He looked away. "Nothing. Just . . . come back and see me after breakfast, okay? We should talk."

"Okay . . . I'm going to take a look at how the ballroom setup is going—"

<I'm coming with you.>

[As am I.]

"Oh, come on. You two can't shadow me all day—how's it going to look?"

Tango narrowed her eyes. *<Whiskbroom follows you around like he's on an invisible leash, and you never complain.>*

[That's different. I accompany her as part of a regular routine. A cat, however, thinks the word *routine* means *not completely random activity*.]

"He's right, Tango. Besides, we can't give in to paranoia; being aware of a possible threat doesn't mean we let it dictate every action we take. We have precautions in place, we're all on alert—we'll be fine. If it makes you feel better, we'll hang out in shifts: Whiskey can do the morning, you can take the afternoon. That we can probably get away with."

<Hmmmph. I guess.>

I gave Ben a goodbye smooch and made my way to the ballroom. Well, we call it the ballroom, but depending on ZZ's current hobby, it can also function as an indoor lacrosse court, roller rink, rock-climbing space, or robot battleground. Right now, there was a pile of equipment cases, lights on stands, and plastic crates of various sizes in the center of the hardwood floor. Neither Maxine nor Summer was there yet, so I moved on to my next stop: paying a visit to another of our guests, Esko Karvenin.

One of the things ZZ has a passion for is science and cutting-edge technology. That, of course, could take many different forms, ranging from the mechanical to the biological. Karvenin was an expert in one of ZZ's latest interests and had set up shop in the billiards room.

Oscar was already there, which was something of a surprise; he wasn't exactly an early riser. Well, if he was expecting to get in some snooker before lunch, he was going to be sadly disappointed; the billiards table was covered with a sheet of plywood, and Karvenin's equipment was spread out on top of it.

Instead of a complaint, however, all I got from Oscar was a friendly nod and a cheerful "good morning, Foxtrot." Oscar was dressed as nattily as ever, in cream-colored slacks, a blue Oxford shirt, and highly shined leather slippers—but for Oscar, this was the equivalent of jeans, an old T-shirt, and flip-flops. For once, he didn't seem to have a drink in his hand.

Casual clothes? Up early? Non-inebriated cheer?

Uh-oh.

Oscar was to scheming what hot, evaporated water was to early locomotion—in other words, a scheme engine. He loves diving into a new scam the way ZZ loves delving into a new hobby, and the two all-too-frequently collide. Remind me to tell you about ZZ's Siamese Fighting Fish and Oscar's plan for a Worldwide Federation of Mixed-Maritime Arts.

"So are you up and running?" I asked Esko. He was wearing a lab coat this morning, though it was a decidedly un-lab purple and decorated with a variety of pins and buttons.

"Not quite yet, I am afraid," he said. The words were softly pronounced but carefully enunciated, giving everything he said a simultaneous gentleness and intensity. He would have made a great DJ. "I have run into something of a snag. The printers utilize a variety of materials, but as some of them are quite weighty, I required a different shipping company than I used for the printers themselves. They have yet to make delivery—and therein lies the problem."

I frowned. "Right. Rocket ships are on the pad, but the fuel tanker hasn't shown up yet."

Oscar sidled over. "Really, Foxtrot. A spaceship metaphor? A much more accurate one would be a simple cement mixer and a building site. This isn't science fiction; this is a highly viable, widely available mechanism, usable by almost anyone. A license to fly a rocket is not needed."

There are certain phrases I've learned to dread hearing from Oscar, and *highly viable* is one of them. When

Oscar decides to vie for something, security alarms start to blare at the local vie oversight office.

I glanced around the table. "Looks like you have all your equipment set up, though, right?"

"Yes, I have. All I require now is something to print with."

I nodded and pulled out my phone. "Let me see if I can help. What was the name of the company you used?"

"I have all the information right here." Esko handed me a piece of paper.

"I'm sure Foxtrot will have your shipment here before the day is out," said Oscar. "Her skill with the mundane is quite extraordinary. If she ever turns her attention toward more lucrative opportunities, I've no doubt her own wealth would soon exceed mine."

I sighed. "This is the part where you try to get me to eat an apple, right?"

"Apples are an excellent comparison. If you'd invested in them at the right time—"

"Right fruit, right metaphor, wrong apple. Just tell me, Oscar. I can always tell when you have something cooking; *eau du avarice* wafts through the house like freshly minted money."

He shrugged. "Very well—3D printing is going to be one of the most important technologies of the twenty-first century. I believe Esko and I have devised a most ingenious way to profit from it."

I glanced over at the table full of equipment. Most of them were the size and shape of milk crates, with a small platform on the bottom and open front and sides—though there was one that reminded me of a cross between a sewing machine and a coffee maker. One common feature almost all of them shared was a mobile printing head mounted on a slide rail across the top, though the printheads themselves varied in appearance. A few of the larger

ones looked more like lathes or photocopiers to my inex-
perienced eye.

"Occasionally," continued Oscar, "Mother and I agree
on a trend's importance. You understand the basic principle of how a 3D printer works?"

"Sure—same as an inkjet. The printing head moves
back and forth, spraying a thin coating of—whatever it's
using—building a three-dimensional object one layer at
a time."

"Correct. A secondary process ensures that the layers
set properly—a strong ultraviolet light or even a laser is
used in some processes but is not always needed. Thermo-
plastics, for instance, can simply be extruded and allowed
to cool. Depending on the material being printed, a bond-
ing agent may be used between layers, and some industrial
printers bake the finished object in a kiln as a last step.
What's fascinating, though, isn't that one can use this to
create almost any shape—it's what you can create that
shape out of. Not just plastic, but nylon, wax, glass, metal,
ceramics. And others."

"Why do I get the feeling this will all end with a visit
from the Treasury Board and a large shipping container
full of extremely new hundred-dollar bills?"

Oscar chuckled. "No, no, my dear Foxtrot. Counterfeit
currency is not the aim here. The items we plan to print
will be much more exotic than mere money. 3D printers,
you see, can also print with *biological* materials."

At my feet, Whiskey made an unhappy sound. [Good
Lord. Please tell me I'm not going to have to invoke the
Frankenstein Protocols.]

"The *what* now?" I said.

Karvenin looked up from the printer he'd been tinkering with. "What my esteemed business partner is talking
about is known as bioprinting. A researcher named Naka-
mura realized human blood cells are the approximately

the same size as the drops of ink in a standard inkjet; this eventually led to bioprinting cardiac tissue and functional blood vessels. But the truly amazing thing is this: when printing a bio-artifact—like, say, an organ—it's not necessary to get the fine details accurate. Once the appropriate cells are approximately placed, life takes over; the cells organize *themselves* into a more precise arrangement."

[Never mind, false alarm. Let me know if he starts tinkering with lightning, will you?]

"That's incredible," I said.

"*Inspiring* is the word I'd use," said Oscar. "It opens up all sorts of possibilities, particularly in regard to personal branding."

"Designer kidneys?" I hazarded.

"Not as such. We're thinking more along the lines of implanted DNA. What, after all, is more representative of who you are than your genetic code?"

"Me? My bookshelf. Exactly whose DNA are you talking about?"

Oscar smiled. "*Celebrity* DNA, Foxtrot. The famous sell proxies of themselves in a wide variety of mediums, from scents to clothes to jewelry, and the public eats it up. What better way to endorse the object of your adulation than to own something made from their very substance?"

I blinked. "What sort of objects, exactly?"

Karvinen cleared his throat. "That has been a topic of much debate, Foxtrot. I believe the high-end market would be best suited to this endeavor; Mr. Zoransky is of the opinion we would be better served by a mass-produced, lowest-common-denominator model."

"Examples?"

Oscar inclined his head. "Very well. Esko would like to recreate singular, iconic items such as the gemstone in the *Titanic* movie or Indiana Jones's hat, imbuing them with the DNA of the star they are associated with: Leonardo DiCaprio or Harrison Ford, in this case."

I frowned. "Even if you could convince either of them to sign on for this, you're going to run into licensing problems with the studios."

Oscar nodded. "Exactly my point. Whereas if we concentrate on something more mundane—the type of sunglasses favored by Bono, perhaps—we could secure those rights much more easily. And with a little bit of Bono in each one, they would sell like *mad*."

"I fail to be convinced," said Karvinen. He fiddled with the printer head of one of his machines. "The beauty of the 3D printer is not in its potential for mass production; it lies in creating the custom-designed and singular, in spinning the fantastic into the real. Like this."

Karvenin bent down and rummaged in a bag at his feet then pulled out . . . a skull. Its proportions were lifelike, but it seemed to be made of an intricate lacework of filigreed white—a lacework that extended through the body of the skull itself, an intricate interior maze. He held it out to me, and I took it carefully.

"No need to be gentle," he said. "It's quite sturdy."

The skull weighed very little. Up close, I could see it was made from plastic, though if I'd seen it in a museum, I'd have guessed bone or ivory.

"It is an amazing object in its own right," said Karvenin. "But equally amazing is the fact that the artist and the object have never been in the same room. The original skull parameters are by way of Holland, from a man who used a simple smartphone app to take pictures of the real thing. He sent them to a woman in Iceland who designed the final look and then emailed the file to me. From template to design to creation—a collaboration that spanned three continents, cost almost nothing, and was accomplished in the space of a few days, done using equipment both commonly available and inexpensive."

I turned the skull over in my hands, studying it. "That's pretty spectacular," I admitted.

"Yes," said Oscar. "But it would be even more spectacular if it were based on Matt Damon's skull and contained his DNA."

Karvinen didn't reply to that, but he didn't look like he agreed. "In any case," Karvinen said as he took the skull back, "It is true that the range of materials used by this technology is integral to its importance and versatility. But, as with any transformative technology, there's also the potential for abuse."

"Sure," I said. "3D printed guns are the one people seem most worried about."

Karvinen grinned, but his eyes weren't happy. "They're thinking too small. There's a big movement in 3D printing right now to print robots."

"Robots?" I said.

"Yes. Not terribly sophisticated ones, not yet—but it doesn't take much sophistication to run a 3D printer. Can you envision where this is heading?"

"Robots making more robots. Yeah, no way that could go wrong."

Oscar shook his head. "That's the sort of alarmist reaction that always stands in the way of true innovation. Society has had industrial robots for decades, and none of them have ever decided to rise up against their human masters and establish a new world order."

Karvinen put the skull down on the table, resting his long, spidery fingers on it gently. "Industrial robots are just machines. Big, expensive, highly specialized machines. The robots I'm talking about are open-source—freely available plans disseminated over the internet, easily assembled by nonprofessionals, using parts they're creating themselves. When the *machines* can assemble their own bodies, the process will be self-sustaining. And sooner or later, that *will* happen. It's inevitable."

Oscar frowned. "Even so, what's the harm? It simply means that making robots will become easier. It doesn't logically follow that they'll become a threat—that's the stuff of paranoid science-fiction movies. We're nowhere close to creating artificial intelligence."

"You don't need intelligence to be a threat," Karvinen said quietly. "A swarm of bees isn't intelligent. Neither is a colony of army ants. All they really know how to do is gather supplies, build basic fortifications, reproduce, and advance. Over and over and over again. And, of course, how to defend those fortifications."

Oscar blinked. He's not an unintelligent man, but I think he has a knee-jerk reflex that keeps him from thinking too hard about consequences. "I . . . see," he said slowly. "You're saying they might become an *ecological* threat?"

Karvenin regarded him coolly. "Is it so hard to imagine? Swarms of self-assembling robots programmed to do simple tasks like identify and gather simple building materials—plastic will do—and bring them back to a central base where they're turned into more robots. They don't have to be very strong or complex—just numerous. And the same kind of defenses insects use would work even better for them; poisons and acids are extremely easy to synthesize from common materials, and—depending on the chemicals you choose—the robots would be immune to both. Or you could build bots that generate mustard gas, which is lethal to anything with lungs—"

"We get the idea," I said. "But it seems far-fetched. Why would anyone build something like that?"

Karvenin looked down and stroked the filigreed skull with one long finger. "Because they could," he said. "If it is in the realm of possibility, sooner or later someone will try to drag it into the real world. That's what we do."

It was hard to argue with that; he had most of human history on his side. "Well, try not to start the robot apocalypse while you're here," I said. "ZZ's very tolerant, but even she would have a problem with the estate being turned into a Terminator factory."

Karvenin smiled. "I'll do my best to keep things under control."

When Whiskey and I left, Oscar was staring at the printers in a very different way. If I didn't know him better, I'd say he looked worried—but he was probably just considering ways to turn Karvenin's predictions of calamity into profit. Personalized robot deactivators, maybe.

"What's your take on all that, pooch?" I asked Whiskey as we headed upstairs to my office. I expected him to have some droll, dismissive comment to offer, but he surprised me.

[Worrisome,] he said after a long pause.

"Really?"

[Yes. Life is that which survives and thrives. What Mister Karvenin was talking about is exactly that—but his comparison of machines to insects is inaccurate. He was describing the actions of a virus. Mindless, soulless, devoid of emotion, existing only to consume and grow. More like a forest fire than a life form.]

"Funny. I was thinking it sounded like a corporation . . ."

I knew something was wrong the second I touched the doorknob of my office. It was ice cold.

But the rest of my body hadn't quite caught up with that realization; it was engaged in the mundane, everyday routine of opening a door, something I'd done thousands upon thousands of times in my life and expected to do a few thousand times more—unless whatever was waiting for me behind that door had other ideas.

By the time my brain and body had sorted out what I should do, it was too late. I stopped in the doorway, my hand still on the knob, and froze.

Someone was waiting for me. And she wasn't happy.

Teresa Firstcharger stood in front of my desk, her arms crossed. The look on her face was even colder than the room, which hovered somewhere just above zero. If I hadn't been holding my breath, it would have escaped from my lips in a warm, foggy cloud. Possibly for the last time.

"Maxine Danger is an Unktehila," Teresa said. "But that's not exactly news to you, is it, Foxtrot?"

Here we go . . .

Chapter Five

I stared at her for a second before replying, "I don't appreciate the trick with the temperature. Turn it back up to normal, then we can have a civil discussion. Failing that, you'd better have some coal, a carrot, and two sticks with you." I said this in my most genial, nonthreatening tone, because that's how you deal with an aggressive alpha who's angry with you. Showing weakness is bad, and provoking them is worse, so I usually go with firm politeness and a dash of cognitive dissonance. Sometimes the best way to derail anger is distraction.

Teresa, though, was too quick on the uptake for my comment to even slow her down. "I'm not here to build a snowman, Foxtrot. I'm here to find out why you didn't come to me immediately when you discovered we had one of those *things* under our roof."

I sighed and closed the door. Whiskey had already trotted past me and now stood quite deliberately between us.

"Two reasons," I answered. "First of all, it's not *our* roof. You're a guest here, and you better remember that. Second, for exactly the same reason my office has suddenly become a deep freeze. You didn't even realize what you were doing, did you?"

Her eyebrows twitched downward, just enough to let me know I was right. "I was doing my best to stay . . . cool."

I desperately wanted to cross my arms against the cold, but I resisted. I needed my body language to be as open as possible. "Exactly. And that affected your immediate environment without you being conscious of it. I've seen the same thing happen with Ben, especially if he's feeling really emotional about something."

"You were worried I'd lose control? Destroy the house in a weather tantrum?" She was trying for sarcastic, but I could hear a hint of genuine worry hidden in her voice. For all her regal poise, her own abilities still scared her—as well they should. There are more powerful forces on the planet than weather, but not many.

"You're a very powerful woman, Teresa, but that's not the relevant fact here. You're also extremely smart. You don't seriously think I'd try to keep this a secret from you, do you?" I raised my eyebrows to emphasize the question.

"No. You'd wait for the appropriate moment to let me know, in a setting where I'd feel comfortable but would have to stay in control."

I gestured with a hand. "Like my office, maybe?"

"You should have told me last night."

"No, I should have let everyone—including me—get a good night's rest and a decent, cordial breakfast. Which is what I did. How'd you find out?"

"Ben told me during our training session. Don't blame him; it was a difficult decision for him to reach. But this is the fate of our entire *species* we're talking about, Foxtrot. And not just ours, but yours, too."

So that's why Ben had been a little weird this morning. I should have been angry, but I saw his point all too clearly: according to Thunderbird lore, the last time the Unktehila got out of hand, they'd left the deep, blue seafood buffet for a little trip to the salad bar on dry land. The Thunderbirds had no problem with them eating buffalo, deer, bears, moose, or anything else they could get their jaws on . . . but when they started snacking on people, the Big Birds drew the line. The Unktehila refused to listen, the Thunderbirds called down the lightning, the snakes retreated to the sea.

And now they were back. The question was, were they still hungry?

"I realize how serious this is," I said. "All the more reason for caution. Look, you've known Maxine Danger for a while now—has she ever done anything to harm you? Has she ever done anything to harm *anyone*?" The temperature in the room had started to rise, and I wasn't sure if that was a good thing or not.

"How would I know?" Teresa snapped. "She can change her shape, she can influence minds. She could be this country's most prolific serial killer, and no one would even *suspect*."

[If I may interject?] Whiskey said. [That's hardly likely. The fact that Miss Danger makes her living as an escape artist suggests she uses her talents in a very different way. And being in the public spotlight is hardly a good strategy for multiple homicides.]

Teresa gave Whiskey an annoyed look. "Isn't it? Traveling from city to city, able to look like anyone? It might be the perfect cover."

"So why reveal herself now?" I said. "We need to hear her out, at the very least. If she wanted to hurt you—or any of us—she's had plenty of opportunity. But she hasn't."

"That doesn't mean anything! The Unktehila are by *definition* masters of deception—even if her plan isn't obvious, her motives are. She's trying to win our trust so she can betray us later. That's what they *do*."

I kept my tone calm. "Do they? Are you speaking from personal experience or from stories you were told? Because that's the funny thing about ancient, tribal conflicts—each faction tends to exaggerate the other side's crimes. Or maybe you've never experienced that sort of prejudice . . ."

I watched that one hit home with a certain amount of satisfaction I didn't show. Teresa blinked, opened her mouth, then closed it again. Like I said, she was a smart woman—and a political one.

I waited. She only took a moment to collect her thoughts and then said, in a much cooler tone, "Perhaps I am being a little presumptive. There's an old Iroquois saying: *In our every deliberation, we must consider the impact of our decisions on the next seven generations.* If I seem overly hostile, it's because I'm thinking of those next generations. I want to ensure they'll exist."

I nodded. "Then we're on the same page. I know the Unktehila are dangerous, and that they've done some terrible things in the past. But Maxine could be telling the truth. We should judge her by her actions, not as a member of a group but as an individual. So far, she hasn't done anything wrong."

"True," Teresa admitted. "Very well, let's say for the sake of argument that she's telling the truth—it means a war is imminent. That's hardly better news."

I stepped around her, pulled out my office chair, and sat down. The seat was still extremely cold, but it was better, psychologically speaking, than being on my feet; sitting behind my desk put me in a position of authority. "No, but it's better than hearing war has already been declared. So let's talk about what we should do next."

"Obviously, we need more information. We have to sit

down with Maxine immediately and hear what she has to say—then we can decide what to do about it."

"Before or after I talk to Lockley Hades?"

Teresa frowned. "Good question. He's supposed to contact you, correct?"

"Yes, but he didn't say exactly when, just sometime today."

"I think we should wait until we hear from him. We'll need to consider whatever he has to say very carefully before we talk to Maxine." Teresa gave her head an irritated shake. "This is maddening. Every instinct I have is telling me we should go on the offensive instead of having our enemies pour lies into our ears."

"Look on the bright side: most likely it's only fifty percent lies and fifty percent vital information. All we really have is a labeling problem."

Teresa gave me a grudging smile. "That's one way to put it. Just try not to let that sunny optimism color your more analytical abilities. We'll need them."

I smiled back. "Don't worry about that. I'm harder to snow than my office."

Teresa glanced around. "Please. This is barely an early frost." She opened the door and paused. "Let me know when Hades gets in touch." The door closed softly behind her.

[That went better than it could have.] Whiskey jumped up on the couch and made himself comfortable.

"Sure, in the sense that the house is still standing. But what happens if those two run into each other now? Teresa's a ticking bomb."

[Comparing her to an explosive device is not accurate—or fair. She fully acknowledges her animal nature, and thus it does not control her.]

Control. I could use a little more of that myself—there were too many factors at play, and I didn't have my hands on the steering wheel of any of them. I couldn't talk to Maxine until I'd talked to Hades, I couldn't talk to Hades until he got in touch with me, and my only source of insider knowledge was a talking snake who pulled a disappearing act before I could ask him anything useful. About the only thing I could do was go talk to my boyfriend—and considering how frustrated I was feeling, that wasn't a conversation that would go well: *Hi, honey! What's new? Besides you blurting out confidential information to your hot-tempered supernatural teacher who was this close to starting the war we're trying to forestall? What? Oh, I totally understand that you're feeling conflicted and you thought it was your duty and I don't feel betrayed AT ALL.* Uh-huh.

"All right, let's go back to the Crossroads and look for Granddaddy Slither," I said. "It's probably the closest thing to being proactive we can manage right now. Other than strangling my boyfriend, which might prove to be counterproductive."

[Agreed. Let's leave our feline accomplice here, shall we? I think she was a little abrasive with him last time.]

I got up, slipped my tablet into a bag, and slung it over my shoulder before opening the door. "*Our* Tango, abrasive? Don't be silly. The next thing you know, you'll be telling me that sandpaper is rough and a forest fire can be a trifle warm . . ."

I took the long way around in order to avoid both Ben and Tango, out the front door and around the side of the house.

The air was brisk but fresh, with that lovely springy smell to it. Purple crocuses lined the front walk, green buds tipped the ends of branches, and the local bird population was in an insanely cheerful mood.

I caught Whiskey studying a particularly outspoken

sparrow in a nearby oak as we strolled along. "Any idea what he's saying?" I asked.

[You'd have to ask Tango—that's her specialty, not mine. I'm more interested in form than phonetics.]

I peered at the sparrow myself. It cocked its head to the side and peered back. "And what, exactly, is so fascinating about this bird's form?"

[Nothing, really. If it's genuine.]

I shook my head. "You are becoming a 'noid, both you and Tango."

[Excuse me?]

"And the two of you together? Paranoids."

He grunted in a very doglike way. [You really should have saved that one for her. I fail to be impressed by puns.]

"And I'm not impressed by seeing the world through ruse-colored glasses. You can't be suspicious of every living thing we encounter, Whiskey. You told me yourself once that shape-shifters have their limits, like anything else. I mean, should we be afraid of every bug that flies by, too? How about bacteria, for that matter? I mean, I get that we're talking about the supernatural, but if the Unktehila were *that* versatile, they would have taken over the whole planet a long time ago."

He gave me the canine Look of Shame™. [You're right, of course. I shall endeavor to keep my worries to a more reasonable level.]

When we reached the graveyard, we headed for the last place we'd seen Grandfather Serpent. No luck.

"Well, that takes care of the obvious approach. I guess we just cruise around for a while? Maybe talk to anybody we see that's scaly?"

[I concur. And get that look off your face; I can tell you're thinking of ways to play with the word *concur*.]

"Busted," I muttered, and off we went.

There are worse ways to spend a sunny spring morning

than roaming around a graveyard brimming with animal ghosts. It might sound spooky—if you ignore the sunny part, anyway—but it was really the opposite of that. See, animal spirits *shine* in a way nothing else does; it makes neon seem like the dim glow of a dying flashlight in comparison, even in bright sunlight.

The reason for that suddenly struck me: what I was seeing was pure life force stripped of any external container. They may have been ghosts, but in a way, they were *more* alive than they'd ever been. The pure, gleaming energy at the heart of biology, freed from the machine it used to power. Far from being mysterious or scary, it was glorious.

[You're in an awfully chipper mood,] Whiskey said, [considering the situation.]

I leaned down and ruffled the fur on his head. "Gather ye rosebuds while ye may, and all that. I know the outlook is on the dire side—when isn't it?—but even so, let's just take a moment to look at the Big Picture. Beautiful day in a universe filled with possibility. And what's this I'm surrounded by? Actual evidence that not only is death not the end, but that Paradise is plural. Plurals? A plurality? Whatever. Plenty of Heaven to go around is what I'm saying."

Which, of course, was when I heard a bellow of extreme unhappiness.

The ghosts were pretty quiet, overall, but this wasn't a ghost. It was a very human cry, in a vocal range I was familiar with: frustration and exasperation, angry with a side of anguish. Angrish.

[That sounds like Keene.]

"So it does. We'd better see what's bothering him."

We found him not far away, at the gravesite of a galago called Jeepers. Keene claimed that this particular galago was also his muse, that the spirit of the animal helped him get into a creative groove; I sometimes found the singer perched on Jeeper's headstone, strumming a guitar and scribbling things in a notebook.

Not at the moment, though. The guitar was nowhere in sight, and the notebook lay on the ground, unopened. Keene lay prone beside it, his shaggy head resting on the grass. He wore tight-fitting jeans, sneakers, a beat-up, black leather jacket that was too big for him, and a look of despair.

"Are you actually up this early, or did you sleep there?" I said, stopping beside him.

"Go away. I'm *working*."

"Are you? This is a graveyard, you know. You're actually supposed to be doing the exact opposite—*de*composing."

"I *am* decomposing. Also uncreating, antiwriting, and generally accomplishing nothing of artistic merit. In fact, that sentence is the most creative thing I've managed all morning."

I dropped into a cross-legged squat. "I see. Don't you generally have your guitar with you when you're song-writing?"

"Yes. It's over there." He pointed without looking. "We had a disagreement."

I peered in the direction he'd indicated. "I think I see it—part of it, anyway."

"It made the most amazing sound when it hit that statue of a horse. I spent half an hour trying to turn it into a melody."

"I take it you were unsuccessful."

"Extremely. Now be quiet. I'm *trying* to listen to worms."

Whiskey snorted. [Good luck with that. I'm not saying it can't be done—just not with miniscule ears like *that*.]

I glanced around but didn't see Jeepers. Not that

Keene could see him even if Jeepers was present; Keene's abilities were strictly non-supernatural. "I'm not really an artistic type myself, but I'm a little dubious on the inspirational effect of worm noises."

"I'm not listening for inspiration. Inspiration and I have parted company. I just wanted to focus on something natural and organic and completely unmusical, because clearly that part of my life is now over. Also, if I lie here long enough, the worms may take pity on me and devour my brain."

"Highly unlikely. Worms are notoriously pitiless, much like professional assistants. And I thought you said you were working?"

He sighed and raised his head slightly to look at me. "That was just to make you go away. You're not going away, are you?"

"Nope. Like I said, pitiless."

He groaned and put his head down again, facing away from me. "It won't come, Foxtrot. The music. My skull is as empty and dark as a cave, minus the echoes. Even the bats have packed up and left."

"Sounds bad. Is it bad?"

"It's bad."

"Hmmm. I've never known you to have writer's block."

"That's a bit like saying you've never known me to have Ebola. You only get it once."

I nudged him with the toe of my shoe. "Oh, come on. I've been around plenty of creative types when they've been blocked, and all of them pulled out of it sooner or later. It's a nasty head cold, not flesh-eating disease."

"Easy for you to say. Making music is not just who I am, it's *what* I am. Not being able to do it is like suddenly depriving a kangaroo of the ability to hop majestically across the Serengeti."

"The Serengeti's in Africa. And lacks kangaroos."

"See? I can't even whip up a proper metaphor."

I resisted the urge to point out that his comparison was actually an analogy. "Anything I can do to help?"

He turned his head and peered up at me. "I'm not sure. What do you suggest?"

"Not to smack you over the head with an obvious metaphor, but standing on your own two feet would be a good start."

He considered this for a moment then put his head back down. "Not sure that's the right approach for me. I like it down here. It's peaceful. Calm. Devoid of strife—ow! Stop that!"

I nudged him in the ribs with the tip of my shoe again. "Nope. Strife equals conflict, conflict provokes action, action leads to achievement. I'll quit strifing you when you're back on your feet and glaring at me in that adorable way only a British pop star can manage."

He surrendered to the inevitable and reluctantly got to his feet.

We looked at each other. I smiled, he glowered.

"Not bad," I said. "I mean, you're no hungover Rod Stewart at six a.m., but that's a pretty decent glare all the same."

Which then wilted. "Ah, bloody hell. I'm sorry, Trot. You're doing your best and all, but I think this is going to require more than even your considerable skills."

"Oh, I'm just getting started. I can ramp up from merely annoying to full-on nuisance at a moment's notice."

He shook his head. "Thanks, but I believe I'll try something a little less . . . murdery first."

"There you go. *Murdery* is a great start. In terms of creativity, I mean, not as a general adjective for ongoing activities."

"Think I'll go see if Coop's home. Have a chin-wag and

a cup of tea." Cooper was the graveyard's caretaker, an old hippie that lived on the grounds in a small bungalow.

For a second I was hurt that he'd prefer Cooper's company to mine, and then I understood what he meant by a "cup of tea."

"Ah. Well, I guess that's one way to get the brain revved up."

"Sometimes. But I'm not holding out a great deal of hope."

He waved a bleary farewell, turned, and trudged away. I almost felt sorry for him then remembered he was young, rich, and famous and was mostly complaining about having a few difficulties doing something most people couldn't do at all. He'd figure it out.

Whiskey and I resumed our search. We had no luck finding the snake we were looking for—but then another one found me.

I'd taken the tablet along because Hades had said he was going to Skype me, and now it chimed with the tone that told me I had a video call coming in. I pulled out the tablet and opened the app.

A window popped up. Lockley Hades, on what appeared to be a huge iron and granite throne, with flames from an even larger fireplace flickering behind him. He was dressed all in black: leather pants, turtleneck, boots. He had a sharp, vulpine face, with a short, neatly trimmed ginger beard and a high widow's peak of reddish hair. His eyes were as dark as his outfit.

"Good morning, Foxtrot," he said. "I hope you slept well."

I peered at the tablet. "If you're trying to inspire trust, you should fire your interior decorator. Where are you broadcasting from, Dracula's castle?"

He grinned. "Do you like it? It's the set for my latest

show. It should be a huge success—if, you know, by the time I start the tour, civilization is still a thing. Anyway, you're not exactly in a position to criticize; you seem to be standing in a graveyard. What, the morgue wasn't available?"

Interesting. Apparently he didn't know about the Great Crossroads—or at least wasn't admitting it. "It's a long story and not relevant at the moment. So, here's where we are: I've talked to Maxine, and she's claiming pretty much the same thing you are, only she says she's trying to prevent the war and you're trying to start it. Care to respond?"

He didn't look surprised or even concerned. "It's what I'd expect from her. We're very good at this sort of thing, you know. Infiltration, manipulation, multiple levels of deception—you could probably find Unktehila DNA in ninety percent of the intelligence operatives alive today."

I resisted the obvious joke about politicians. "Again, not helping in the trust-gaining department. Why should I trust you and not her?"

"Because I'm going to give you actual information as opposed to vague innuendo. Otherwise, this is nothing but an exercise in finger-pointing and paranoia."

"I'm listening."

Hades shifted his position, leaning forward and resting his forearms on his knees. "The Unktehila have a large-scale plan in place. They've put agents close to every Thunderbird they could identify, and they've identified a lot. They're going to take every one of them out at once—a mass assassination. Once that's done—well. With no Thunderbirds to stop them, the Unktehila can pretty much take over the world. *And no one will even notice.*"

He was right. Shape-changers that can influence people to trust them? They could replace every leader in the world without trying. All that was standing in their way was a little genocide . . . of a group that included my boyfriend and his mentor.

"Sounds apocalyptic," I said. "Let's say you're telling the truth. How do you propose we stop them?"

"Two methods come to mind. One, I betray my own race to our ancient enemies and they do their best to wipe us out first."

"Which is pretty much exactly the war we're trying to prevent. Option two?"

"We convince both sides to sit down and talk. Broker a truce."

"Much more reasonable. But a lot harder to pull off."

He shrugged. "True, but we've got plenty of incentive to do so. You know how much time and effort I've put into staging this upcoming tour? All for nothing if the world ends in a frenzy of assassinations, tornadoes, hurricanes, and lightning storms."

That was hard to argue with. "I don't suppose you can get your hands on a list of proposed assassinations?"

"I might be able to, yes. But the real question is, should I give that list to you? The Thunderbirds could use it to kill my people instead of the other way around."

He had a point; Teresa had been in an awfully bloodthirsty mood before I calmed her down. "What do you propose, then?"

He leaned back against his throne. "A meeting between Teresa and myself. I'd prefer face-to-face, but Skype works for me. Whatever she needs to feel safe."

"Skype might be a better idea . . . so what about Maxine?"

"You're going to have to decide which one of us to trust, of course. Meet with her, see what she has to say. If you mention the list, don't be surprised if she claims she can deliver the same thing. You understand why she's there, don't you? Why she's gotten close to Teresa First-charger and Zelda Zoransky?"

I felt a chill run down my back. "You mean—"

"Yes. She's there to kill Teresa—and Ben Montain. Two Thunderbirds with one stone . . . think about that, Foxtrot. Goodbye."

Chapter Six

After the call ended, I put away my tablet and sat down on the nearest headstone. I needed a moment to collect my thoughts.

[I don't trust him,] said Whiskey. [Do you?]

"Of course not. But he could be telling the truth. We need to talk to Maxine and see what she has to say."

[True. But we also need to talk to Grandfather Serpent. Any insights he has into the Unktehila and how they operate could be invaluable.]

I shook my head. "We need to split up. You try to locate the ghost snake, I'll go talk to the shape-shifting one—"

[Absolutely not. My place is by your side.]

"That's adorable, doggy, but not practical."

[Maybe we could get Maxine to join us in the graveyard for a discussion?]

"Good idea, but I don't think it'll work. She's performing the escape stunt tonight in the ballroom, so she'll be super busy getting ready. A long, rambling walk among the tombstones while we look for the spiritual ancestor of her entire race isn't going to be on her agenda—and what happens when we find Grandaddy Snake? Talk about awkward.

*Oh, hi, this is your great-great-great-times-infinity-great
grandfather. We just want to have a little chat with him
about any possible weaknesses you might have. Would you
mind waiting just out of earshot? 'Kay, thanks.*

[Then we should talk to Maxine first. There's no telling if or when Grandfather Serpent will show up, and I
refuse to let you negotiate with an Unktehila alone.]

I could see that he wasn't going to give in, and unlike
an ordinary dog, there was no way I could make Whiskey
do anything he didn't want to. I sighed and gave in to
the inevitable. "Have it your way. We'll talk to Maxine
first. But I've got a busy schedule myself; I can't spend all
day roaming through the Great Crossroads waiting for a
ghostly anaconda to show up."

[Then I suggest we leave immediately.]

I had a lot to mull over on the walk back to the mansion. It didn't really make sense that Maxine would reveal herself to me if she'd been sent as an assassin—but
maybe that was *why* she'd revealed herself; she didn't
want to be a killer.

And then there was the whole idea of the list. Did Teresa know about every Thunderbird on it, or had the Unktehila discovered Thunderbirds that even Firstcharger
was unaware of? Either way, if a single Thunderbird died
because I hadn't informed Teresa in time, she'd have my
head on the end of a lightning bolt.

I walked a little faster.

Maxine was in the ballroom with Summer, setting up the
equipment. This seemed to mostly consist of Summer using a forklift to jockey a large, metal tank onto a platform
of steel grid work about three feet off the ground. Unlike
the finery of last night, today they were each dressed in
baggy jeans and T-shirts, hair roped into ponytails and
corralled under baseball caps.

"Hey there," I said from the doorway. "Anything in here I'm not supposed to see? Because it's totally too late."

"A bit more to the right," said Maxine to Summer. "Good, good. Hey yourself, Foxtrot. Come on in; don't worry, we've got nothing to hide."

"Not yet, anyway," Summer said with a grin.

"I know you're busy," I said. "But I need a word. Can you get away for just a minute?"

Maxine saw the look in my eyes and nodded. "Of course. Getting away is my specialty, after all. Summer, take a break—go get another of those Danishes you've been lusting after."

"Yay! Carbohydrates!" Summer shut down the forklift and leaped off the seat; she was out the door before Maxine and I were.

"Your chef has a real way with pastry," said Maxine.

"Among other things. Let's go to my office."

Whiskey never took his eyes off her the whole way there—and once we'd arrived and closed the door, he sat upright exactly halfway between Maxine on the couch and me behind my desk.

"So," I said. "I want to trust you. I definitely *don't* want a war. But Lockley Hades is telling me one thing, and you're telling me another. Before I let the snake out of the bag, I need to decide which of you I should listen to."

Teresa and Ben already knew, of course—but Maxine didn't know they knew. If she did, it might force her hand, and I didn't want that. Not yet, anyway.

Maxine studied me calmly. "You know about the Unktehila ability to influence people's actions, don't you?"

"I do."

"Then you should be able to tell that I'm not using that ability at the moment."

"Not as far as I can tell, no."

"But the fact that I *could* damns me before I say a

word, doesn't it? How can you decide in my favor if any favorable opinion of me is suspect?"

"Good point. And since I've only talked to Lockley Hades on the phone, he doesn't have the same problem."

She nodded. "Which is exactly why he's doing it that way. What else has he told you?"

"I'm more interested in what *you're* going to tell me."

"Fair enough. There's a plan to take out all the Thunderbirds in one stroke. A group assassination."

The same thing Hades had told me. "That would be difficult to organize, wouldn't it?"

"They've spent years setting it up. Figuring out who the latent Thunderbirds are and putting people next to them. Most of the targets don't even know what they're capable of—or didn't until recently."

"Right. And which target is yours?"

She met my eyes and didn't flinch. "My primary objective is Teresa Firscharger. Lockley Hades is supposed to kill Ben Montain."

"But you had a change of heart."

"I'm not the only one. Many of the Unktehila think this is a bad idea, but Hades leads the faction that thinks eliminating our old foes is the answer."

"I see. There must be a list of targets, then . . ."

She hesitated then said, "Yes. But I'm not sure if I should turn it over. What if the Thunderbirds' reaction is to kill all my people?"

So Maxine wouldn't give me the list to prove her good intentions. Hades claimed he would—maybe—but there was no guarantee the list he'd give me was genuine. One of them was doing their best to deceive me, while the other wanted to help. . . . but which was which?

"I need something concrete," I said. "Something that *proves* you mean what you say. If there are other Unktehila that feel the same way you do, you must know some of the other targets."

She grimaced. "I do. But if I tell you, this whole thing could escalate out of control. We need to defuse it by getting the leaders on both sides to agree to a truce. Anything else is too dangerous."

"I think I can get Teresa to agree to that. But how can I do the same with Hades if he won't even admit to being in charge?"

She shook her head. "I don't know. I think he's just stalling for time."

Or maybe she's the one stalling. Maybe this was just her strategy for getting Teresa and Ben in the same room at the same time—after all, Teresa seemed to be the closest thing the Thunderbirds had to a leader. But why go to all this trouble when neither Ben nor Teresa even suspected what Maxine really was before this?

My phone started warbling "She Blinded Me with Science," meaning it was Karvenin calling. "Mr. Karvenin, what can I do for—"

"I'm leaving," he said. "I have had serious concerns about this project from the beginning, and I am afraid the dictates of my conscience have now outweighed my desire for financial compensation." His soft, sardonic voice was tinged with regret. "Please offer my apologies to Mr. Zoransky and Ms. Danger. I am truly sorry to miss her performance this afternoon, but I will be departing immediately. I'll be in touch concerning the transportation of my equipment."

Uh-oh. An unhappy guest meant a big checkmark in the FAIL column of my job description. "That's a shame. Is there anything I can do? I know Oscar can be a bit . . . profit-motivated, but he's not all bad. I'd be happy to talk to him—I've been able to make him see reason before."

"That's very kind, but my mind is made up. I'm already packed, and I've called a taxi."

"All right, then. We're sorry to see you go."

I put my phone down. "Well, your audience just shrank by one. Esko Karvenin is leaving, but he specifically said to tell you he's sorry to miss your performance."

Maxine frowned. "That's too bad—but the show must go on. Speaking of which, I really need to get back to work. Some of the technical aspects of this stunt are . . . challenging."

"I understand. I'll talk to Teresa and set up a meeting for afterward, say around four? Does that work for you?"

"As long as I survive." She smiled then sighed. "I'll see if I can arrange for Hades to attend remotely. I doubt I'll be successful, but I'll try."

After she left, I asked Whiskey, "Well? Can your amazing, supernatural nose tell you anything about what she told us?"

[I'm not a lie detector. She smelled anxious, but considering the situation, that's perfectly normal. What's more worrisome to me is the fact that she also smells completely human. No trace of serpent at all.]

"Which either means she's lying about being an Unktehila—or they're undetectable by scent."

[Precisely. And it's difficult to say which is more troubling.]

Teresa wasn't on the estate. Apparently not trusting herself around Maxine—or not trusting Maxine around her—Teresa had driven into town to do some shopping. When I called her, she agreed to the sit-down, but she didn't sound happy about it. "We're being manipulated, Foxtrot. Regardless of which one is telling the truth, one of them isn't. Hell, maybe both of them are lying and this is only part of some even more complicated scheme."

"Try not to let your imagination run wild, okay? If she had something evil in mind, she could easily have attacked you when you didn't know what she was. Let's see what they have to say."

"Very well. I'll be back in time to see her "performance." But if anything seems at all suspicious, there'll be a lightning bolt at my fingertips."

Terrific. Like having someone with a loaded gun aimed at you as you turn the crank on a jack-in-the-box. "I'll see you then. Do me a favor and stay away from caffeine until then, okay?"

She hung up without answering.

I'd sent Whiskey back to the Crossroads after talking to Maxine, and now I heard his telepathic voice in my head: [Foxtrot? A total lack of surprise. I've just located Grandfather Serpent.]

If you're going to be braincasting from the graveyard, at least try to work your password into the conversation, will you? You know the Crossroads amplifies psychic communication.

[Very well. It is with a total lack of surprise that I note you still haven't given me your password.]

Umwhirligig.

[Thank you. I especially appreciate how skillfully you worked it into the natural flow of dialogue.]

Let me try again. I used to have a dog until he was accidently run over by a late-model umwhirligig.

[Not really credible.]

Which I was driving.

[Better. I'll wait for you by the statue of the horse.]

When I arrived, Whiskey was sitting in front of the statue, staring intently at the horse's feet. This was because Grandfather Serpent was wrapped around the statue's front legs, apparently enjoying the sun. Oddly, though the statue was in a high-traffic area, there were very few spirits around, only a few turtles seemingly plodding in the opposite direction as quickly as they could.

"Hello, Grandfather Serpent," I said. "I'm glad to see you again."

"Are you?" he replied. "Then I suppose you've thought about what I said the last time we spoke?"

"You told me information itself was less important than what we do with it. And while I agree, it's difficult to know what to do when you don't know which information to trust."

The snake moved its head from side to side in a very human way. I thought he looked a little different from the last time I'd seen him—longer, maybe? Or was it the pattern of scales that seemed to have changed?

"It is not information that requires trust. It is those you obtain it from."

"Very true. Any ideas on that subject?"

His tongue flicked at me. "I have a story you might find illuminating. Do you wish to hear it?"

I leaned against a nearby headstone. "I'd love to."

"Very good. The story begins, as many do, with someone who was unhappy. This person lacked those most basic of characteristics: limbs. Having neither legs nor arms, the snake was forced to crawl on his belly through the mud and over the unforgiving rocks. He complained bitterly about this, so the other animals tried to cheer him up. *Fish don't have arms or legs either*, a bear told him.

"*Fish don't need them—they move through the water like birds through the air*, the snake replied.

"*Snails don't have arms or legs*, a blue jay said.

"*Snails have a shell to protect them*, the snake replied. *I have nothing.*

"After a while the animals gave up and left him alone. What else could they do?

"So the snake made the best of it. He learned to swim.

He learned to climb trees. And most of all, he learned to pay attention to everything that was going on around him. He became very good at keeping still, even better at being hidden, and in these ways he discovered much about the world that many of its other inhabitants were unaware of."

Grandfather Serpent watched me as he continued speaking, and I pictured his story in my mind.

"The snake's knowledge eventually led him to a garden where life was easy. There was no shortage of food, the weather was excellent, and the gardener took such care in her property that it was always lush and beautiful. Such a garden attracted many other animals of course, and the gardener had built a high and sturdy wall to keep them out. The observant snake had found a hole beneath the wall made by a rat, and thus, not only gained entrance but a tasty dinner at the same time.

Indeed, the biggest problems the gardener faced were rodents and birds, for a wall kept out neither while the abundant fruit of the garden's trees attracted both. This suited the snake just fine, for he much preferred eating mice and sparrows to peaches and plums. Over time, this arrangement led to him and the gardener becoming good friends. The snake would often wrap himself around the lower branches of a pomegranate tree and chat with the gardener as she pruned and weeded and watered.

But then, one day, two new intruders appeared in the garden. A man and a woman who had managed to climb over the wall.

They were clearly as scared as they were hungry. They grabbed some overripe fruit that lay on the ground and disappeared back over the wall as quickly as they'd appeared.

The next day, the snake told the gardener what he'd seen. The gardener paused in her work and frowned. "That's not good," she said quietly.

"Why? They took very little, and of that, only what lay

on the ground and would have rotted anyway. What's the harm?"

"The harm, little snake, is that human beings learn even quicker than you do. They will begin with the fruit on the ground and then move to the fruit hanging lowest on the trees. They will bring baskets with them to carry as much as they can, for they will fear that others will eat the fruit first. They will take more than they can use, for they are clever and will soon realize they can trade fruit to others for furs or meat or weapons. Sooner or later they will pick every tree bare, for their cleverness does not outpace their greed." The gardener sighed. "Their intelligence seems to get them into as much trouble as it finds solutions for. Sometimes I wish they'd just stayed up in the trees . . ."

"Can I help?" the snake asked, since he appreciated all the gardener had done for him.

The gardener studied the snake. "You do a good job of keeping the birds and rats under control. Perhaps you could frighten the humans away."

"How? I have no claws like the lion, or jaws like the crocodile, or talons like the eagle. I am hardly fearsome."

The gardener smiled. "It isn't what you can do, little snake. It's what others *believe* you can do." And she told the snake what to say to the man and the woman when they came back.

And yes, they did come back, the very next night. The snake was waiting for them, curled in the branches of the pomegranate tree. He waited until they came closer, and then, very softly, said, "You should not be here."

The man and the woman froze. "Who's there?" the man demanded. His voice only shook a little.

"A friend. And I must warn you about this garden and what is in it."

"We know what's in it," said the woman. "Food. And we're hungry."

"What this garden grows is not food but death. The fruits, the nuts, the flowers—all are poisonous. The wall is there for your protection."

"You lie," the man said. "We ate the fruit from here before, and we yet live."

"You were lucky," the snake replied. "You took only fruit that had fallen to the ground. The toxin inside is the first thing to decay, and thus the fruit does not poison the soil of the garden. But you don't have to take my word for it; go ahead and try some of the fruit still hanging from the branches for yourselves."

The man and woman did not move.

"Then if we eat only fruit from the ground, we will be safe?" the woman asked.

"Yes," the snake said, for the gardener had told him she didn't mind if they did so. And so the man and woman gathered up what fallen fruit they could find, though much of it was half-rotten and full of insects. And then they departed—but returned again the next night.

For a while, everything was fine. The man and the woman took only the fruit on the ground, and the snake watched them. He found them to be fascinating creatures; curious, clever and playful, they soon lost any fear of the snake and would talk to him freely.

"Doesn't being so close to the poison make you nervous?" the woman asked him one night, as the snake slithered past a ripe pomegranate. "If they could poison the very ground, surely they could poison a snake."

The snake hesitated. He was going to tell the woman another lie, that he had lived in the tree for many years and thus built up an immunity to the poison—but he saw her studying the ripe pomegranate, fear warring with hunger in her eyes, and took pity on her. "This tree is different from the others," he admitted. "Its fruit will not harm you."

The woman was wary at first, but she and the snake had become friends, and she trusted him. She picked the pomegranate, grinned with delight, and ran back to tell her partner. The man looked skeptical, but they took the fruit with them when they left.

One tree, the snake thought to itself. *One fruit. What's the harm?*

And there was no harm, not at first. But soon the fruit on the ground was gone, and the fruit in the pomegranate tree hung heavy from the branches. The man and woman ate sparingly at first, as if convinced some traces of poison must surely remain—but as their health remained robust, they devoured more and more. Indeed, soon they spurned any of the fruit on the ground at all.

"There's a nice-looking apple over by the edge of that bush," the snake tried to point out.

The man barely gave it a glance. "Brown spots. Probably got a worm inside, too."

The snake sighed. But the pomegranate tree was large, and there were only two of them; how bad could it get?

The next night, they brought baskets.

He tried to convince them it was a bad idea. He tried to tell them they'd get in trouble and get him in trouble as well. They had quite the argument, and in the end they accused him of lying to them and being on the gardener's side all along. Which was, of course, quite true.

The gardener found the snake curled up beneath a bush the next morning, looking miserable. "You're not in your usual spot," she said.

"No," the snake said.

"Then again, neither are any of my pomegranates. The tree currently contains neither reptiles *nor* fruit; would you care to explain?"

And so the snake did. He told the gardener how he'd taken pity on the man and the woman, and how they'd responded by taking the pomegranates. "When I tried to persuade them not to, they wouldn't listen. Eventually they got very angry and chased me away with a stick."

The gardener sighed. "Poor little serpent. Well, we've all learned a lesson here, haven't we?"

"I suppose," said the snake. "Though it doesn't seem like the same lesson for all of us."

"It never is, little snake. It never is . . ."

"What do we do now?"

"Now? Well, they won't be back for a while—they've taken all they can. But eventually, they'll start to think about all the other fruit in the garden and realize you lied to them about that, too. And then they'll be back."

"How will we stop them?"

The gardener smiled, but it was a cold and hard thing. "We will have to make some changes," she said. "Starting with giving you a way to defend yourself. Not everything you told them was untrue, you know."

"You mean some of the fruit *is* poisonous?"

"Oh, yes—and not just the fruit. There are all kinds of poisons in the world: some slow, some fast, some subtle, and some not. Even words can be a kind of poison, if mixed and delivered correctly; in that sense, we all carry poison within us, all the time."

"Even me?"

"Oh, yes, little snake. Right now you feel angry and betrayed, and that is a recipe for the worst poison of all. I will teach you how to concentrate and store this poison; I will teach you how to deliver it. And then, little snake, it will be time to teach those thieves *another* lesson . . ."

Grandfather Serpent stopped. I realized after a moment that it wasn't just a pause, and he was actually done.

[An unusual variation of a very old story,] said Whiskey. [I'm not sure what the relevance to our situation is.]

"The variation of a story," said Grandfather Serpent,

"often depends on whose point of view it is told from. Indeed, the entire meaning of a story can change simply by looking at it through a different set of eyes. Perhaps your own story should be looked at in another way."

This time I spotted the hole before he slithered down it, at the base of the statue—though I could swear it wasn't there before. In another second he was gone, leaving behind more questions than answers.

Chapter Seven

"So," I said as we walked back to the mansion. "Garden of Eden, right? Adam and Eve and Original Sin."

[Yes. But in this case, the positions were reversed; the Serpent was the one who disobeyed, and the humans were the betrayers.]

"It wasn't that simple, though. The Serpent's disobedience was an act of kindness, and the humans didn't really betray anyone; when they discovered they were lied to in the first place, they got angry."

[And violent. And then went back to stealing what they'd been stealing before.]

"Yeah. So what's the takeaway? Humans are less trustworthy than snakes?"

[Perhaps. Or it could simply be that both species are capable of generosity and selfishness.]

"Also, God is female. And not terribly nice."

[I have no comment on that statement.]

"*There's* a surprise."

[Speaking of surprises—watch where you're about to step.]

The warning came a second too late. My shoe squelched

down on something brown, squishy, and—I realized a moment later—smelly.

"Oh, for—who lets their dog crap in a graveyard and then doesn't clean it up?" I wiped my shoe furiously against the grass, but that just mushed it up worse and somehow raised the level of stink.

Whiskey sniffed carefully at the offending substance. [The owner of a three-year-old Welsh terrier, I surmise. In fair health but has recently been dewormed.]

"I'll deworm *him*—"

[Her. In both cases.]

"So, the arrogant owner of a Welsh terrier thinks she can use *my* graveyard as their own personal toilet? This will not stand—it may stink, but it won't stand. Whiskey, can you tell which way they went?"

[The trail is at least a day old—but yes, I think I can.]

He put his nose down and started snuffling around in a big circle around the offending pile before angling off in one particular direction. I followed. We tracked the perpetrators right to the entrance of the graveyard and a short ways up the street, where the trail vanished. [Sorry, Foxtrot. They must have gotten into a vehicle and driven off.]

I called Cooper, the groundskeeper, and let him know about the doggy-do. He assured me he'd clean it up right away.

We returned to the house, where we updated Ben and Tango on what Grandfather Serpent told us. Ben's reaction was frustration—understandable, since we hadn't really learned anything useful—while Tango seemed unsurprised. <*A snake taking the side of the Devil. Of course.*>

"There was no actual Devil involved," I said. "I think it was just a metaphor to show us that the Unktehila have their own side of the story. Maybe we should focus more on trying to understand them and less on trying to find ways to destroy them."

<That makes sense. It's always good to know your enemy's weaknesses.>

I sighed and didn't bother with a rebuttal. Instead, I mentioned the unpleasant surprise we'd found afterward.

Tango was unsurprised. *<Dogs are disgusting. Who leaves their droppings out in the open like that? Dogs, that's who. And birds. And rodents. And horses. Come to think of it, most animals are disgusting when it comes to their personal habits.>*

"How about humans? We invented indoor plumbing."

<True. But you have so many other failings, that hardly makes up for anything.>

I glowered. "Well, they better not come back. I might be overworked, but that doesn't mean they can disrespect the Great Crossroads like this. Whiskey, keep your nose peeled whenever we're in the graveyard; if they return, I want to know about it."

[I shall stay alert.]

Tango snorted. *<Like they'll ever come back. Why should they? They've got a whole world they can treat like a litter box.>*

Sadly, I couldn't disagree.

Lunch wasn't well attended. Karvenin had left, Summer and Maxine were holed up in the ballroom—I sent Consuela with sandwiches, but they didn't answer her knock, so she left them at the door—and Keene was presumably still hanging out with Cooper. That left the Japanese lockmaker, Masuda, and Amos Clay, the forensics specialist. They seemed happy enough with the pasta salad and crab cakes Ben made for them, though Clay grumbled a bit about crustacean populations and sustainable aquaculture practices. Masuda seemed a little distracted, though that might have just been about his role in the afternoon's presentation. Oscar put in a brief appearance but only to grab a plate and vanish again, muttering something about wire feeds jamming and clogged nozzles.

Teresa Firstcharger was notably absent. Ben told me she'd returned from town but then left for Thunderspace, and he was joining her once he'd cleaned up after lunch. "Don't expect either of us back for a few hours," he said. "She told me I need to do more than just train."

"What's *that* mean?"

Ben looked grim. "She wants to talk about war strategy."

Great. Better to be prepared, I guess . . . but I hated it.

After lunch I went back to my office to catch up on some paperwork, and both Whiskey and Tango came with me. The performance was supposed to start at two, and I kept expecting Maxine or Summer to call me with some last-minute request—but apparently they had everything under control.

"You two stay up here," I said, getting up from my desk.

[Why?]

<Yeah, why?>

I leaned over the couch where they sprawled at opposite ends and gave each of them skritches behind the ears. "Because ZZ told me you had to. She's worried that one of you will mess up the performance. *I* know you won't, but that's hard to explain to her."

<Hmmmph. I'm not interested, anyway. So she can escape from a trap she built herself? How is that impressive? I could do the same thing.>

[Please. I've seen you get yourself trapped in a laundry hamper.]

<Okay, first of all? Laundry hampers shouldn't even have locks. Who's worried about someone stealing their dirty laundry? And second, I wasn't even consulted about the design of said hamper. >

[What you call a *lock* others call a *latch*. I believe it's mostly there to keep the lid closed so oblivious felines don't try to add it to the list of odd places they've fallen asleep in.]

<There's no such thing as an odd place to fall asleep. Just places I have and places I haven't. Yet.>

"I'll just be downstairs. I'll leave the door ajar, and if anything weird happens, I'll give a big, old telepathic holler. All right?"

[Very well.]

<I guess.>

I went down and joined the group clustered outside the ballroom's doors. Oscar was now wearing a white yachting jacket with a blue cravat, while ZZ was in a plain (for her) pink jumpsuit and white sneakers. Keene wore the same clothes he had at the graveyard, along with a glazed look in his eyes and a strong aroma of cannabis. Amos Clay, in the same off-white cargo shorts and safari shirt that was his usual uniform, was grinning and chatting to ZZ. The serious expression on Hironobu Masuda's face matched his dark-blue business suit; he kept both hands clasped behind his back as if awaiting a firing squad.

The second I stepped up, the ballroom doors opened wide. Maxine's assistant Summer, wearing what seemed to be a sequined cheerleader's outfit, motioned us inside with a bow and a flourish.

"Welcome!" she said, beaming. "Prepare to be wowed by the amazing Maxine Danger and . . . the death-defying Ice Escape!

Maxine's voice called out from behind her. "Glacier Escape!"

Summer rolled her eyes. "We haven't settled on a title card yet. Anyway, come on in and make yourself comfortable."

In the center of the ballroom stood the red metal platform I'd watched them putting together earlier. A low set of steps had been added, and a row of folding chairs was set up a few feet away from the front of the stage.

On the stage was a large, open safe. It was big enough to hold maybe three people standing upright. It stood on a block of solid, transparent material that raised it another foot and a half or so above the metal floor of the stage.

Maxine Danger stepped out of the safe. She was dressed in a very skimpy, ice-blue bikini, which everyone tried not to stare at and mostly failed.

"Greetings," Maxine said formally. "If you're wondering why I'm dressed like this, it's to show that I have nothing to hide. This is a Pendergrass 10–19 vault, renowned for its unpickable locking mechanism. Can you confirm this, Mr. Masuda?"

Masuda nodded then stepped forward and turned around to face the rest of us. "The body of the Pendergrass is composed of twelve inches of hardened steel plate. The lock utilizes a special magnetic key that is impossible to pick by any known method. I have examined the safe myself and can verify that it has not been tampered with in any way."

Oscar sniffed. "And we'll just have to take your word for that, I suppose?"

Masuda regarded Oscar gravely. "Not at all. Please examine this." He withdrew a folded piece of paper from the inside pocket of his suit and handed it to Oscar. "This is a notarized contract drawn up by Ms. Zoransky's legal firm. It states that should I be found to utter any false statement concerning this performance or my professional evaluation of any component of it, I can be held legally responsible for fraud, with a penalty payable to the complainant of one million dollars."

Oscar studied the document the way a hungry rat studies cheese. "I see . . ."

"Is that safe—er, *safe*, resting on that block of ice?" asked Keene, casting a nervous and somewhat bloodshot eye at the stage. "It couldn't slide off and crush someone in the audience?"

"Oh, that's not ice," said Maxine. "It's a slab of bullet-proof glass. Durable and transparent. During the actual stage show, we'll add a little dry ice to enhance the illusion. No, the reference to ice in the name is more about showmanship than anything else. Which brings us to this . . ."

Summer had been standing off to one side; she now stepped behind the vault and reappeared on the other side pushing a wheeled stand as tall as she was, which was draped with a purple velvet cloth. She brought it to the front of the stage and then stepped aside once more.

Maxine pulled the cloth off in one quick, smooth movement. What stood revealed was a waist-height angular metal table, holding a three-foot-high glass column filled with some sort of thick, transparent liquid; tiny bubbles were suspended throughout, and wisps of vapor rose from the open mouth of the tube. Beneath the table stood a thick, metal canister labeled DANGER: EXTREME COLD. Four insulated hoses led from the canister to each corner of the table, where four nozzles were angled up at the tube. A metal pipe around three feet long with a wheel on the end of it jutted sideways from the top of the canister.

"The clear column on top is filled with polymethyl methacrylate," said Maxine. "Otherwise known as Lucite. A clear, strong acrylic currently being heated to a temperature of three hundred and twenty degrees Fahrenheit— just enough to keep it in a liquid state."

I could smell it now, the odor of hot plastic that I always associated with fried electronics.

"Please," continued Maxine, "feel free to inspect the vault from any angle for any secret exits or trap doors. There's a step ladder around back if you want to take a look at the top."

Amos Clay and ZZ accepted her invitation, climbing

onto the stage and circling the vault with critical eyes. Oscar peered under the platform itself, while Masuda seemed content to remain where he was.

"Mirrors," Keene stage-whispered to me. "I knew a chap, used to open for my band back in the day. Told me all about it."

"If you can find a single mirror, Mr. Keene," said Summer, suddenly materializing at his side, "I'd be happy to eat it."

Keene stared at her then grinned. "Now you've given me the munchies," he said. "I fancy something crunchy. And . . . reflective."

"I'll get Ben to whip you up some fortune cookies," I said.

Despite my far-too-paranormal lifestyle, I'm a pragmatist at heart; I couldn't resist conducting my own examination, including climbing the step ladder and inspecting the vault's roof. If there was a hidden trap door, I couldn't find it.

"I should add," said Maxine when we were all satisfied, "that Mr. Masuda has also inspected the vault and certified it tamper-free. What you see is what you get: a big block of steel with a pick-proof lock. Now—on to the finer details. Mr. Masuda?"

Masuda reached into his pocket and produced a small sealed envelope. He ripped it open and emptied the contents into his hand: a single key, which he held up between his thumb and forefinger so all of us could see it. It was slightly larger than an ordinary key, with a thick shaft.

"This," said Maxine, "is a magnetic key. It works the same way as a regular key, with one major difference. You see these circles?" She stepped forward and pointed her finger at four evenly spaced discs along the shaft, taking care not to actually touch them. "These contain powerful magnets. They are arranged so that each of them either attracts or repels a corresponding pin inside the lock. When the key is inserted, the pins are pushed or pulled into the correct alignment to open the lock. Mr. Masuda—can you confirm that this sequence, created by you, has never been revealed to me or anyone else?"

"I can," said Masuda formally.

"And that this is the only key to this lock in existence?"

"Yes."

"Excellent. And do you have the other piece of equipment, as specified?"

"Yes." Keeping the key carefully in sight, Masuda reached into the side pocket of his jacket and produced a short length of wire.

"Good. Please attach the wire to the key using the loop in the key's head."

Masuda did so.

"And now for the last piece of equipment," said Maxine. "Summer?"

We glanced over at Summer, who had taken advantage of Maxine's spiel to gobble some noodles from a take-out container. She froze, swallowed guiltily, then handed over one of her chopsticks. "It's only a little greasy," she said.

Maxine sighed. "Mr. Masuda. Please wind the end of the wire around the middle of the stick, and then—carefully!—lower the key into the glass tube with the chopstick across the top."

Masuda did so. I could see tiny bubbles of air stuck to the surface of the key once it was immersed in the hot, liquid plastic.

"Very good," said Maxine. "Any attempt by me—or anyone else—to retrieve and use that key will result in serious burns as well as hopelessly gumming up the lock—which I should point out has regular pins and tumblers in addition to its magnetic features. Not that I have anywhere to hide a lockpick on me at the moment—"

"Ahem," said Summer. Her noodles had vanished, replaced by a short metal wand familiar to anyone who'd flown on an airplane in the last twenty years; a handheld metal detector.

Maxine rolled her eyes theatrically. "*Fine*," she mock-groaned. "And just to prove we're not cheating, one of *you* can use it on me." She waved in our general direction. "But make sure you use it on yourself first, to eliminate any doubt. Who wants to have a go?"

Keene bolted forward like a boy who'd just been offered ice cream, but Maxine stopped him with a look. "Let's leave this to an adult, shall we?" she said. "Foxtrot, how about you?"

"Absolutely," I said. "I just hope your check clears."

This got me a deadpan stare; I guess I should leave the one-liners to the professionals. I took the wand, ran it over myself, and got mechanical squeals from my phone, my belt buckle, and my necklace.

"Seems okay," I said. I ran it over Maxine's body, then down her arms—

SQUEEEE.

I stopped. The wand had erupted while going over one of her outstretched hands. She tried to look innocent, then sighed, and said, "Okay, *fine*." She grabbed her middle finger with her other hand and pulled.

It came off.

No blood, but a few suspicious metallic things stuck out of the base. She handed it over: an almost perfect fake finger with several lockpicks in place of bones. Her actual finger had been curled against her palm. How on earth had I not noticed it earlier?

Because she's very good at what she does, I told myself.

No. Because she's a shape-shifter, you idiot, I replied.

"Now this part's *really* cool," said Summer. "From

three hundred and twenty to *minus* three hundred and twenty, in fact. A plunge of *six hundred and forty degrees Fahrenheit*." She walked over to the table with the column while holding the key and grabbed the metal wheel that stuck out a yard away from the table itself. "This tank is filled with liquid nitrogen," she said. "Any idea what will happen when we blast a tube of near-boiling liquid acrylic with it? 'Cause I have *no* idea. But I can't wait to find out!"

And before anyone could say anything, she'd cranked the valve open.

Four jets of white vapor blasted the column, obscuring it for a few seconds. There was a loud CRACK! as the tube shattered and fell away in several large pieces. Only a solid tube of acrylic remained, with a sheen of white frost on it. The key was still clearly visible, trapped in the column.

"Now that we've gotten that out of the way," Summer said, "can we get to the really fun part? Well, fun for me, anyway." She was already pushing her boss toward the vault.

"Okay, well, I guess we're ready—" Maxine said, suddenly looking nervous. "This should take—"

"Enough talking! Showtime!" yelled Summer, shoved Maxine inside, and slammed the door shut.

We all looked at Summer. She grinned.

And then her phone went off.

She pulled it out and answered it. "Hello? Oh, hi, Mom. No, nothing special. Sure, I can talk. Just a sec, lemme grab some privacy . . ."

She strolled off the stage and past us, talking the whole while and ignoring our befuddled stares completely. "So, how's Pop? Oh, still with the sleepwalking? Tell me he didn't get arrested again . . ."

She paused at the door, turned back, and said, "Don't worry, she's got air for at least ten minutes. Five minutes? Something like that. Anyway, I'll be back. Toodles."

And she walked right out the door.

We just stood there for a moment. I'd felt awkward silences before but never one with an undercurrent of panic at the same time.

"I bet she pops out the bottom," said Keene, peering underneath the platform and waving his hand under it as far as he could reach. "Or the top. Or the side. No, wait! *I bet she was never here in the first place*."

"Don't be ludicrous," said Oscar. "Or at least any more ludicrous than you usually are. Clearly, she—well, she—"

Amos Clay laughed, a big, barrel-chested guffaw. "Hah! I have absolutely no idea how she's going to pull this off and neither do you, my friend. But I can't wait to see her do it!"

"I doubt that we'll see anything," said ZZ, looking around the room avidly. "She'll just appear—maybe in a puff of smoke, or *right behind us*—"

She ducked her head and looked behind Keene, who yelped and spun around in a panic.

And then the lights went out.

"Nobody panic!" Keene said in a panicky voice.

"Nobody is," replied Oscar, sounding bored. "In case it hasn't penetrated your addled brain, this is clearly part of the trick—"

"I can vouch for that," I said. "None of the emergency lights have come on, which should have happened automatically. Also, they really should have told me before messing with those."

"Oh, I think we'll be all right," ZZ said. "Where's your spirit of adventure, Foxtrot?"

"Safely packed away with my passport, my immunization records, and a copy of my birth certificate," I answered. "In other words, exactly where it should be and I can access it whenever I need to. Or I could, if I weren't enveloped in complete darkness—"

The lights snapped back on.

"That's better," said Amos Clay. "Now, let's see what's up."

The vault was still locked. The key seemed to be untouched inside its Lucite prison. We looked around, but Maxine was nowhere in sight.

"What now?" Oscar asked.

"I think I know," I said. I stepped onto the stage and pointed at the vault door, to a small, yellow square right in the middle of it that hadn't been there before. It was a Post-it note with two words scrawled on it: OPEN ME.

"How very *Alice in Wonderland*," said Oscar. "I do hope there isn't a Jabberwock inside."

Though I didn't say anything, so did I.

Amos Clay was the one who discovered that the solid block of Lucite wasn't actually solid; only the exterior was. The key was still encased in ultra-hot plastic, though. He fished the key out. Hiro Masuda produced a handkerchief to wipe the molten acrylic off it, though he burned one of his fingers in doing so. When we were finally ready, ZZ insisted on being the one to unlock the vault.

The heavy door swung open with a tug. Maxine Danger was not inside.

But the vault wasn't empty, either.

A body lay just inside, crumpled on the floor. A naked, male body.

"What the deuce?" said Amos Clay.

"Is this part of the act?" said ZZ. "Who *is* that?"

I knelt beside the body. There was a knife in its chest and a slowly spreading pool of blood beneath it, which I carefully avoided as I checked for a pulse. No luck.

But while the presence of the body itself was a shock, that was nothing compared to who it was: Lockley Hades.

"Um," said a worried voice behind us. Summer Coyne stood in the open doorway to the ballroom, wearing the same outfit Maxine had been dressed in. "Maxine should be standing right there, right about now . . ."

She strode past us and up the steps of the stage. When she saw the body, her eyes went wide. "Oh my God," she said. "That's—that's Lockley Hades. What the hell is he doing here? *And where's Maxine*?"

"I have no idea what's going on," said Keene. "Is anyone else having this problem, or is it just me?"

Now came the part where we notified the local constabulary—which in this case is in Hartville, the nearest town and barely large enough to even have its own police force—and they sigh, say, "Again? Really?" and send out Officer Forrester to examine the scene, take notes and pictures, shake his head a lot in disbelief, and give us looks that are supposed to be accusatory but aren't because, by now, his eyebrows are mostly stuck in the up position. He gave up rolling his eyes a while back because they started spinning like slot machine windows and made all of us dizzy.

Okay, maybe it's not *quite* like that. But this has happened often enough that we have a permanently open file at the police station, the coroner has us bookmarked, and the surprise of discovering a corpse has faded somewhat from highly disturbing to mildly unpleasant. We're all a little jaded, I know.

But just as local law enforcement has gotten used to us, we've gotten used to them. And, being the highly prepared sort of person I am, I devised a set of protocols for my assistants when such a thing occurs.

Step one: telepathic alert to Whiskey and Tango. *Code X! We have a Code X in the ballroom!* (There was a discussion concerning various codes and which ones would be appropriate to the situation. This was made unnecessarily long and contentious by Tango, who raised objections to almost any word suggested by Whiskey as being inherently prejudicial against felines. This somehow morphed into an argument about *every* word being inherently biased against the idea of murder itself, which Tango thought unfair and worth examining. Honestly, I think she was just bored; Tango is perfectly capable of stalking, pouncing upon, and tormenting a concept if no rodent or bird is available.)

I heard a feline yawn in my head. <*Password?*>

Umwhirligig!

[A total lack of surprise! On my way!]

<*Heading for the roof. I'll try to stay awake.*> Tango's job is to keep a lookout for anyone—like cops—arriving and anyone—like a murderer—trying to flee. Whiskey's job is to immediately converge on the crime scene to, with his doggy senses, pick up any traces a normal forensic team might miss. This goes beyond the usual canine supersensitive nose; as a ghost, Whiskey has access to a supernatural library of scents recorded by other dogs over the entire history their race has existed. A smellbrary, I suppose. It's come in useful more than once.

As an ectoplasmic being that can shape-shift into any dog breed, Whiskey can pretty much go wherever he wants. There are dogs big enough to push open even heavy doors and dogs tiny enough to squeeze under them. He has to be cautious around people who don't know what he is, of course, but even if one of the staff sees a greyhound bolting down the stairs, by now they're used to that level of wacky.

It helps that I'm nominally in charge, at least until Shondra—our head of security—arrives. But she's already busy talking to the cops on the phone, and crowd-control is my job by default.

So default was definitely mine when a tiny, mouse-gray terrier zipped past everyone's heels, through the door, and into the crime scene. Fortunately, nobody noticed a thing—they were all too busy trying to make sense of events by talking amongst themselves in a huddle just outside the ballroom. ZZ was counseling patience, Keene was babbling nonstop, and Oscar was desperately trying to find someone to get him a drink. Hiro Masuda and Amos Clay were talking quietly to each other, and Summer Coyne was standing a little off to one side looking extremely upset.

I shut the doors with Whiskey inside. Nobody seemed to notice or care. I sighed to myself and started talking to my ghost dog in my head.

Here's what happened, I began. I gave him a quick rundown of the events that led up to the discovery of the body. *And now we're waiting for the authorities.*

[We *are* the authorities, Foxtrot. The only ones that matter in this sort of case, anyway.]

Careful you don't step in any of the blood.

[Please. I won't disturb so much as a hair—including the one I just found.]

Where? And can you tell who it belongs to?

[Just inside the vault. And its owner was a *Gorilla berengei berengei*—a mountain gorilla.]

Except, of course, it really wasn't. It was an Unkhetila, right?

[Impossible to know for sure. The scent from the hair is authentic, but we already know the Unkhetila can mimic another animal perfectly. It does suggest that the form was chosen for strength and manual dexterity.]

The better to steal a key and commit murder with? But how did the body get in the vault—and if Maxine was the killer, why kill Hades in such a public way, when all suspicions would naturally point toward her?

Tango cut in, <Heads up. The police officers arrived.>

[I'm about done in here. The only other scent is one lingering in the air of the vault itself. Very faint, but definitely marine-based.]

A fish? How the hell does a fish fit into all this?

<Oh, you can always fit in a fish. They're not that filling.>

I groaned and went to greet the police at the front door. Again.

Chapter Eight

Lieutenant Forrester, a man in a dark-blue suit with the build of a linebacker and the face of a character actor stuck playing the angry police chief, sighed as he sat down with us in my office. Shondra—our head of security, dressed all in black—sat down to his right. Together with me behind my desk, we formed a perfect triangle of offense, defense, and a ball trying to appear helpful while really not cooperating at all. Spectators were Whiskey lying at my feet, staring intently at each of us in turn, and Tango on the windowsill, pretending to ignore everyone. Game on.

Forrester threw the first pitch—er, pass. Serve? You know what, I'm just gonna drop the sports metaphors and stick with English. "Okay. I've looked over the crime scene. I've got my partner taking pictures, prints, any evidence she can pick up and put in a baggie. The medical examiner's on his way for the body. Now it's time for my favorite part; Twenty Straightforward Questions, followed by at least Seventeen Ridiculous Answers and Three Half Truths. What exactly happened here?"

"Maxine Danger was demonstrating her new escape," I

said. "She was locked in the vault. The lights went out for a minute or so. When they came back on, we opened the vault. The body was inside. Maxine's assistant appeared at the door to the ballroom a second later."

"Shondra?" Forrester said.

Shondra is ex-military, a no-nonsense woman who could clean a gun blindfolded and stare down a tank. She nodded and said, "Security cameras indicate no one has left or entered the estate other than police personnel since the murder. Whoever did this is still here."

Forrester looked at me. "I've talked to all the witnesses. They all tell the same story—except Summer Coyne. She insists she and Maxine are innocent but refuses to divulge how the escape was done—and claims she has no idea how the body of Lockley Hades got into the vault. Maxine Danger is missing and presumed to have fled. Needless to say, she's my prime suspect."

Shondra gave him a look I found hard to interpret—cool but not cold, sharp but not cutting. Like she was poking him with a frozen carrot rather than stabbing him with an icicle. "Can you tie the weapon to either of them?"

"Not yet."

"Motive?"

"Hades and Danger are well-known professional adversaries."

"*Professional* adversaries," Shondra said, leaning forward slightly in her seat. "Meaning their feud was largely staged and beneficial to both of them. And its public nature meant an escalation to murder would be extremely stupid for either to consider. How many professional escape artists tend to be stupid?"

"Not many, I bet," I tried to interject, but I may as well have not been in the room at all. Forrester was staring at Shondra with a slight grin on his face.

"Granted. But even artificial wars can turn nasty. Could be a crime of passion—which is still motive."

She arched one eyebrow and gave him the barest trace of a smile back. "Which brings us to opportunity. Clearly Maxine Danger was able to escape from the vault, even if we don't know how she did it. The question is, how did the body get in?"

"The same way Maxine got out?" I ventured.

"Not necessarily," said Forrester. "Getting to the top of a building from the bottom isn't the same as getting to the bottom from the roof."

"Yes," said Shondra. "You can throw a body off a roof, but you can't throw it *onto* a roof."

[Not true,] said Whiskey's voice in my head. [I heard about a case from a colleague in a Russian circus involving a human cannonball and a penthouse swimming pool—]

Quiet. I'm trying to follow this.

"And," added Shondra, "There's the question of whether or not the murder was actually committed in the vault or the body moved from elsewhere."

"That one I can answer," said Forrester. "The blood pool under the body indicates the murder took place in the vault itself. Single knife thrust to the heart, and the knife was still there. We're trying to lift prints off it, but I'm not hopeful."

"Doesn't sound like enough for an arrest," said Shondra, leaning back.

"It's not," admitted Forrester. "I've got local and state cops on the lookout for Ms. Danger, and I've asked your guests not to go anywhere for the next few days until I can investigate further. They've all agreed. All except for Esko Karvenin—I understand he left earlier today, before this all happened?"

"Yes," I said. "But his leaving had nothing to do with Maxine's act—he and Oscar had plans for a business venture. Apparently, on further consideration, he found it a little too unsavory for his professional ethics."

Forrester was aware of Oscar's penchant for fly-by-night schemes. "Ah. Well, unless my investigation turns up a connection between Karvenin and Hades, I think we can rule him out for now. In the meantime—you know the drill, Foxtrot."

"Right," I said. "Nobody leaves the estate unless it's with a police escort. Nobody new to be admitted to the grounds other than previously vetted delivery people until you give the say-so."

"Or I do," said Shondra. She smiled at Forrester, but there was an edge to it. "You trust my judgment, right?"

Forrester didn't hesitate. "Of course. And I think that about wraps things up for now." He got to his feet. "I'll see myself out."

"Bye," said Shondra. She didn't get up, but her eyes followed him out the door.

"How long?" I asked when the door shut.

"Two weeks," said Shondra.

"He a keeper?"

"Don't know yet," Shondra said. "Signs point to yes."

"We're going to figure this out," ZZ told me. We were in her version of an office, an eclectic space currently decorated with large Warhol prints on the walls, bright-orange shag carpeting, and numerous multicolored beanbag chairs.

"Yes, ma'am," I said.

"Don't *yes, ma'am* me, I took acid with the Doors. Well, most of them—Jim Morrison spent the entire trip having an animated conversation with a Boston fern."

"Yes, ZZ."

She paused for thought, staring out the window that took up most of one wall, and said, "Any ideas?"

"Wait until the police catch Maxine and she confesses?"

ZZ snorted. "Don't be ridiculous. She's a professional escape artist, Trot. She's escaped, past tense. I don't think she'll surface until we clear her name."

"But—she's the prime suspect. Actually, she's the *only* suspect."

"What about her assistant? Maybe this is a way to replace Maxine. Or revenge for something Maxine did."

"Still wouldn't explain why Maxine ran."

"Maybe she didn't," said ZZ slowly. "Shondra told me the security system doesn't show her leaving. She could still be here."

"That's an interesting theory," I admitted. In fact, I'd already came to the same conclusion—but I knew Maxine was a mind-bending shape-shifter, meaning hiding in plain sight was a lot easier than anyone knew. Well, anyone except me, Teresa Firstcharger, Ben, Whiskey, Tango, Eli—okay, so a whole lot of people knew. Didn't mean Maxine couldn't pull it off, though; she was a professional illusionist, after all.

Ben had finally shown up a few hours after the discovery of the body, along with Teresa Firstcharger. They were shocked, but at least I could eliminate them as suspects; there was no way Ben would lie to me, and being together in an alternate dimension while the murder occurred gave both of them an alibi. The fact that time flowed more slowly in Thunderspace reinforced this—even if one of them slipped away from the other, returned to the earthly plane, killed Hades, and then went back, the passage of time would be exaggerated; a few missing minutes would become something closer to an hour.

But that still left a whole lot of other suspects—any of which might be a murderous shape-shifter posing as someone *else*.

Yeah. ZZ was right. We had to solve this. And if we

didn't do it quickly, the killer might strike again—possibly at my boyfriend.

"I'm on it," I told ZZ. "Whiskey's got a keen nose, and we've got stuff that has Maxine's scent on it. If she's hiding anywhere on the grounds, I'm sure he can track her down."

ZZ looked relieved. "Of course! I should have thought of that myself—nice work, Foxtrot!"

"Don't thank me yet," I said, heading for the door. "Let's see how our pooch does, first."

Whiskey and Tango were both waiting for me just outside the door. <Great plan, Toots. You know, if the plan was to make Whiskbroom look bad. Sorry, I meant worse.>

They paced beside me as I strode down the hall. [It's not my fault Unkhetila can disguise their scent as easily as they do their appearance,] Whiskey grumbled.

<True. Cheer up, pal; unlike the many, many things that are your fault, this ain't one.>

Where to begin . . . talk to the guests? See if Eli has any insights? Try to track down the elusive Grandfather Serpent for more elusive wisdom? Search the grounds for the missing Maxine? Ask my boyfriend if his mentor might also be a murderer?

Sometimes, when you're overloaded by myriad, contradictory information, the best way to start is to attack the first problem in front of you . . . and then just keep going.

I rounded a corner and almost ran down Hironobu Masuda. "Oh! Mr. Masuda, I'm so sorry—I'm a little preoccupied at the moment."

Masuda took a step back, gave his head a little shake, and muttered, "Not at all. Today's events have been . . . most unsettling."

"Of course. I was just heading to the parlor for some tea. Would you care to join me?"

"I—yes. Yes, that would be agreeable."

I pulled out my phone as we walked and ordered a large pot of jasmine green, Mr. Masuda's favorite. It arrived no more than a minute after we'd made ourselves comfortable in the parlor—Ben's quick on his feet, and it was a long walk.

Whiskey, I thought at him, *take a look around the grounds, and see if you can pick up any sign of Maxine.*

[I shall.] He trotted off.

Tango, go check out the zoo. See if any of the animals saw anything out of place.

<You got it, Toots.>

The parlor's a large room with an immense, stone fireplace at one end, Persian rugs on the floor, and a number of overstuffed armchairs and sofas that managed to look antique and modern at the same time; ZZ liked to find genuine old pieces and then have them completely reupholstered in fabric that *looked* authentic but on closer inspection proved to have a fine pinstriping of miniature skulls wearing sunglasses.

Masuda settled back into a plush chair of green baize with a sigh; only careful study would reveal the ghostly pattern of dinosaur skeletons skulking through the weave. "This has been . . . quite a day. Quite a day."

I poured tea for both of us. "Yes, it has. Again, I apologize for all the . . . unpleasantness."

Masuda picked up his tea, took a long, careful sip, then placed it back on its saucer. "No apologies are necessary. I was aware that Ms. Zoransky's gatherings can be . . . eventful. I just never thought I would actually be present when one such event occurred."

His phrasing struck me as odd, and when I parsed it, I realized what he was implying. "Wait a minute. You mean you *knew* there might be a murder?"

He froze for just an instant, but for someone with my skill at reading people, that was plenty. "No. Don't be absurd—"

"You did. You totally did. How? Did Maxine tell you something was going to happen? Are you *part* of this?"

People from different cultures respond differently to being questioned; a lot depends on not just how the questions are phrased but who's asking them. For a middle-aged, Japanese male, having a female subordinate go from friendly subservience to outright accusation can produce the equivalent of cultural whiplash—it's such a shock to the system, it can generate a brief, uncontrolled burst of emotion. Which emotion tends to depend on what the subject is feeling at the moment.

The emotion I saw on his face was panic.

"I—I am not! I am only a . . . a *fan*."

There was something about the way he said *fan* that made me squint at him suspiciously. Apparently my squint has become a lot more dangerous through years of careful honing, because it was enough to make him break right down. That, or the gnawing fear that he'd become an accessory to murder in a country that was not his own.

"You don't mean a fan of Maxine's, do you?" I said.

"Not . . . exactly. I am a fan of . . . certain events."

And then I got it. I'm quick like that. "The kind of events that sometimes happen here," I said. "Like murder."

He looked intensely uncomfortable. "Please. I did not know what would happen. I did not know if *anything* would happen. But there are certain places where such things are more statistically likely."

Great. He's a murder-mystery fan. And now that he's right in the middle of an actual locked-room—scratch that, locked-*vault*—mystery, he should be in heaven.

Only, he's not. Because he's way too close to the real

thing and just starting to realize how deep this end of the pool is. Time to march him out to the end of the diving board and make him look down.

I started with a theatrical sigh. "Oh, Mr. Masuda. While it's true that our salons have attracted their share of mayhem, that's not what we want to be known for. ZZ values social, intellectual, and artistic discourse; physical violence is the last thing she wants to publicize."

"I know that! And devotees of my hobby prize discretion above all else—"

"Is that so? I'm afraid I find that hard to believe, Mr. Masuda. After all, notoriety is what brought you here, and that's nothing but gossip in stylish clothes. No, I'm afraid legal steps will have to be taken."

He paled. "Legal steps? You mean . . . the police?"

I shook my head. "Worse. Ms. Zoransky's lawyers will have to be involved. You see, her reputation—and by extension, the reputation of this estate—is very valuable to her. You understand that, don't you?"

I knew that he did. He understood publicly losing face, too. "Now, in order to save Ms. Zoransky from ridicule, social ostracizing, and financial ruin, she's going to need assurances from you—in writing—that you will not discuss, disclose, or otherwise disseminate any information uncovered or made available to you during the duration of your stay. Am I being clear?"

He swallowed. "Yes."

I smiled but didn't let it reach my eyes. "Good. Then as long as you comply, you're not in any trouble. You may stay and even observe such parts of the investigation that may occur in your presence—as long as you don't actively interfere or withhold any pertinent information. Are these terms agreeable to you?"

"I—yes. Yes, they are."

"Excellent." I turned the warmth of my smile up a few

degrees. "Then, please, relax and try to enjoy yourself. I need to ask you a few questions, if that's all right?"

He took a deep breath and then let it out. "Yes. You may proceed."

I knew I had him. After all, actually being part of a murder investigation was part of his fantasy; and as distasteful as I found the idea, I could still use it to my advantage. "Okay. What can you tell me about Maxine's latest escape?"

He hesitated then shook his head. "Very little, I'm afraid. There was no cheating, if that's what you're after. I was hired by Ms. Danger to do exactly what she specified in front of all of us: to construct a magnetic key-and-lock combination for the vault you saw. I revealed the magnetic combination to no one, and the key never left my possession until it was placed in the vat of Lucite. She made me sign contracts to that effect as well. I can show you my copies—they're with me, in my room."

"I'd appreciate that. So, she never told you anything at all about how the trick was going to be performed?"

"No. To be honest, I never even asked. I value a sense of . . . the mysterious."

My attitude toward him softened a little. Sure, an obsession with people's untimely demise was kind of creepy—but who didn't have at least a touch of fascination with the unknown? With using your wits to battle the danger lurking out there in the dark? That was on the resume of pretty much every primitive human that ever managed to survive coming down out of the trees. "Okay, Mr. Masuda. I'll need to look at those contracts, and then I think we're done for now."

"Ah. Thank you." He gave me a nod that was more of a bow and then got to his feet. "I will be right back."

After he left, I drank my own tea and thought. Masuda didn't seem to know much, but I thought he was telling the truth. And if he was being up front about his hobby, then he had every incentive to assist me however he could.

Of course, if he was actually Maxine in disguise, then I was so outconned, I wasn't even in the game . . .

After talking to Masuda, it seemed obvious who I needed to speak with next: Summer Coyne. The police had spent more time questioning her than anyone else, which made sense; she obviously knew how Maxine escaped from the vault, which presumably meant she knew how Lockley Hades wound up in her place. Forrester had told me she refused to give up the secret, citing an NDA she'd signed that identified the methodology as Maxine Danger's intellectual property; legally, she couldn't share that information, even to the police. Forrester seemed to have his doubts about the legality of that where a murder was concerned, but he wasn't pushing it for now. Maxine—wherever she was—had enough money to hire lawyers the town of Hartville couldn't afford to fight. A civil suit could literally mean a few years from now the place would be called Dangerville.

But when I went looking, I really didn't expect to find her lounging by the pool.

Not that it wasn't warm enough; even though it was only April, the temperature was more like June. The sky overhead was a clear, untroubled blue, and there was no wind at all. Summer Coyne was stretched out on a red-and-white chaise lounge, wearing a neon-orange bikini and matching sunglasses. She was sipping on a tall, bloodred drink with a straw in it and reading a paperback one-handed.

"Summer," I said. "Hello. Do you have a minute?"

She looked up, gave me a dazzling smile, and put the book facedown on the short table next to her lounger. "Sure, Foxtrot! Always happy to help out a fellow facilitator. What do you need?"

I pulled up a folding deck chair and sat down. "Answers, I'm afraid."

She pulled her sunglasses down and peered at me over the top. "Ah. You too, huh? You know I can't do that."

"You haven't heard the questions, yet."

"No, but I have a vivid imagination. I can't talk about the gag, Foxtrot. Large, ugly lawyers will appear and eat me."

Which is when Tango chose to make her appearance, doing that cat thing where she casually strolls up, apparently materializing out of thin air. *<Oh? Or would you eat them?>*

This was the telepathic equivalent of jumping out of a bush and yelling, "Boo!" It caught me off guard—but Summer didn't react at all.

Well, not to that, anyway—she reacted to my reaction, instead. "Oh, don't be embarrassed for asking, Fox. It's just that my hands are tied, ha-ha, no joke. There's nothing I can tell you."

<No? Then howzabout you let me know how you taste?> my cat said and stalked forward with an intent look in her eyes that I'm sure was the last thing hundreds of small birds and rodents ever saw in this life.

"Tango!" said Summer. "C'mere, kitty. Lemme give you some love." She put her hand down in the universally acknowledged gesture of sniff-my-finger-first. Normally, Tango would do so then decide whether she'd deign to receive some affection from the offering human.

But Summer wasn't necessarily human. And clearly, Tango had her own test for that in mind.

I jumped out of my chair and scooped her up before she could put her plan into motion. "Ah, you should probably avoid her for now. I just put some of those flea drops on her."

Summer looked slightly taken aback, but she shrugged it off. "All right. So, anyway—"

I sat down with Tango in my lap. I could feel she

wanted to bolt, but I held her firmly and used my Outdoor Telepathic Voice. *Hey! Attacking the guests is not on the approved activities list!*

<*Lemme go! Snakes are cowards—I take a chunk out of her and we'll see what she really is!*>

Tango, she does the same job I do—*only hers involves locks and chains and extremely sharp pointy things. This is a bad plan, kitty—either you're right and she'll have to kill both of us, or you're wrong and we'll have pissed off someone who's easily as capable as I am.*

She made an annoyed sound on my lap but stopped struggling. <*Okay, okay. I'll be good.*>

"I get it," I said to Summer. "I deal with NDA stuff all the time. Nondisclosure agreement? More like No Duh, Always. But there are all kinds of things you can tell me *without* telling me a thing."

She raised her eyebrows. "I get you. Go ahead."

"For instance, if I were to suggest the trick involved cleverly disguising Maxine as someone else, you would certainly laugh in my face."

She stared at me for a moment and then said, "Ha, ha. I certainly would."

<*Was that a yes?*>

I think it was, kitty.

"And," I continued, "if I were to suggest that hiding in plain sight is a good strategy, you could hardly disagree."

She gave me the barest of smiles. "I don't suppose I could."

I took a deep breath. "And if I were to point out that performing this trick clearly required actual elements of the supernatural, you probably wouldn't believe me."

She frowned. She pushed her sunglasses back up to cover her eyes. "Now you've lost me. I mean, the supernatural? You're right, that's the wildest thing you've said so far. And I really don't see the point of this, Foxtrot."

Huh. So either Summer didn't know what Maxine was—or she wasn't prepared to admit it. Which left me pretty much stuck, with nowhere to go.

"Sorry," I said. "This is frustrating for both of us. Look, I'll leave you to your book—but if there's anything you want to tell me, I'm always available. And very discreet."

She picked her book back up. "I'm sure you think you are, Foxtrot. But in my world, your version of discreet barely qualifies as 'kind-of-sort-of-private.' But I'll keep your offer in mind."

"Thank you." Tango jumped off my lap, and I got to my feet. I glanced at the cover of her book as I turned to go, and managed—I think—to keep my reaction from showing on my face.

It was called *The Serpent and the Rainbow*.

<*I still think you should have let me draw a little blood,*> Tango said sulkily as we left.

I didn't tell her that I was starting to think she was right.

Chapter Nine

When Whiskey and I stopped in at the kitchen to speak to Ben, I discovered Teresa Firstcharger had found him first.

She and Ben were in the middle of a heated exchange when I walked in. "—well, wiping out half the planet isn't a viable option, either!" Ben snapped.

Teresa saw me and bit off her own reply. "Foxtrot," she said coolly. "Have you caught the Unktehila yet?"

"Caught? I haven't even identified them. But Whiskey tells me he hasn't found any scent of one on the grounds."

"I thought they smelled like whatever they're mimicking," said Ben. He picked up a large steel bowl and started whisking what was in it vigorously.

"That's true," I said. "But it means the Unk hasn't changed into its snake form while here, or Whiskey would have smelled that."

"So?" snapped Teresa. "What does that even matter? Why would it reveal itself as a giant snake when there are almost an unlimited number of forms it could take instead? It could have become a deer and run off by now."

"I'm . . . not sure," I said. "I don't have all the facts yet when it comes to exactly how their abilities work."

"Well, there's at least one form an Unktehila can't take—and that's one of a Thunderbird. So at least it didn't fly away."

[I can also assure you that no creature of the approximate body mass of a human being has left the grounds since the murder—other than the authorities.]

"We need more information," Teresa said. "We can't fight a war blindfolded!"

"Is that what this is?" I asked. "Let's not escalate the situation into something worse. One murder doesn't make a war."

Teresa folded her arms. "Tell that to Archduke Ferdinand."

[The next time I see him, I will.] Whiskey's telepathic voice tends toward the formality of the British, and no one can deliver a deadpan line like a Brit. [But I can give you his response now: when it comes to war, he's against it.]

"Nobody wants a war," said Teresa. "But there's clearly a power struggle going on amongst our enemies, and if the wrong side comes out on top, a war is what's going to happen. We have to be prepared."

"You're right," I said quickly, seeing the look on Ben's face. When Thunderbirds argue, storms tend to break out indoors; I could already smell ozone in the air. "As a matter of fact, I'm heading to the graveyard right now to talk to a . . . source. It should shed some more light on the Unktehila and their objectives."

"What source?" Teresa asked. "No, never mind. But if it's that damned crow, he won't tell us any more than he has to. He never does."

I didn't bother correcting her—Eli was the one who directed us to Grandfather Serpent, so technically the information was coming from the white crow. And she was right; Eli always played his cards very close to his feathered vest.

"We've just gotten back from a meeting in Thunder-space," Teresa said. "Everyone's on edge. This could be the start of a war or the beginnings of a move toward reconciliation. We need to find out which Unkhetila faction is in charge, Foxtrot—or if there even *are* factions."

"I'm doing my best to gather information," I said. "I'll find Maxine, I promise. Just give me some time."

"What choice do I have?" Teresa said.

I didn't respond, because the only answer that came to mind was, *Well, you could raze the entire mansion and grounds with lightning.*

I didn't have to say it, anyway. I could tell she was already thinking it.

"Then we better get going," I said. I nodded to Ben, and Whiskey and I left—out the kitchen door and into the back grounds.

Where we were promptly ambushed by Tango. She bounded out of the hedge with something in her mouth—something long and wriggling. *<I've got a prisoner!>* she announced telepathically.

[You've caught a worm,] said Whiskey. [At last you've found a conversational equal.]

<Shows what you know. This isn't a worm, it's a snake. A guarder snake, to be exact.>

I sighed. "I think you mean 'garter' snake, kitty. And why do you have one, exactly?"

She dropped her prize and used one quick paw to promptly pin it to the ground just behind its head. *<Gonna interrogate him, of course. And it's clearly pronounced* guarder, *as in to guard something. I want to know what this one was guarding, and why.>*

[No, it's *garter*, as in the item of women's clothing. You—]

<*What item of women's clothing?*>

Whiskey gave his head an annoyed shake. [It's a sort of little belt, worn around the upper thigh—]

Tango gave me a suspicious look. <*You wear snakes around your upper thigh?*>

"What? No! I mean, I sometimes wear garters, under the right conditions—"

<*And what exactly are they guarding? No, wait, upper thigh. Never mind.*>

"That's not what it's guarding—I mean, that doesn't need guarding—"

<*Sure, sure. Of course not. Why would it?*>

"Wait. Why *wouldn't* it?"

<*Beats me. You're the one that brought it up.*>

"But you—"

[Foxtrot. Stop. There is a large sign directly ahead of you on this path, proclaiming MADNESS AHEAD. Proceed at your own risk.]

I took a deep breath, and looked down at the little snake squirming desperately under Tango's paw. "Okay. You sure your snakelish is up to it?"

<*I know how to parse the tongue.*>

"Then go ahead with your questions—just don't hurt him. And you're letting him go right afterward."

<*Spoilsport. Don't worry—I'm just going to squeeze him a little.*>

One of Tango's talents is the ability to speak an inordinate number of animal dialects—anytime I need a translator, she's up to the task. I watched as she bent over her captive and started hissing.

The snake stared at her, clearly dumbfounded, then hissed back.

"What did he say?"

<He said, "What? You speak Snake?">

Well, duh. "Ask him . . . ask him if he's seen any strange snakes around lately."

More hissing. *<Nope. But he just woke up from his winter nap, so he's a little groggy. Also, he thinks this whole thing might just be a dream.>*

Well, that made me feel a little better. Always good if you can convince your interrogation subject the whole thing didn't really happen. In my book, anyway.

Lots more hissing, along with some vigorous tongue-flicking on the snake's part. <Ah-hah!>

"Ah-hah? *What* ah-hah?"

<This is no ordinary snake. This snake claims to be . . . cold-blooded.>

Ever hear a dog groan? I have.

[Oh, for the sake of . . . Tango, *all* snakes are cold-blooded!]

<Yeah, right. Just believe whatever the squirmy little monster says, is that it? You are so gullible.>

"Tango, it's the truth. All snakes *are* cold-blooded."

She looked confused. *<But—wouldn't they just turn rock-solid in the winter?>*

"You got me there. Whiskey, you have any snake-biology tips you want to share?"

[I'm afraid my knowledge on the matter is somewhat limited. I know how to tell the difference between a black mamba and a Gaboon viper, but it's hard to put into words.]

"Then I think we should declare this interrogation officially over, as well as being a colossal waste of time. Tango, let the poor thing go."

She lifted her paw and the snake instantly wriggled through the grass and disappeared.

<Cold-blooded, huh. What a weird creature.>

[Look who's talking—]

"Enough, both of you. Let's go find a snake who actually has something useful to tell us, shall we?"

The Great Crossroads was oddly quiet.

Not that the silence itself was odd—that was pretty much a given. As ghosts, the hordes of animal spirits that normally flowed through the place made very little noise—none at all that an ordinary, living human could hear. When your senses have been enhanced to take in the supernatural—as mine have—it's a different story; but even then, spirits don't tend to make much of a racket.

No, what I meant was that there weren't that many of them around to make noise. No multicolored rivers of guinea pig ghosts streaming from one portal to another; no flocks of rainbow-bright parakeets swarming overhead; not even the squeak of Piotr the circus bear's ghostly unicycle. The graveyard was . . . well, dead.

"This is weird," I said out loud. "Isn't this weird?"

<It's kinda nice, if you ask me. This place is always way too busy.>

[Yes, the ominous, foreboding emptiness is a refreshing change of pace.]

It didn't last, of course. Even if all the other spirits were mysteriously absent, one of them still remained.

Grandfather Serpent.

He was wrapped around the headstone of Davy's grave. The snake seemed considerably larger than the first time we'd met, and the scales of his body glinting in the sun seemed a more vivid, richer red. I noticed for the first time that his eyes, despite being bright yellow, were disturbingly human in shape.

"Greetings," he said. His voice still held that tinge of a Punjabi accent but also seemed deeper, more sonorous.

"And to you, Grandfather," I said. "We've been thinking about the story you told us when last we met."

[Two of us have, anyway.]

"I see. And what did you think of it?"

"I think that the Unkhetila are no different than any other creature. They don't want to destroy or conquer the world; they just want to be able to live in it."

<That is not *how cats see the world—>*

Quiet, you.

"Very good. Things in the supernatural often come in threes, and as this our third meeting, it is an important one. At our first, I simply wanted you to see snakes as living creatures that can have a positive effect on the world as well as a negative one; at our second, I attempted to show you how even the best intentions can go terribly wrong. Now, the time for parables is past. You may ask me any question directly, and I will do my best to gift you with the information you seek. Think before you ask; even my patience is not endless."

I couldn't believe it. At last, some straightforward intel on the situation and what we might do about it—as long as we asked the right questions . . .

<When a snake swallows something whole, does it tickle going down? From, you know, legs twitching and whatnot?>

Ever hear a dog and a human groan in harmony? I have.

"Yes, sometimes," said Grandfather Serpent. "Unless we're eating another snake. Then, not so much."

"The Unkhetila," I said. "Are there any rules governing their supernatural abilities? What they can and cannot do?"

This time, there was no doubt what I saw on the snake's face was a smile. "A very good question, indeed. And the answer is yes. Pay close attention; this is important."

He slithered closer. I realized he could easily gulp down Tango as an appetizer, me as the main course, and Whiskey as dessert. His head reared up until his eyes were level with mine, and I swallowed. Visions of Kaa from *The Jungle Book* flashed through my mind, though my mental version was considerably less Disneyfied.

"An Unkhetila is more limited in what they can do than you might think. The form being mimicked must be approximately the same mass, though there is some leeway possible by using compressive or expansive techniques. Other than that, the form must be duplicated exactly—including its scent and chemical composition. And, of course, there must be room within the skull for the Gem of Influence."

"That's what lets them control minds?"

"Not control—influence. It is a power that suggests, not demands."

"Is there anything they *can't* duplicate?" I asked.

"Many things. In fact, only living forms can be copied—clothing, weapons, or ornamentation cannot. Neither can supernatural abilities like controlling the weather. There is also a limitation on how many forms they have available at any given time, other than their snake and human form—three. To learn a new form requires discarding the pattern of one of the former and requires at least twenty-four hours of study in close proximity to the subject."

<What about mental manipulation? Is there any way to tell if an Unkhetila is trying to control you? Is there any way to fight it?>

"All it takes is an alert mind; awareness of the danger allows you to defend against it. An Unkhetila uses its brainstone to coerce, and this can only be safely done while in its serpentine form; otherwise, there is the danger of mental confusion. The brainstone can also probe a subject's mind as well as their body, especially if the subject is asleep. In this way, knowledge can be duplicated as well as shape. However, this ability comes with its own dangers—a duplicated mind will sometimes overcome the Unktehila's own identity, causing them to be trapped forever. This can happen even if only the form and not the mind is copied; the longer an Unktehila remains in a copied form, the harder it is to revert to their usual one."

Tango snorted in disgust. *<Great. This is seriously going to screw up my napping schedule.>*

[Not to be indelicate, but—how hard are they to kill? Can they use their shape-shifting abilities to heal wounds?]

"It is a fair question. The answer is no—while my children can shift shape almost instantaneously, any injuries sustained in one form are passed on to the next. And should the injury prove fatal, the Unkhetila will revert to its base form."

"A giant snake?"

"No," said Grandfather Serpent. "A human being."

His tongue flickered out, tasting the air, and I wondered what flavor he was getting from me—fear? Determination? Curiosity? Because I was feeling a mix of all three.

"One last thing," said Grandfather Serpent. "Of the three forms an Unkhetila can hold at any one time, one is usually reserved for fighting, one for fleeing, and one for subterfuge. It is the third one that is most dangerous."

<One last thing? You haven't told us the most important thing of all—how to kill one!>

The look he gave Tango was sad. "You are wrong, little hunter. I told you that the very first time we met. The universe kills all beings, sooner or later; it is not a problem to be worried about. Delaying this process is much more important . . ."

I expected the same disappearing act he had pulled twice previously, but he simply returned to the headstone of Davy's grave and draped himself over it once more. "If you will excuse me," he said, "I would like to enjoy the sun for a while. I am very old, and it takes longer for the heat to penetrate these ancient bones than it once did."

I wondered how much heat a ghost could even feel, but I kept that question to myself. I knew the interview was over.

<What a bust,> Tango grumbled as we returned to the house. <I was hoping for some tips that were a little more . . . >

[Lethal?]

<I was going to say assassinational, but okay.>

"Assassinational is not a word, kitty."

<Sure it is. If organizational is a word, so is mine. And it is mine.>

[Nobody here is arguing with that.]

"I think we learned a lot," I said. "And remember, the point isn't to kill anyone; we're trying to stop a war, not start one."

[We may already be too late. Whichever side Lockley Hades was on, they're going to be unhappy. And almost certainly retaliate.]

"We need more information. We need to find Maxine."

[I believe she is still within the grounds. Even if she'd shifted forms to something enabling her escape, I'd have scented it.]

"No way she'd go near the Crossroads. Eli or one of the prowlers would have spotted her for sure."

<Well, I haven't had a chance to question every single creature in the menagerie—but I doubt that's where she is, anyway.>

"Oh? Where do you think she's holed up?"

<In plain sight, obviously. She's an Unkhetila. She's replaced one of the guests—or the staff.>

I had to admit she had a point. If Grandfather Serpent's rules were accurate, Maxine had been here long enough to duplicate any of us. At least the possibility of mental coercion seemed diminished—as long as all of us were on our guard, we couldn't be controlled.

But that only protected those of us who were aware of the threat. Which meant only me, my two partners, Teresa, and Ben were safe. That left far too many potential targets for duplication. And what would happen to the original, if the duplicator didn't want to be found out?

I knew the answer to that question. And wished I didn't.

[Ah, Foxtrot—do you recall that scent you told me to be on the lookout for?]

"Maxine's? What, do you have something?"

[Not hers, no. Two other females—one human, one canine. A Welsh terrier, to be exact.]

Right, the woman who'd let her dog crap in the graveyard and hadn't bothered to clean it up. "Which direction?"

[From the scent, it appears the perpetrators have returned to the scene of the crime. And repeated themselves.]

"Let's go!"

I dashed off in the direction of the last incident, Whiskey running beside me. [Ah, Foxtrot—you might want to slow down.]

"Why? Are they armed or something?"

[I detect no traces of gunpowder, gun oil, or high explosives. Clubs and edged weapons do not generally have a distinctive aroma. However, that is not the relevant point. The relevant point is that, once more, the trail is cold enough that they have almost certainly left once again.]

I got to the site and glared down at the evidence. "That's twice. Twice they've . . . desecrated this place."

[I beg your pardon? It's a simple biological function, Foxtrot. I doubt any of the animals buried here mind at all. In fact, I doubt if they even notice.]

"Well, I notice, and I mind. You're ectoplasmic and don't need to poop—but if you did, I'd make sure to clean up after you. This person is clearly bringing their dog here *specifically* to do their business—and then refusing to take any responsibility. I won't have it, Whiskey. I *will not* have it."

[Understood, ma'am. Loud and clear.]

"Don't *ma'am* me. I used to manage a heavy metal band."

Twice. *Twice.*

But the third time was going to be the last.

Chapter Ten

Usually, ZZ's dinners were the highlight of the day. Her guests were chosen for their interesting and varied backgrounds, and ZZ encouraged debate and discussion of every kind, with plenty of social lubrication available in the form of an open bar—one, thanks to automation, that actually came to you. The drinks trolley, christened *Al the Uber-Boozer* by Keene, rolled around the table and dispensed alcoholic libations freely. It wasn't humanoid—more like a glorified Roomba topped with a robotic arm—but it could make anything from a James Bond martini to a Singapore Sling. It would retreat to a recessed alcove to fetch more esoteric choices, say a particular brand of beer or vintage of champagne, but it had rarely been stumped; this was not due to a gigantic robot brain but research into the guest's preferences by me before they arrived.

Tonight, though, the atmosphere was strained and the conversation muted. One of the guests was missing, another had departed, and the specter of murder hung over the event like a shroud.

This, however, did not stop Keene from getting spectacularly drunk.

He was still in the throes of a creative funk, and there's nothing quite as self-absorbed and pathetic as an artist who cannot art. It's not that Keene lacked empathy—in fact, he was one of the most empathic people I knew—it was simply that pain makes people selfish. It turns your eye inward so that all that you notice is your own hurt and not the suffering of others. The fact that Lockley Hades was a stranger to all of us was another factor; it didn't feel so much as if a killer had struck in our midst than as if a corpse had been forced upon us from the outside, like a FedEx package you didn't order showing up on your doorstep full of rotting fish. Nobody here wanted it or knew what to do with it, but we could all agree the smell was terrible.

"I believe I shall sample the cooking sherry," said Keene, pronouncing every word with exaggerated care. "Al? Some of your most mundane, if you please."

"I have a Lustau Solera Reserve Dry Amontillado," Al said in a decidedly non-robotic voice. "Will that do?"

"What?" said Keene. He stared at the trolley in bleary-eyed consternation. "I want a good, cheap, working-man's drink, and you offer me something Edgar Allen Poe killed a bloke with? Bloody hell, no."

He glanced around and saw us all wince at his choice of words. "Whoops. Not killed, no. Merely bricked-up in a wall. Which is nothing like being murdered inside a sealed vault, is it?"

"It is almost *exactly* like being murdered in a sealed vault," said Oscar. He took a long sip of his own drink, a gin and tonic in a tall glass. His own drinking had not sped up to match Keene's but neither had it slowed down; Oscar liked a nice, steady buzz to carry him through the day. "But at least you brought it up. Anything's better than sitting here in silence pretending it didn't happen."

"In that case, I'll have some absinthe," Keene said.

"Proper drink for someone in the depths of creative despair, that is."

"Oh, get over yourself," Summer said. "My boss is missing, and a colleague is dead. I think that's a little more serious than a case of writer's block."

"Easy for you to say," Keene grumbled, accepting a glass of greenish liquor from Al. "Not likely you're going to forget how to pick a lock or escape from a trunk. Me, I may never work again."

"That's a bit melodramatic, dear," said ZZ. She was wearing one of her billowy caftans, but it was a muted shade of copper instead of the usual neon brilliance ZZ favored. "You'll pull through. The same can't be said of poor Mr. Hades."

Summer snorted. "Poor? Hardly. Hades's last tour topped fifty million dollars. That may not seem like much compared to movie box office receipts, but in our world, it's a hefty income. He was one of the most successful illusionists working."

"Do I detect a note of envy, Summer?" said Oscar, spooning up some of his soup. "Or is that disdain?"

"Neither," said Summer. "It's genuine dislike. Hades was an unpleasant man, both greedy and arrogant. I didn't like working with him, though it didn't seem to bother Maxine."

That raised eyebrows around the table. "So the feud between Maxine and Hades *was* manufactured?" I asked.

"Of course. It was just business—show business. Two performers trying to outdo each other is always good for attendance. They were both careful about never being seen together in public, but in private they were friendly. In a completely professional way, you understand."

"So Ms. Danger," said Hironobu Masuda, "had no reason to want Lockley Hades dead." He had been quiet until now, and I was a little startled to hear him speak. I suppose his initial shock at becoming part of the investigation had turned into interest—it was his hobby, after all.

"None that I knew of," said Summer. "They were both making money, that's all I can tell you."

Amos Clay finished his soup and put down his spoon. "Oh, I think you can tell us a great deal more than *that*," he said. "It's more a question of what you're willing to talk about."

Summer gave him a cool glance. "That's true, Mr. Clay. Professional secrets remain so, even into the grave."

"Or in the wind," said Oscar. "Which is where Maxine seems to be, to borrow the CSI vernacular."

Amos frowned. "That's a generic expression, not a CSI term. I should know." Clay was an expert on animal forensics, and usually put his expertise to work catching smugglers of exotic animals or their parts. "Anyway, you don't have to reveal your secrets, Summer; as a scientist, I can deduce a few things about the performance we witnessed without you violating your code of ethics. If you don't mind?"

"Go ahead. If there's one thing a professional illusionist is used to, it's people trying to figure out how we do things. They usually get it wrong."

Amos smiled. "I'll do my best not to embarrass myself. I'm no prestidigitator, but I do know science. And I can tell you one thing: hitting a column of heated liquid acrylic with a blast of liquid NO_2 wouldn't produce the effect we saw. It should have failed—spectacularly."

Keene had finished his drink and signaled Al for another. "Spectacular failure—I'll drink to that."

"What do you mean, exactly?" said ZZ, leaning forward intently. "What should have happened that didn't?"

"Well, glass undergoing thermal shock of that magnitude might have exploded, not merely broken and fallen away. But even if it didn't, there simply wasn't enough time for the temperature differential to cool the Lucite to a solid state. We should have seen hot polymethyl methacrylate flowing onto the floor, with many chunks of broken glass stuck to it. But that's not what happened."

"No, it's not," I said. "So what's the explanation?"

"Two layers of glass," said Amos. "A thin one on the outside, designed to break away and shatter when it was hit with the liquid nitrogen, and a thicker, stronger one on the inside with a low temperature coefficient—probably Pyrex. The inner tube would be invisible to the naked eye, and once revealed, everyone would assume it was simply the outer layer of acrylic, now frozen solid."

Summer said nothing. The enigmatic smile on her face could have meant anything from *you are so far off, it's taking all my self-control not to burst out laughing* to *even though you nailed it exactly, I will never give you the satisfaction of admitting it—*

And then she spoke. "Even if you're right—and I'm not saying you are—it would have very little to do with how the trick itself was performed. All you're talking about is a little stage management, designed to get a few *ooohs* and *ahhhhs* from the audience."

"I remember those," said Keene, now slumped morosely in his seat. "Like little sonic kisses. Unlike the *boos* and *get offs* I'm more likely to hear from now on."

ZZ sighed and crossed her arms. "Mr. Keene."

"It's just *Keene*, ZZ. You wouldn't say Mrs. Madonna, would you? Because—aside from the obvious internal theological contradiction—she doesn't respond well to it."

"*Mister* Keene," said ZZ firmly, "I will—and have—put up with all sorts of behavior at my dinner parties. I have endured threats, insults, leers, and blackmail attempts—but I draw the line at self-pity. You are a professional, sir, with more gold records than you have fingers. Everyone hits a slump now and then; that's no reason to impose such self-indulgent theatrics on those around you. Not to put too fine a point on it, but . . . quit being such a buzzkill."

There was silence around the table for a second, and then Oscar burst out laughing. "Ha! My God, the life of the party is dead, long live . . . well, me, I suppose."

"Oh, please," said ZZ, with a withering look. "You could suck the air out of a zeppelin."

"Zeppelins were filled with hydrogen, not air," said Oscar. "And when it comes to sucking down large quantities of things that aren't air, you're clearly the titleholder at this table."

The silence that followed was more stunned than the first, as if the conversation had just received a thunderous uppercut and was deciding if it should fall down.

"Oh, for—" said Oscar testily. "*Marijuana.* I'm talking about her penchant for inhaling massive amounts of burning ganja, you gutter-minded hooligans."

"Well, I can see I'm not wanted," muttered Keene, getting unsteadily to his feet. I wondered if he was more offended by the buzzkill comment or the insinuation that ZZ could smoke him under the table. "Lovely dinner, ZZ. Especially the salad of cruelty, sprinkled with . . . with cruel-tons. I'm off to sulk in my tent."

And with that he tottered away, only pausing to shout over his shoulder, "Homer! The Odyssey! Look it up!"

And then he was gone.

When dinner was over, I followed Amos Clay into the study. There was a fire burning in the hearth, and I asked him if I could join him for a glass of brandy in front of the flames.

"Please do, m'dear," he said, sinking into an overstuffed armchair. "And be generous, will you? I have no problem taking advantage of ZZ's hospitality."

I poured us two snifters—Al was relegated strictly to dining room duties—and gave him one before taking a seat on a divan. "That was pretty sharp, how you figured out the two-glass-tubes bit."

He chuckled. "Oh, you don't have to flatter me, Foxtrot. I know what it means when an attractive young woman seeks attention from an old fossil like myself."

I took a careful sip of my brandy. "And what's that?"

"You want my advice. That's how I prefer to look at it, rather than 'the old coot knows something, and I've got to get him to cough it up.' I may be a forensics man, but I was in academia for many years. I've dealt with my share of undergrads."

"Busted," I admitted. "I was wondering if there was anything you noticed—something you might have been reluctant to say in front of a crowd."

"Something controversial, you mean? Or even accusatory?"

"ZZ's never shied away from controversy."

He nodded, staring into the fire as he considered his answer. The flames highlighted the ruddiness of his skin and gave even the white of his beard a faintly red tint. "I suppose," he said at last, "the question that's been preying on my mind is simple. Why? Why would anyone, least of all Maxine Danger, kill Lockley Hades in such a public and provocative way? This was no mere murder, Foxtrot; this was a message."

He didn't know how right he was, but of course I couldn't tell him that. "Any idea to whom? Or what the message is supposed to be?"

He frowned. "Animals kill for very simple reasons—to survive, mainly. Humans are more complex—we're capable of killing a fellow human simply to send a warning. If that's the case here, Maxine Danger would seem to be the intended recipient—though the message might be more brutal than a simple cautionary statement. *You're next* would be my interpretation."

That sent a chill through me, despite the warmth of the fire. I hadn't considered that the Unkhetila were potential victims instead of victimizers. If true, my primary suspects now consisted of two people: Teresa Firstcharger . . . and my boyfriend.

"However," said Amos, "The only thing more unlikely than an escape artist being killed inside another escape artist's trap is the idea that someone is systematically killing escape artists. Unless they're some sort of demented genius trying to demonstrate just how clever they are, I suppose. You wouldn't believe some of the ingenuity demonstrated by animal smugglers—sometimes I think there's some sort of hidden competition among them, just to see who can pull off the most outrageous method."

"Oh? Such as?"

He took a sip of brandy before replying. "Well, there was this one case—a woman in a long skirt who was making her way across a border. Only the person she presented her documentation to kept hearing this strange, *flipping* noise coming from beneath her skirt. Upon checking, it was revealed she was wearing a custom-made, many-pocketed apron underneath, with fifteen water-filled bags inside. She was smuggling over fifty tropical fish."

"That's pretty bizarre."

"Oh, that's nothing. Are you familiar with the novelty gag 'snakes in a can'?"

"Sure. The snakes are made out paper, with springs inside. When you open the can, the springs propel them into the unsuspecting victim's face."

He chuckled. "Well, somebody must have taken inspiration from the original joke. King cobras coiled into potato chip canisters, three of them. Fortunately, the customs officer that discovered them opened the containers *very* carefully."

Snakes. Why did it have to keep coming back to snakes?

I was just ready to go home—I'd collected Whiskey from where he was napping upstairs and said good night to Tango, who prowled the mansion at night—when Keene found me. Or rather, I found him: he was passed out on top of my Prius.

[Oh, splendid. An alcoholic hood ornament.]

"Um," I said, nonplussed. "When you wake up, I'm going to need that."

"I'm not unconscious," he said, his eyes closed. "I'm *thinking*."

I studied his prone body, which was wearing an understated pink suit with white pinstripes. "I see. Do you have to do it on top of a vehicle, or just mine?"

"I was waiting for you, Foxy."

"Don't call me Foxy. Why?"

"Because, Ms. Trots, I think you can help me with my problem."

I sighed. "Don't call me Ms. Trots. Is this problem the same one you've been moaning about all week?"

"I am an internashull—intentional—*world-renowned* rock star, Boxtop. I shout, I scream, I holla. I do not *mooooooaaaaaan*."

I added an order of eye roll to my next sigh. "If you're going to commit onomatopoeia in public, don't get vowels all over my ride. How am I supposed to be of help in this particular scenario?"

[You could tell him he'd be more comfortable underneath the car than on top of it.]

He sat up on the hood. "You can fix me, Trot. I know you can. You fix *everything*, all the time. That's practically your job title—fixer."

I unlocked my door and put my bag inside. Whiskey jumped into the back seat. "I can fix many things, Keene, but unclogging your fount of inspiration is beyond my purview. You need . . . well, I don't know *what* you need, but I'm not it."

He rolled himself off the hood and managed to make a not entirely ungraceful landing on his feet. "But you are. See, I've figured it out. What I need is just someone to *listen* to me."

[Don't do it, Foxtrot. And get him to move away from the vehicle; my nose is telling me he's flammable.]

I paused, still holding the open door. "You're young, rich, and famous. People listen to you all the time."

He shook his head, dark ringlets of curls bouncing around his boyish face. "No, no, no. Employees don't count. Fans don't count. *Groupies* don't count. They all have an agenda. They'll tell me what they think I want to hear, or what they want me to know, or what they want me to think. I need . . ."

"Objectivity?"

"Not exactly. I need a sounding board, Trot. I need to talk to *myself*—but I also need to have someone there to listen, to really *hear* me."

"Mmmm. And call you on your bullshit?"

"Yes! Absolutely. And you are extremely, extremely *excellent* at that."

"This is true." I thought about adding a third sigh, realized it was unnecessary, and said, "All right. I'll give you half an hour, and then I'm going home. Without you, if that's not clear."

"How about an hour?"

"Forty-five minutes, tops. If I start yawning, we're done. C'mon back out, Whiskey."

He shot me a baleful look as jumped out. [At least I'll get another walk in. You, I feel sorry for.]

Keeping the guests happy is part of my job, I thought at him as I closed the door. *Even the whiny, drunk ones . . .*

We wound up walking through the graveyard.

There was a half-moon in the sky, and only a few clouds keeping it company. The night was cool, but the air smelled lovely: freshly-mowed grass, budding flowers—spring in all its pollenated glory. Graveyards lend themselves naturally to a sort of Zen-like calm, as long as you're not overcome with feelings of grief or remorse. Or, you know, you can't see teeming hordes of animal ghosts everywhere. But I'm good at focusing in distracting circumstances.

Here's the thing about Keene: he's always been attracted to me, in the I'm-attracted-to-anything-pretty-and-they-always-fall-down-at-my-feet sort of way, and the fact that I refused to made me even more desirable. In the beginning, I'd used my professionalism to keep him at arm's length—having once managed a touring rock band, I was used to doing that—but since Ben and I had become a couple, my relationship with Keene had become the semi-flirty thing that good friends sometimes have, an acknowledgement that maybe in an alternate universe we might have a thing but definitely not in this specific reality. In other words, we genuinely cared about each other, but there were boundaries we were careful not to overstep.

And an isolated, moonlit stroll with too much booze in one of us was pushing it.

"The problem is that there's no problem," he said, managing to walk in a fairly straight line. "D'you see? Classic rock star conundrum. A song, a really good song, has some pain in it. But what pain? What do I have to complain about? Nothing. Ergo, no song."

I watched Whiskey sniff at the grave of someone's pet opossum and back away when the spectral possum in question popped out of the gravestone like it was an open door. It eyed him suspiciously then waddled on past once it was sure he wasn't going to use the grave as a rest stop.

"You could always write about that," I suggested.

It was his turn to roll his eyes. "Oh, brilliant. I expected better of you, Trot. That's Classic Response Number Two to the Rock Star Conundrum, write about the fact that there's nothing to write about. De do do do, de da da da, in other words. D'you know how overwritten that trope is? I've got nothing new to add to it."

"What's Classic Response Number One?"

"Writing about all the problems that come with success. You know, my tax accountant's ripping me off, the seventeenth woman I slept with this week gave me herpes, my Maserati does one-eighty-five, but I lost my license, so now I don't drive. That sort of thing."

"Ah. You don't want to sound petulant."

"No."

"Or self-absorbed."

"Of course not."

"Or whiny."

"I don't—oh, wait. I see what you're doing. Stop that."

"Sorry. Brutal honesty being turned off. I am a still, reflecting pool."

"And I am . . . broken, Foxtrot. I am *broken*."

Normally, this is where I would prod him about how rich, successful, and generally lucky he was . . . but there was too much pain in his voice. Real pain, not just drunken maudlinism.

I put my hand on his shoulder. "I'm sorry, Keene. I am."

"Thanks, Trot. You're a good friend. And very good at solving other people's problems, which is why I asked you for help. But I don't know if you can fix this. I think *I* have to—but I don't know *how*."

"You might just have to give it time. These things can resolve on their own—"

He sank down onto a grave and slumped against the headstone. "I don't *have* time, Trot. My label is howling for a new single, and I've got nothing. If I don't come up with something brilliant, they're going to drop me."

"Oh, they're probably bluffing."

He shook his head dismally. "Not this time. I've put this off for too long. My last release only did so-so, and in this business you're either headed up or going down. I need this, Trot."

I crossed my arms and leaned my hip against the headstone. "That's probably half the problem, right there. Too much pressure to perform."

"I know, I know. But knowing that doesn't make the pressure go away." He drew his knees up and hugged them. "It's me versus my own head, Trot. And it's a wily bugger, I'll give it that."

Whiskey came over and sniffed the headstone. [He's about to start talking about himself in the third person. I can tell.]

"But you won't beat me, brain. Keene is more than just a squishy three-pound lump of misfiring neurons—"

[Told you—]

"—Keene is also a collection of endocriminy—ethnocrine—*hormones*. Yes. Testasterossamine and adrenaline and, and, that one that makes you go all funny when you smell something."

"Pheromones?"

"Maybe. Point being, Keene is more than just his upstairs tenant. He is also his heart, and his bodily fluids, and his *spleen*!"

"His spleen?"

[Sssshhh. He's on a roll. If he really gets going, he may let us leave.]

"Yes! And they are all going to help me in my battle. A battle against *my own brain*."

He abruptly lurched to his feet, steadied himself against the headstone, and reached into his jacket pocket, pulling out a flask-size bottle. He looked around, spotted what he was after, and tottered over to a headstone with a flat top. He rummaged in another pocket and pulled out what seemed to be an oversize metal shot glass but proved to be four shot glasses nested within each other. Keene separated these one by one and placed each carefully in a row along the top of the headstone. When he was done, he unscrewed the top of the flask and began to fill each of the glasses in turn.

As I watched him do this, I said, "I'm not going to ask you why you have four shot glasses with you, as you'll simply tell me it's always best to be prepared, and who am I to argue with that? But I will say I'm not about to start doing shots when I'm about to drive home."

"Shots. Yes, that's it exactly. Shots fired in the war that's about to begin. Me versus my cerebelliam. Cerebrus. Whatever."

[It would appear that the initial skirmish is being won by Mr. Keene's brain.]

"What is that, anyway?"

"Mezcal. If the buzz doesn't shake something loose, the hangover will show my brain who's boss." He finished filling the glasses, sealed the flask, and put it back in his pocket. He picked up the first one and held it high. The moonlight glinted off the silver metal. "Ready, aim . . ."

"I think this is a bad idea," I muttered. "But who knows? This kind of thing worked for Hemingway."

". . . *fire!*" He downed the shot, gasped, and immediately picked up another one.

"Keene, you've already had too much to drink. Another three shots and you'll be comatose."

"Sounds like a victory to me," he said and downed the

second shot. "Whooo! Maybe not. I think I should fall down now. I mean sit."

[I wonder if he'll throw up. This night may not be a total loss.]

If you mean what I think you do, that's disgusting. Shame on you.

[I just meant it would smell interesting, that's all. There's a whole range of aromas humans don't appreciate. You can enjoy a finely aged Bleu cheese, but the meat equivalent makes you nauseous. I hope you can at least appreciate the irony in that.]

If he does the Technicolor yawn, the only thing I'm going to appreciate is some distance and being upwind.

But Keene's stomach—and his sense of balance—were apparently stronger than Whiskey gave him credit for, as he remained both upright and non-vomiting. He swayed a bit, but that was it. And he already had the third shot in his hand. He raised it, just as he had with the last, and said, "A toast. To the downfall of the tyranny of reason. To the death of neuroses, and anxiety, and overthinking every damn thing. To . . . to not giving so many damns that you feel like a beaver with a messiah complex. To hell with . . . with all that. Shalom."

He downed the third shot.

Then he sat down again. Or slid down, more precisely, using the headstone as a backstop. He blinked a few times and hiccupped once.

"Oh, boy," I said. "I'm going to wind up hauling you back to the house by your heels, aren't I? There's never a taxi around when you need one."

Keene looked up at me and grinned. "Hello, Foxy-woxy. When did *you* get here? F'that matter, when did *I* get here?"

"Look!" I said, pointing. "The moon!"

While he was busy staring at the sky, I grabbed the last

shot and dumped it out, quickly putting it back before he noticed.

"Thass no *moon*," Keene muttered. "It's a pop culshur ref'rence up inna sky, thass all . . . Y'know, Foxy, there's something I never tol' you," Keene said, refocusing his bleary gaze on me. "You prolly don't wanna hear it, but I should really tell you anyway."

[Ah, here it comes. Do you think he brought a ring to go with the proposal, or will he improvise with a bit of string?]

"That's okay, Keene. Why don't you tell me tomorrow? If you tell me when it's this dark, I'll probably forget." One of the techniques I picked up during my first professional assistant gig—working for a rock band—was how to keep a drunk confused enough to stop them doing whatever dangerous and self-destructive thing they were trying to do. Injecting a little gibberish into a reply was often able to befuddle them just long enough to redirect their actions. Part social-engineering, part Bugs Bunny.

But even Bugs doesn't have a 100 percent success rate.

"T'morrow I won't have the nerve," he said. "Trots, I promise I won' ever try t'take you to bed."

That wasn't what I was expecting to hear. "What?"

"You're too good for me," he said, pronouncing his words carefully. "I know what I am, which is a silly man who sings. You, though—you are something special. You make the world a better place, Foxtrot Lancaster. And I— everybody, really—are lucky to have you."

"I—" Damn it, that caught me off guard. And I knew that he meant every word; alcohol diminishes inhibition, it doesn't replace truth.

"That's it. Thass all I'm gonna say. Now help me up, will you? I think m'gravity's broken."

[Hmmm. Mr. Keene shows an unexpected level of perception.]

Artists will do that. Even silly ones who sing.

I collected the empty shot glasses—Keene seemed to have forgotten all about the last one, anyway—and then helped him to his feet. I got him to put one arm around my shoulder then led him away. "C'mon, silly man. Let's get you back to the house. You can have a nice lie down and dream about the moon."

"Thank you, Trot," he said. "You . . . you're the best."

He leaned heavily against me, but I was in good shape and Keene was skinny; it wasn't hard to support his weight at all.

Support, after all, is what I do.

Chapter Eleven

I got Keene back to the mansion and into his guest bedroom without any trouble. He was incoherent by the time we got there and asleep within seconds of hitting the mattress. I made sure he was sleeping on his side, not his back—rock stars have a bad tendency to choke on their own vomit while passed out—and went home.

The next day started much as they always do: Whiskey and I had breakfast, and then I drove to work, arriving just after eight. After checking in with Tango, who assured me nothing Unktehila-related had occurred during the night, and making sure Keene was still breathing, I went up to my office to take care of some paperwork. Regardless of whatever disaster was unfolding within it, the household required constant attention all the same, and constant tweaking to that attention as well. Okay, the tweaking was maybe a little OCD-ish on my part, but that didn't mean it wasn't necessary—I have my own needs, too.

I was engrossed in the annual food and beverage budget—man, did we go through a lot of fancy food—when my phone started up with the ringtone I had reserved for my boss, a catchy little number by a band out of Texas known for their wild beards and sunglasses. "Good morning, ZZ. What's up?"

"Foxtrot?" The connection was bad; she sounded faint and far away. And sort of like she was yelling. "Foxtrot, can you hear me?"

"Barely. Where are you calling from, the bottom of a well?"

"I'm in my workout room. I'm . . ."

"ZZ? Are you still there? Hello?"

The next few words were inaudible. Then: ". . . I'm stuck."

"Well, that's why you hired me, remember? How can I help?"

"No, I'm *stuck*. I'm . . . oh, never mind. Just get up here, will you?"

"Right away, boss." I hung up and turned to Tango, who was lounging on the couch, and Whiskey, who was sprawled out on the floor. "That was strange. C'mon, guys—I think you should tag along."

Whiskey jumped to his feet. [At your service, m'lady.]

Tango yawned. <*That's within thinking distance. Give a mental shout if you really need me.*>

We headed up to the third floor, where ZZ had a garret room set up as a miniature gym. Some people like to stick their exercise equipment in the basement, but ZZ figured, why waste a great view? She had two floor-to-ceiling windows set into the curving wall, letting her look out over the gardens on one side and over the hedge into the animal graveyard on the other.

The door was closed—and locked. I banged on it. "ZZ? Are you in there?"

"Yes!" She sound a little stressed.

"The door's locked. Can you let me in?"

"Use your master key!" Yep, definitely stressed. Starting to feel worried, I pulled out my master key, unlocked, and opened the door.

To find my boss standing in the middle of the room in a set of old-fashioned stocks.

You know the kind I mean? Big, wooden thing like a yoke for oxen, locks around a person's neck and hands? Used to be used for petty criminals back in Colonial days so villagers could pelt them in the face with mud and rotten vegetables? *Those* things.

"Hmmm," I said, standing in the open doorway. "Bad date last night?"

"Close the door!" she hissed. "Before somebody else sees! This is embarrassing enough as it is . . ."

I closed the door behind me and then looked around. I spotted ZZ's phone glowing on top of a bar fridge in the corner. "How'd you manage to call me?"

"You're not the only assistant I have, you know—some of them are digital. Now, can you get me out of this? The key's on the floor."

I spotted it, bent down, and picked it up. "Sure. Say, now that you have a moment, would it be a good time to bring up a raise?"

She groaned. "I suppose I should have expected that."

I fiddled with the lock. "Oh, you should expect a lot more. If I were feeling really mercenary, I'd take out my own phone and snap a few pictures."

"No, you wouldn't."

"No, I wouldn't. Lucky you." I got the lock open and popped the top half of the stocks up.

ZZ straightened up with a relieved sigh. "Luck has nothing to do with it. I hired you precisely because I knew you weren't the sort of person who would ever take advantage of me—no matter what."

I shrugged. "Responsible, compassionate, and ethical to the bone—you got me. Curse my unwavering moral compass . . . How did you manage to get yourself stuck like that?"

"I had the key in a string around my wrist, and it slipped off when I was trying to pick the lock," she said. "But I had the phone on as a backup. I'm not a complete idiot."

"No, ma'am."

"Don't *no ma'am* me. I had a threesome with Jimi Hendrix and Janis Joplin."

"Oooookay."

ZZ rubbed her wrists. She looked troubled, which was unusual—regardless of how well or disastrous her experiments turned out, she never lost her enthusiasm. "Foxtrot, there's something you should probably know. Maxine swore me to secrecy, but since she's disappeared . . ."

"What is it?"

"Esko Karvenin, the guest that left. Oscar wasn't the one that invited him, he just took advantage of his presence. He actually came with Maxine—in fact, they were working together. I promised Maxine I'd act as if they didn't know each other."

"Why? What was Karvenin doing for her?"

ZZ shook her head. "I don't know. Something to do with 3D printing is my guess—but I don't know what. And now that he's gone, we can't ask him."

"I could reach out with a phone call or an email."

"I already tried that—no response. He's not answering his phone, and he's ignoring my messages. He could be anywhere by now."

"Thanks for letting me know, ZZ. I'll see if I can track him, or someone who knows him, down."

"Thank you, dear. I knew I could count on you."

"Can I go now, or are you planning on slipping into

a straitjacket and hanging upside down from the chandelier?"

"If I do, I won't need rescuing."

"Of course not."

I left, ZZ muttering about my generation's lack of respect for the counterculture and something about Andy Warhol.

[Well, that was diverting,] Whiskey thought at me as we walked back to my office. [What on earth would Maxine Danger need with a specialist in 3D printing?]

"I'm more interested in what she had printed. Something sharp and pointy, perhaps?"

[That seems like an awful lot of trouble to go to for something as common as a knife.]

"Maybe, maybe not. Maybe it was made out of a special material—something lethal to an Unkhetila, for instance."

[Grandfather Serpent didn't mention anything like that.]

"Grandfather Serpent seemed more interested in preventing fatalities than detailing ways to cause them. Which is admirable, and I totally agree with the sentiment—but whoever killed Lockley Hades clearly didn't."

[The man himself is gone, but isn't his equipment still here?]

I beamed down at him. "Yes it is, pooch. Trucking company isn't supposed to pick the stuff up until later this afternoon. Plenty of time to do a little investigating . . ."

The billiards room was still filled with Esko Karvenin's equipment; he hadn't bothered packing any of his 3D printers before leaving. That struck me as a little odd; while I could see the man having an attack of conscience, it didn't track that he would leave the care and handling of specialized, delicate machinery to some random delivery service.

I looked around curiously. There was a stack of boxes near the door that hadn't been there before, no doubt the delivery of supplies that Karvinen had been expecting. I found the manifest sticking out of a plastic envelope taped to the top container, pulled it out, and read it. The boxes contained spools of a variety of materials: thermoplastic elastomer, polyethylene terephthalate, polycarbonate, and plain old nylon.

But that wasn't all. There were also composite metal and plastic filaments; powdered bronze, nickel steel, aluminum and titanium; carbon fiber and carbon nanotubes; paper; and even yarn. To me, it looked like a demented shopping list for an arts-and-crafts obsessed robot—which it kind of was.

"Ah, Foxtrot," came a familiar voice behind me. "Come to see the fruits of my genius?" Oscar walked up, dressed in what was, for him, rags: a pair of jeans so new, I could almost see the tags, a blue chambray shirt, and penny loafers. If I'd taken his picture right then, he probably would have expired in a shriek of embarrassed pride.

"This isn't your genius, it's Mr. Karvenin's," I answered. "And don't get too used to it—it's all being packed up and shipped off this afternoon."

"Oh, but that would be a terrible waste," said Oscar. "I think we should purchase and keep at least some of this fine equipment, and I'm going to argue the point to Mother over lunch. You're welcome to join us."

"I'll do that," I said. Oscar could be very persuasive, and I found it best to keep myself in the loop when he tried to convince ZZ to fund his endeavors.

"Excellent," he said, beaming. "Now, I require some privacy. I have preparations to make for my presentation."

I hadn't expected that, and I didn't know what to say. "What are you planning on doing?"

"I'm afraid I can't say," Oscar said with a mischievous grin. "But all will be revealed at lunch. I'll see you there, correct?"

"Right. I'll . . . see you there." And then he ushered me and Whiskey out of the room and shut the door on our confused faces.

[What just happened?]

"Oscar outmaneuvered us. Somehow."

[Perhaps we should simply knock on the door and demand to be let back in.]

"And say what? We're investigating the murder and think the equipment was somehow involved?"

[That's a good place to start.]

He was right. I squared my shoulders and knocked on the door.

No answer. I tried the door; locked. I tried my master key, but he'd bolted it, too.

I considered my options. Oscar was entirely capable of ignoring me—in fact, I'm sure he was relishing the opportunity. Which meant that whatever investigating I was going to do concerning the printers would have to wait until after lunch.

Since I couldn't examine the 3D printing equipment, I decided I'd go talk to Ben instead. However, I couldn't find him—I assumed he was training in Thunderspace with Teresa. Strike two.

I went upstairs to my office and spent some time trying to locate Esko Karvenin but had absolutely no luck in tracking him down. Strike three.

I sighed and joined Tango on the sofa, where she immediately walked onto my lap and snuggled in. "Today is not going my way, kitty," I said.

<Skritches will make everything better.>

"Maybe, but who's going to skritch me? Ben's missing in action."

<Ssshh. Less talking, more skritching.>

[Oh, yes, listen to the self-involved feline. I'm sure she has all the answers.]

<I don't hear you offering any.>

So I gave in to the inevitable, rubbing under Tango's chin and just over her eyes until she was purring so loud, she sounded like a little chainsaw. And, strangely enough, it did make me feel like I'd actually accomplished something. Sometimes doing something for someone else can make you forget your own inadequacies for a while.

I decided to go down to the ballroom and look around; both my companions came with me. Local PD had finished up their examination, and the crime scene tape had been taken down. The vault was still there, up on the stage, along with the heated Lucite column that the key had been suspended in—though whatever was heating it had been turned off, and the Lucite had cooled into a solid block. The blood was still there, too, and the broken glass—I'd probably have to call in specialists to clean it up. Fortunately, New York wasn't far away, and they surely had any number of services with experience in exactly this sort of scenario.

I walked around the stage, careful of the shattered glass, examining things from every angle. How had she done it? The escape, I mean, not the murder. There was no way out of the vault without the key, and the key hadn't been touched.

Or had it?

I remembered Maxine reaching out her hand toward the key, though she hadn't actually made contact. No matter how good she was, I didn't think any sort of sleight of hand was possible under those circumstances—but I could be wrong. Was Hironobu Masuda an accomplice in the trick? I didn't think so—he'd signed legal documents saying everything he'd done was exactly as it appeared, with no subterfuge.

It was frustrating. Like the key itself, it felt as if the answer was tantalizingly close but just out of reach. I could see the key, but I couldn't touch it . . .

I frowned. Living with a dog with a supersensitive nose had taught me that information could be relayed in ways that weren't always obvious, at least not to those without specialized resources. And who had more specialized resources than a professional magician?

"Whiskey, I want you to do a scent search of this room."

[Very well. What am I seeking?]

"Traces of Summer or Maxine. I want to know everything they handled or touched, and if possible, where they did so."

I stood back and let Whiskey work. He took a long time, going over every single inch of the stage, the vault, and all the equipment. Every time he got a positive hit, he'd tell me: [Maxine touched this here. Summer handled this, with both hands.]

There were no surprises, not at first. Both of their scents were all over the immediate area, and none of the places they'd touched seemed unusual.

Then Whiskey widened his circle. I told him to be careful of the glass, but he reminded me he was actually made of ectoplasm, not flesh—cuts were something he could more or less ignore, since they just sealed themselves up like soft cookie dough after you poked a hole in it.

Then he found something the cops had apparently missed.

It was an empty can of pop, sitting on top of an equipment case, on a table off to one side of the stage, along with a rolled length of cable. [Foxtrot. There's something not right about that can.]

"Oh? In what way?"

[It's been handled by both Maxine and Summer—and it does not smell like a carbonated beverage. More like plastic, glass, and electronics.]

I reached up and grabbed the can. Sure enough, it wasn't what it appeared to be; closer examination revealed that the entire top popped off like a lid, and what was inside seemed to be a tiny camera with a lens concealed in the exterior logo.

"This was angled so it got a clear view of the key in the Lucite," I said. "And look." I pointed. There was another can positioned across the room on another equipment case at exactly the same height. It proved to have the same electronic guts as the first one.

"Two cameras, aimed at the key," I said. "Between them, they'd be able to capture the shape of the key itself."

[Presumably this would let them duplicate it somehow—]

"The 3D printers," I said. "Scans of something can be sent from a remote location, remember? Karvenin must have been in charge of printing a duplicate key."

[I believe I understand. These cameras take a picture of the key, which is transmitted to a 3D printer hidden nearby. The printer creates the duplicate key—which Summer retrieves when she leaves the room.]

"Exactly!"

Tango's voice broke up our celebration. <Wait a minute. I thought there was something special about that key that couldn't be duplicated.>

"Oh. Right. The magnets." I'd forgotten about the embedded magnets. No way these little cameras would be able to tell which magnet was aligned where, which meant any 3D-printed key would be useless. What I really needed to do was get into the billiards room and get a closer look at all those 3D printers—but I supposed I could wait for lunch.

Lunch was attended by ZZ, Hironobu Masuda, Amos Clay, and myself; Keene was still sleeping off his bender, Teresa was presumably off somewhere with Ben, and Summer was mysteriously absent. Not that a guest missing lunch was unusual; only supper was mandatory, and our guests frequently decided to take advantage of our other amenities—like the stables, the pool, or the tennis court—instead of the noon meal.

There was no sign of Oscar, though, which was strange; he'd seemed almost gleeful with anticipation. Well, it was hardly out of character for him to put in a late appearance.

When Oscar did show up, it wasn't in a way I expected.

He came in from the main hall, pushing a silver serving trolley. He wore a spotless white apron and a ridiculously large chef's hat. On the trolley was the large half dome of a serving cover—the kind that usually hid a full roast turkey or something equally massive.

"Good afternoon, everyone," said Oscar with a wide grin. "I do hope no one minds, but today's menu of petit fours and a soup course will be supplanted by something a little more . . . original."

ZZ's look was equal parts suspicion, apprehension, and annoyance. "Oscar, what on earth—"

"Tut, tut, mother. All will be revealed momentarily. But first, if you'll permit me, a brief introduction."

He drew himself up, radiating the utmost dignity, which was almost completely subverted by the absurd hat perched on his head; it look like an oversize egg-white soufflé that was about to explode.

"I have been many things in my life," he began loftily. "But the word that best describes me, I think, is *entrepreneur*. I possess the ability to see—nay, to foretell—the direction any particular trend will go. I have had . . . *mixed* results in my past ventures, but—"

"*Mixed* is one way to put it," ZZ said. "Perhaps you'd care to share your brilliant plan to market rotating treadmills for small dogs?"

He stopped and gave ZZ a stern look. "The idea was sound. Mechanical difficulties beyond my purview prevented them from attaining financial viability—"

"They were hamster wheels hooked up to dryer motors," I said. "Lent a whole new meaning to the phrase *tumble dry*. Only, half the time the dog would wet herself in terror, so the dry part isn't all that accurate—"

"Regardless," said Oscar, attempting to regain his momentum, "Past endeavors aside, I have something quite new and quite wonderful to show you—not to mention *delicious*. And so, without any further ado, allow me to present . . ."

He lifted the lid of the serving tray with a flourish. "My *mother*!"

We all stared.

On the tray was a pizza.

And the pizza was ZZ. It was, in fact, a piZZa.

A perfect likeness of my boss's face, and one I recognized: it was a copy of the oil painting hanging in the main foyer, the one of ZZ dressed in a green, velvet gown and pearls, which is the probably the most conservative image of her that exists.

"This pizza is entirely 3D printed," said Oscar. "From the dough that forms the canvas to the various sauces used as pigment. The red background is of course tomato, while the green is pesto. The flesh tones are a blend of mozzarella and parmesan, all finely ground into a paste before being applied via the spraying mechanism. I understand bakers use a similar process to transfer a photo onto a cake, but powdered sugar is a much easier medium to work with."

ZZ, for once, seemed at a loss for words. "I look a little . . . puffy."

"Yes, that tends to happen with the cheese," said Oscar. "We're still ironing out a few bugs, but it's quite the achievement, don't you think?"

"I think it's bloody marvelous," declared Amos Clay. "Seems a shame to cut it into pieces, but—it certainly smells good, too."

"I call it the Selfie Pizza," said Oscar, with a wide smile. "Send the restaurant one of you and your friends, and an hour later, you'll be able to devour yourself."

"I don't know how good the pizza is," I said, "but that's a damn good metaphor for something. Okay, I'll bite. If you'll serve me up a piece, that is."

Oscar produced a pizza knife. He promptly handed it to Ben, who had appeared at his elbow. As Ben sliced up the pizza, he said, "Don't worry, I supervised the whole thing. Nobody's getting food poisoning or inkjet disease or anything like that."

"What a rousing recommendation," Oscar said drily. "Really, don't feel you have to oversell it."

"There's pepperoni mixed with tomato sauce in it, too," Ben said. He began placing slices onto a pile of plates, which Oscar took around to the guests. "So the texture might be a little grainy. To make up for the lack of cheese coverage, we baked some into the crust, around the rim. Should make for a good balance."

And I had to hand it to Oscar—the pizza was surprisingly good. A lot of that was due to Ben's influence, I was sure, but I let Oscar have his moment. The entire thing was eaten, and to top it all off, Oscar rolled in a four-foot high Eiffel Tower made entirely of chocolate, which was also impressive—especially when he informed us the entire thing had been printed and assembled in less than an hour.

"I would imagine the most difficult part is manipulating the melting point," said Masuda. "Especially considering the delicacy of some of the structure."

"Yes, we had to move the entire printer into the walk-in freezer," Oscar said. "Fortunately, the machine itself isn't that large or heavy—or, for that matter, expensive. Adding this equipment to a standard pizzeria wouldn't require a large outlay of money, and the rewards would be substantial—"

ZZ sighed. "Ah. Here comes the investment speech."

"Really, Mother, I'm simply offering your guests a once-in-a-lifetime opportunity—"

"You know the rule, Oscar. No pestering the guests at dinner."

"Ah, but this *isn't* dinner. It's lunch."

ZZ opened her mouth to argue then threw up her hands in surrender. "Okay, you win. That was very tasty, I will admit. I have no idea how you're going to get health inspectors to sign off on a piece of equipment that sprays food all over the place, but if you think you can convince anyone here to invest, go right ahead. Who knows, maybe you actually have something."

"At least until later this afternoon," I said. "That's when the shipping company shows up to crate up all the equipment and ship it back to Esko Karvenin."

"A mere technicality," said Oscar loftily. "I no longer need Mr. Karvenin's expertise to continue with this project. What I do need is a modest influx of cash . . ."

And that was when Ben caught my eye and motioned

with his head toward the kitchen. He was smiling, but I could tell something was bothering him, bothering him a lot.

I had no idea just how much—but I was about to find out.

Chapter Twelve

I joined Ben in the kitchen. As soon as the door swung closed, he turned around and said, "I've got some bad news."

"How bad?"

"I don't know yet. It's about Maxine Danger. Trot, the Thunderbird Council wants to have her brought in."

"Brought in?" I frowned. "As a suspect? I'm pretty sure the police are already working on that. Me, I'll settle for just figuring out where she is—"

"Not as a suspect. As a prisoner."

That stopped me for a second. "A prisoner? But—she said she wanted to *stop* a war from happening!"

Ben's voice was grim. "And she might have been telling the truth. Or maybe she wasn't, and Lockley Hades was murdered before he could give up the list of planned assassinations. The Thunderbird Council has decided it can't risk that."

"The Thunderbird Council? Who, exactly, is the Thunderbird Council, anyway? You and Teresa are the only ones I've ever met."

"There are more. The council consists of six leaders,

chosen by consensus. They make decisions that will affect the entire Thunderbird Nation."

"And Teresa sits at the head of the table, right? She's the one behind this decision?"

Ben shook his head. "This isn't just her, Trot. Everybody agrees that we can't be operating blind with this kind of threat hanging over our heads. Maxine needs to be brought in and questioned."

"Interrogated, you mean. By a group that hates and fears what she is." I was starting to get angry. I didn't know if Maxine was guilty of murder or conspiracy to commit the same, but I knew the kind of reasoning going on in the council's heads. "And what if she decides that giving up the list is going to wind up with most of her race dead and the rest at war? What if she won't do that? What then?"

Ben wouldn't meet my eyes. "Then they'll do their best to . . . persuade her."

"No. Not 'them,' Ben. *You. You'll* be responsible for what happens, just as much as they are."

He started pacing back and forth. "You don't think I know that? You think I *like* it? But dammit, Trot, I just can't see any other way—Maxine is on the run, and that doesn't look good. With her resources, if she gets off the estate, she could disappear forever. And this standoff isn't going to last forever. Sooner or later one side is going to blink, and then there'll be a massacre. Innocent people are going to die, not just Thunderbirds and Unktehila, but ordinary people caught in the crossfire. You think climate change is bad now? Wait until we've got tornados ripping through towns trying to exterminate an enemy that might not even be there."

I crossed my arms. "I know how bad it looks. But Maxine came to me first, remember? She wanted to prevent this, not incite it. She must know how bad this looks."

"Then why not come forward?" he demanded. "Why not just sit down and talk to us instead of hiding?"

"Maybe because hiding is what she's done all her life. Maybe because she's afraid that the council will do exactly what they're planning on doing. Maybe because she doesn't want to make a misstep that could have horrific consequences."

"Well, hiding is no longer an option. It makes her look guilty as hell."

I could feel my stare becoming a glare. "You've already made up your mind, haven't you? You agree with the council."

Now he did meet my eyes and refused to look away. "Yeah, I do. The fuse has been lit, Foxtrot, and it's getting shorter every minute. If she comes in on her own, I can protect her to a certain degree—and believe it or not, so can Teresa. But if Thunderbirds start dropping dead, all hell is gonna break loose. And there's nothing I or anyone else can do to stop that."

"You're wrong," I said. "*I'll* stop it."

He still looked angry, but there was a note of pleading in his voice. "How, Trot? *How*?"

"Because handling shitstorms is what I *do*, Ben. And I'm not about to hand in my letter of resignation now. Excuse me."

I turned on my heel and walked out of the kitchen. By the time my face was back in the dining room, it had an unconcerned smile on it.

Because when things break down, I don't.

By the time lunch ended, Oscar had persuaded at least one guest—Hironobu Masuda—to look at his proposal, though nobody had pledged any funds. Considering that this was a far higher level of success than Oscar's business ventures usually received, he was practically ebullient.

Me, I made it through by gritting my teeth and pretending everything was fine, even though it wasn't. Only ZZ noticed—she's hard to fool—but she didn't say anything, only gave me the occasional concerned glance.

Afterward, I decided to take Whiskey for a walk. I wasn't in a good mood, and from the ominous gray clouds hanging around overhead, I could tell Ben wasn't, either. "Stupid Thunderbird weather powers," I muttered, jamming my hands in the pockets of my jacket. "If it starts raining, I'm going back and shooting him in the face with a Super Soaker."

The rain held off though, and I was so lost in my own thoughts that it took Whiskey two tries to get my attention telepathically. [Foxtrot. Foxtrot!]

"Hmmm? What is it, Whiskey?"

[The Welsh terrier and her owner. I believe they've struck a third time—and they're still here.]

I grinned, feeling a little like all three bears at once; I finally had Goldilocks where I wanted her. Or whatever color her hair was.

I headed straight for the spot where she'd struck before. I was not in a good mood. In fact, if I were a Thunderbird, I'm pretty sure lightning would be crackling around my head and little icicle daggers would be shooting from my eyes. Okay, that sounds a little more like a 1940s cartoon than a mystical animal spirit, but I was also in no mood to keep my metaphorical imagery on point. I was, in a word, pissed.

The terrain of the graveyard was dotted with low hills, and as I crested one, I spotted her down at the base. White leather jacket, short matching skirt, oversize sunglasses, lots of wavy, red hair. The Welsh terrier, a medium-size, black-and-tan dog with short, curly fur, was sniffing at a gravestone with a cremains urn mounted on top of it; it meant that where the pet was interred, the pet's owner had elected to store their cremated remains as well.

I stalked down the hill to where she stood and stopped a few feet away. Whiskey and the Welsh terrier immediately opened canine diplomatic relations: slow, careful circling, heads lowered, and then the sniffing of butts. The woman looked at me coolly, as if I were a server she'd ordered a drink from and hadn't received it yet.

"Excuse me," I said, pointing to the still-steaming evidence. "Is that yours?"

She glanced down then back again. "No, it's hers. I'm just a bystander."

I'm not going to say my skin turned red and my blood boiled; I'm just going to mention that any plant within ten feet of me wilted. "Bystanders in this graveyard are expected to clean up after their pets."

"I'm afraid I forgot to bring a plastic bag with me."

"You must be suffering from dementia, then. This is the third time."

Her elegantly arched eyebrow was just barely visible over the curve of her oversize sunglasses. "You're keeping track? What a novel hobby."

"Oh, my hobbies are a lot more interesting. This is my job."

"What a rich and fulfilling life you must have. I'm going to leave you to it, then."

"You're not going anywhere unless you take that with you."

"Oh? Is that a threat? Because I prefer to let my lawyer do my fighting. He's much better at it than I am, and always eager."

"Oh, my boss—you know, the one that actually owns this property?—has lawyers that will eat yours for a light snack. The fine for not picking up after your dog in this county is five hundred dollars, but I'm sure your lawyer's fees will be considerably higher. So if you really want to blow a few grand on being an inconsiderate bitch, I guess I can't stop you. But I can make you pay."

She considered me for a moment, expressionless. "Why do you care so much, anyway?"

"Like I said, this is my job."

"I don't think so. You're not dressed like a caretaker. You know this is my third time here, which suggests you've been waiting for me—that's above and beyond, even for the most dedicated employee. And how do you know the other two times weren't somebody else?"

"Other than the fact that it happened in exactly the same place? My dog has a very sensitive nose. He's identified you as the culprit, and I believe him." As I said it, I realized how ridiculous it sounded.

So did she. She glanced down at Whiskey and the terrier, who had concluded formal negotiations, decided neither of them was a current threat, and were now pretending to ignore each other. Somewhere in their brains, nuclear codes were being hastily reviewed in case they were suddenly needed. "You must be very close. I'm sure that when he's called on as an expert witness, the court will pay close attention to his every word."

[Most vexing, isn't she?]

No, she's a pleasant, refreshing breeze. Can you eat her?

[Not as such. But it's tempting to try.]

"Let me tell you how this is going to go," I said pleasantly. "You're going to leave your disgusting little present right here, showing a complete disregard for other people's property or rights. You're going to walk away, down to whatever showy, overpowered SUV or sports car you drive, and I'm going to follow you there. I'm going to take pictures of you, your car, and the poop. And then

I'm going to call my friend—the local cop—and tell him about you. He likes me and doesn't know you. After he issues the ticket, I will personally see to it that it is delivered to your place of residence. Then I'll sit down with those hungry lawyers I mentioned earlier, and we'll explore New York case law re: desecrating graves—"

And that's when I noticed she was crying.

Her expression hadn't changed at all. But two big, fat tears had escaped from behind those oversize shades and were rolling slowly down her cheeks. "Desecration," she said. She didn't say it unbelievingly, or mockingly, or even with a question mark attached. She said it the way someone else would say, "Finally."

"Yes," I said. "This is a graveyard, you know."

"Oh, I know," she said. "I know exactly where we are. Do you? Do you know who's buried here?"

In fact, I didn't. The headstone bore the name CARLOS but nothing else.

"Carlos was my father's parrot. He had him since before I was born. Carlos lived to be eighty years old, and I was twenty-five when he finally died."

"I'm sorry—"

She continued as if I hadn't spoken. "Carlos was always there, on my father's shoulder or on his perch. Never in a cage. You see this?" She held up her hand; there was a nasty, three-inch scar on the back of it. "Carlos was a biter. He did this to me when I was six. Do you have any idea how powerful the jaws of a parrot are? They can crack Brazil nuts with no trouble. My father was angry at me, because he had to pay for the stitches."

Her voice had the flat, affectless tone of someone recalling past trauma; treating it distantly was the only way she could look at it without breaking down. "My father was a cruel man. He beat me. I think Carlos was the only thing he ever loved, and even that was a twisted, dark sort of love. He loved it as a possession, not a living being. He used to teach it to say the nastiest, filthiest things. But that wasn't the worst. Oh, no. The worst was how Carlos liked to imitate the things I said when my father hit me. The sounds I would make. I can't describe how it made me feel, to hear that days or weeks later. I don't want to."

Ever feel like you've been running headlong and just screeched to a stop, because you realized you'd run into a field full of landmines? Well, if you haven't, I can tell you exactly what it feels like.

"When my father was diagnosed with cancer, he bought a plot for Carlos here. He arranged for his own cremated remains to be affixed to the headstone. Then he had Carlos put down. 'Who else is going to take care of him once I'm gone?' he said. 'You?'"

She took off her sunglasses, then, and wiped her eyes with the back of her hand. "I hated that parrot," she said. "But I didn't blame it. It was only an animal, doing what an animal does. But my father? He made choices. He could have treated the bird differently. It would have been a very different creature, I think, if he had. Or if it had been raised by someone else. But it wasn't, and it was what it was."

"I see," I said. I didn't say it gently, because that's not what she needed. She needed to be seen as an equal, not someone pitied. Not as a crying, six-year-old girl.

"He didn't leave me any money. I made that on my own. And I bought Sophie, because I needed to teach myself how to love an animal instead of hate it. And sometimes, that isn't enough, and then I come here and . . . well, you know. So yes, *desecrate* is exactly the right word. But it's not Carlos's grave I'm really desecrating. He just happens to be the one who has the headstone."

"I'm so sorry," I said, because those are the words that

you say at times like this, and as you say them, you know how hollow and empty they are, but they're all you have.

"So am I," she said, and for the first time, there was a trace of emotion in her voice. It was weariness, more than anything, and I understood that; carrying that sort of emotional weight around is exhausting.

"Listen, I know the groundskeeper—I'll arrange to have your—offerings cleaned up, okay? Don't worry about it."

She looked at me then, her tears drying on her cheeks, and said, "Thank you. I don't know how long I'm going to do this."

"As long as you need to," I said. "I'm Foxtrot."

She nodded and sniffed back the last of her tears. "Emily. Thank you, Foxtrot."

"Hey, cleaning up other people's shit is what I do anyway," I said.

"Don't we all?" Emily replied, and I didn't give her an answer, because she didn't need one.

And neither did I.

Chapter Thirteen

By the time we got back to the house, a light rain was actually falling. Not the thundershower I was expecting but more like a melancholy mist, as if the air itself were depressed. I guessed Ben wasn't feeling any better about our fight than I was, just less angry.

Most of my anger was gone, though. Meeting Emily had put things into perspective, somehow; even though I was grappling with these huge problems, I couldn't lose sight of the smaller things—the important ones. Things like respect, and dignity, and compassion for others who were suffering—even though you might have no idea what they were going through, everyone was going through something.

And there were always choices to make.

The choice I made—after calling Cooper and explaining the doggy-do situation—was to see if I could finally get into the billiard room and examine the 3D printers Esko Karvenin had left behind. Now that Oscar didn't have himself bolted inside, it should be easy.

And it was. Oscar was there, fiddling with one of the

machines, but thankfully Ben was not. I was in no mood to resume our argument.

"Well, well, Foxtrot. Come to congratulate me on my resounding success?"

I sighed. "Congratulations, Oscar. You put on quite a show. The pizza was good, but the chocolate Eiffel was amazing."

He beamed at me. "Yes, it was, wasn't it? That's the problem with edible art—it looks so good, you don't want to destroy it by eating it. But nothing lasts forever, alas."

I looked over the machine he was adjusting. "This is the one that printed the pizza, right?"

"Correct. It can also create cakes, pasta, and a variety of pastries. Esko and I were working on a candy bar infused with celebrity DNA, but I believe the specter of faux cannibalism was what finally drove him away. A pity, but his expertise can be replaced." Oscar examined a spout critically and added, "In any case, I wasn't serious about contacting Babe Ruth's estate."

"Meaning you were, and then you talked to someone with actual ethics and/or a law degree, and now you aren't."

Oscar frowned. "The forefront of science is one constantly on the move, Foxtrot. Today's deceased-ballplayer-infused candy bar is tomorrow's cure for Lou Gehrig's disease."

"Wow. You've been waiting for a chance to use that one, haven't you?"

He gave me a cool look. "Opportunity is a fickle mistress. One must be prepared for her knock."

I walked around the room, looking at each unit in turn. Some were designed for heavier material like metal or minerals, others for textiles like nylon or yarn. But which one would have been used to print a key?

On closer inspection, the metal printer actually used a metal-infused wire—and it didn't appear to have been used, or even completely assembled; parts of it were still packed into Styrofoam-cutouts next to it. Also, there didn't seem to be anything connected to it that could be used to run it remotely, which would have to be the case if it were printing something scanned in from the ballroom. The thing wasn't even plugged in.

"So, no need to be coy," said Oscar. "I know why you're here."

"You do?"

"Yes. Clearly, you can see the brilliance of my plan and want to invest. As practically a family member, I can offer you a sizeable return on your investment—"

"Sorry, Oscar—you've got your wires crossed. I just came to check out the equipment—professional curiosity only."

He looked a little disappointed but took it in stride. "I see. And what is it about a 3D-printing concern that interests a professional assistant?"

I smiled. "They're capable of spinning something elegant yet strong out of the most basic of materials, in almost no time at all. I do that practically every day . . ."

"Touché," he said and gave me a little bow.

After I left the billiard room, it was time to grab an umbrella from the stand next to the front door, find Tango, and tell her we needed to check out the menagerie.

She wasn't keen. *<Haven't you noticed? Cold, wet, death is falling from the sky.>*

"Oh, come on. It's only a little rain."

<Only a little rain? That stuff will kill you if you give it half a chance. It is, without doubt, the second most vile substance in existence.>

[I await your pronouncement of what holds first place. Eagerly.]

She gave Whiskey a sidelong look. *<You're covered in it. Or to be more precise, you* are *it.>*

[Ectoplasm? How provincial of you.]

<Dog ectoplasm, to be exact. How is it possible for something that's basically unreal to smell so bad when it gets wet?>

[The unwavering, diligent work of hundreds of dog scientists, working tirelessly through the centuries.]

<Dog scientists? You guys are still confused over who exactly owns your own tail.>

[That's hardly an unmuddied legal area. Our lawyers have argued the point for—]

"Dog lawyers?" I interrupted. "Dog scientists? Okay, I like a good leg pull as much as the next gal, but I can tell when I'm being bamboozled. And you two are both pro-level bamboozlers."

<Never mind the Canine Professional Association. The point is, it's wet out there and dry in here, and guess which one I'm staying close to?>

It's a well-known fact that you can't out-stubborn a cat. You can, however, bribe them—especially if you have a certain brand of cat food stashed away for emergencies.

<Oh, that is so unfair,> she yowled. <I swear you buy that stuff just to torment me. You know I'll do anything for it.>

[Anything?]

<Anything that I was intending to do anyway, I mean. But I'll give it a higher priority.>

Whiskey scratched himself behind one ear with one leg, a notoriously rude gesture in the animal world. [So you're willing to slightly alter your timetable—but not your actual agenda—in order to get your paws on this food you desperately crave.]

<I know. It's humiliating.>

[It's illuminating. The words proud, stubborn, and

headstrong can now all be retired in favor of a single adjective: *cat*. Thank you so much for your service to the
English language.]

<*You're welcome. All right, I'll go, but I want three
tins of Royal Feline Feast right now, and you hold an
extra-large beach umbrella over me the entire time.*>

"One tin when we get back, and the umbrella will be
regular."

<*Fine. But I don't do my best work when I'm sulking.*>

[Then when do you do it? Please let me know; I'll rear-
range my entire schedule in order to bear witness.]

"C'mon, you two. You can argue on the way."

The reason I needed Tango along, of course, was because
of her facility with other animal languages. I was never certain exactly how many dialects she spoke, but I hadn't seen
her stumped yet.

I wanted to canvass both the menagerie and the graveyard, but I thought I'd start with the living creatures; the
Great Crossroads was a much larger, more complicated
project.

Our first stop was the ostrich pen, where Oswald was
kept. Oswald, despite being a large, flightless bird with
a tiny brain, was nonetheless a master of escape. In fact,
when we first arrived, I thought he was gone again; I finally spotted him hiding behind the enclosure in a tiny
area barely large enough to hold his bulk. We circled
around and caught him scratching industriously at the
ground at the base of the fence. He stopped and stared at
us guiltily as we approached then pretended to be preen-
ing one stubby wing.

<*Okay, what do you want to ask him?*>

"Ask him if he saw anything on the afternoon of the
murder. Someone running away from the house, for instance."

Tango emitted a series of hisses that made her sound like a deformed, deflating balloon. Oswald cocked his head to one side, listening, then emitted a similar set of sounds.

"Well?"

<He says he's never seen anyone run away from here, ever. Who would want to leave this wonderful place? Surely not him, of course.>

I groaned. "Not helpful. Tell him . . . tell him we will happily leave him alone to do whatever it was he wasn't doing when we walked up. But before we go, we need to know if he saw anyone leaving the house in a big hurry yesterday afternoon."

More noises, which sounded to my ear more like a velociraptor trying to whistle than a bird. Well, ostriches are descended from dinosaurs—and their lineage is easier to see than most avian species. Long neck, powerful legs, nasty clawed feet—give 'em a few teeth and some scales, you've got yourself a thunder lizard.

I wondered, briefly, if Thunderbirds were descended from dinosaurs, too—and if so, which ones.

<Oswald says he might have seen someone dressed in a sparkly outfit hotfooting away around the time of the murder. Headed toward the graveyard.>

I frowned. "The graveyard? That seems unlikely—Eli would know if she took refuge there, wouldn't he?"

[Almost certainly. But then, we haven't specifically asked him, have we?]

"That's true," I said slowly. "And Eli never tells more than he absolutely has to. So maybe we should go see him, ask a few pointed questions—"

At which point there was a loud, annoyed huff from behind me.

I glanced back, but it hadn't sounded like either of my

partners; this was a low, guttural noise, one with a lot of implied menace in it. I've heard bulls make that noise, and tigers, and even a hippopotamus.

But it wasn't any of those. It was our resident homicidal maniac—Owduttf, the honey badger.

Honey badgers are South African, but that wasn't the derivation of his name; it was an acronym for One Who Does Unspeakable Things to Foxtrot, an appellation the badger had chosen for himself. And while it was true that Owduttf had never managed to make good on any of his promises, that didn't mean he'd stopped making them. Tango wouldn't translate half of what he said to me, on the grounds that it would give me nightmares. Try to imagine Hannibal Lecter as played by Danny DeVito and you've got a pretty good idea of what he's like.

And, unfortunately for me, honey badgers aren't all talk. They eat king cobras for breakfast, rob lions for lunch, and attack wildebeests for dinner. They are probably the most fearless creature on the planet, with jaws strong enough to deform steel, fur thick enough to deflect small arms fire, and a natural immunity to snake venom. They sound like something a science-fiction writer would create after seventeen shots of espresso and a late-night slasher movie binge . . . but they're real, and we have one.

We keep a very close eye on him, too. The only creature in our zoo better at escaping than Oswald was Owduttf. He's one of the reasons I preferred not to sleep at the estate. . . . though having a thunderbolt-throwing boyfriend and a ghost dog that can transform into any breed gives me a certain sense of security. Most nights, anyway.

I turned and walked up to Owduttf's enclosure. Concrete and steel, top to bottom, with a reinforced steel-plated base buried under the ground. "Hey, Owduttf," I said. "You have something you want to add?"

He uttered a series of whines, barks, and grunts. *<He says the ostrich is lying.>*

Interesting. Owduttf didn't usually bother with mere slurs like *liar*; he liked to jump straight into gory, descriptive threats. "Ask him why he thinks so."

More guttural noises. *<He says he saw the female, and she didn't go toward the graveyard.>*

"Oh? Which way did she go?"

<He says that'll cost you.>

I sighed. "Okay. One raw chicken, but the information better be useful—hey, wait a minute."

<What?>

"Since when does Owduttf speak Ostrich?"

Tango sat down and began licking her paw. *<He doesn't. He overheard enough of our conversation to pick out the relevant details. Or so he says.>*

"Oh, so now he speaks English, too?"

<I'm just relaying what he said to me, toots.> She paused in her grooming to listen to a few more grunts and snuffles then said, *<And he wants three chickens. Giblets included.>*

"Yeah, I don't think so. This information he's offering seems less than reliable."

[I agree, Foxtrot. He simply wants a free meal.]

More grunts and barks. *<He says if he wanted a free meal, he'd just eat you. Free of brains, muscle, or gonads, anyway.>*

Whiskey edged closer to the cage and growled. Owduttf turned and farted loudly in his face. Then he made what sounded suspiciously like laughing sounds and trotted into the low burrow that served as his house.

[I really don't care for that fellow.]

<Yeah, I'm sure that keeps him awake at night. Boo-hoo,

Whiskey doesn't like me. I think I'll chew on this bison skull to console myself.>

"We should try to locate Eli and see what he has to say," I said. "But since we're already here, let's do a quick circuit and talk to a few other residents."

So we did. The birds in the avian enclosure hadn't seen anyone like Maxine in the last two days; neither had the hippos in their muddy pool, or the lizards basking in the sun, or the giraffe, or any of the others.

<Can we knock this off, please?> Tango said. *<My throat is killing me. Some of these dialects are hard on a gal.>*

Even her telepathic voice sounded raspier than usual. "Of course, kitty. C'mon, let's go back to the house, and I'll get you some milk."

<Milk, nothing. I was promised Royal Feline Feast!>

"Right, right. How could I forget?"

I kept the fancy cat food in my office, for which I was grateful; it meant I didn't have to go into the kitchen, where Tango was usually fed.

After she'd gobbled down her treat—and then complained bitterly about how small the portion was—we set out for the graveyard.

I don't know why I assumed Maxine wouldn't bolt for here—with her disguise abilities she could make herself blend right in. Not as a ghost, of course, but maybe as a former pet-owner or a larger animal like a deer—we get them occasionally. I guess I think of the Great Crossroads the way you do a city, with authorities in charge that oversee its safety and monitor any threat. Eli was its de facto mayor—and I didn't think he'd allow a killer to hide on his turf.

Only problem was, I was kind of the chief of police.

So, clearly, I needed to have a conversation with my

boss. This could prove to be a problem, since there was no reliable method of contacting him; he had a knack for just showing up when I needed him, but sometimes he and I disagreed what constitutes need. Invariably he's right, which is both inconvenient and annoying. Also unfair: he has access to information I don't. Eli may be a lot older than me, he may be a powerful supernatural being, he might have tons more experience in certain matters—but that doesn't mean he should keep me out of the loop.

I think he knows this. I get the sense that his wings are tied in certain matters by his own superiors and that he finds that as frustrating as I do. I understand his position . . . but that doesn't mean I like it.

The Great Crossroads amplifies psychic communication, making it easier to do the telepathic equivalent of shouting. However, there's something undignified about a cat, a dog, and a woman roaming through a graveyard shouting, "HEY, ELI!" at the top of their brain-lungs, so we didn't do that. I had Whiskey pop through a portal to the dog afterlife, where he passed on a message from us through official channels. I didn't know exactly how that worked, but I couldn't shake the image of a long row of stern-looking dogs in police hats sniffing each other's butts in turn. One Chihuahua's hat kept falling off.

In the meantime, Tango and I checked the perimeter, keeping an eye out for anything unusual. About the only thing we spotted was a new prowler, a llama. Prowlers are ghosts of animals that fall between the cracks; they aren't quite wild, aren't quite domesticated. Often they come from zoos, or small farms, or circuses or aquariums. The Great Crossroads pulls them in; it radiates love and acceptance of a type the prowler never quite got enough of in life. Prowlers are often confused and don't realize they're dead.

The llama was standing next to the border hedge, eyeing us suspiciously while pretending to munch on leaves. It must have been a dull brown in life; becoming a spirit had changed that to a glowing, burnished bronze. I wondered if she had come from a farm upstate—there are a few that raise them for their wool. I could tell she was a prowler not only because she thought she could still eat but from her general attitude—animal spirits tend to be in a hurry to get from one portal to another in order to visit the people that loved them while they lived. Few just hung around and tried to eat the scenery.

"Hi," I said. I communicate with most spirits without any help, though the farther away from mammal they get, the more difficult it usually becomes. "I'm Foxtrot. This is Tango."

The llama chewed at me suspiciously. She didn't look impressed.

"Do you know where you are?" I asked.

She stopped chewing and stared at me flatly. {I don't know you. Do I know you? No, I don't think so.}

"Like I said, my name is Foxtrot. I'm kind of the sheriff around here."

<*Oh, and I suppose that makes me your deputy? Uh-uh.*>

{Sheriff? What, you gonna arrest me now? I ain't doing nothin' wrong.}

"No, no, nothing like that—"

{Why don' you just leave me alone? You *and* your freaky cat. Lemme have my lunch in peace.}

<*I'm not her cat. I'm my own feline.*>

The llama nodded judiciously. {Mm-hmm. I see that. I see that. So what are you, if you ain't no deputy?}

<Private security consultant. Ongoing contract basis.>

{I feel you. So what's the deal around here, anyway?}

Tango favors the direct method. <You're dead. Kaput. A ghost.>

{Whaaaat? No way. I'm just taking a little walk, that's all. This is kind of a weird neighborhood, but it ain't the afterlife. Pffft.}

"Oh?" I said. "And where is it you call home?"

{Tourist trap up in the hills. All kindsa people go traipsin' around, lookin' at a bunch of old rocks all piled up. Got tired of people wantin' to take my picture all the time, so I went for a wander. Almost fell off a cliff once . . .} She kind of trailed off there, and I guessed that at that point in her travels, she trailed right off the edge of a hill. But I had no idea where she was talking about; there weren't any petting zoos of that description nearby. Of course, *nearby* doesn't mean much to a prowler; unlike human spirits, which are often bound to a place, animal spirits are much more likely to be bound to another living being—and if not, they're free to roam.

{Say, how did you two learn how to talk Llama? I mean, your accent is *awful*, but I can understand you okay.}

"We're not talking Llama. This is the common tongue of the dead."

She eyed me skeptically. {Oh, so you two are dead, too, huh?}

"Well, no—Tango's reincarnated, and I'm the official Guardian of the Crossroads—"

{Guardian of the what now?}

"The Great Crossroads. It's a place where spirits of dead animals can cross over to the human afterlife to visit their previous owners."

The llama's eyelashes were enormous, and they bounced

slightly when she gave me one slow, unbelieving blink.
{Uh-huh. Right.}

"Well, how do *you* explain where you are and what
you're experiencing?"

She'd gone back to chewing her nonexistent lunch, her
jaw moving methodically from side to side. {Oh, that's
easy. It's these leaves. See, sometimes when you eat the
wrong kind of leaves, it makes you sorta crazy for a
while. See and hear all sortsa things, most of which ain't
real. So, this is that.}

I sighed. "So this is an extended drug trip, and we're
just hallucinations. You know, I'm finding it hard to come
up with a way to prove you wrong."

The llama snorted. {I gotta say, as hallucinations go,
you two are kinda disappointing. You ain't glowing, or
floating, or doing any kinda crazy stuff.}

*<That's because we're on the edge. All the interesting
stuff happens further in.>*

{Now that sounds like the kinda thing a hallucination
would say. Always tryin' to get me to do things I regret
later. Nope, not this time. Think I'm gonna just hang
out here and keep on havin' lunch. Y'all can just move
along.}

There was no point in trying to change her mind—
either she'd accept her new reality or she'd continue to live
in her own. Which, I suppose, is something we all have to
do, sooner or later. "Before we go—that tourist trap you
mentioned. What was it called?"

{Matthew Pikachu, I think. Something like that.}

"Macchu Pichu, maybe?"

{Yeah, that was it. You helpful for a hallucination, you
know that?}

"All part of my job. C'mon, kitty, let's keep moving."

We strolled on, leaving the llama chewing on leaves

that ignored her. "Macchu Pichu. That's in South America, Tango—Peru, to be exact. That llama's been travelling for a long, long time."

<Maybe she hitched a ride part of the way. I used to know this ghost raccoon that rode the rails in the thirties. Spooked more than a few hobos—they still tell tales about the Yellow-Eyed Ghost of the Haunted Boxcar.>

"I guess anything's possible. Still, I think that's the farthest anyone's ever traveled to get here. Even Piotr died close by."

Piotr was a fixture around the graveyard, riding around on his unicycle, usually juggling at the same time. Not a prowler, just a performer who needed an audience—and one who had performed all over the world.

We finished our perimeter check by running into Two-Notches, the great white shark that was just finishing her own. Two-Notches thought she was in an aquarium and wouldn't go outside the grounds—that's where the glass was. She and I had a bit of a misunderstanding when I first got here, but since then we've become—if not exactly friends—professional colleagues. Also, she no longer tries to eat me.

Two-Notches had nothing unusual to report, other than she'd spotted the llama, too. Hadn't tried to eat her, wasn't sure why.

We moved into the interior of the graveyard, which is where we finally spotted Eli. He was perched on the lower branches of a cherry tree, almost invisible against the white blossoms.

"Eli! I'm glad we finally found you."

"Hello, Foxtrot. I understand you're worried about the Unktehila escaping."

No surprise there—Eli was always one hop ahead.

"Yes. If she were hiding in the Great Crossroads, would you know?"

"Oh, I suppose I would—which means she isn't. Nor has she crossed the grounds since her disappearance. Other than that, I'm afraid I have no new information for you."

Damn. Not really unexpected, but not really helpful, either. Maxine could still be on the grounds of the mansion, or she could have figured out a way to sneak out without being noticed—

As if he'd read my mind, Eli said, "She's still in the vicinity, though. I'm quite sure of that."

"Oh? Should I ask why?"

"Yes."

"Why hasn't she run? Is it because she's physically incapacitated in some way?"

Eli hesitated. Anyone that hadn't spent a lot of time with him wouldn't have noticed, but I have and I did. "That's not it. She needs to convince the Thunderbirds not to start a war but isn't sure how. Put yourself in her head: if she gives up the list of assassination targets, she puts her own people at risk. If she doesn't, those assassinations may actually occur. If she runs, the balance will tip one way or the other. By staying in hiding, the situation remains unstable but undecided. She needs help, Foxtrot. From you."

"Me? What am I supposed to do? It sounds like if I find her, I'm just forcing the situation to a resolution—and not necessarily a good one."

<There's a time for waiting, and a time to pounce,> Tango said. *<Waiting time is almost over.>*

"Yes," said Eli. "It's not Maxine you need to be searching for. It's the truth—about Lockley Hades."

As soon as he said it, it seemed obvious. If you have

two devious, mind-influencing shape-shifters and one
disappears, you investigate the other—even if he's dead.
Lockley Hades's corpse could probably provide me with
more reliable information that a live Maxine Danger. Except, of course, that the body was currently in possession
of the county morgue. But I had my ways . . .

Chapter Fourteen

One phone call later—to a friend of mine, a corpse-wrangler at the coroner's office—and I learned they'd found traces of foreign animal matter in the wound in Lockley Hades's chest. Since he'd been stabbed with a knife, this was noteworthy. I had a brilliant idea and tracked down Amos Clay in the study, reading a book.

"Amos," I said, "you use genetic typing to identify animal evidence all the time, right?"

"I do," he said, slipping a bookmark between the pages of his hardcover and setting it down next to him. "We have a large database of animals from all over the world."

"Do you think you could arrange access to that database for an associate of mine? It's about the Lockley Hades murder."

"Of course, Foxtrot. Just give me the relevant details."

Within the hour, I'd arranged for the sample to be tested by the nearest Fish and Wildlife field office, which promised results by tomorrow. I didn't know what, if anything, the information would tell us, but any data at all was a good thing to have. I suspected the sample would prove to be from a silverback mountain gorilla, just like the hair Whiskey had found, but I was perfectly willing to be proven wrong.

It was getting close to dinnertime, and I dreaded facing Ben. I avoided the kitchen and hoped there were no fires inside—literal or otherwise—that I had to put out.

Keene finally made an appearance around four. I was expecting a squinting-at-the-light, hungover version but was surprised to find him alert and energetic—perhaps a little too much so.

"Hullo, Foxtrot," he said, gliding down the stairs like a duchess making an entrance. He wore a long, flowing robe of purple, sandals, and a headband to tie back his hair.

I studied him for a moment then said, "If ZZ finds out you've been raiding her closet, she's going to be pissed."

"Not at all, Foxy. She lent me these, in fact; said they were saturated with good vibes. It'll help put me on the right path for my journey."

I groaned. "Have you joined a cult? Because deprogramming really eats up the woman-hours, and I'm already swamped—"

Which is when I noticed the dilated pupils above the beatific smile and realized that while he was indeed on a journey, it wasn't one that led into a heavily fortified compound out in the woods.

"What did you take?" I asked him bluntly. "I need to know, just in case."

Which is when I saw Cooper, hurrying down the stairs behind him. Coop's an old hippie, much like ZZ, and the groundskeeper for the graveyard. He wore his long, white hair pulled back in a ponytail, and a pair of denim overalls over a tie-dyed T-shirt. "Hey, Foxtrot. Don't worry, we've got this all under control. Peace and light and mellow vibrations, all the way. Strictly organic edibles, derived from nothing but the best hydroponic strains."

That mollified me, somewhat. Cooper, despite his proclivities, was thoroughly professional in his duties and knew his way around pharmaceuticals. "Edibles. So this is a pot-cookie and hash-brownie kind of trip?"

"Don't be a Neanderthal," said Keene loftily. "THC-infused gummy worms are the new neon orange. Or possibly lime green."

"And how many of these worms did you ingest, Chicken Little? Because edibles can be tricky—I know, I've seen roadies feed them to groupies. You eat one, wait an hour, and feel no effects, so you eat two more—and an hour after *that*, you're so high, you're counting individual molecules in the air. And it seems to last forever—or so I've been told."

"Don't worry, Foxtrot," Cooper said. "He did exactly twelve on an empty stomach, and he won't get any more. I'll keep an eye on him."

"So you're the shepherd on this passage through High Valley?" I asked.

"Yes, ma'am. We're taking a scientific *and* philosophic approach to Keene's problem. A guided visionary trip to inspiration itself."

"I see. Well, try not to break anything, will you? Especially the guests. That includes you, Keene."

He beamed down at me. "Oh, the only things I intend to break are my own limitations, Fox. Gonna take a little jog through the star stream, pluck a few mind-daisies. Know what I mean?"

"Not even a little," I said. "Just keep him safe, Coop. And have fun, right? Good luck smashing that writer's block to smithereens."

Keene frowned. "Smash? Smithereens? No, no, no— that's all wrong. Too destructive. I'm going to make *friends* with the block. Investigate its blockiness. Find out what it's hiding under that blank, impenetrable exterior. It's going to be quite the excursion, I can tell you."

I didn't know what to say to that, so I just smiled, nodded, and waved. He smiled, nodded, and waved back, then floated down the rest of the stairs and out the front door, Cooper on his heels like a faithful flock of one behind a newly minted messiah. The rain seemed to have cleared up nicely; hopefully, that meant Ben was in a better mood.

I went upstairs. It was time to do some serious research on one Mr. Lockley Hades, deceased.

Tango and Whiskey joined me, taking up positions on opposite ends of my couch.

<She's got that look again.>

[Indeed. And the scent as well.]

"Oh, cut it out. I still refuse to believe that my smell changes when I'm about to go data-spelunking."

<It's not just the smell. Your body language changes, too. You become more alert but less focused on what's happening in your immediate vicinity. Those two contradict each other, which sends confusing signals that are easy to pick up but hard to interpret.>

"You don't seem to have any problem," I said, sitting down behind my desk.

<I'm an expert.>

[There's a mathematical savant that lived in China one hundred and seven years ago. He was known to go without sleep for days when he was on the trail of a particularly difficult equation, eating only fruit and drinking only tea. His endocrine level would change significantly during the process.]

"Right. And let me guess—I smell like him."

[No. But I'm oddly reminded of the case, just the same.]

"Hilarious," I said, and dove in.

Lockley Hades, it turns out, was a very interesting fellow. His name at birth was Herbert Smudge, Junior, and his parents were naturalists. He grew up on the road, traveling from cloud forest to high desert to wetland, getting steeped in one exotic location after another. His interest in stage magic began in India, with fakirs who could charm snakes and lie on beds of nails without harm. Learning that these were tricks rather than actual miracles didn't faze him at all; it drove him to want to create illusions of his own. He studied with magicians all over the world, eventually settling on escapology as the main focus of his work.

He toured extensively, both in America and Europe, gradually building an audience that exploded once the Internet discovered him. The trick that made him famous involved his being welded into a suit made of thick chains then lowered into a tank filled with deadly vipers—only to climb out of an identical tank twenty feet away, also filled with snakes.

Knowing he was an Unktehila made the feat less impressive. Once hidden by the bodies of the snakes, he became one himself, wriggled through what I assumed was a concealed pipe connecting the two, and then returned to his original form. I'm guessing the vipers were close personal friends.

But whose side was he on?

He'd traveled the world, experienced many different cultures firsthand. For most people, that would enhance empathy; that sort of broad exposure to a wide range of people and how they lived—especially at a formative age—made it hard to be provincial or narrow-minded. Tyrants rarely leave their own borders, at least not as children.

But every rule has its exception.

The public persona Herbert created for himself wasn't a cuddly one. He toyed with monstrous or cruel imagery and generally did his best to scare the hell out of his audience. In most interviews, he came across as more Darth Vader than Luke Skywalker—except one.

From a trade magazine for magicians called *Legerde-main*, I found this:

HADES LOCKLEY is enjoying a quiet lunch. He eats a Paleo diet, high in protein, and it is at least partly responsible for his lean, muscular physique. Of course, a lot of the credit must also go to his daily regimen of exercise, a combination of yoga and running that promotes endurance. "Endurance," he says between bites of an enormous, bloody-rare steak, "is probably my defining trait. Certainly it's the one responsible for my success."

He has a point. Lockley Hades's touring sched-ule for the last five years has been grueling, to say the least—over fifteen hundred shows, in thirty different countries. From all accounts, he puts as much effort and showmanship into wowing a three-hundred-seat venue as he does one that holds two thousand, and his fans are as loyal and outspoken as the groupies of a heartthrob boy band. "He al-ways gives a thousand percent on stage," says one, a young man with a beard styled suspiciously close to Hades's own. "No matter how many times you see him, he always keeps you on the edge of your seat. You always wonder if he's going to be able to pull it off."

When asked how he manages to keep his fans entertained yet afraid, Hades simply shrugs. "It's human nature. We're all worried about what's going to kill us, so we're drawn to any spectacle that dem-onstrates the answer. It doesn't matter how unlikely it is that you're going to be strapped down and killed by a hydraulic press—your lizard brain still wants to know if it's possible to survive the process. That's why people still come to see escape artists; part of them thinks there's wisdom—or at least survival skills—to be learned."

When asked what he thinks is most likely to actually kill him, Hades laughs and strokes his ginger-colored, pointed beard. "Climate change," he says, with no hesitation at all. "It's transforming the planet. We're dumping more and more energy into a self-contained system, and of course it's having major disruptive effects. The Earth may become uninhabitable for human beings in our lifetime—and unless we do something about it, it's not just going to kill me, it's going to kill all of us."

Which raised a very interesting question: did Lockley Hades blame Thunderbirds for climate change—or did he want to enlist their help in fixing it?

I did some more digging and found an interview with his father in a popular science magazine. Reading it made me see Lockley Hades in a very different light. It made me . . . sad.

His father didn't seem to think much of his son's accomplishments. Oh, he hid it well enough; there was no outright criticism, more like contempt disguised as sarcasm. I think the most telling quote from Herbert Smudge Senior was this: "Herbert has always had the ability to do anything he wanted to. I'm not sure why he chose the life he has—but it fits him very well."

It fits him very well. He might as well have said, "Herbert has a desperate need to escape." But escape from what? His father, perhaps?

Not exactly hard evidence. But I let my mind wander, exploring the possibilities. Herbert Jr. is desperately unhappy, dragged from one locale to another, his innate oddness making it hard to make friends. His father is distant, the mother . . . well, I didn't know what she was like.

What I did know was that she died when Herbert was only eleven, in India.

Drowned, during a tropical monsoon.

That raised many more possibilities, none of them heartwarming. Was the Unktehila gene passed down from father to son? Did either of them blame a Thunderbird for the death of Herbert's mother? At what age did Herbert learn about what he was and what he could do?

The opposite reasoning could also hold, of course. Hades could simply be a stage persona designed to provoke; he might see his mother's death as a tragic accident and vow to enlist the help of his kind's ancient enemies to prevent such a tragedy from happening to anyone else. I simply didn't know.

My phone emitted a catchy little pop tune that Keene hated, even though it had been his biggest hit. "Hey, Keene—what's up?"

"I am."

Well, of course he was—edibles had a much longer-lasting effect than plain old weed. "Uh-huh. If you're experiencing cravings of the munchable variety, I can give you Ben's number—"

"No, Foxtrot. I mean I am *extremely* high, as in being at an elevated height—"

"So you're an elevant?"

"This is no time for clever wordplay! I am not only a great distance above the ground, I am *trapped* up here. You've got to help me!"

On the couch, two sets of ears perked up. Both Tango and Whiskey were capable of overhearing both sides of a conversation on a phone—especially if one of the people was loud and panicky. Which Keene was.

"Okay, just calm down. Where are you, and what happened to Cooper?"

"I sent him on a run to get . . . supplies. He wouldn't

go unless I promised him I wouldn't stray more than ten feet from a particular tree."

"And?"

"I kept my promise! Technically, I am *very* close to said tree. If I had ropes or Velcro or even glue I would be even closer, but all I have are my hands, feet, and knees. All but one of which are currently occupied in doing their best to keep me attached to the tree."

"I see. You kept your promise, but only in a horizontal vector."

"Yes, very good. A precise assessment of the situation, as always. Now will you please send someone to *get me down from here?*"

I sighed. Having a guest fall to their death from one of the estate trees would not look good on a resume. "Hang on. I'll call Cooper—I'm sure he's already on the case."

I hung up on his protests and tried the caretaker. No answer on the landline to his cottage, and straight to voice mail on his phone. Cooper's not always the most reliable when it comes to modern technology and often forgets to charge his phone or take it with him.

Tango got to her feet and stretched. *<Keene's stuck in a tree? We should go help.>*

[I don't believe he needs your help, actually—he's already stuck.]

<You can stay here. If the tree needs watering, we'll call you.>

I called Keene back. "Okay, we're on our way. Couldn't locate Cooper, but I'm sure there are ladders in the garage. One way or another, we'll get you down."

"One way or another? I envision a group of clowns holding a mobile trampoline with a bull's-eye painted on it."

"Sorry, no clowns—not in the budget. We'll have to make do with a chainsaw and some throw pillows. ZZ never did like that tree, anyway." I was already halfway down the hall, my partners at my heels.

"What? You don't even know which tree I'm in!"

"Which brings me to my next question—Keene, what tree are you in, exactly?"

"Just a second, Fox, let me check the serial number. It's engraved right here on the trunk, you know, very handy for someone in my situation, really have to hand it to the forward-thinking lads in the tree-assembly factory—"

"Does sarcasm help you hang on? If so, please continue."

"No, but it does take some of the focus away from my impending doom, which I can say I was barely even thinking of until just this second thank you *very* much—"

"Don't mention it. And don't—"

"Don't say it. Don't you dare say it. It's bad enough I'm stuck in this bloody tree without becoming a cliché on top of it—"

"The tree, you mean?"

"Yes, of course I mean on top of the tree, that's where we're broadcasting from, bloody station K-double E-N, bringing you the very best in mindless panic and blathering pointlessly on—"

"Can't argue with you there. Don't say *what*, exactly, Lord Blatherington?"

"Don't say 'don't look down.' It's like saying, 'don't scratch that itch,' or 'don't eat the last kipper.' Next thing you know, you're scratching like a mad fiend with a mouthful of smoked fish and no self-respect."

"Don't worry. I'm not going to say that, because it's exactly what I need you to do. Look down."

"*Are you mad?* Do you have any idea how far up I am? I passed a chap wearing a halo around the halfway mark. I'm having to duck passing satellites. I can see other *continents* from up here—Perth just rang me up and asked

what the weather's going to be like later today. AND I
BLOODY TOLD THEM!"

I paused, and let him catch his breath.

<Tree fever,> Tango said. *<He's got it bad.>*

[I thought you said cats never get trapped in trees.]

*<We don't. But occasionally one of us makes less-
than-wise decisions about when to come down.>*

"Listen, Keene. I only need you to look down if you
can't tell me where the tree is. Can you tell me that?"

Silence.

Then: "Um. Sort of. It's in the corner."

"I'm gonna need more than, 'it's a tree in a corner.'
I'm looking for actual coordinates here, not directions on
Christmas decorating."

"Well, excuse me. It's a tree, for God's sake, surrounded by a bunch of other trees, none of which have
convenient little signs on them. Wait. I feel like I'm repeating myself. Am I repeating myself?"

"Well, you are now."

"Marvelous. Marvelous."

"Aaaand now you're going to stop. *Which* corner,
Keene?"

"The one near the graveyard but away from the road.
There's a stone wall. Or at least there was when I went
up here. God knows what sort of crumbled ruin is left by
now."

"Yes, it's been ages, hasn't it? Don't worry, meerkats
run everything now. The world is a safer, saner place."

"Meerkats?"

<There's nothing mere about cats.>

[Not 'mere cats'; *meerkats*.]

"Yes, meerkats. There's an entire artistic subcul-
ture devoted to popping your head out of a hole in the
ground, looking around, and popping it back in again.

Groundhog Day is a national holiday observed all over the world."

"You've gone all strange, Foxtrot. And me trapped in an arboreal hell and all."

"Maybe, Mr. Keene. Or maybe I just wanted to keep your attention focused on me while I zeroed in on your location. Which I haven't quite done, but I'm moving in the right direction. Good news, bad news time: Which one do you want first?"

"Does the bad involved me crashing to the earth and waking up in a body cast?"

"No. Well, probably not."

"Then I'll take the good news first."

"Okay. The good news is that I'm now almost certainly somewhere underneath you. The bad news—"

"Hang on. Is the bad news absolutely necessary? Is there any sort of mediocre news you could use as a buffer, first?"

"No. The bad news is that I'm not exactly sure which tree you're in. These are evergreens, which mean the foliage is so thick that I can't see you and you can't see me. Excellent for climbing, not so great for visibility."

"I could try throwing something down to you. My keys, maybe."

"They'll just get stuck in the branches. No, I've got a better idea."

<Forget it.>

I haven't even asked you yet, I thought at Tango.

<I hate climbing pine trees. The resin gets my claws all sticky.>

[You mean you hate climbing down them.]

<That's the hardest part!>

Look kitty, you won't have to go all the way up. Just high enough to spot Keene—then at least we'll know which tree he's in. It's got to be one of these. I indicated with a sweep of my hand the circle of trees we were now standing beneath, having navigated our way there while Keene was talking.

"*Are you down there?*" Keene's voice called out, sounding high but not too far away. Fifty feet, maybe?

"Yes!" I shouted back. "*We're just trying to figure out how to*—oh, bugger this." I put my phone back to my ear. "No point in yelling, is there?"

"*What? You must be very far away—I can hardly hear you!*"

I let out the sigh that had building in me for the last ten minutes and yelled upward, "Use your phone, moron!" Calling guests names is not something I usually do, regardless of how much they deserve it, but Keene was a special case. He's the sort of friend that expects a certain amount of abuse, and it hurts his feelings if he doesn't get it.

Which was right about when I heard a low rumble of thunder.

Getting a guest electrocuted—while it's not like it hasn't happened before—is something ZZ definitely frowns upon. I needed to get Keene down out of that tree in one, unbroken piece, and I needed to do it now.

"Hang on, I'm going to try Coop again." I disconnected then rang the caretaker. "Hello?" Success!

"Coop? You haven't by any chance waylaid a certain very high rock star, have you?"

"I'm sorry to say I have, Foxtrot. He sent me off to get something, and he was gone when I got back. Have you seen him?"

"Not as such. But I have a definite idea where to find him . . ."

I told Coop where we were and what Keene had managed to get himself into—or up to. Coop told me he knew where to get his hands on a really long ladder and would have it around to us in about twenty minutes. I thanked him and hung up.

Another rumble of thunder. And I still didn't know which tree held my wayward celebrity.

Well, first things first. I braced myself and called Ben. If he was still in a mood, he might not answer, but I got lucky. "Yes?"

"Hi to you, too. Look, I've got a weather problem, and I need your help."

"What, the guests complaining they can't use the tennis courts? I've got better things to do, Foxtrot—"

"No, this is serious. Keene's trapped himself at the top of a very tall tree, and I'm hearing thunder. Think you can put the kibosh on that before he Frankensteins himself?"

There was a pause. "Oh. Well, I disagree on your definition of 'serious'—sounds like typical Keene idiocy to me—but no, I don't want to see him fry. I'll have a chat with the local storm system."

"Thank you."

"I live to serve." Click.

Ouch. Well, that was a little cold but not subzero. He'd come around.

Then it started to rain. Not heavily, just a damp little drizzle. Okay, maybe he was still pretty miffed. At least the thunder had quit.

[Oh, for—the one thing cats are better at than dogs, and you refuse to help?]

<*I'm not refusing to help. I'm just directing my energy in a different direction.*>

[You've been insufferable ever since you put on that play.] Tango had directed a group of animal spirits in a graveyard production of her own devising, specifically for my benefit.

<*Suffering is something I'm extremely familiar with,*

thanks to you. And cats are better at WAY more things than dogs.>

[No, you're not. Dogs have been trained for literally hundreds of different tasks—]

<Trained? TRAINED? That's a curse word in Fe-line, you know. It means, 'too stupid to understand the word no.'>

[That's—that's just *so*—I can't even—]

And that was when my dog—whose default form is that of an Australian cattle dog—used his ectoplasmic abilities to transform into a different breed altogether: it was around the same size but a tawny orange in color, with a fox-like face.

And with a single bound, he climbed into the lowest branches of the nearest tree.

[The spine of the New Guinea singing dog is ex-tremely flexible,] Whiskey stated. [And so are their front and back legs, which can spread sideways up to a ninety degree angle.] He bounded up to the next branch, using his paws to wrap around it and pull himself up. [As you can see, I can now also rotate my paws more than most other breeds. All of which is to say: dogs may not be bet-ter than cats at climbing trees, but that doesn't mean we can't do it.]

<Hey! No fair! That's supposed to be my job!>

[Having a job implies training. Clearly, that leaves your entire species out.] Up another branch.

<Yeah? Well, I don't need any stinking training to do a job. Watch this.> And with that, Tango sprinted up an-other tree. It didn't take her long to pass Whiskey, who was still setting a pretty good pace.

I didn't bother telling either of them to be careful. Tango knew what she was doing, and Whiskey was made of ectoplasm—I was reasonably sure he could reach the top of the tree and fall off without hurting himself.

In seconds they were both out of sight, lost in the thick foliage. *Hey*, I mentally called out, *whoever finds him first, let me know—*

My phone sang at me. Keene's ringtone. I answered and said, "Don't worry—help is on its way—"

"Foxtrot. There's a dog in this tree with me."

Uh-oh.

Chapter Fifteen

"Don't be ridiculous," I said. "Dogs can't climb trees."

[Oh, dear. He's spotted me. Drat this shifting wind—]

Don't panic. Just get back down here. "I suppose the dog can climb backward as well, ha, ha."

"Yes, it bloody well can! Now I can't see it anymore—Foxtrot, I looked right into its eyes, and they were the strangest shade of green—"

Green?

[Yes, another peculiarity of the breed. Can only be seen in a particular light—]

Tango, I need Keene paying attention to you instead of Whiskey. How about a little song?

<Sure thing, Toots. Another thing cats can do better.>

At which point a tremendous yowling burst forth, clearly audible not just from Tango's tree but from my phone as well.

"What the funkadelic?" Keene yelped. "That's no dog—it's a screaming demon from Hell, and it just jumped into another tree! Get out of here, Foxtrot! Save yourself!"

"No, that's just a raven. They're tremendous mimics,

and there's a local one that likes to torment cats by imitating them. Maybe that's what you saw, too."

"Foxtrot, I may be on the equivalent of half a pound of high-grade chronic, and I may be stuck up in a tree, but I'm not hallucinating. What I saw did not have wings, and it wasn't black. Ravens are still black, right?"

"As far as I know." I squinted up into the tree and saw Whiskey climbing back down. When he got within twenty feet of the ground, he simply jumped and changed back into his normal form on impact. Tango continued to serenade us from on high, which was a sound I could really do without. *Okay, you can stop now.*

<*But I was just getting to the best part!*>

[You stopping *is* the best part.]

"Keene," I said into my phone, "Do you even remember why you climbed the tree in the first place?"

"Perspective, Fox. Perspective. And aromatherapy."

"That *almost* makes sense. Get any pine-scented inspirations?"

"Yes. Being high and getting high are two different things, and one shouldn't combine them. Especially while high."

"Well, that's *almost* poetic. Are you sure you couldn't work that into anything?"

"Oh, being stuck up here has worked wonders for my focus, Foxtrot. And what I'm focused on is *getting down*. And not in any disco-related sense."

"Just hold on. I think I see Cooper coming."

I did, and not only did he have an extendable ladder with him, he had two safety harnesses and a great deal of rope. "Oh, good," I said as he approached. "Once we get him out of the tree, we can use that to hang him."

"I'm real sorry, Foxtrot," Cooper said. "Never thought he'd do something like this, that's for sure."

"Don't sweat it," I told him. "Rock stars are like puppies; they're gonna go where they're gonna go, and somebody else will have to clean it up. Luckily for us, we get paid nicely to do so."

After that, it was just a matter of getting the ladder into place and sending Coop up it. Keene was so happy to get down, he didn't even balk at the safety harness, and before too long, he was back on solid ground, which he promptly lay facedown on. "I am never getting that . . . *vertical* again," he said.

"You're going to get pine needles up your nose like that," I said.

"Small price to pay. I'm putting my penthouse on the market as soon as I can remember the name of my real estate agent. Pembroke? Pemberton? Pemmican? Something like that."

"C'mon, my flightless little bird. Let's get you back to the house while Cooper puts the equipment away."

Keene let himself be helped to his feet; I noticed Tango stealthily making her way back down her tree behind him. *Thanks, kitty.*

<You're welcome. Any excuse to sing is always a good one—>

[Oh, please. Calling that singing is like calling a car accident an improvisational sculpture.]

<I notice she didn't ask you for a performance.>

[I was the one she was trying to draw attention away from!]

<Sure. Just keep telling yourself that. If he'd heard you open your mouth, he would have jumped just to escape the racket.>

[They used to string rackets with cat gut, didn't they? I'm beginning to understand where the word came from.]

Enough, guys. Whiskey, you're with me—Tango, stay

out of sight while Keene's with us. There's enough going on without him wondering why you're hanging around instead of a raven.

Between us, we managed to get Keene back to the house, where he made his way upstairs and announced his intention to collapse into bed and meditate until dinnertime. Which, I realized, it was almost time for; the day was almost done, and I was no closer to solving the multiple mysteries of not only who killed Lockley Hades but which side they were on—and what they were going to do next.

"Foxtrot!" said ZZ. "How lovely of you to join us. How is Keene?"

I smiled as I took my seat and said, "He's fine. Said he was coming down for dinner, but he may be a little . . . distracted."

"That's putting it mildly," said Oscar. He wore a natty, white dinner jacket over a pale-peach silk shirt, and my imagination kept adding an ascot that wasn't there. To his left sat Amos Clay, wearing almost exactly the same outfit he'd worn yesterday, and to his right was Hironobu Masuda in his tux. ZZ, as usual, was at the head of the table and wore a stunning, low-cut gown of something white and diaphanous, with little silver stars and crescent moons worked into the material.

I wore an off-shoulder black dress I kept in my office for just such occasions and a simple necklace of pearls. Whiskey, at my feet, was dressed in fashionable brindle-colored fur, draped over a russet base. His one blue eye clashed terribly with his one brown one, but he had the insouciance to pull it off. Tango had not deigned to join us for dinner, but she rarely did.

Rack of lamb was the main course, with a medley of roasted vegetables for those who preferred to eat vegetarian. Keene showed up just after it was served, dressed in ripped jeans, a purple, paisley tailcoat over a black T-shirt and sporting cat-eye sunglasses; he slid into his seat as if not entirely sure of the local gravity and proceeded to stare at his wine glass as if it were speaking to him.

"I see that Summer is still absent," said Oscar. "Has she finally left the premises, or have the police decided to charge her?"

"Bit premature for that, don't you think?" said Amos Clay, attacking his lamb with gusto. "Just because she was involved in the performance of the trick doesn't mean she's guilty of murder."

"Indeed. What would be her motive?" asked Matsuda.

"Professional jealousy?" suggested Oscar. "He and Maxine were rival performers, after all."

"Not according to what I've discovered," I said. "The rivalry was all faked to generate publicity. No reason for either side to end it, either—it was working exactly the way it was supposed to."

"A lover's quarrel?" suggested Oscar. "The fact that the body was entirely unclothed is suggestive of . . . something."

I knew the answer to that one, but I couldn't tell them: Lockley had clearly been in another form when he was killed—most likely a mountain gorilla, according to the scent Whiskey had picked up. But why?

"It'll turn out to all be about money," said Keene, who had altered his focus on his wineglass to the food in front of him. "Always is, especially in the entertainment industry. Somebody's manager's agent's lawyer will turn up with a detailed contract about how they get X percentage of all proceeds in the unlikely event that their client dies naked in a ballroom during an attempt to escape from a steel vault. Seen it happen a dozen times before."

"Money is often the motive," said Masuda. "Who benefits? Does Lockley Hades have any heirs?"

"Not that I can tell," I said. "No siblings, only a father he's estranged from. But it's hard to tell who'll benefit without seeing his will, and that's beyond my capabilities. I would imagine the estate is sizeable."

"Unless he had vices we don't know about," said Oscar. "Gambling debts, perhaps. A previously unknown child by a former relationship. Compulsive shopping binges—"

"You're far too good at listing bad habits," ZZ said, taking a sip of her wine. "An overabundance of field research, I think."

"I take a different view," said Oscar. "Bad habits are simply good ones that haven't been properly trained through rigorous practice."

"The killing might have been motivated by revenge," pointed out Clay. "Everyone has enemies. Who were Lockley Hades's?"

"None that I could find," I said. "Nothing obvious, anyway. No nasty lawsuits or public feuds—other than the one he staged with Maxine."

Keene suddenly sat bolt upright. "A fan," he blurted out. "It could be a deranged fan. Someone who didn't know the feud was a fake. Someone who thought they were defending Maxine's honor."

The table fell silent as we all considered this. "It does make a certain amount of sense," ZZ admitted. "Some fans will go to ridiculous lengths for the object of their desire. Climb fences, break into homes, stalk the people closest to them."

"You would know, Mother," said Oscar. "Please, regale us again with the story of how you snuck into Keith Richards' hotel room dressed as a maid."

ZZ chose to ignore that. "And a fan would be likely to know something about escape artistry—maybe enough to stage a performance of their own . . ."

Fan was, of course, short for fanatic. I stole a glance at

Hironobu Masuda, but he was carefully avoiding looking at me, suddenly engrossed in his meal. I already knew he was a fan of mysterious murders—the question now was, how big a fan?

"I've had fans do some bloody weird stuff," said Keene. "One woman kept sending me eggs. Hand-blown ones, painted up in Easter colors. Hold one up to the light, and you'd see a little piece of paper inside with a poem written on it." He paused, remembering. "Lovely eggs. Terrible poems."

"Still, our security is quite good," Oscar said. "Shondra does a marvelous job. I very much doubt an intruder could sneak onto the grounds without being detected."

If Oscar knew about shape-shifting snakes with mind-influencing powers, he'd be a lot less sure of himself, but that gave me an idea—I could check the security footage from the cameras on the estate and see if any large animals had breached the perimeter in the hours before the murder. Shondra had gone home for the night, but I had access to her office. It wasn't much of a lead—even if I found something, all it would prove was that Lockley Hades had managed to sneak onto the grounds, which was something we already knew. Of course, if I *didn't* find anything, that was an entirely different matter . . .

"None of which answers the question: Where is Summer Coyne?" Amos Clay pointed out. "Is she still here or not?"

"Good question," said Oscar. "The rules, established by Mother and written in Old Testament stone, are that guests must attend the nightly soirees. Exceptions have been made in extreme circumstances, but the mere fact of being a suspect in an ongoing murder investigation does not qualify. Why, if we allowed people to use that as an excuse, the dining room would be become a desert, bereft of all company save our trusty drinks trolley, trundling over sand dunes and around empty chairs . . ."

"Very picturesque," said ZZ. "But—astonishingly—you bring up a good point. Summer really should be here."

"She hasn't left the grounds, as far as I know," I said. "That truck she drove in, with the trailer attached? Pretty sure it's still in the lot."

"Perhaps she's inside?" Keene suggested. "When you're touring, the trailer becomes your second home. Place to retreat to when things get a bit much as well."

"Maybe we should check on her," said ZZ, looking worried. "She must be finding all this tremendously stressful. Foxtrot, would you mind?"

"Not at all," I said, getting up. "I'll take Whiskey with me for moral support. C'mon, boy."

[Please don't call me *boy*,] Whiskey thought at me as we left the dining room. [I'm old enough to be your father.]

Is that in human or dog years?

[In experience. In any case, it's hardly an appropriate appellation.]

Okay, okay. I bow to your accumulated wisdom and alliteration.

We went outside, to the parking lot just off the main entrance. Maxine's truck and trailer were still parked there, the bright-red truck emblazoned with her logo in big, showbiz letters. The trailer, though, was much less showy, little more than a long, gray box with a hefty air-conditioning unit on its roof. In fact, it looked more suited to industrial use than travel; it didn't even have any windows, just one featureless door near the back.

I studied it for a second then said, "I sort of assumed this trailer was just for equipment, but I've never actually been inside. Maxine and Summer were kind of cagey when they unloaded it, too. I wonder if the cops have been in it."

And suddenly, Whiskey was at full attention. Ears

pointed straight up, eyes intent, tail motionless. [I very much doubt they have.]

"And why would you say that?"

[Two reasons. First, I assume Summer would insist on a search warrant, citing professional concerns. Second—I believe this trailer holds a dead body.]

"What?"

[Yes. The refrigeration unit has slowed down and masked the decomposition, but at this close range it's unmistakable. There's a corpse—a human corpse—inside.]

I swallowed. "Then I guess there isn't much point in knocking, is there?"

I tried the door. It opened easily.

Most of the trailer was empty space, with tie-downs along the walls for containers. At the very back of the trailer was a blank, gray wall, with a push broom mounted lengthwise on two hooks.

[It's a false wall. The smell is coming from behind it.]

I walked forward, studied the wall. I took the broom off, tried twisting one hook, and then tried the other. There was a click, and the door swung open.

Cold mist spilled out of the refrigerated space. There were only two things in it: a 3D printer . . . and sprawled at its base, the body of Summer Coyne.

[I believe,] said Whiskey, [that ZZ will find this an acceptable excuse for missing dinner.]

Chapter Sixteen

"Another one?" Lieutenant Forrester said, scratching his head. "I think you guys need to throw fewer dinner parties."

The police had cordoned off the trailer, and I'd already given Forrester my statement. "It's not the dinner parties that kill them," I protested. "In fact, if she'd come to the party, she'd still be alive. Probably."

Forrester shook his head. "I doubt that. Hard to tell when a body's frozen how long it's been dead, but it takes a while to get as . . . *solid* as she is. She's been dead for hours, at least. Single stab wound to the chest, looks like—just like the last one."

The last time I'd seen her was poolside, yesterday afternoon. So it was possible she'd been killed shortly thereafter—but by who, and why?

"Things aren't looking good for Maxine Danger," said Forrester. "First her rival, then her assistant? I'd say she's either next on the list—or she's the one making it."

I hadn't touched anything, but I'd taken a quick look around before calling Forrester. It looked to me as if Summer Coyne had been stabbed the same way Lockley Hades had—once, right through the heart. But what was really puzzling to me was that she was dressed in the same outfit she'd been wearing when she and Maxine had performed the vault escape—that is, the one she'd been wearing at the start, before she reappeared.

That, and the 3D printer.

I'd studied it without touching it. I'm no expert, but it looked to me like the equipment attached to it was some sort of remote access setup—which meant this was where the signals from the ballroom had been sent. The hidden scanners took pics of the key sealed in the Lucite column, and this printer made the duplicate key.

Out of ice.

My research had taught me ice was one of the mediums 3D printers could work in. Now I knew at least part of how the trick was done and even how the key was disposed of—a wet spot on the carpet is hardly noticeable, especially amongst a bunch of broken glass. But how they figured out the alignment of the magnets and duplicated them was still a mystery.

Forrester told me he'd need the statements of the dinner guests, and I arranged for him to interview them one by one in the library. I knew it wouldn't take long; after all, what was there to say? I supposed everyone would have to account for their whereabouts during the day, but I was sure there would be gaps; guests tended to move around the grounds, taking in the zoo or the stables or the tennis courts or the pool, and I was guessing there would be gaps in everyone's story, periods of time they couldn't account for when they were alone. Heck, even I spent large amounts of time locked away in my office, with no one but Whiskey or Tango to alibi me—and I wasn't about to use the testimony of a talking dog or cat.

By the time everyone had wrapped up their statements, it was full dark. The body had been examined, photographed, and taken away. If you ignored all the crime scene tape, it was almost as if nothing had happened at all.

Except that a young woman was dead.

I'd liked Summer Coyne. She was bright, and talented, and a wise-ass with an impeccable sense of timing. She was a big part of why Maxine Danger was successful, and she was no longer on the planet. Where she might be now I was a little unclear on; while I knew there definitely was an afterlife—for humans, that is—Eli kept me firmly in the dark on any particulars. My purview was the Great Crossroads, and the various animal afterlives it connected to. About the only chance I had to talk to Summer's spirit would be to locate a treasured pet she had as a child and convince them to go interview her for me. For a brief moment, I considered the idea then realized how ridiculous it was. For starters, I didn't know much about her beyond her professional abilities.

So I did what I always do when I feel things are spiraling out of control: I went upstairs and did more research. Whiskey came with me, but Tango had disappeared into the night. I wasn't worried about her; she was a cat, after all.

What can I say about Summer Coyne?

It wasn't her real name, of course. She had begun life as the much more ordinary-sounding Jennifer Talbot, though she obviously thought she needed something a little flashier for showbiz. She'd done a part-time gig in radio for a while, but it was clear from the beginning that her heart belonged to magic; I found a photo of her in the classic fishnet-and-top-hat look that she'd worn for the talent part of a beauty pageant.

I was struck by something as I surfed through the bits

and bytes of her online presence, through all the milestones of her professional and personal life: though my intention was to get a clearer picture of Summer as a person, the task I was performing was essentially the same as someone gathering information for a eulogy.

Because what is a eulogy, other than a condensed history, a collection of high points and moments, trying to evoke the spirit of someone with words and facts? Went to school here, worked there, accomplished this and this and this—but more than that, more than just dry, obituary paragraphs. A eulogy is a tribute, and it tries to do more than just remind; it tries to recreate, in a very short period of time, the best of someone.

I found myself trying to do this as I researched Summer Coyne, looking for more than just cold data. And as I did, I felt cheated, somehow; I felt that Summer was someone I could have been friends with, someone I could have admired and even confided in. She was smart, she was persistent, she was brave; she had to be, to break into the world she wanted to be part of.

And she'd done it.

For many years, female magicians had been almost nonexistent—at least as far as the public was concerned. They'd been used as props, as clever distractions that helped the male illusionist perform under the limelight. But that was an illusion itself; the assistants were an integral part of the magic, and always had been. They didn't receive the same glory as the one they were supposedly "assisting," but they worked just as hard and deserved as much of the glory.

I wondered about that. Summer was a prominent part of the act—but it was still Maxine's name on the marquee. Did she resent that? I hadn't sensed any tension between them, but professionals can hide such things.

As I looked through the online details of Summer Coyne's life, I got the picture of a bright, driven girl who craved the spotlight. She'd gotten some of it—but was what she got enough?

I didn't think so. Which raised the question: What exactly was Summer willing to do to get that fame? Could it include knocking off Maxine's competition? In order to do what? Replace him, maybe?

Something at the back of my brain had been itching at me, and I suddenly realized what it was. Lockley Hades didn't have an assistant.

Oh, I'm sure he had plenty of employees, and the title "assistant" was probably attached to a few of them—but he didn't have the equivalent of Summer Coyne. That bothered me, and I knew why.

Assistants—like myself—are what power things behind the scenes. We have many names, from secretary to facilitator to parent, but what we *do* is . . . everything. We're jugglers and diplomats and organizers and dispatchers. We get things moving and then make sure things move where they're supposed to. Summer Coyne was one of us, and she'd died. I owed it to her to find out who'd done it and why.

The fact that Lockley Hades didn't have a visible version of Summer Coyne standing beside him smelled like arrogance to me, and maybe the inflated ego to go with it. That revelation didn't bring me any closer to catching his killer, but it was something.

I leaned back in my desk chair and stretched. I had more questions than answers, the beginnings of a headache, and a sore back. Plus, my boyfriend and I weren't getting along, there was a killer still on the loose, and two supernatural factions were about to go to war with each other. Yeah, pretty typical day.

Which is when I got the telepathic summons from my cat.

<Toots, you gotta get down here. I think I just broke this case wide open.>

Really? Where are you?

<Down in the zoo. I just finished talking to Owduttf, and man, did he spill his guts.>

Weird. The honey badger generally preferred spilling the guts of other animals, and then consuming them whole—including massive wildebeests. *I'll be right down.*

Whiskey yawned and jumped off the couch. [This should be entertaining.]

"Oh, you don't think she's actually found anything?" I said as we headed downstairs.

[I think Owduttf's found something. A gullible feline.]

Through the foyer and out the front door. "Oh, come on. He's given us reliable information before."

[He's also made up wild stories in order to get whole raw chickens.]

"True . . ."

We strolled down to the end of the grounds where the menagerie began. Tropical birds cawed at us, and a fennec fox peered at us suspiciously from the entrance to its den before darting back inside.

However, we were still a few pens away from Owduttf's enclosure when Tango padded out of the shadows. *<There you are! Took you long enough.>*

[For a creature who prides herself on patience, you are exceedingly impatient.]

<You just don't understand the definition of the word. Patience is when I'm waiting for something I want in the world. Impatience is simply me letting the world know it isn't working fast enough.>

[Because, of course, that always speeds things up.]

<Naturally. Otherwise, I wouldn't bother.>

[But a demand for speed is the opposite of patience—]

<No, the opposite of patience is waiting for something I don't *want. Waiting, for instance, for a dog who doesn't understand a simple concept.>*

"I'm about to lose *my* patience," I said. "C'mon, what have you got? Besides a raging case of impatience?"

Tango sat, curled her tail around herself, and regarded me calmly. *<I have found not one but two more witnesses present on the day of the murder. Can you see why I might be a little impatient?>*

"What? That's amazing. Who are they?"

<Follow me.>

[Hmmph. I'll believe it when I see it.]

Tango led us to a cage that held a long-tailed lemur, related to a monkey. It had a black face with a fringe of white fur around it and was perched high up in the tree in its pen. It peered down at us warily as we walked up.

<This is Ernesto. He admits he was here when the murder occurred.>

[Well, of course he was here. Where else would he be? He's in a pen.]

<The point is, he saw something. Didn't you, Ernesto?> Tango screeched something in what I assume was Lemur, and Ernesto screeched something back.

<He says,> Tango translated, *<that he doesn't know what I'm talking about, and who are you people, anyway.>*

[I see. Well done. Very revealing.]

<Shut up. I'm going to explain that we're investigating a murder and imply that he's a suspect.> More screeching, with a few yowls thrown in. Ernesto's reply sounded incredulous to me, but maybe that was my imagination.

<*He says, and I quote: "What? I didn't see nothing.
Nothing happened, and if it did, I didn't see it. I wasn't
even looking that way. I never look that way. I wasn't involved, I don't want to be involved, and you can't make
me."*>

[Bravo. You've cracked the case. It's so cracked, it's
practically fragmenting into pieces. Somewhat like your
brain.]

More Lemur-speak from Tango. <*I just told him,
"Look, monkey boy. We know you saw something, and
the more you deny it, the guiltier you look. Tell us what
you saw, and maybe we'll put in a good word with the
warden."*>

"I don't think Carol will take kindly to being called a
warden."

<*Then we won't tell her.*>

Abruptly, the lemur swung down from his branch to
our level and stared at us furiously. He uttered a series
of low grunts and squeaks while waving his hands about
like a conductor.

<*Aha. He says, "Look, you don't understand. I could
get in trouble. These walls have ears, you know? And
sometimes teeth and claws, too. I'm not saying another
word."*> And with that, he shot off the branch and into a
hole in the wall that led to his indoor quarters.

[That was illuminating,] said Whiskey. [In the same
sense that a brick weighs very little or water is exceedingly
dry.]

<*Don't you get it? He's admitting he saw something,
even if he won't say what. He's just too scared to talk.*>

"That *is* what it sounded like," I said. "But it doesn't do
us a lot of good if he won't tell us what he saw. And I'm
a little confused—I thought you said it was Owduttf you
got the information from."

<I'm getting to that. Follow me.>

Tango led us to the next pen, an enclosure that held a brown bear. A rather overweight one—apparently his previous owners had overfed him. Carol, the vet that oversaw the zoo, had him on a strict diet. The bear regarded us curiously as we approached.

Tango didn't wait but launched right into an ursine dialogue. The bear listened intently then replied with a series of growls, grunts, and other bearlike noises.

<I'm going to translate directly,> Tango said. *<"Hello again. These are my helpers. We'd be very interested in what you saw the other day."*

<"Greetings, Cat Person. I welcome you and your assistants. I am unsure as to what you are referring, as many things occur within my field of view that are both intriguing and memorable. Could you perhaps elaborate on the specifics of the event, so as to stimulate my recollection?"

"I will do my best to provide you with a proper frame of reference. It occurred two days ago, when the sun was high in the sky. A being of indeterminate type was seen fleeing from the large house behind me. Does this description parallel any of your recent memories?">

[I had no idea the Ursine language was so formal,] Whiskey muttered.

<"I'm afraid I can neither affirm nor deny this description. While it's certainly within the realm of possibility, the actuality of the occurrence remains in doubt. Many factors are in play, only some of which can be positively identified. Thus, the shadow of uncertainty remains over the sequence of events.">

"I may not speak Ursine," I said, "But I know obfuscation when I hear it. Tango, are all bears this obtuse, or is it just this one?"

<You nailed it, Toots. He knows something, but he's

*not telling. And bribes won't work either—I already tried
that. Both he and the monkey are scared of something,
but they won't say what. I think I might know, though.>*

And now Tango led us to Owduttf's enclosure—where
we discovered the honey badger waiting for us, staring
through the bars of his pen in a very unsettling way.

I've talked about honey badgers before, but some facts
bear repeating: this beastie is one of the more fearsome—
and fearless—creatures on the planet. They've been
known to take kills away from lions, they treat venom-
ous snakes as a light snack, and their jaws are so strong,
they crunch through hooves and horns like potato chips.
Honey badgers have also been known to dig up and eat
human corpses, which shouldn't make them any scarier
but does. They are the psychopathic serial killers of the
animal kingdom, and we had one in residence.

He made his usual noises, barks and grunts and chuff-
ing sounds, and I almost expected Tango to translate it as,
"Hello, Clarice."

But no. What he said was, "Are you ready to give me
my five chickens yet—or do I have to come get them?"

"It was three, not five, and they aren't on the menu,"
I answered. "And neither is anything else in the immediate vicinity. Have you been threatening the other
animals?"

Owduttf made chuckling noises, which turned out to
mean, "What a ridiculous idea. Even if I have picked up a
few words of Bear or Lemur, I certainly wouldn't use that
to intimidate anyone."

I grimaced. As I mentioned, another thing honey badgers are famous for is escaping—Owduttf was nearly as
good at getting out as Oswald. And if the other animals
knew that, they'd be inclined to keep quiet as opposed to
becoming dinner. Even a brown bear would think twice
before pissing off Owduttf.

"Okay, so maybe you saw something, and you're bullying the other animals into being quiet so you're the only one who gets rewarded," I said. "But you're devious enough to bully them into shutting up about seeing nothing, which would let you make something up and get the same result. You see my problem?"

"No problem at all," was Tango's translation. "You give me my chickens, I tell you what I saw, you decide for yourself whether or not I'm telling the truth. It's really all up to you."

"Not so fast. How about you tell me what you saw first—I'll decide *then* if I believe you, and you'll get rewarded appropriately."

"That hardly seems fair. You could learn some very valuable new information and then decide to keep the chickens for yourself."

I shook my head and wondered for a brief moment about the arc of my life and how it had led me to arguing the finer points of chicken-bartering with a bloodthirsty South African carnivore. "I can have all the chickens I want, Owduttf, and I don't have to spin tall tales in order to get them."

"So you say. From my point of view, chickens are a rare and valuable commodity. For all I know, there's a chicken drought and you're bargaining with the last five chickens you own."

Damn it, he had me there. I wondered if this would be going any better if I did it as a PowerPoint demonstration, with big color pictures of poultry farms and a pie chart showing robust growth in the chicken industry, then realized I was getting a little punchy.

"Look, Owduttf, it's clear we have a trust issue here. Whatever it is you know, you don't believe I'm going to cough up the bird carcasses once you tell me. And I have no way of knowing if your information is actually useful, though I strongly suspect that if I just give you what you want, you won't bother reciprocating with anything at all. So we're at an impasse."

Owduttf seemed to be thinking this over. He resumed after a moment: "How about a compromise? You give me two chickens, I tell you some of what I saw, and then you can decide if the remainder is worth three more."

That actually seemed reasonable, which made me suspicious. But what the hell, all it was going to cost me was two chickens. And having to convince my boyfriend to part with them.

"Okay, you've got a deal," I said. "I will go and get the chickens forthwith. Uh, they may be frozen."

Tango paused, listened then continued. *<He doesn't understand the word* frozen.*>*

Hmmm. Well, of course he didn't. It gets plenty cold here in the State of New York, but Owduttf's pen is heated, and he's from a tropical country. He's never had to deal with meat the temperature and consistency of a block of ice—though I have no doubt he'd make short work of it regardless. "Tell him it might be a little chewy until it warms up. Nothing he can't handle."

Tango did so and then got a reply. *<He says he doesn't care how chewy it is, as long as he gets to eat it.>*

"Sounds like we've got a deal. Let's go get some chickens."

Tango said our goodbyes, and we headed back toward the house.

[I can't help but wonder,] said Whiskey, [what the other animals will tell us once they're no longer terrified of doing so.]

"I don't know if that's possible. Even once he gets his way, Owduttf's still going to be the monster next door. I think they'll back him up regardless of what he tells us."

<Too bad a cat didn't see anything. We're not scared of anyone.>

[No, of course you aren't. You know honey badgers can climb trees, don't you?]

<They cannot!>

"Yeah, I'm not so sure about that one," I said. "*Eat* trees, I'm willing to believe."

It didn't take us long to go back to the mansion, locate a couple of frozen chickens in the walk-in freezer—fortunately, Ben didn't seem to be around—and return to Owduttf's enclosure. He was waiting patiently for us, grooming one deadly front claw with his teeth.

"Okay," I said, hefting the chicken in one hand. "Here comes the first one." I pitched it over the top of the enclosure; it hit the ground and bounced to a stop at Owduttf's feet.

I thought he might sniff it, bat it around a little, try an experimental chew on a wing. Nope. He pounced on it like Tango on catnip and proceeded to quickly rip it apart using his teeth and claws, gobbling down chunks as he went. It was like watching a hungry chainsaw.

"Um," I said. "Well, he is certainly . . . efficient."

[And almost finished. Better toss the next one in before he becomes . . .]

<What, more bloodthirsty?>

"I don't think that's possible," I said. "Here goes."

Poultry carcass number two went up and over. Same result as the first one—fast, deadly and *loud*: the crunching was like listening to tree branches break. In another minute or so, the second one was gone, too. I wondered how long it would have taken him to eat them if they weren't frozen and shuddered. I was increasingly seeing the brown bear's point of view.

"Okay, we made good on our end of the bargain," I said. "Your turn."

Owduttf regarded me with beady, glittering eyes, licked his lips, and gave me his reply, which Tango translated: "I saw a person running from the house. They changed into a bird and flew away."

I stared at him. "What kind of bird?"

"I'm not telling you that until I get the other three chickens."

"Damn it," I said. "You know, you almost had me. Almost."

"I will tell you more once I have the other chickens."

I shook my head. "No, you won't. Because what you just told me is impossible. You might have seen a shape-changer, but the Unkhetila are limited by mass and weight—they're too heavy to change into something that can fly. They only way you could have seen something change into a bird is if it were a Thunderbird—which I'm told is a trick the Unktehila can't pull off."

"I know what I saw."

"Then you're telling me a Thunderbird committed the murder—and I happen to know the two Thunderbirds involved in this case were in another dimension at the time, which gives them supporting alibis for each other."

<Uh, he doesn't really understand what you just said. But he's insisting you're going to want to hear what he knows.>

"Forget it. I'm talking more to myself at this point than him. Tell him he's lucky he got the two chickens, and that I won't fall for this again." I turned on my heel and strode off.

I was mostly angry with myself, but that wasn't all. Teresa Firstcharger and Ben were supposedly in Thunderspace when the murder occurred . . . but time flowed differently in that place, hours passing there while minutes ticked by here. If either of them had slipped away to return here, even for a short while, the one left in Thunderspace would have noticed. Ben hadn't mentioned anything like that.

I couldn't believe that Ben was the killer. But was it possible he was covering up for his mentor? It looked like I was going to have to have a serious conversation with my boyfriend sooner rather than later . . .

Chapter Seventeen

I walked back to the mansion in a foul mood. Conned by a pint-size glutton, forced to talk to my significant other when I really needed time to cool off, frustrated by my inability to get anywhere in not one but two murders . . . nope, I was not in a happy frame of mind.

Fortunately, I had friends.

I had no sooner walked into my office when Tango said, *<Foxtrot. Make a lap.>* Her tone indicated she didn't want to be argued with, so I planted myself grumpily on the couch.

Tango immediately sprang up, made straight for my thighs, and got comfortable. *<Skritches, please.>*

So I gave her skritches, she relaxed and purred, and Whiskey curled up at my feet. After a couple of minutes, I felt a little better.

"Thanks," I said. "You guys are great." I reached down and rubbed Whiskey just between his right front limb and his belly, a secret spot that he'd confided to me all dogs share. Yes, if you really want to make friends with a canine, forget about rubbing them on the belly or scratching them behind the ears or even above the tail; instead, go straight for the armpit. I'm just glad that dogs don't sweat.

<One of us is. The other is merely passable.>

"Passable? That verged on a compliment, kitty. Are you feeling all right?"

<How I'm feeling is not the question, Toots. How are you feeling?>

"Stressed. Too many things, going in too many directions."

[Bah. You've handled far worse.]

I wasn't so sure about that. Everybody, no matter how good they are, will reach a point of overload. Had I finally hit mine?

I thought about it. Put up a mental list of all the things I had to take care of and all the things currently close to spiraling out of control. Strangely enough, making such a list didn't make me feel overwhelmed; instead, it put things in perspective. There were a lot of things on that list, but the list wasn't endless—and it was divided into subheadings. Under subheading one were things I could do something about, under subheading two were things I couldn't, and under subheading three was only a single item.

Subheading three listed things I could do something about but didn't want to—namely, talking to Ben.

Well, there was no sense in putting it off. I needed to know if Teresa's alibi was solid, and by extension, if Ben's was, too. Not that I really believed my boyfriend was a killer—but the first victim had been an ancient enemy of his kind, and we were on the brink of a war. Under those kinds of conditions, people could do strange things.

It had gotten late. All the guests had gone to bed. Ben had his own quarters, but I didn't have to go there to find him; he was in the main kitchen, scrubbing down the meat slicer, dressed in cook's whites splattered with food stains.

"Uh, hello," I said. "Can we talk?"

He gave me a guarded look and said, "Sure. You mind if I work while we do?"

"No, no, go ahead."

He kept at it, rubbing down the metal with a blue-and-white cloth.

"So," I said. "Wild day, huh?"

"Yeah."

"Look, I just wanted to say that I'm sorry if I came across as a little . . . arrogant, the last time we talked."

"Arrogant?" He kept rubbing as he talked. "No, arrogant is when your mouth writes a check your ass can't cash. You don't do that. You always have more than enough in your account."

"Not always. My mouth is pretty loose with the checkbook."

He shook his head and started wiping down the blade with short, even strokes. "You shouldn't be apologizing, Trot. You're just doing what you do—which is everything, by the way. And now this whole mess from my life comes along, and you're stuck in the middle. It's not fair. I'm sorry I got a little short with you."

"It's okay—"

He stopped what he was doing, tossed down the rag, and picked up another one that he used to clean his hands. "No. It's not. Whatever happens, I want you to know one thing. I'm on your side. Whichever side that happens to be, whatever goes down. I need you to know that."

He stepped forward, took my hands in his. "You and I lead crazy lives. Crazy things happen. But no matter what happens, you're always there. You always come through.

I need to tell you that I recognize that, that I see it. And I want you to know how much it means to me."

He met my eyes and held them. "Ever since I found out I was a Thunderbird—hell, even before that—my life has been . . . turbulent. Lots of ups and downs. But not since I met you. Not since we've been together. You know how there's an eye in the center of a hurricane, a place where it's calm? Well, that's you in my life. You're the eye of my storm."

I blinked. I didn't know what to say.

"I trust you, Foxtrot. I trust you with my life—and with the lives of others. So, whatever you need to do, whatever you decide, I'll back your play. All the way."

I still didn't know what to say, so I kissed him.

A lot.

Sometime later . . .

I snuggled into his shoulder and caught my breath. "Whew. Have I told you I'm glad your quarters are so nearby? Although they do seem a bit chilly."

He pulled the blankets over us. "Here. I tend to keep things a little cooler than most people like. One of the side-effects of being a Thunderbird, I guess. Among others."

"Oh?" I propped myself up on one elbow. "Like what?"

"Like . . . well, this is weird, but I think I'm starting to see electricity."

"And what does electricity look like?" I traced a finger over his chest.

"That's hard to describe. I don't see it visually, exactly—more like sense patterns of it. Like when you put your hand in running water and feel it moving past you? Like that, but at a distance."

"Currents. You can feel currents."

He grinned. "I guess. Anyway, I can tune it out most of the time—which is good, because it's pretty much around everywhere, in some form—but sometimes a stray bit will catch my attention and nag at me. Very distracting."

"Oh, we wouldn't want you distracted."

"That's *very* distracting . . . anyway, the other night I went into town to catch that movie you had no interest in?"

"The one with the cars and the guns and the things getting blown up?"

"That's the one. And I realized, sitting alone in the dark, that I can sense people's cell phones. I have to concentrate, because they're not putting out a lot of power, but I know they're there. And they're all turned off—or at least down—except for this one guy's. He's sitting about three seats away from me, and he's just texting away during the movie."

"How rude."

"I know, right? So I ask, real polite, if he would mind not doing that during the movie. And he says, 'Yeah, actually I do mind,' and totally ignores me."

"Uh-oh. Please tell me our body count didn't just go up to three."

He gave me a look of mock chagrin. "A sweetheart like me? I never laid a finger on the guy. In fact, I didn't even talk to him again."

"I'm sensing something, too—that there's more to the story."

"Well, I already knew I can throw around thunderbolts. But I wondered if I could do something on a much smaller scale. Microvoltage. So I just sort of reached out with my abilities and gave his phone a tiny, little nudge."

"Tiny."

"Yep."

"Hardly did anything at all."

"Well . . ."

"Uh-huh. So how bad was it?"

"I want to state right now that the battery did *not* explode."

"Of course not. And there was no fire."

"There wasn't! Just a few sparks . . . hardly worth mentioning, really."

"So you fried his phone?"

"'Fraid so. Completely and utterly. Turned it into an expensive glass brick."

"Good," I said. "I hate guys like that."

I snuggled back into his shoulder. "Listen. We still need to have a serious discussion."

"Go ahead. I'm about as relaxed as I'm going to get."

I told him what Owduttf had told me. "Now, I know that hairy little murder machine can't be trusted, but just in case there's a shred of truth in what he's saying—is there any possibility Teresa could have slipped away from you while you were in Thunderspace on the afternoon of the murder?"

Ben shook his head. "No way. We went straight to the meeting, she was there the whole time, and we left Thunderspace together. Whatever Owduttf saw—if he saw anything—it wasn't us."

"That's what I thought. Thank you."

I got out of his bed and started getting dressed. This was met with groans of disapproval and statements of general dismay, which I put down with a firm look. "I really need to go home, Ben. I'm still wearing my evening dress from dinner, for God's sake."

"Looks good to me."

"Good, yes. Professional, not so much."

He threw up his hands in defeat. "Okay. But you should

start thinking about maybe keeping a change of clothes here. I mean, you do it for the dinners."

"Hmm. Good point. You are at worth at least as much as one of ZZ's soirees. Make room in your closet, please."

It was his turn to blink at me. "Just like that?"

"Yep. You silver-tongued devil, you."

And with that, I collected my patiently waiting—and oddly quiet—dog and went home.

Usually Whiskey is pretty self-sufficient when it comes to walks, but we have a regular route we follow in my neighborhood for the sake of appearances and because Whiskey likes to catch up on the local gossip. We took a leisurely stroll around the block when we got home and were about halfway when Whiskey said, [I don't think I'll ever understand human love.]

"You and me both," I said.

[You and Ben are mismatched in many ways. He tends to be more emotional and impulsive, whereas you are eminently practical. Yet you manage to maintain a relationship.]

"It's a mystery to me, too, doggo. But there's something to be said for opposites balancing each other out. I guess that's what me and Ben are about."

Whiskey stopped to sniff a mailbox then carefully marked it with his own brand of postage. [I suppose. Please don't take offense, but I'm glad that canine pairings don't work that way. I don't think I could stand being in a long-term relationship with someone so utterly different from me.]

I did my best to keep a straight face—but I must have released the mental equivalent of a chuckle.

[What?]

"Nothing."

[Clearly, you have something to say.]

I grinned and shook my head. "Don't make me say it. It's sooooo obvious."

[I don't—are you talking about Tango and me?] He stopped and looked over his shoulder at me accusingly.

"Come on. You two are definitely opposites, you definitely care for each other, and you're in a long-term relationship—"

[A *professional* relationship!]

"Of course, of course. That's exactly what I meant."

[It's not the same at all!]

"Nope. Not the same. At all."

And then the walk was over, and it was time for bed.

I arrived for work the next day determined to make some progress. I checked on breakfast, made sure everything was running smoothly, then went up to my office with Whiskey to greet Tango and start the day. I decided I needed a recap of events to clarify exactly what had happened and where I was in my investigation.

So. This had all started when Lockley Hades called to warn me about an impending war between his race—the Unktehila—and the Thunderbirds. He claimed to have a list of Unktehila agents that were poised to strike at Thunderbirds everywhere. He also outed Maxine Danger as an Unktehila and said she was on the side of the bad guys.

Maxine admitted what she was but claimed she was the good guy and Hades was the bad. Teresa Firstcharger was ready to go ballistic on both of them, with the Thunderbird Nation behind her.

Then, in the middle of an escape performance, Maxine had vanished, and Hades had turned up, naked and dead. Summer had been killed the next day—and I still didn't know which side either of the Unktehila were on.

I sat and thought, turning the various puzzle pieces

over in my head. And what I came up with was this: "Why kill Summer?"

[Good question,] said Whiskey. [Presumably, the killer was covering their tracks.]

<If it was the same killer,> Tango pointed out.

[There's no need to complicate things with a second killer.]

"No, she has a point," I said. "Things have a tendency to get complicated around here. But for now, let's assume it's the same killer covering their tracks. What did Summer know that was worth killing her for?"

[The identity of the killer is the most obvious answer.]

<That makes no sense. If she knew the killer's identity, why wouldn't she tell the police?>

"Because the killer may well have been Maxine. Summer knew how the trick was performed, so presumably she knew how Maxine could not only escape but murder Hades and leave his body behind as well. That's the sort of information that could get you killed. But . . ."

<But what?>

"But what was Lockley Hades doing here in the first place? And calling me beforehand to warn me—it smacks of a setup. Plus, I just don't see Maxine committing murder and then sticking around to kill her assistant because she knows too much. Summer was more than just Maxine's employee—they were partners. Maxine trusted Summer with all her secrets; why would that trust suddenly end?"

<Maybe because she found out her boss was a shape-shifting snake?>

"That's a possibility," I admitted. "Or maybe somebody else did. Blackmail is always a good motive for murder."

[Who would be in a position to find such a thing out?]

"How about someone who dealt closely with Maxine

Danger? Somebody with an acknowledged fascination with murder?"

[Hironobu Masuda?]

"Hironobu Masuda."

I found Hironobu Masuda in a sunny nook just off the library, sipping tea and eating toast with marmalade. I asked him if I could join him, and when he nodded his assent, I pulled up a hair and joined him at his small table. He wore a long-sleeved black shirt and a dark-gray tie.

"Good morning," I said. "I hope you slept well."

"As well as could be expected under the circumstances, thank you."

"Yes, it's terrible what happened to Summer. Did you know her well?"

He hesitated before he answered. "Not terribly well, no. Our relationship was a professional one."

"So it was Summer you dealt with concerning the lock? Or did Maxine handle that part personally?"

"I—I dealt with both of them. They seemed quite inseparable, to me."

That seemed an odd way to put it, but I didn't comment on that. "And were you privy to the secrets of the trick itself?"

At this, Masuda seemed quite shocked. "No! I would never betray the confidence of the audience like that. My participation was exactly as it seemed—I provided a lock that could only be opened with a magnetic key. I had the only copy of that key."

"Had?"

"Yes. I had to give it to the police as part of their investigation. They were quite . . . *thorough* in their questioning."

He seemed a little upset at that, though he tried to hide it.

"Well, it is a homicide investigation," I said. "Personally, while I have no idea how Maxine escaped the vault, I'm more interested in how Lockley Hades's body got in there."

"You'd think the police would have the same interest. But they seem to be focusing on the second murder even more intently than the first."

"They're probably just more at ease with the circumstances surrounding it. A corpse found in a refrigerated trailer is a lot easier to explain than one that appeared out of thin air."

"I suppose . . ."

I hesitated then asked, "Just out of curiosity, Mr. Masuda—where were you Tuesday afternoon?"

He stiffened before he forced a smile onto his face. "I took a short trip into town. ZZ's chauffeur drove me."

"I see," I said. "Well, I'm sure the police will figure all this out before long."

I got to my feet, thanked him, and left him to finish his breakfast. Whiskey, as usual, waited until we were out of sight before offering his insights. [Mr. Masuda was definitely nervous.]

"I didn't need canine instincts to pick up on *that*," I murmured. "But what, exactly, is he nervous about?"

I headed for the front door. "C'mon, pooch. Let's go have another chat."

[With who?]

"ZZ's driver. Not that I think Masuda's necessarily lying, but there's something he's not telling us . . ."

ZZ's chauffer was a man named Victor Hausen, a tall, fit German with short-cropped, iron-gray hair. He was out in the garage working on one of ZZ's sports cars—she has two or three but almost never drives. Victor's legs, dressed in white overalls, stuck out of the bottom of the car like an ice-cream truck victim of a hit-and-run. The car itself was lemon yellow, as smooth and curvy as an Italian super-model and shinier than new money. I considered rapping on the fender to get his attention, but that seemed impolite—like throwing pebbles at a stained glass window. I coughed loudly instead and said, "Victor? Got a minute?"

"Just a moment, please." I heard mechanical ratcheting sounds, a thump, and then a soft swear word in German. More ratcheting, and then he slid out from under the car on the little wheeled dolly he was lying on. He got to his feet with the mechanical precision of his own tools, then immediately grabbed a rag from a nearby bench and began wiping his hands. His white overalls were cleaner than my dress shirt.

"Victor. I was wondering if you can confirm something for me."

"I shall if I am able, Ms. Foxtrot." Victor was the only one who called me Ms. Foxtrot. "How can I help?"

"I was wondering if you gave one of our guests, Mr. Masuda, a ride into town Tuesday afternoon."

Knowing Victor, the answer should have been a curt *yes* or *no*—he was as direct as he was efficient, and he was very efficient. But instead, there was the barest pause—and then he said, "At what time, exactly?"

"I'm not sure. Sometime between lunch and dinner."

He nodded, as if that cleared up any inconsistencies. "Then, yes. One o'clock, approximately. We were back by five."

I'd seen Summer alive after one, and the frozen state of the body when it was discovered meant she must have been killed not long afterward. Therefore, Mr. Masuda was in the clear. Except . .

"Even with travel time, that's quite a while to spend there," I said. "What did he do? Where did he go?"

Victor's sharp features seemed to get a little sharper. "I

do not know the specifics. Antique shopping, perhaps. I believe he said something about that while we were driving there."

"So you just dropped him off and picked him up again?"

". . . Yes."

I nodded. I had never realized what a terrible liar Victor was before, but then, he'd never lied to me before. Or if he had, his skills had depreciated a great deal since then. I suppose someone that prides themself on their eye to detail must find it difficult to deliberately blur those details or make up entirely new ones.

"Victor, how long have you worked for ZZ?"

"Seventeen years, Ms. Foxtrot."

"She values you highly. You know that, right?"

"I believe I do."

"I would never say anything to her to undermine that relationship, Victor. It's important to ZZ to have trust between herself and the people that work for her. But sometimes, the facts aren't black and white. They're open to interpretation. And usually, when that happens, I'm the one that does the interpreting. I'm the buffer between what ZZ wants to know and what she needs to know. Are you following me?"

"I'm not sure." Was that a flicker of panic I saw in those pale, Teutonic eyes?

"It's simple, Victor. If there were some small discrepancy between what you just told me and the truth, I wouldn't necessarily tell ZZ. But that would depend on what the discrepancy was—and whether you admitted to it or I had to find out later from another source. Is that a little clearer?"

A look of resignation crossed his face. "Yes, Ms. Foxtrot. I understand."

"I don't care what Mr. Masuda was actually doing in town. I just need to know that he was actually there. I need to know it for certain, Victor."

"He was there, Ms. Foxtrot. But not for the length of time you mentioned. I can, however, vouch for his whereabouts from one o'clock onward. He was with me."

"With you?"

"In my quarters." He indicated his apartment over the garage with a quick jerk of his head. He looked slightly uncomfortable, which on Victor's face was practically a nervous breakdown.

I knew Victor was gay, though he was so circumspect about it that most people might have guessed him as asexual. He wasn't ashamed of his sexuality, as far as I knew; he was simply very private about it. ZZ knew and of course had no problems with it—but that wasn't what Victor was worried about.

"Okay," I said. "Victor, you're not in any trouble. I don't care if the guests and the employees get up close and personal, and neither does ZZ. All I needed to know was Masuda's whereabouts during that time, and you've given me that. Thank you."

He nodded, and a little of the uncertainty left his features. "I apologize for misleading you. I did not wish to cause Mr. Masuda any problems, either."

"Well, you've done just the opposite—you've cleared him of murder. One of them, anyway."

I thanked Victor again, and let him get back to work. He was back underneath the car by the time Whiskey and I left the garage.

"Now we know why Masuda was acting nervous," I said as we returned to the house. "I guess he's still in the closet. Or maybe it's a class thing—doesn't want people to know he's sleeping with the help."

[What an odd thing human sexuality is. Dogs don't make such a fuss over who does what with whom.]

"We're weird creatures, all right. No argument there . . ."

Chapter Eighteen

I had no sooner grabbed myself a mug of tea and returned to my office than I heard a knock on my door. It was Shondra with some news about Esko Karvenin. Apparently he'd been reported missing; nobody had seen him since he'd left ZZ's.

"And you know this how?" I asked, blowing on my tea to cool it.

Shondra sat down on the couch to give Tango some attention. "I've got a little spy in the sheriff's department," she told me, using two fingers to rub the spots just forward of Tango's ears. Tango closed her eyes and purred. "He's generous with that sort of thing."

"Thanks for letting me know," I said. "Now we've got two missing people—Maxine and Karvenin."

Shondra shook her head. "With no connection between them, other than the fact that they were both here. They didn't know each other, did they?"

"Pretty sure they met here for the first time."

Shondra got to her feet. "Well, 'pretty sure' often leads to 'not sure at all.' You might want to follow up on that."

"I guess I should."

After she left, I started snooping around the Internet to see what I could discover about Esko Karvenin that I didn't already know. There was quite a bit there: his name was littered through all sorts of news about 3D printing, going back to when it first started becoming popular. He had his own company, Tri-Dee Enterprises, which was both a retail outlet for 3D printing supplies and a private service offering to build things for customers. Yelp reviews were largely positive.

I kept coming back to the fact that a 3D printer had been an integral part of the trick. No way that could be a coincidence—the devices were becoming more and more common, but they were still relatively rare. That meant Karvenin was involved, though I wasn't sure how. Covert technical support in case the device needed fine-tuning? I was pondering this when my phone chirped at me.

"Hello, Foxtrot? This is Amos Clay. I was wondering if we could talk."

"Certainly. I'm free right now, if you have a moment."

"That would be fine. I'd like to do it in person, if you don't mind."

"Not at all. I can come to you. Whereabouts?"

"I thought we could take a stroll through the animal internment grounds, if you wouldn't mind."

A somewhat unusual request, but not really; many of the guests found walking around the graveyard to be calming. "Sure. Do you want to meet at the gate?"

"I'm inside already. Do you know the bench close to the statue of the bear?"

"I do. Shall we say a few minutes from now?"

He agreed and said goodbye.

<Very interesting,> said Tango. *<I knew there was something unfishy about that guy.>*

[You have that backward. You mean *fishy*.]

<I know exactly what I mean, and that's not it. Fishy

*is clearly a positive description, while unfishy is not. And
this guy is* unfishy.>

"Whiskey, you're with me," I said. "Tango, if you're so
inclined, you can come, too—maybe your feline instincts
can pick up on something Whiskey can't. Maybe hang
back a bit and keep an eye on things."

<*You mean you want me to stalk him?*>

"Sure. Why not?"

I headed out to my rendezvous, grabbing a light jacket
along the way; it looked a little brisk today.

The Great Crossroads looked the same as it usually
did to me, with multicolored, glowing animal phantasms
crawling, hopping, loping, and soaring among the graves;
Whiskey and I made our way through them to the bench
Amos Clay had mentioned, which was not far from the
statue of Piotr the circus bear. Piotr himself—a near-
constant, juggling fixture on his unicycle—was currently
not present.

Clay, of course, was unaware of any of this. He thought
he was just sitting on a bench in a neatly mown graveyard
with only a slight breeze moving through it.

I walked up and joined him on the bench. Despite the
slightly cooler weather, he wore only a T-shirt and jeans.
His skin was ruddy and weather-beaten, the outer hide of
an outdoorsman. He smiled and nodded at me. "Thanks
for meeting me. I'm more at ease outside than in. Result
of a life spent in the field, I guess."

"The graveyard is one of my favorite spots to spend
time in," I said truthfully. "It has a certain . . . essence to
it that's very appealing." In fact, I found it one of the most
life-affirming places I knew of—but it would be difficult
to explain that to anyone without giving up the place's
secrets.

Clay leaned forward, clasping his hands and resting
his elbows on his knees. "Here's the thing, Foxtrot: one

of the principals in this mess was not exactly a stranger to me. I haven't said anything until now because I didn't think it was relevant. And then Summer was killed . . ."

"Wait. You knew Summer Coyne?"

"No. I hadn't met any of the guests before I arrived. But I did know the other victim—Lockley Hades. Sort of."

"Sort of?"

He frowned and shook his head, as if trying to clear it. "I know his father, who's a naturalist. I met Lockley back when he was still called Herb, and no more than nine or ten. Before his mother died."

Right. In a torrential downpour that might have been caused by supernatural forces. I wondered exactly how much of that Clay knew about.

"Herb and his father haven't spoken in years. Herb blamed his father for his mother's death, for dragging her out into the jungle with him. I knew there was more to it than that—his mother loved traveling, loved seeing the world in its raw state—but that's a hard thing to communicate to a ten-year-old boy or a teenager who's still grieving. Herb's father has mostly watched his son's success from the bleachers, seeing him gain fame and fortune through his own hard work. He's very proud of him."

"I see. But his son didn't know this?"

Clay shook his head, his eyes fixed on some indeterminate point in the sky. I wondered what he'd say if he knew he was looking at the spirit of a large bird soaring directly through his line of vision; some kind of eagle, it looked like, though not a bald one. "Herbert was the one that cut off communication when he was old enough to be on his own. His father's tried over the years to reach out, but nothing's ever come of it. He sent me to make one last effort—I suspect he's got some sort of serious health problem. And isn't that always the way? We get close to the end of the game, and we get desperate. One final roll of the dice, one more chance to fix things. But those things rarely work out, do they?"

I looked up at the eagle, a gleaming, golden brown even at this distance, and said, "Oh, I don't know. I think we get more final chances than we know."

"That's a lovely sentiment, but I don't think it applies here. His father pulled some strings to get me an invitation, but then I found out Lockley Hades wasn't even going to be here—Maxine Danger was. Still, his father was sure Herb would put in an appearance—how he knew that, he wouldn't say. But I'm pretty sure he wasn't expecting his son to turn up as a murder victim."

"And forgive me for asking, but—why are you telling me this instead of the police?"

His clasped hands slipped down to hold one knee. "Two reasons. First of all, I don't want Herb's father dragged into this—this is going to be hard enough on him as it is. Secondly, I recognize competence when I see it, and I see it in you. Assistants are the unsung heroes of the world, from commerce to academia, and I've met both secretaries and undergrads who could run rings around their bosses or professors, all while keeping out of the way of the work— whatever work that is. You're one of those. If anyone can figure out why Hades Lockley was here—and who killed him—it's you. And you can do it quietly, in the background, because that's what you excel at."

"Thank you. I do my best."

"And your best is extremely good. So—do you have any ideas who killed my colleague's son?"

The eagle circling overhead was getting closer. "Right now, the evidence points to Maxine Danger," I said. "But evidence can be misleading. The rivalry between the two was fake, so Maxine didn't have a motive. And why would she kill Hades in such a publicly incriminating way?"

"Hmm. Well, I don't know how useful this will be—it

doesn't make any sense at all, to me—but my contact at the Fish and Wildlife lab got the results you wanted from the autopsy. There was a trace of foreign animal matter in the chest wound of Mr. Hades. Believe it or not, it belonged to *Aetomylaeus bovinus*, better known as a bull ray. Usually found off the coast of Europe or Africa. They can mass up to two hundred and fifty pounds and have a wicked barbed tail. In fact, that's what they found in the body—a fragment of the tail. Meaning Mr. Hades was stabbed to death with a very odd, handmade weapon and not the dagger found beside the body."

More like Unktehila-made. Even though I couldn't admit it to Clay, it was another spike in the coffin lid of Maxine Danger's guilt. Two Unktehila, traces from two exotic animals, and one body; it added up to a brief but violent clash in the dark, one that ended with a barbed tail driven through Lockley Hades's chest.

"That's very strange," I said. "But then, this whole affair is strange. I wonder who would have access to such an unusual weapon."

"Me," Clay said.

"Excuse me?"

He laughed at the look on my face. "Don't worry, I didn't lure you out to the graveyard to admit my guilt and then kill you. I'm just saying that I have access to all sorts of strange animal bits. Hell, I could have committed the murder with a narwhal horn or a walrus tusk. But if I had, I certainly wouldn't be sharing that information with you, would I?"

There was a flash of golden brown beside me, and suddenly we were sharing the bench with a large, ghostly eagle, who perched on the back of it with powerful-looking but immaterial claws. Yes, I know that sentence makes no sense, but that's the world I live in.

I must have jumped a little, because Amos Clay gave me an odd look. "Are you all right?"

"Sorry, just a twinge from a sore back," I said. "Think I overdid something yesterday. Anyway, thank you for the information. Even though I have no idea what it means, any data is useful."

"Spoken like a true scientist," he said. "Hopefully, that meaning will reveal itself sooner or later."

The eagle cocked his head at me, fixing me with a penetrating avian glare. He was perched closer to Clay than me.

"You must run across hundreds of different species in your work," I said. "Both living and dead."

Clay leaned back on the bench, draping one arm over the back of it. It now almost looked as if the eagle were perching on it. "I do. More dead ones than alive, I'm afraid. Smugglers—even those trying to smuggle live specimens—have a high attrition rate among their stock. But sometimes we get lucky and can rewild what we apprehend."

"You ever rewild any . . . large birds?"

"A few. There was a golden eagle we managed to intercept this one time, being smuggled inside a golf bag. She was pretty banged up, and a wild bird refuge had to hold on to her for a while until she healed. I got kind of attached to her, actually—went to visit her whenever I could. Almost fooled myself into thinking she was grateful for what we did for her." He laughed. "Just projection of emotion, I know. But when you deal with so many abused animals, sometimes you need to feel that you're making a difference. Just human nature, I suppose."

I stared into the fiercely protective gaze of the eagle and smiled. "No," I said. "Just nature."

Tango rejoined Whiskey and I as we returned to the house. *That man is being haunted by a bird.*

"Not exactly haunted," I said. "More like shadowed. I mean, I didn't get the feeling that the eagle meant him any harm."

<Really? What gave you that impression? Was it the giant, hooked beak, or the immense, ripping talons?>

[Oh, please. You can't judge a creature simply because it's evolved the proper equipment to bring down prey. *You* have teeth and claws, too.]

<Not like that! That thing is a flying murder machine!>

"I had no idea you harbored such ill will toward birds of prey, kitty. If anything, I thought you'd appreciate their skills as hunters."

<Skills? What skills? Skills are things like stalking and pouncing. What that engine of destruction does is like dropping a brick from the sky. How is that fair?>

[Hmmph. Since when do cats prize the idea of what's fair? You think fair means you getting fed every twenty minutes while having your chin rubbed.]

<That's ridiculous. Once every hour is perfectly fine.>

[And the chin rubs?]

<Skritches—back or ear—are an acceptable substitute.>

[You're just upset because a bird that can eat a cat is the exact opposite of what you're used to.]

<Of course that upsets me! It's backward!>

Back at the house, I was intercepted before I could head upstairs by a despondent Oscar. "Foxtrot, a moment of your time?" He was standing in the foyer by a balding man in a suit and tie, who had a clipboard in his hand and a sour expression on his face.

"This is Mr. Benning," said Oscar. "Ms. Lancaster is in charge of day-to-day operations here at the house. I'm sure she can clear up any misunderstanding."

"Hello," I said. "How can I help you?"

The balding man scowled at me. "You can tell this guy

how much trouble he's in and exactly how long he can expect to spend behind bars."

I gave him Smile #23, the one that was really a sigh of exasperation in disguise. "Before we lock him up and throw away the key, how about telling me what he's done?"

"He's in the process of breaking about a dozen FDA regulations," Benning said. "Including a few that haven't been invented yet. And on top of it all, he tried to bribe me!"

"What?" I said, trying to look shocked. "I'm sure there must be some mistake. Oscar, what's going on?"

Oscar gave me a strained smile. "It turns out there are certain hoops one must be willing to jump through in order to obtain the proper licensing for my planned venture. I was attempting to comply with said necessities when I—ah—might have misspoken."

Benning's scowl deepened. "First of all, these 'hoops' you're talking about are laws. Second, embedding human genetic material in *anything* breaks any number of these laws. Third, trying to bribe a federal employee is—"

"It wasn't a bribe," interjected Oscar. "I was just offering Mr. Benning a chance to sample the product before the general public did."

"You offered me a chance to sample human flesh!"

"No, no, we're not at that stage yet. This was merely the chocolate base the DNA was to be infused with—"

"Oh, no," I said. "Oscar, you said you weren't serious about the Babe Ruth candy bar."

"It was only an idea—"

"You can forget about the FDA signing off on anything to do with your—your *idea!*" said Benning. He was fuming so hard, I could almost see steam rising from his ears. "And if I ever hear about you trying to peddle your cannibal candy to the public, I'll be back with an arrest warrant so fast, it'll make you dizzy!"

"Understood," Oscar said, looking pale. "My deepest apologies for the misunderstanding—"

"Look, Mr. Benning," I said. "Nothing happens under this roof that I don't know about. And I can promise you that no such 3D printing of foodstuff for commercial use is ever, ever going to go forward here."

Benning took a deep breath and got himself under control. "I'm a baseball fan, you understand? I deal with all sorts of nastiness working for the FDA, but— manufactured cannibalism of one of the great icons of the sport? That's a new one on me."

It took a few more minutes of listening to Benning and assuring him there wouldn't be a problem before he finally agreed to let Oscar off with a warning. "And don't use the one you've got set up already, even for yourself," Benning added. "That room it's in doesn't meet FDA standards for food safety—it looks more like a machine shop than a kitchen."

He finally stalked off, clipboard under his arm, muttering darkly under this breath about the current state of civilization in general. When he was gone, Oscar thanked me profusely and promised his 3D project was at an end. "Such a shame," he sighed. "The pizzeria idea seemed terribly promising."

"Oscar, you were about five minutes away from offering that guy cash," I said. "I know your methods, remember? You're lucky I was able to calm him down."

"Yes, well, I've certainly learned my lesson—"

I frowned and held up a finger. "Wait a minute. That remark he made about a machine shop—are the other printers still in the billiards room?"

"Yes. Where else would they be?"

"On a large truck, taking them back to Tri-Dee Printing." I walked down to the billiard room and peeked inside.

All the machinery was still there. "Excuse me—I have to make a phone call . . ."

One phone call later, I'd learned that Esko Karvenin had never arranged to have the machines returned—only delivered. I tapped my phone against my chin, thinking.

"Esko Karvenin," I said, leaning back in my office chair and staring at my two furred companions. "An unusual man. Interesting personal style. Clearly thought of himself as a visionary. On the cutting edge of a new technology. Does he seem like the kind to just abandon a bunch of expensive machinery?"

[Perhaps. Visionary types sometimes ignore mundane details.]

"Not when they're the basis of their business," I said. "And now that I think about it, his departure seemed very abrupt. He claimed it was over ethical concerns, but he must have been aware of those long before he committed himself to coming here. No, something's off here."

<Humans are always doing weird things for weird reasons, though.>

[On this subject, we are in complete agreement.]

I made a few more phone calls and discovered that Esko Karvinen was still missing. Now it seemed as if he hadn't just disappeared—it was like he'd planned on disappearing all along . . .

And suddenly it made sense.

"Oh my God," I said. "Esko Karvenin was never here. But Lockley Hades was."

<What are you talking about?>

"That's how Hades got onto the grounds—he shapeshifted into someone that had an invitation."

[But he left before the murder.]

"No, he didn't. He changed his appearance again. Unktehila can take on three additional forms, remember?

One to get onto the grounds—Karvenin—one to attack Maxine—the mountain gorilla—and one to slip away afterward. But things didn't go according to plan . . ."

Tango gave a large, feline yawn. *<Do they ever?>*

Chapter Nineteen

What I needed to do was locate Maxine. I found it hard to believe she could still be on the grounds, but after scouring Shondra's security footage—we had excellent coverage of pretty much the entire perimeter—I had to admit the possibility. Nothing big enough to be a disguised Unktehila had left since the murders.

The reason she'd stuck around after the first murder seemed obvious—to kill her own assistant. And if she was still here, it seemed equally obvious that she had another target in mind: the resident Thunderbird, or perhaps his mentor.

Despite the mounting evidence that Maxine Danger was the killer, I still wasn't sure if she was for the impending war or against it. All I knew was that she was still in hiding and probably nearby.

Three forms, Grandfather Serpent had said, in addition to human and serpent. One of Maxine's had apparently been a bull ray. What were the other two? And what did she look like right now?

I remembered that Unktehila could switch to a new shape once they'd had at least twenty-four hours to study one. It had been more than that since the last murder; she could look like any of the other guests or staff by now . . . except for Ben or Teresa. Unktehila couldn't imitate Thunderbird abilities, thank God.

It was a lot to think about—but I had mundane tasks to take care of, too: staff scheduling, emails, a meeting with the zoo's resident vet about her budget, and dozens of other minor details. Just because two people were dead didn't meant the rest of the world was about to slow down so I could catch my breath.

The day went by in a whirl. Croquet was played on the back lawn. High tea was served. Phone calls were made and returned. ZZ asked me to look into one of those vertical wind tunnel things people go into to simulate skydiving, indicating she was shifting gears to another hobby. I ordered things online.

But in the midst of all this routine, the strangest thing kept bobbing to the surface of my mind—and it had very little to do with the case.

I took Whiskey for a walk just before dinner, through the graveyard. The Great Crossroads was as busy as ever— Grand Central Station for the animal afterlives, thousands of souls making their way from one portal to another. The graves with human cremains in urns led to the human afterlife—or afterlives, possibly; I didn't know the details, and Eli had made it plain he wasn't about to share any.

But maybe he would be more forthcoming about something else.

I made my way to the grave of the parrot, Carlos. The one that had the abusive owner, though it hadn't really been Carlos who'd been abused. I stood there and said, "Eli? Are you around?"

I couldn't always summon him that easily, but he seemed to know when I really needed to talk. This was apparently one of those times, because a few moments later, the white crow came swooping out of the sky behind me and landed on a headstone nearby, flapping his wings to break his momentum.

"Hello, Foxtrot," he said. "What's on your mind?"

"Something you probably can't talk about," I said. "But I figured I'd ask, anyway."

"Go ahead."

"I know the souls of animals have their own afterlives—even their own gods. These afterlives are their versions of Heaven. What I want to know is . . . are there places for animals that aren't as nice?"

"I'm not sure what you mean. Animals that aren't nice, or places that aren't?"

"Both."

Eli cocked his head to one side. "Ah. You want to know if there are places that are . . . the opposite of Heaven."

"Yes."

He hopped along the headstone, a little closer to me. "What do you think?"

"I think that you're going to deflect the question by asking me one. Like you just did."

He gave a little avian shrug. "That predictable, am I?"

"Yes. And you just did it again."

"I suppose I did. But you have to understand, that's the nature of our relationship. I'm not here to tell you what to do; I'm more of a guide that's supposed to point you in the right direction. And when it comes to answering the big metaphysical questions? That's definitely an area I have to be careful about."

"I get that. So if you can't answer me outright, how about a helpful analogy? I'll even settle for a parable."

"Hmmm. Let's see. Animals are not the same as human beings, Foxtrot. Even though they think, they are more creatures of instinct than thought. They have will, but it is less free. Therefore, they are not entirely respon-

sible for any actions they commit. Would it be fair to pun-
ish an alligator for being an alligator, even if its actions
might seem monstrous to a human point of view?"

"Of course not."

"An animal's afterlife is not a reward for making good
choices, Foxtrot. It is simply a reward. Does that answer
your question?"

"I think so." I hesitated, thinking about Carlos. "And
if a pet loved a human who didn't earn that kind of
reward?"

Eli looked at me and blinked. "Then their afterlife
would be a lonelier one. No system is perfect."

"Yeah," I said. "That's kind of what I thought."

I stared at Carlos's grave. Poor parrot, I thought. He
didn't ask for a crappy owner, but that's what he got. I
hoped he was enjoying his parrot afterlife and that he
made lots of parrot friends.

I thanked Eli, and then I made my way back to the
house. It was almost time for dinner.

"I am going to hold a séance," Keene announced.

His news was met around a variety of responses around
the table: amusement, interest, wariness, and incredulity.

"Really?" said Amos Clay, finishing off his salad. "In
this day and age?"

"Why not?" countered ZZ. "There are more things in
Heaven and Earth than are dreamt of, etcetera, etcetera.
Sounds like it might be fun."

"But not in good taste, surely," said Hironobu Masuda.
"An attempt to contact the dead, in light of recent events?"

Keene held up a single finger. "I should make clear
that I am in no way trying to talk to those unfortunate
victims of recent circumstance. No. What I would like to
do is hold a séance to try to contact my muse."

Oscar took a long sip of his drink. "Let me see if I

have this right. You believe your muse is not just absent but deceased? How very postmodern. What happened, was she struck and killed by a unicorn?"

"Technically, my muse was already dead," said Keene, undeterred by Oscar's sarcasm. "In fact, my muse happens to be more of an animal totem than anything Greek. It's the spirit of an animal colloquially known as a bush baby."

"Your muse is a dead galago?" said Clay. "Well, that's just bizarre enough to be intriguing. How did you come by such an . . . arrangement?"

"It was quite by accident," said Keene. "I was out in the graveyard, just going on a walkabout and reading head-stones, when I saw one that called to me. It was Jeepers—that was his name in life. I started humming a melody, quite spontaneously, while I stood there. That was some time ago, and Jeepers has never failed me since." He stopped and sighed. "At least, not until now."

"Galagos do have an interesting sonic relationship with the world," Clay said. "*Nagapies* are what they're called in Afrikaans, which means 'little night monkeys.' Large, bat-like ears, which are very sensitive. Different species of galago each have their own 'advertisement call'—used for identification and communication—and those have all been scientifically cataloged."

"Well, Jeepers has always been a great listener," said Keene. "And sometimes, that's all you need to produce a good song—just someone to listen to it."

"Isn't that putting the cart before the horse? Or the nagapie before the . . . whatever?" said Oscar. "How can you play something before it exists?"

"Oh, quit trying to be all sciencey on me," said Keene. "No offense, Mr. Clay. It's just that trying to describe a process that's intuitive and artistic doesn't always neatly fit into a rational framework."

"None taken, Mr. Keene. I know science has its blind spots."

"Really, Amos?" said ZZ. "I'm disappointed. Surely a scientist like yourself has strong opinions about such mystic mumbo-jumbo?"

Clay laughed and raised his glass of wine. "Sorry to let you down, ZZ. My colleagues say I'm too open-minded for my own good."

"How do you propose to do this?" asked Masuda.

"At Jeepers's grave," said Keene. "It seems a nice evening for it. I thought we could spread out a blanket, light a few candles, see what we can invoke."

"Um," I said.

"Yes, Foxtrot?" asked ZZ. "You have an opinion on this?"

I did, but it wasn't one I could really say out loud. It went something like, "Hey, this is an actual focal point for some very potent supernatural forces and none of you have any formal training in the occult and maybe you don't want to accidently summon something like, oh, I don't know, the spirit of a fifteen-foot great white shark that swims through the air and is a little unclear on the fact that it doesn't need to eat anymore?"

But I couldn't blurt that out, so I didn't. What I said was, "Let's see how the weather looks, okay? I thought I saw some rain clouds heading our way. Wouldn't want to get caught in a sudden downpour." Especially not one I could arrange.

"Nonsense," said ZZ. "The sky was perfectly clear before we sat down to dinner. I think it sounds like an entertaining outing, and I think we need one. Foxtrot, make sure Keene gets everything he needs. Shall we all meet half an hour after dinner, down by the entrance to the graveyard?"

And, just like that, I was in charge of preparing for a séance.

The first thing I did was to scoot down to the graveyard to see Eli. Luckily, he was still around, perched on the gray granite head of a horse statue. "Hello, Foxtrot. I sense you have more questions."

"You could say that." I laid out the scenario for him. "What's the protocol here? Should I allow this? I could get Ben to whip up a quick rainstorm—even Keene would surrender in the face of a good downpour."

Eli shook his head. "No, that won't be necessary. It sounds as if they don't know enough to do any real harm. It might even work."

For some reason, that dumbfounded me. It was like the head of an automotive company saying, "Sure, let the ten-year-old have a car. What's the worst that could happen?"

"But—couldn't something go horribly wrong?"

"Things can always go in unexpected directions. That doesn't mean we stop trying. Let them have their séance. They might learn something . . . or maybe *unlearn* something."

"Okay," I said. "You're the boss."

It didn't take me long to track down what we needed—ZZ had plenty of candles in decorative holders, there were a bunch of folding chairs in storage, and I found a large, tie-dyed wall hanging that would serve as a blanket. I hoped the spirits wouldn't be too disoriented by the color scheme. I set everything up—and abruptly realized I needed a lighter for the candles. Whiskey and I headed back to the house.

And then—speaking of disoriented—I ran into Keene.

He was in an upstairs hallway just outside his room, staring at himself in a large, oval mirror. He was dressed in jeans, a faded, black T-shirt that looked older than he was, and sandals.

"Nice shirt," I said. "Is this what the modern rock star wears to a séance these days?"

"It's from the very first concert I ever went to," said Keene. His voice sounded a little hollow, and he was still staring into the mirror. I took a look myself and understood why: his pupils were so dilated, they were like little black dimes.

"Oh, terrific," I said. "What are you on now?"

"I," he intoned solemnly, "am on. A great deal. Of psychedelics. Wonderful word, don't you think? Sy. Ko. Dell. Icksssssssss . . ."

"Does every attempt to break your writer's block have to involve messing with your brain chemistry?"

"It's all brain chemistry, Fox. From yoga to delta-wave inducement machines. We're just a bunch of neurons plugged together walking around on nervous systems wired to stilts. I just need to find the proper tools to do a bit of rewiring, that's all."

"As long as I don't have to rescue you from another tree."

He laughed, a high, dreamy laugh that sounded a little spooky. "Not to worry, my dear Foxtrot. I am in the perfect condition to undertake a psychic journey to the land of the dead—dead animals, I mean. I just hope I can contact the right one; graveyard like that, must be jam-packed with spirits. I could wind up with the ghost of somebody's pet turtle or something."

He didn't know how right he was—and I wasn't about to tell him. "I've set out a blanket, some chairs, and some candles. Is there anything else you need?"

"Oh, yes, I nearly forgot. Hang on just a second." He ducked back into his room and came out holding a skull— one intricately filigreed with a variety of occult sigils.

"Picked this up in Mexico city," he said. "Not the real thing, of course, but it is carved from ivory. Should be a good focal point for getting in touch with old Jeepers."

I eyed the thing dubiously. "If you say so."

We left the house together and walked to the grave-yard. It was dusk, the far side of the horizon already deepening from blue to black, the first stars barely visible. ZZ, Oscar, Hironobu Masuda, and Amos Clay were already there, sitting in the chairs I'd set up. Whiskey joined them, sprawling at ZZ's feet where he knew he'd get some skritches.

Also present were the usual denizens of the Great Cross-roads: lots of cats and dogs, of course, but also lots of birds, fish, and everything in between, their fur or feathers or scales gleaming with brilliant, otherworldly color. A few looked at our little group curiously, but mostly they were busy travelers, on their way from somewhere to some-where else; we attracted no more attention than would a busker in a busy train station. But then, we hadn't started playing yet.

I'd placed candles on Jeepers's headstone and a few others nearby, and as I began to light them, Keene walked to the center of the blanket I'd spread over the grave it-self and dropped into a cross-legged pose with the skull cradled in his hands. "Thank you all for coming," he said. "I appreciate you—*indulging* me in my somewhat hare-brained pursuit. I'm going to ask one more thing of you: try to really focus on what we're doing. I'm not asking that you change your whole belief system or anything, just be open to the flow of energies around you."

"And what exactly are we supposed to be focusing on?" asked Amos Clay. "That hunk of ivory in your lap? Which I hope you didn't get from a proscribed source— ivory smuggling is a real problem."

"I'm told it came from a licensed antiques dealer and

is made from a walrus tusk," said Keene. "Now, are there any questions before we begin?"

Oscar took a small, silver flask out of his pocket. "Any objections to my toasting the occasion?"

"Not at all. Proceed." Keene stared at Oscar as if he were about to burst into flame and the skull he held was a fire extinguisher.

"Then here's to all the dearly departed that surround us," Oscar said, lifting the flask into the air. "May they forgive us our sins, remember our kindness, and live on in our hearts."

He took a healthy swig from the flask then resealed it. ZZ was staring at him as if he'd just pulled a rabbit out of his pocket. Oscar noticed and said, "Oh, don't look at me like that. I have a sentimental side, too, you know."

"Oh, I know," said ZZ. "It's just that usually I only get to see it when there are large quantities of cash involved."

"Please join hands," Keene said. "We are going to begin."

I sat and took ZZ's hand on my left and Hironobu's on my right.

Keene closed his eyes and intoned, "I call upon the powers of the five elements: water, earth, fire, air, and spirit. I call upon the sacred power of this place, and upon the good intentions of those gathered here."

I glanced around without moving my head. Sure enough, some of the animal spirits had stopped in their tracks and were eyeing us intently.

"Most of all, I call upon the spirit of Jeepers, the galago," continued Keene. "I call upon his guidance and assistance."

A ghost collie bounded over and sniffed at Amos Clay's knee His leg twitched, ever so slightly, like a bug had landed there and he was trying to dislodge it.

[I can't believe Eli signed off on this,] Whiskey thought at me. [We're drawing all sorts of attention.]

<I think it's funny, myself.>

I could hear Tango's voice in my head, though I couldn't see her. *Where are you, kitty?*

<Not far. Just hanging out a few graves over. Hey, should I wait until things really get rolling and then start to yowl?>

Absolutely not, I thought at her.

<Spoilsport.>

More and more ghost animals were gathering around us: a school of luminescent goldfish flickered past, a pair of glowing ferrets scampered around Masuda's feet.

"Jeepers," said Keene, "I'm calling out to you from the other side. I . . . I need your help." His voice shifted from the deep, sonorous tone he'd been using to something more conversational. "I'm having some problems, mate, I really am. I know you don't owe me anything, but I'd really appreciate some assistance."

Then the birds arrived.

Tropical ones for the most part, because those are the most popular breeds for pets: parrots, macaws, parakeets, all of them glowing with the brilliant shades of the afterlife. They lit on the graves around us, perched on the backs of chairs—a pair of lovebirds even landed on top of ZZ's head. She shivered and said, "I just felt the strangest sensation."

I kind of wished I could tell them about the unearthly beauty that surrounded them, but that was a definite nonstarter. What I didn't see was a monkey-like creature with enormous eyes and bat-like ears.

<What's with all the flying snacks?> Tango asked.

[Whatever Keene's faults, he's a singer by trade. No doubt they sense a kindred spirit.]

<So this is working, kind of. You think Jeepers will actually put in an appearance?> Tango asked.

[Doubtful. I think the relationship Keene has with him is mostly in his head.]

"I know we've had some good times together in the past," Keene continued. "Remember the tune to 'Coco Blues'? We came up with that one together, right here."

<Kind of cynical, coming from you. I mean, you've made new friends with the living since you passed on.>

[In a professional capacity, yes.]

Hey! I thought at him. *I'm a little offended by that. We're more than just work friends.*

[Of course we are. But our relationship began on a professional footing.]

<Footing, shmooting. You're a ghost, and you made friends with the living. What's wrong with that?>

[Nothing. I was just trying to say that—]

And that was when Jeepers showed up.

He didn't make a grand entrance or anything. A swirling sort of portal thing appeared in the gravestone, and he popped out—which is exactly how all the other spirits traveled, when moving between worlds. Normally, at this point he'd make his way to a different grave—one that held human cremains in an urn—another portal would open, and he'd go through that. Don't ask me how they know which human grave to use or if it even makes any difference which one they travel through.

But Jeepers didn't amble away. He just crouched there for a second then hopped up on the gravestone itself, scattering several parrots. They flapped their wings indignantly but made room. They didn't indulge in a lot of squawking, though; the Great Crossroads is mostly a quiet place.

Then Jeepers just stared at Keene. And if there's one thing a bush baby excels at, it's staring. Those huge, round eyes of theirs, like little saucers.

"Are you there, Jeepers?" Keene continued. His own eyes were closed, now. "I think I feel something . . . but that could be the chemicals talking. Oh, now I've got animated molecules chasing themselves around inside my head . . . wait. Are they chasing you? Or am I one of the molecules?"

"Technically, you're a bunch of molecules," Amos Clay said. "Then again, so is everything."

"Never mind him," ZZ said. "Keep concentrating on Jeepers."

The deceased animal in question cocked his head quizzically at Keene—then leapt onto his shoulder. I did my best not to react, though I may have squeezed ZZ's hand a little hard.

The galago peered around at the rest of us, as if trying to figure out who we were and what we wanted, then turned his attention back to Keene. He poked one long, thin finger into Keene's long hair as if searching it for bugs; if Keene felt the phantasmal intrusion, he gave no sign.

Keene opened his eyes and sighed. "I don't think this is working," he said sadly.

"Don't give up so easily," I said. "C'mon, we just got here."

"I wish I had your faith," said Keene. "But I need to face facts. Even if the little bugger shows up, he can't fix me. Whatever logjam I've got going on in my noggin, it's not going to get knocked loose by a long-dead galago. This is just an excuse to find someone else to blame, and old Jeepers deserves better than that." He got to his feet, the filigreed skull in one hand and said, "Sorry, mate. I know you did your best. And thank you, everyone, for coming along and helping out."

And with that, he walked away, deeper into the Great Crossroads and the falling night, his spectral muse on his shoulder. Jeepers looked back at me, and I swear he winked.

"Well, that was anticlimactic," said Oscar, pulling his flask out. "Back to the house for brandy, anyone?"

A cold wind gusted through, and I noticed some dark clouds on the horizon that hadn't been there a few minutes ago. "Good idea," I said. "The weather looks like it's taking a turn for the worse . . ."

Chapter Twenty

By the time I'd gathered up the blanket, chairs, and candles, the wind had turned chilly and damp. I hurried back to the house behind the guests and wondered if I should return to collect our resident moping rock star as well; in the end, I decided to leave him where he was. A little cold rain would either suit his mood perfectly, or it would inspire him to come in where it was warm and dry.

"A little cold rain" turned out to be an understatement. What we got, minutes after we got inside, was a downpour. Heavy, hard rain, falling almost straight down. I wondered if my boyfriend had anything to do with it and tracked him down in the kitchen to ask.

"Don't look at me," Ben said. He was cleaning up after dinner, stacking plates in an industrial-size dishwasher. "I mean, I'm not responsible. Not personally, anyway."

"What's that mean?" I said, leaning against a counter.

"It means that another Thunderbird is kicking up a fuss. I can sort of feel it."

"Another Thunderbird? Who?"

"Who do you think?" he said, plunking forks into a

plastic holder next to the plates. "My mentor. She's on her way here, and she's not in a good mood."

Sure enough, Teresa Firstcharger walked through the door not five minutes later, and I was there to greet her. "Good evening, Teresa. Here to see Ben?"

"Not exactly," she said grimly, taking off her long jacket and handing it to me. "I'm here to see both of you."

Tango picked this moment to saunter up to Teresa and see if she could get some skritches. It's not that my cat is bad at reading moods; she just doesn't care, not as long as skritches—or kitty treats—are involved. I could see her cheerfully cuddling up to Jack the Ripper while having her head rubbed.

"Let's go into my office, where we won't be disturbed," I suggested. "I'll go get Ben."

A few minutes later, I was behind my desk, and Ben and Teresa were seated on the couch. Ben looked nervous; Teresa looked resolute.

"Foxtrot, we've waited long enough," Teresa said. "The Council of Thunderbirds needs this to be resolved. All of us are tired of jumping at shadows and sleeping with one eye open."

"That's understandable," I said. "But what am I supposed to do?"

"Bring us Maxine Danger."

"How? I'm not sure she's even still here."

"The council feels she is. The second murder surprised them, but now they think the killer isn't finished. Maxine Danger is clearly an assassin, and that means she's going to go after her true target—a Thunderbird."

"You mean me?" Ben asked. "Or you?"

"If she comes after me, she's in for a surprise," Teresa said evenly. "Ben is the more likely target because of his lack of expertise."

"Hey!" said Ben.

"*Relative* lack of expertise," she amended. "But he's more exposed, too. This location provides plenty of opportunities to get him alone and attack."

"I won't let that happen," I said.

"That's commendable, but so far you haven't even been to locate the Unktehila, let alone prevent it from killing."

"Her," said Ben.

"Excuse me?"

"*Her*, not *it*. We may be enemies, but that doesn't mean we should dehumanize them."

"They're not human," said Teresa coldly. "And neither are we, for that matter."

"Speak for yourself," said Ben. "I may have lightning in my veins, but I'm still a human being. And Maxine might have serpent blood in hers, but I'm betting she grew up as human as I did."

"That's not your bet to make."

"He's just saying you might have more in common than you think," I said. "Something to think about."

"What I'm thinking about is the survival of my species," said Teresa. "And so should you."

"My species?" I said. "We're just the ones caught in the middle."

"Exactly," said Teresa. "Don't forget that the Unktehila view human beings as prey. Saving the human race from becoming snake food is how the last war between them and us started. How do you think things are going to go if the Unktehila win?"

"That sounds pretty paranoid to me," I said. "I mean, they're not just going to start gobbling down people on the street, are they?"

"That's just it—there's no telling what they'll do. With their abilities, they could easily insinuate themselves into positions of power. They probably already have."

"Sure, like a famous escape artist," I said. "Poised to take over Las Vegas in a ruthless coup."

"Celebrities have access to other celebrities," Teresa said, her voice stubborn. "There's no telling what kind of contacts she's cultivated—or who she could kill and replace."

I didn't want to admit it, but she had a point. Keene liked name-dropping the different famous people he'd rubbed elbows with, as did ZZ. Who's to say Maxine couldn't pose as either of them? And once you started playing six degrees of separation, it was a short slither to just about anyone in the world.

"The Thunderbird Council has come to a decision," said Teresa. "You've got twenty-four hours to produce some results, Foxtrot. After that, we're going to have to act."

"Act? What does that mean? What are you going to do?"

"Take action to drive them out into the open. Unktehila are basically cowardly creatures; make them afraid enough, and they'll show their true colors. Thunderbirds have the power to do that."

I shook my head. "So you're going to do what? Mess with the weather until they panic?"

"Something like that. If the Unktehila think we're ready to boil the seas, they'll put their plan into motion. They'll try to kill as many of us as they can."

"That's insane," I said. "What if it doesn't work? You could cause a global catastrophe!"

"We will illuminate the world," said Teresa calmly. "Electricity flows through all beings, including the Unktehila. When we summon the World Storm, we will be connected to everything living through the lightning in our veins. They won't be able to hide, then; their electrical patterns will be plain to us."

"The World Storm?" said Ben, his eyes widening. "The council's really considering that? The amount of power you're talking about is—I mean, I can barely wrap my head around it. You're talking about electrifying the entire planet!"

"The entire planet is already electrified," said Teresa. "We're merely going to up the voltage."

"That sounds extremely hazardous," I said. "How much collateral damage is there going to be?"

"I won't lie to you—damage will be severe. Lives will be lost. But to finally rid ourselves of our ancient enemy, no cost is too high."

I glared at her. "I disagree. And you know what? I think you're taking this personally. You're angry that you let Maxine get close to you, and now you feel betrayed."

Teresa crossed her arms and glared back. "Of course I feel betrayed! How would you feel if someone you considered a friend turned out to be a shape-shifting monster planning on murdering you?"

"You don't know that for sure—"

"I'm pretty damn sure. And so is the council." She got to her feet. "Twenty-four hours, Foxtrot. That's what you've got before the storm breaks."

She marched out of the room. It would have made a great dramatic exit, if not for the fact that she then had to wait for me to retrieve her jacket and give it back to her. And then, just after she put it on, the door opened, and Keene staggered in.

He was drenched and incoherent, muttering about eyes in the rain and Technicolor puddles. I nodded goodbye to Teresa, who still looked furious, left Ben with her at the door, and hustled Keene into the study, where a fire was blazing in the hearth.

"I don't know, I just don't know," Keene said. "It's like I had all the notes in a bag, but it broke open and spilled onto the ground." He held up wet, muddy hands. "I tried to scoop them all up, but they were so *slippery*."

"It's all right," I said. "I'll get you a blanket and some hot tea. Fix you right up. And don't worry about the notes—they'll come back."

"Will they?" he said, his voice distracted. "They seemed awfully cross with me when I left. You haven't been cursed out until you've been cursed out by a D minor, let me tell you . . ."

I got him a blanket and wrapped it around his shoulders. "That's better. Tea will be ready in a moment."

Keene stared into the fire. "Beautiful little world you've got there," he murmured to it. "Much better than the watery one, I think. Did you know fire is a gas? A gas, gas, gas, said Jumping Jack Flash . . . I had it demonstrated to me at a festival once. I was staring into the flames of a bonfire, just like I am now, when I noticed they were flickering in time to the music. Thought it was the drugs at first, but no. Music is just the air vibrating, did you know that? And fire is a gas, just like air, so when you play loud music near it, you can actually *see* the vibrations instead of just hear them. Fire makes music visible. Isn't that amazing?"

"It is," I answered. "Inspiring, even."

"Oh, I don't know about that," he said vaguely. "It's just science. Science is all about what we know. My problem isn't what I know—it's changing what I *know* into what I *feel*. Or maybe the other way 'round."

I left him there, mumbling into the firelight, and went to the kitchen to make the tea. Ben was already there, and he'd put the kettle on. "So. Twenty-four hours, huh?"

"Ticktock," I said, getting out the tea. "Well, it's not the end of the world. Just large portions of it."

"I don't know how you can joke about this."

I measured the tea out into a ceramic pot. "Survival mechanism. Beats crying in your beer. You do that, the world still ends, but you die with salty beer."

"Seriously, Trot—what are we going to do?"

"Solve this," I said. "But I'm also going to do my job—taking care of the guests."

I put the teapot, a mug, a teaspoon, a small pitcher filled with cream, and a bowl with sugar in it onto a tray, and brought it out to Keene. He was sitting straighter in his chair now and seemed a little more clearheaded.

"Thank you," he said when I set the tray down on a table beside him. "Just what I need, I think. I just wish you hadn't brought me something quite so . . . swirly."

Which was when Tango appeared out of nowhere, meowing softly. Keene stared at her for a moment. "Hello, kitty. I'd offer you a lap, but mine is rather damp at the moment—"

Tango promptly jumped up onto said lap. I half expected Keene to freak out, but he seemed calm; he let Tango get comfortable then started to slowly stroke her fur. "Ah, cats," he said. "They are little bundles of magnificence, aren't they? Can always sense when you need a little cheering up—or mellowing out."

<Of course we do. We are also fierce, loving, clever, and exceedingly beautiful.>

"That's quite the purr she's got going," I said.

"Yes. Like holding a tiny, soft buzz saw."

"Hmmmm. That sounded suspiciously close to a metaphor. Maybe your method is working, after all."

"D'you think?" he said hopefully then looked crestfallen. "No, that's no good. Words but no melody. The purr is nice, but you can't dance to it . . . in fact, it's becoming a little too intense." He gently picked Tango up and put her down on the floor, where she immediately stalked away as if she'd been intending to do so the entire time.

<Hmmmph.>

"Can I tell you something, Foxtrot? I have a terrible feeling. Something is coming—something *bad*."

I've done my share of talking down people on bad trips—I used to wrangle a heavy metal band—so I knew what to say. "That's just the drugs talking, Keene. You're in a safe place, with safe people. You'll be fine. Have some of your tea."

He picked up the mug and took a slow, careful sip. "Thanks, but—a safe place? Have you not been paying attention to what's been happening? Two people have died. Any of us could be next."

He had a point. "Whatever's going on, I very much doubt you'd be a target—"

"Why not? Both the victims were performers. I'm a performer. Maybe the killer has something against talented extroverts." He drank some more tea, almost gulping it back, and I was glad I'd picked a decaffeinated variety. "I'm telling you, Foxtrot, something is *off*. I could feel it in the graveyard, and it got worse once the weather turned. That storm—it almost felt *personal*, the way it drenched me."

It seemed as though whatever he'd ingested was indeed ramping up Keene's personal psyche; talking him down off this particular mental ledge was going to be harder to do than I thought.

I tried another tack: "Well, let's look at this logically. Storms are huge. You—in comparison—are very small. Isn't it more likely that whatever the storm is pissed off about, you just happened to be in its way? I mean, I'm sure an ant takes it personally when it gets stepped on, but it's usually an accident that goes completely unnoticed by the one doing the stepping."

He clutched the mug with both hands, as if it were about to float away and he needed to keep it earthbound. "But what about the murders, Foxtrot? I think . . . I think the storm is *angry*. Angry about the murders . . ."

"I think you're getting a little carried away," I said.

"But let's say you're right. *You* had nothing to do with the murders, so the storm can't possibly be angry at you. Right?"

He considered and drank a little more tea. "I suppose," he said slowly. "But what you said about storms and how big they are—what happens when the storm is angry at one particular ant, and that ant lives in an anthill, a very nice anthill with tennis courts and stables and a robot that dispenses drinks, and the storm doesn't notice any of that because it's a storm, a huge hurricane monster of a thing, and it just wants to kill this one particular ant? What happens to the other ants in the anthill, Foxtrot? The ones that just want to play rock and roll and drink too much and try to salvage their dying musical careers? They get washed out with the rest of the poor bloody anthill, don't they?"

"Keene," I said firmly. "Listen to me. *Storms don't get mad at ants.* Got that?"

He looked at me for a second, and I saw the panic in his eyes. "I want to believe you," he said. "I really, really do. And I'm starting to think adding peyote to the mix wasn't a terribly wise choice. At least animals haven't started talking to me . . ."

I stayed with him, by the fire, and we talked. I managed to steer the conversation in a less ominous direction, and he slowly calmed down. By the time I left, he was back to staring into the fire, seemingly hypnotized by the dance of the flames, and quite peaceful.

And now I had less than twenty-four hours to make sure everything I told him was true—or all of us ants were in big, big trouble. . . .

Chapter Twenty-One

I didn't know what to do next, so I did what usually do: I took my dog, went home, and went to bed.

I could have stayed with Ben, but I knew he'd be up early to do breakfasty things, and with the condition I was in, I'd probably keep him awake half the night worrying out loud. I had a deadline now, and deadlines always amp things up.

I slept badly. Lots of dreams, the kind that blur into each other and are completely nonsensical yet seem perfectly lucid while you're having them. A walk on the beach with a stork, who happens to have lightning bolts for legs, and then I was having dinner with a bunch of penguins who were all wearing disguises, only I'd ordered the wrong kind of pizza, and now I was going to have to go into the woods to find the jeweled brooch my third grandmother had given me. And so on, and so on, and so on.

I finally got up an hour earlier than I usually do, took Whiskey for a walk, then had breakfast with a cup of tea, and did a little scrolling through the internet.

Things were not looking well, weather-wise. Hurricane

warnings in the Atlantic, heat waves in Brazil, freak snow-storms at China. All over the planet, weather systems were starting to act wonky. The Thunderbird Council, warming up—and in some cases, freezing down.

In my own neighborhood, the sky overhead was a dark, threatening gray. I let Whiskey stick his head out the window as we drove to work, and he reported that everything still smelled just amazing, thank you very much.

However, he could tell that I was worried. [Foxtrot, this ultimatum has to be a bluff. Mmmmm, cow manure.]

"I know what a bluff looks like, Whiskey. Teresa did not look like she was bluffing."

[It makes no sense for them to attack the planet. Dead squirrel? No, groundhog.]

"Talking to you while you're doing that is like trying to make sense of the dreams I had last night. As in, it's extremely confusing."

[I apologize for my lack of focus, however—garbage truck! Garbage truck!]

I wrinkled my own nose and raised his window, making sure he didn't get stuck. He gave me a reproachful look. [Was that really necessary?]

"I'm afraid so. Look, when people feel threatened, they do things that aren't completely rational. Right now, the Thunderbirds are feeling extremely threatened. They're acting out of base instinct. You can relate to that, can't you?"

[I can, but being technically dead gives me a certain emotional distance from such things.]

"You don't seem to have a lot of distance from taking delight in disgusting odors."

[Perhaps not. But when one's pleasures are few, they became heightened.]

We arrived at the mansion, parked, and I went inside to start my usual routine. The air had that heavy, oppressive feel that often precludes a major storm.

Tango was nowhere to be found, but I wasn't worried; she, like many cats, had the tendency to appear and disappear with no warning.

Conversations over breakfast touched briefly over the unusual weather happening worldwide, but then moved on to other things. It's funny how people can take such momentous events for granted, as long as said events aren't happening on their own doorstep.

That would change.

After breakfast I took a quick meeting with ZZ to go over a few things, and then I grabbed Whiskey and took him for a walk down to the graveyard. Time to report in to my other boss and let him know the situation.

I found Eli over by the statue of Piotr, perched on top of the statue's head. "Eli," I said. "I assume you've heard the news?"

He cocked his snow-white head to the side and said, "About the ultimatum? Yes." He didn't tell me how he knew, and I didn't pretend to be surprised. I've come to take as a given that Eli knows more than I do at any given point.

"I need to talk to Grandfather Serpent," I said.

"He can't stop this," said Eli. "And neither can I."

"I didn't think it would be that easy. But I need his insight into the situation. Maybe he knows something that will help me solve this."

Eli preened a wing feather. "Hmm. I suppose he might."

"Can you arrange another meeting? Soon-ish?"

"I'll see what I can do," Eli said and abruptly took flight. In moments he was out of sight behind one of the Crossroads's low hills.

I took a slow saunter around the graveyard, keeping my eyes open for a giant snake—you'd think such a thing would be hard to miss, but there's so much colorful motion happening at any given point that even a gigantic serpent can get lost in the mix. I thought I spotted what I was looking for once, but it turned out to be a sinuous train of multi-colored ghost gerbils snaking their way down a path.

And then, coiled in large pile on a slab of white granite that marked the grave of a thoroughbred, I found him.

"Greetings, Foxtrot," said Grandfather Serpent as I walked up. "And to you to, Whiskey."

[Hello.]

"Good morning," I said. "Except it's not really that good at all. Can I take it for granted that you're aware of the current situation, or do you need a brief rundown?"

He lifted his scaly, red head above his coils and regarded me with his bright-yellow, human-shaped eyes. "I am an old snake. Please, assume that I know nothing of your current troubles, and inform me concerning them."

"The Council of Thunderbirds is about to wreak havoc on the entire planet in an attempt to flush the Unktehila out of hiding."

A black, forked tongue flickered out, tasting the air. "I see. This is unfortunate."

"Yes, it is. They also believe a group of Unktehila assassins are poised to strike at them. They've given me twenty-four hours—ten of which are already up—to catch one of these assassins for questioning."

"Not very much time."

"No. And before she disappeared, the assassin I'm looking for claimed to be on the side of the Thunderbirds and wanted to turn over vital information about the other assassins."

"But she did not?"

"No. Instead, she seems to have killed another Unktehila—who was making the same claims she was—and then vanished. Plus, her assistant was killed the next day."

The giant snake nodded his head. "Very complicated.

An intricate network you must untangle. How may I be of assistance?"

"I was wondering if you could shed any light on the situation. I mean, you have more experience with the Unktehila than anyone else. Any insights would be welcome."

"Ah. I see. You wish to peer into the souls of your subject, the better to understand their actions."

"Something like that."

"I believe I can illuminate at least some of what you desire. To do so requires I tell you a story, a very important tale indeed: the story of the first war between my children and the Thunderbirds . . .

"It happened long, long ago, before men had begun to write down what had occurred and when. In those days, monsters prowled the dark, and men and women huddled close to their fires at night. The Thunderbirds owned the skies, and none dared challenge them; the Unktehila had no desire to do so, for their own abilities kept them well fed with little effort. They could lure prey by taking on an innocuous shape and beguile the simple-minded beasts with their mental abilities as well. The humans they left alone, for they were harder to trick—as well as being under the protection of the Thunderbirds.

"But every tribe has those who chafe under rules, who wish to do as they desire without restriction, and who believe themselves wiser than their elders. So it was with an Unktehila named Sillak.

"Sillak preferred to take the form of an injured doe, the better to lure in a single hunter such as a cougar or coyote. He would then switch his form to that of an enormous wolf and attack without warning. There were much easier ways to hunt—and easier prey to bring down—but Sillak relished the joy of battle, pitting his fangs and claws against an opponent with weapons of their own. And over time, he acquired an appetite for the taste of other meat-eaters.

"Inevitably, this led him to preying upon humans. They were harder to trick, and they had weapons that could kill from a distance—but Sillak enjoyed the challenge and found it made the meat taste all the sweeter.

"When it was discovered what Sillak was doing, the other Unktehila were very upset. Sillak was admonished and told to stop what he was doing. He agreed to this, for he had no desire to be banished from the company of his own kind.

"But his resolve was not as great as his hunger, and before too long, he found himself hunting humans once again.

"He took the form of a large turtle and pretended to be sunning himself on the banks of a river. He knew that a young human woman came to the river to wash clothes on the flat rocks, and he was determined to devour her.

"The young woman's name was Sunseeker, and her father was chief of a local tribe. She was strong-willed and clever, and Sillak knew that it would not be easy to trick her.

"The first time, he simply allowed her to see him while she was some distance away, and then he slipped into the river and swam off. He knew she would be intrigued, for he was surely the largest turtle she had ever seen. She might even mistrust her own eyes.

"The next time, he let her get a little bit closer before sliding into the water and swimming away. Now he knew that she had seen him.

"The third time, he did not swim away but stayed where he was, lying in the sun. Sunseeker approached cautiously and then began to do her washing on the banks of the river."

After a time, Sillak said, "Hello, woman."

Sunseeker was startled, but after a moment she replied, "Hello, Turtle."

"I see you here every day, doing your washing," said Sillak. "But the rocks here are uneven and sharp. There is a much better place on the other side of the river."

"That may be, but I am on *this* side of the river."

"You could swim across. The current is swift, but you look like a good swimmer."

"Yes, the current is swift. And even if I were as good a swimmer as you think, I would still have no way to carry my washing."

"Ah. That is a problem."

They both fell silent for a time, and Sunseeker did her washing, pounding her clothes against the flat rocks.

After a little while, Sillak said, "I know of a way for you to cross the river safely."

"Oh? And how is that?"

"You could ride on my back and carry your washing in your arms. I would have no trouble in carrying you across."

Sunseeker smiled, for she was not naive. "That is kind of you, Turtle. But what do you expect in return for this favor?"

"Why, nothing at all," said Sillak. "I am merely trying to do a favor for another living being."

"I see. And what if you should tip me off your back in the middle of the river and I should drown?"

"Why would I do that?"

"Perhaps you want to eat me."

"Eat you? I am a turtle, not a wolf. I eat fish, and frogs, and sometimes the young of birds—have you ever even heard of a turtle eating a human being?"

Sunseeker had to admit she had not. "How about this," she said. "Tomorrow I will bring a stout rope and tie it to a tree on this side of the river. I will make a loop in the rope that you can hold in your mouth, and I will hold the rope as I sit on your back. That way, if I fall into the water as we're crossing, I can grab the rope and pull myself back to shore."

Sillak considered this, and then he agreed. That night, his dreams were full of the taste of tender human flesh.

The next day, Sunseeker arrived with her washing in a bundle and a long, coiled rope over her shoulder. She tied one end of the rope to an oak tree and made a loop in the other end. She gave this loop to Sillak, who took it in his mouth. Then she climbed aboard his broad back, and he crawled into the water.

Sillak's plan was to tumble her into the water and then attack her while she tried to pull herself ashore. He would not even have to change shape to do it; a turtle may not be an eater of men, but their beaks are sharp and powerful. He wondered how many bites it would take.

But halfway across the river, she tightened the loop around his beak, took the knife from her belt, and cut his throat.

His body was heavy, but she was still able to pull it from the river using the rope. She was very surprised to see that he was now a giant snake with the rope caught in his fangs, but meat is meat. Her tribe was very happy, and her father proud.

"And that would have been the end of the story—except the story of how a human had killed an Unktehila spread, from person to person, tribe to tribe, and finally back to the Unktehila themselves. Stories have a way of doing that; they move, and they grow, and as they do so, they change. Before too long the story was about how a treacherous human woman had tricked an Unktehila to his death in order to eat him. After that, it wasn't too long before another Unktehila decided to avenge this death by eating a human.

"And so Sillak became the tragic victim of a story that

was not really about him but about who was more devious—humans or Unktehila.

"More human deaths followed. The Thunderbirds, who regarded humans as under their protection, were angered. They called a meeting of all their leaders to figure out what to do. It was decided that the Unktehila must answer for their actions, and for that purpose, one of their leaders must speak; but the Unktehila were afraid and used their powers to hide, and none would come forward. This angered the Thunderbirds even more, and they decided that an example must be made. They knew of a forest that was home to many of the serpents and told the men and women that lived there to flee; then the Thunderbirds called up a great storm to destroy the forest and to kill every living thing that remained. Lightning strikes started fires and boiled lakes. The Unktehila tried to escape, but only a few managed to make it to the sea, where they could hide in the deep and the Thunderbirds could not reach them. And that is how the great war between the Unktehila and the Thunderbirds began—and ended." Grandfather Serpent fell silent.

"So the war really began because a human killed an Unktehila?" I said.

"No," Grandfather Serpent said sadly. "It began because of selfishness, and pride, and anger. All of these things are wound throughout this story like vines in a thicket. All must take their share of the blame, for do we not all live in the same thicket?"

"I suppose we do."

"But there is another lesson to be learned from this story—which is that stories themselves cannot be trusted. They can inform us, entertain us, and enlighten us—but they can also deceive us. You must ask yourself: Which of the stories you have been told are true?"

"Well, in the beginning I was told the same story twice—but by two different Unktehila. One of them must have been lying."

"Almost certainly. But which one?"

That was the key, right there. Which of the Unktehila was trying to prevent a war, and which was trying to start one? Was Maxine Danger a whistleblower, or was she trying to muddy the waters by claiming to be one before Lockley Hades could reveal his information? There might even be two lists of assassins and their targets. And where could I find those lists?

"Thanks," I said. "But I'm not sure how this helps me stop another war from starting up."

"I am unsure as well. The Unktehila are more clever at hiding than they were before, and now the Thunderbirds are not just angry but afraid. But one thing gives me hope."

"What's that?"

"That all of them—Thunderbirds, humans, the Unktehila—are more alike than not. Both supernatural tribes have blended themselves into the larger human one. If we can make them see that, make them see that they are now merely different parts of the same tribe—then, perhaps, we can stop them from warring against each other. Otherwise . . ."

"Otherwise," I said, "The world burns."

I took a slow, thoughtful walk back to the house; I was thinking about what Grandfather Serpent said about stories and how they can change. At the very beginning of all this, I'd been told two conflicting stories. "You know what occurs to me?" I asked Whiskey.

[In my experience, many things. Often, too many.]

"Yes, I'm an occurrence-rich ground zero—what I meant specifically was the phone call I received from Lockley Hades, back when all this began."

[What about it?]

"He claimed to be on a set for his show. I think he must have used some kind of fake background—maybe digital—to convince me of that. And the only reason I can see for that is because he wanted me to think he was far away—when in fact he was very close."

[That makes sense.]

"And the only reason he'd do that is because he was constructing an illusion. An illusion that he was to be trusted and Maxine Danger was not."

[Which means the opposite was true?]

"Exactly. And if Lockley Hades was lying to me from the beginning, then Maxine was telling the truth. And even more importantly—if Maxine was telling the truth, she must have had the list of Unkhetila targets with her. Whiskey, *that list must still be here.*"

[Which means a search is in order?]

"You got it, pooch. We'll start with the rooms Maxine and Summer were staying in and then try their vehicle and trailer."

So, I had a plan at last. But what if I couldn't find the list—or worse, what if Lockley Hades had found it first and destroyed it?

I didn't know what I would do then.

But I had a little over twelve hours to figure it out.

Chapter Twenty-Two

We began our search in Maxine's room. All of her stuff was still there: several suitcases worth of clothes, costumes, and props, most of it spread around the room on hangers, draped over furniture, or piled on the bed. The maids had done their best to clean around the mess, but even so, it was just that—a mess.

I searched through pockets of clothing, the toiletries on the vanity, and even the wastepaper basket, looking for anything that might be a list. Whiskey applied his nose to the situation, sniffing every square inch of the room for something out of place.

[The problem here is that words don't have a smell,] he complained. [Paper does, and so does ink—but dried ink is so faint as to be almost imperceptible and relays nothing about the content of the writing.]

I was looking inside the toes of a pair of strappy, bright-red stilettos, hoping for something small and scrunched up. No luck. "I know, but maybe the list isn't written on paper. Or in ink."

[What are you hoping for? Something scrawled on sealskin in squirrel blood?]

I scowled. "I don't know. If this were a spy novel, it would be on a microchip or something."

[Or a thumb drive? I know what *they* smell like.]

I brightened. "Yes! See if you can sniff out one of those."

But twenty minutes later, we were forced to admit defeat. No cleverly hidden thumb drives, no cryptic notes hidden inside the pages of a book. I did find a laptop and a cell phone—both with locked screens—and several props I didn't quite understand, including some fancy metal handcuffs and a transparent wand, but if any of them contained any secrets, they refused to give them up to me. Whiskey reported a few crumbs of old cheese in a corner that the maids had missed, and he was pretty sure that someone had spilled a gin and tonic on the bedspread within the last week. That was all.

We checked the shared bathroom on the same floor but had similar results. Then we moved on to Summer Coyne's room.

Summer was much neater than Maxine, her clothes neatly hung up in the closet or stashed away in the bureau. Another laptop, also encrypted against anyone trying to do any snooping. And again, despite our best efforts, we didn't find what we were looking for.

I sat on Summer's bed and leaned back against my hands. "No list," I said. "It could be on either of these laptops—but we can't access them. Or maybe she still has it on her."

Whiskey rested his head on my knee. [Don't surrender just yet. It might be somewhere else in the house.]

I groaned and flopped backward onto the bed. "That's not exactly encouraging. A house this size? Plus, it might be somewhere on the grounds. Or in the graveyard. Or even in the menagerie."

[True,] Whiskey admitted. [But we can't give up.]

"I'm not. I'm just readjusting my expectations downward."

[That sounds suspiciously like giving up.]

"Nope. More like refocusing in order to expand the potential of alternative outcomes."

[You've been reading that book on professional management techniques again.]

"What can I say? It helps me get to sleep. I mean, it increases the possibility of unconscious interaction with my environment."

Another hour gone by, and I wasn't any closer to finding Maxine or the list. I sat up, stood, and said, "Come on. Let's go look through the vehicles."

I had found a key ring in Maxine's room, and the keys on it opened the truck they'd arrived in and the trailer where Summer's body had been discovered. The forensics people had already been over both, but they weren't looking for the same thing I was.

There was nothing in the truck but an old air freshener hanging from the rearview mirror and registration papers in the glove box, but the trailer was much more interesting. There were lots of tools and stage equipment near the door, but the hidden, refrigerated compartment in the back was what I really wanted to explore.

It was still very cool back there, but the refrigeration unit was no longer running; there were little pools of water on the floor, beneath the table that held the 3D printer. I examined it carefully, along with the attached laptop. This was the printer that made the ice key to open the vault—though I still didn't know how they'd figured out a way around the magnets embedded in the key. Did Esko Karvenin set it up for them? I examined the controls but couldn't figure out how to work them. If Karvenin was still here, I could ask him—but he'd disappeared as completely as Maxine had.

The police had taken Summer's phone, so I couldn't check that for possible leads. I'd tried Maxine's phone when she first disappeared, but it went straight to voice mail.

I pulled out my own phone and called my contact at the coroner's office—another overworked assistant who understood what I had to deal with on a daily basis. We chatted amiably for a bit, and then I managed to finagle a little information out of her—it didn't look like Summer Coyne's body had been moved afterward, which means she'd been killed in the truck itself. Someone had lured her into the secret compartment and then attacked her. Both she and Lockley had died of stab wounds to the chest—but Lockley had received his from the barbed tip of a bull ray, courtesy no doubt of a transformed Maxine. But if that was true, why was a knife found stuck as well?

[Foxtrot? You should take care where you're stepping.]

"What? Why?"

[Those wet patches aren't water. They're blood.]

I stepped back hastily. Of course there'd still be blood residue—it must have frozen after the attack, and now that the refrigeration unit was no longer running, it had defrosted. "Let's get out of here, Whiskey. We're not learning anything we didn't already know."

After lunch the weather continued to worsen. There was a brief spate of hail, which drove everyone indoors. Keene continued to mope, spending a lot of his time in a long, silk dressing gown, staring out the window and sighing. I stood beside him and looked out at the white dots that now speckled the ground. "I'd say penny for your thoughts, but you'd probably start bemoaning your impending lack of royalties."

"I don't know what to do, Fox. I'm at the end of my rope, creatively."

"Oh, you've still got plenty of rope. There must be dozens of esoteric drugs you haven't tried yet."

"The drugs seem to be a bit of a dead end, to be

honest. All they're doing is remixing my despair into different flavors."

"And Jeepers was no help?"

"I think Jeepers was a no-show, to be honest."

"Really? That surprises me."

He gave me a wary, sidelong look. "If you're about to make some sort of joke, please don't. I'm not in the mood."

"I'm not. What I was going to say is that I . . . felt something during the séance. Seriously."

He raised an eyebrow. "What, exactly?"

"A presence. And that presence was concerned about you and doing their best to help. I'm surprised you didn't feel it, too."

His gaze shifted back to the window. "It's hard to know what I'm feeling, these days. It's like I'm emotionally blocked up. There's all this stuff I just don't seem able to access—I know it's there, down below the surface. I just can't get at it." The look on his face was miserable. "I'd give anything to be able to, Fox. I really would."

"Then stop running away from it," I said gently.

"What?"

"All the drinking, the drugs, even the séance—I think they're making your block worse, not better. Your block is about something else, something you don't want to think about. Getting wasted is a time-honored tradition for emotional avoidance."

His eyes narrowed. "So what is it I'm avoiding, do you think?"

"Could be all sorts of things. Worry about your career. Grief over losing something. Anger at yourself—"

"Anger? What would I have to be angry about?"

I shrugged. "I don't know, but self-blame can be a heavy weight to carry. Maybe there's something you need to do, or maybe there's something you didn't do and wish you had. You're going to have to think about it—with a clear head."

He gave me a rueful half smile. "Sure. You make it sound so easy."

"Oh, it's not going to be easy. But you've tried all the easy ways, and they didn't work. You're going to have to try something else."

I left him there at the window, grabbed my jacket, and took Whiskey out for a walk. I was running out of ideas myself—and when that happened to me, I did the only thing I knew how to do: kept moving.

The air was warmer than I expected, the hail already melting. Whiskey and I did a tour of the menagerie, peering at all the animals like they could tell me what I needed to know. Even if that were true, it wouldn't do me any good without Tango here; my knowledge of animal language was limited to the universal telepathic speech ghosts used.

Just as I was wondering where my cat had gotten to, I heard her voice in my head: *<Hey, Toots. Where are you? I think I'm on to something.>*

I'm over by the hippo pond.

<Well, get yourself to the ostrich yard. I've discovered something interesting.>

[What now?] Whiskey asked me. [She's probably discovered that ostriches are birds and expects us to be equally astounded.]

"We won't know until we check it out, pooch."

We got there a few minutes later to find Tango sitting patiently just outside the enclosure. Oswald himself was strutting around in the back of his pen, idly pecking at the remaining pieces of hail on the ground like they were some sort of exotic sky popcorn.

"What's the big news?" I asked as we approached.

<He is,> said Tango. *<Watch this.>* She gave a series

of hisses followed by a rumbling noise like a low roar. Oswald stared at her intently for a second then went back to nibbling at hail.

<See?>

"I don't see anything, kitty—or hear anything, for that matter. Did Oswald say something?"

<No, and that's the point.> She got to her feet and started stalking back and forth, the tip of her tail twitching. *<He won't talk to me.>*

[Ah, I see. You've called us over to demonstrate Oswald's impeccable good taste. Well done.]

<You're not getting it. I've tried to start a conversation for the last ten minutes, and all he does is stare at me.>

"Maybe he's got nothing to say?" I said. "Oswald's never struck me as being overly chatty."

<He's not. But this is unusual. I can't get him to engage at all.>

She tried again, emitting that same low, roaring noise. *<See? Nothing.>*

[Maybe he just doesn't understand you. How fluent are you in Ostrich?]

Tango gave Whiskey a disdainful look. *<There's nothing wrong with my speech. I think he's scared.>*

"Scared? Of what?"

<Owduttf, maybe. Which means he must know something useful and Owduttf warned him against spilling it.>

"I guess that's possible. Owduttf's pen is close enough that Oswald could hear any vocalizations he made. And he's threatened other animals before."

I studied Oswald; the ostrich stared blankly back at me and then looked away. "Ask him if Owduttf said anything to him."

Tango made some hissing noises and got no response.

"Try again. Tell him he doesn't have anything to be afraid of, that we'll keep him safe."

Tango made another attempt. Still nothing.

[I think he just doesn't like you.]

<I'm telling you, the ostrich knows something,> Tango insisted.

"You might be right," I muttered. "How about we try some bribery and see if that makes him a little more talkative?"

I knew from talking to our resident animal caretaker that ostriches will eat almost anything, from leaves and seeds to bugs and lizards; I thought I could find something relatively tasty in the mansion's kitchen.

Ben gave me a very odd look when I told him what I wanted, but he shrugged and said, "There are some Danishes left over from breakfast. Will that do?"

"Perfect," I said.

Back at Oswald's enclosure, I lifted my bag of Danishes up and yelled, "Hey! Treats! You want some treats, come and get 'em!"

That got no response, so I had Tango repeat it in Ostrich. Oswald studied us dubiously for a moment then took a few slow steps closer.

He stopped about ten feet away from the fence. I pulled a Danish from the bag, tore it in half, and tossed it into the pen. Oswald plucked it up and gobbled it down immediately.

"Now we're getting somewhere," I said. I held up the other half of the Danish tantalizingly. "Want this? Talk to us."

Oswald stretched his neck out, as if he could just reach out and pluck the treat from my hand, but he was still too far away.

"Nuh-uh," I said firmly. "At least say hello."

Oswald emitted a hiss.

"Close enough," I said. I tossed him the other half, and he caught it in midair.

"Now, I've got some questions for you," I said. "Like—why aren't you talking to Tango?"

Oswald cocked his head to one side and regarded me then blinked.

"Oh, come on," I said. "Tango?"

Tango tried, emitting a series of hisses and moving her own head in a circular way. A lot of animal dialects, according to my cat, are just as much body language as they are sound.

Oswald responded, bobbing his head up and down and scratching at the dirt with one long-clawed toe. I peered at the scratch mark hopefully, but it didn't reveal anything astounding. "What did he say?"

<It's . . . kind of garbled. No talk, still hungry, more food. Not that Oswald is exactly great at conversation at the best of times, but this seems like he's a little confused.>

"Almost like someone's been messing with his mind?"

<I guess. Not that he's got a lot of mind to mess with.>

[Foxtrot, do you think it's possible an Unktehila did something to Oswald? Used their mental coercion abilities?]

"It's possible. Which means Oswald—unlike Owduttf—might have actually seen something useful."

I pulled out another Danish. "Oswald. Did you see anyone—a human being—change into something else?"

Oswald stared at me quizzically, then made some more head-bobbing motions and flapped his short, stubby wings once for emphasis.

<He says, and I quote: Danish yummy.>

I tried again. "Transformation, Oswald. Person changing into something else. Maybe another person?"

More noises and some foot-scratching. *<Oh, this is interesting.>*

"What? What did he say?>

<Giant sky Danish eat me never. No birdseed. Me am not rocks.>

"Really?"

<I'm telling you, that's what he said.>

[I have an idea. What about if I demonstrate some shape-changing and see if he responds?]

Whiskey's transformation skill has been useful in more than one situation. "Sure. Tango, let the bird know this is the kind of thing we're looking for, okay?"

<You got it, Toots.>

Whiskey barked once, to get Oswald's attention—the ostrich was still fixated on my bag of goodies—and then shape-shifted, transforming from his Australian cattle dog form into a gigantic, gray-furred Irish wolfhound.

Oswald stared at Whiskey's new form then shook his head as if trying to clear it. He emitted a new series of noises, accompanied by some head weaving.

<He says: dog Danish bigger now no fair still hungry Danish Danish Danish dusty.>

"Okay, this is getting us nowhere. I think his mind has definitely been messed with."

Whiskey reverted to his normal form. [I agree. But this information does us little good, since we can't get at what he actually knows.]

"True. But at least we know that whoever did this to him was trying to hide something significant—something Oswald saw."

[Something like someone hiding a list?]

"Exactly."

The problem was, Oswald's view encompassed a lot of territory. From his pen, he could see the front of the mansion, a bunch of the grounds, all sorts of trees, and the driveway that led up to the house.

But I had a secret weapon—Whiskey's nose.

I took him around carefully, looking for anything that might smell out of place—more specifically, anything with traces of Maxine Danger's scent on it. I didn't have high hopes, though—the recent rain might have washed anything like that away.

We were still at it when the rain returned, even harder than before. We gave up and rushed back to the house, Tango in the lead. She really, *really*, didn't like rain.

[Well, that was a waste of time,] Whiskey grumbled, shaking himself.

<Of all the disgusting dog behaviors I know, that one is the worst,> Tango snapped.

[What do you mean? I'm just trying to get dry in the fastest, most economical way—]

<Yes, by spraying water all over anyone near you!>

"She does have a point," I said. "You could wait until I got a towel—"

<Or you could clean yourself in a more normal, appropriate way, with your tongue—>

[I don't see what the fuss is all about. Just appreciate the fact that I wasn't wearing my sheepdog form.]

My phone beeped at me, and I saw that I had a text from Keene. "Hmmm. Our resident melancholy rock and roller wants me to come up to his room."

<More angst and self-pity, no doubt.>

[Have a little compassion. He's going through a rough patch.]

<Oh, I feel for him—but we should stay focused on what we're doing. We've got until tonight before the Thunderbirds make good on their threat.>

"Oh, I'm well aware of that," I said. "But we're running out of options—and besides, you know how I excel at multitasking. I can handhold and brainstorm at the same time."

<Fine. I'm finding a warm, dry spot by the fire to curl up in.>

"Good idea. Whiskey, you go with her—I don't really think Keene would appreciate the aroma of wet dog adding to his troubles."

Whiskey gave me a hurt look but trotted after Tango toward the study. Hopefully he wouldn't offend anyone else, either.

I went upstairs and knocked on the door to Keene's room. "Hello?"

"Come in, come in."

He was sitting on his bed, barefoot, with an acoustic guitar in his lap. All the lights in the room were turned on, including the lamp on the desk and the one on the nightstand. "Here it is not even midnight, and look at all the oil you're burning," I said. "Sudden fear of the dark?"

He laughed and shook his head. "No, no. I just wanted to dispel any appearance of this being a seduction. Because it definitely is not."

I crossed my arms. "Oh? And what makes you think I would suddenly jump to this wild conclusion—other than all the other times you've tried, I mean?"

He smiled—the first real smile I'd seen on his face for days. "Oh, that was just flirting, Fox—if I were going to make a serious attempt, there'd be all sorts of props and whatnot. Candles, incense—no, strike the incense, you're not the patchouli type—intense mood lighting, the whole nineteen-and-a-half yards. None of which is in evidence, is it?"

"No, but I remain unconvinced."

"I should have had you bring Whiskey along—nobody tries a seduction while their dog's watching."

"So—if this isn't a seduction, what is it? Has the block finally broken? That guitar looks promising, even if you don't."

"I . . . may have. I have a little something I've been noodling around on. It's something I've been working on for quite some time, actually. And that's been the problem."

"Oh? How so?"

"Please, sit," he said. "On a chair, I mean, not the bed. Honest."

I pulled a chair over and sat. "Okay. Now, tell me more about this problem."

He looked down, let his left hand idly finger a few frets. "It's like this, Fox. There are some songs I start and never finish. A few bars here and there, inspired by some random event—usually, to be honest, an attractive woman. And then I usually realize I'm just copying some other song I already know and let it drop. But sometimes an unfinished melody sticks with me, and I just sort of get used to it. Turns into something eventually, or it doesn't. Except for this one."

He strummed a few chords, and something light and lovely drifted into the air. It sounded vaguely familiar, but I couldn't place it.

He stopped playing abruptly. "That's all I had for the longest time. Couldn't for the life of me do anything with it. For a while, it went like this—" A few stirring notes with a much faster tempo. "And then it mutated into this—" Now it sounded slower, more haunting. "And even this—" Now it was happy, almost chirpy.

"As you can see, none of the bits really go with each other—and yet they do. Can you guess what the name of this convoluted little tune is yet?"

"Keene's Slow-Motion Nervous Breakdown?"

He laughed. "Almost. I call it Foxtrot's Theme."

I opened my mouth and then closed it again.

"It's not a love song, not quite. It's not a heartbreaker, or a march, or a silly jingle. It's all of the above, and more. Because, of course, you defy description."

I swallowed. "I see a single candle and I'm out of here," I managed.

"Nah, Fox, you've got nothing to worry about. You and I are solid. We've got a great friendship, and I really value that. But I'm a romantic soul, and part of me just can't stop pulling at that thread. It's all right if I do it with music—it gives me an outlet, you know? Lot of music gets written about romantic tension. I've written lots of songs about women I'll never be with. But this song. . . . it refuses to resolve itself, and it refuses to go away."

"Wait a minute," I said. "Are you trying to tell me *I'm* the reason for your block?"

"No, no, no. Definitely not. But I think you've given me the tool I need to *break* the damn thing."

"I don't understand."

He shook his head and looked down at his guitar again, his long, curly hair in his eyes. "I realized I had all these great, unfinished bits of songs that I could expand upon. Bits that I wouldn't let myself finish—because once something is finished, it's over, isn't it? And I didn't want these songs to be over. I wanted each one of them to be like you—complicated and contradictory and full to bursting with potential, going a mile a minute one second and then relaxing over dinner the next. I told myself I could never knit all of them together into one piece anyway, but that was just an excuse. Really, I was just afraid. Do you see?"

He met my eyes and didn't look away. I wasn't sure of the emotion I saw there.

"I think so," I said. "You need to . . . let go. And if you do, you can move on."

His smile was one of relief. "Yes. That's it exactly. And I think I can do that, Foxtrot, I really think I can. I just—this is going to sound ridiculous but—I need your permission."

I thought about it for a moment before I answered—

not to be mean, but because I wanted him to see that I understood the weight of his words. "Yes, Keene. I am officially releasing you from the curse of Foxtrot's theme. Turn those little bits of melody into anything they want to be. And I'm sure that whatever they become, they'll be memorable."

He grinned back at me and said, "Oh, you are *so* lucky I don't have any candles right now . . ."

Chapter Twenty-Three

You might think it would be uncomfortable for me to stay there after that, but it wasn't. I felt more at ease, actually. Secrets have their own weight, after all, even when you're not the one carrying them around. Keene's admission that he had little bits of songs he'd hidden away, waiting to grow into something else, was freeing—and I felt good that I'd been able to give that to him. Even the flirtiness was more relaxed, like an old groove we'd found after losing it. I stuck around for another half hour, and he played me all the partial songs and musical riffs he'd been talking about. I had to admit, a lot of them did sound like me, somehow— especially the one that wouldn't have been out of place in a march, or the one that jumped around a lot, or the one that just seemed to have too much happening all at once.

But I liked the slower, more romantic stuff, too— though I didn't admit that to Keene. I'm allowed to have a few secrets of my own.

I left him there, guitar cradled in his lap, looking less troubled and more focused than he'd been in days, and went back downstairs.

Outside, the weather had continued to worsen. It was

midafternoon, but the sky outside was dark as night. Thunder grumbled and coughed, lightning spat; fat, cold raindrops drummed against the roof. I'd built a fire on the hearth in the study, and those of our guests that weren't huddled around it were staring at the flat-screen in the corner, which was tuned to a weather channel.

The news wasn't good. Weather systems all over the world were acting wonky, with at least six different regions reporting unusually heavy weather that ranged from tropical monsoons to tornados to freak blizzards.

Ben and I stood a little ways away from everyone else and talked in low voices. "This is only the beginning," Ben said grimly. "A show of force. Showing the Unktehila they mean business."

"Saber rattling with thunderbolts and hailstorms," I said. "Well, it's working on me. Can you tell your bosses we surrender? Or at least I do."

"You know what they want, Foxtrot."

"I can't give them what I don't have!" I said in a vehement whisper. "Maxine is still missing. And if she wrote down that list of Unktehila assassins, I have no idea where she hid it."

"They're not going to stop," Ben said. "They think they can force the Unktehila's hand—make them strike out of sheer terror or self-defense."

"That makes no sense! It's the rest of us mere human beings who are going to suffer!"

"Don't you think I know that?"

Our discussion was interrupted by Oscar, who was fortifying himself with a stiff drink or three. "I do believe we've broken the planet," he said, his tone light. "Bloody marvelous."

"Isn't it, though?" I said. "Funny how everyone takes weather for granted until it's about to destroy something."

"Oh, I take climate change very seriously," said Oscar. He took a healthy swig of his martini. "Anyone with a brain in their head does. Even those who deny it publicly say otherwise when there are no cameras aimed at them. On some level, everyone knows how bad the situation is; it's just a question of whether or not people are willing to admit it to themselves. It's the ostrich approach, I suppose."

"Right. You know that's a myth, right? Ostriches don't actually hide their heads in the sand and pretend nothing's wrong."

Amos Clay walked up as we were talking, a large snifter of brandy in one hand. "That's right—mostly."

"Oh?" Oscar said. "Do tell."

Amos swirled the brandy gently around in the glass cradled in his hand. "The thing is, ostriches do exhibit behavior similar to that. If an ostrich is trying to evade a predator, it has three choices: it can run, fight, or hide. Usually they run or fight, but sometimes, if neither of those is an option, they will try to conceal themselves. But it's hard to hide when you're a six-foot-tall bird, especially on the flat, arid plains of their native Africa."

"I imagine so," said Oscar. "Rather like Mother trying to appear inconspicuous at a funeral."

Clay chuckled. "She does tend to stand out, doesn't she? As does the ostrich. Well, what the bird does is lie on its stomach, with its neck and head stretched out and flat against the ground. From a distance, they now appear to be just another small, nondescript hill."

"Interesting," I said. "But I don't see how that got turned into sticking their head in the ground."

Clay took a sip of his brandy. "That's probably due to the behavior of the males during egg-laying season. The eggs are buried in small mounds of dirt, you see, and the male will stick his head into the dirt to move them around. Paternal activity, not evasion—"

A loud crack of thunder interrupted his comment,

and we all jumped a little—all of us except Ben, who no doubt had sensed it coming.

ZZ came over to where we were standing, a glass of red wine in one hand "Foxtrot, please tell me that our emergency generator is in working condition."

"Of course," I said "If the power goes out, we won't have any problems. Flooding, on the other hand . . ."

ZZ glanced nervously at the window. "Yes, it really is coming down, isn't it? The grounds will be a mess—not that I should be worried about *that*." She shook her head. "When I think about all the things we protested in the sixties—for civil rights, the environment, against war—we never thought that it would manifest like this. Smog-filled cities and polluted waterways we could envision; hurricanes and heat waves were thought of as natural disasters, not human ones."

"Things change," Ben said. "Sometimes, really big things."

"And we're all a bunch of ostriches," said Oscar. "Even if the folk saying isn't accurate, the metaphor still stands."

"What saying isn't accurate?" ZZ asked, and Amos Clay repeated to her what he'd said to us.

I had the oddest feeling while he was talking. Something about ostriches and pretending not to see the world as it really was as a defense. Tango must have noticed, because she came over from where she'd been sprawled by the fire and butted up against my legs. I took a seat in a nearby armchair, and she jumped on my lap.

<What's up, Toots? Your thoughts feel bothered.>

What, I thought at her, *the enormous storm that's about to engulf the world isn't enough to be bothered about?*

<There's something else. Spill it.>

I wish I could. There's something my subconscious is gnawing at, but I can't see it. I just know it's there.

Over by the fire, Whiskey raised his head [Gnawing? Perhaps I can be of assistance.]

<Go back to sleep. We're talking about actual problems, not bones.>

[Should I be offended by that remark? Most likely. However, I do not believe I will make the effort, as the problem itself is of prime importance.]

Guys, guys. Take it easy. We just need to—

Which was when the doorbell rang.

"Someone out in this weather? How odd," said Oscar.

"I'll get it," I said and hurried to the front door with Whiskey at my heels.

It was Teresa Firstcharger, wrapped in a dark-gray raincoat, her long, dark hair streaming with water from the downpour. Somehow, that detail bothered me more than it should; I thought of Thunderbirds as being immune to weather and all its effects.

ZZ came to the door to see who it was and looked surprised when she did. "Ms. Firstcharger. Did you get caught in the storm?"

"I did," Teresa said. "It's lovely to see you, ZZ, but I actually have some business to discuss with your chef."

ZZ was under the mistaken impression that Teresa was taking cooking lessons from Ben, which accounted for their spending so much time together.

"I'll get Ben," I said.

"Great," said Teresa, flashing a brief smile. "Have him meet me in the kitchen, will you?"

She was early—hours early. But from the look in her eyes, if she had news to share, it wasn't good. . . .

"We're out of time," Teresa told us.

We were in Ben's small office, the door closed behind us. Teresa had taken the seat behind the desk, and we were standing in front of it like recalcitrant students in front of an irate teacher.

"What do you mean, out of time?" Ben said. "The deadline isn't up yet—"

"You should know better than that," Teresa snapped. "Thunderbirds think in terms of seasons, not minutes. Twenty-four hours was approximate at best."

When she put it that way, I felt stupid. What was I expecting, a gigantic clock somewhere ticking down the seconds? We were talking about weather here, not a bomb—although the effects were going to be equally catastrophic.

"Tell me what's going to happen," I said.

Teresa stared at me and then placed her hands flat against the surface of the desk. "Very well. The Thunderbird Council just had a meeting in Thunderspace. We're going to decelerate our control of the systems that are now operating."

"Wait—decelerate your control? What does that mean?"

"She doesn't know," said Ben. His voice was flat.

"Know what?" I asked, puzzled.

"What I asked him to keep from you," said Teresa. "Foxtrot, Thunderbirds aren't responsible for causing the extreme weather around the globe. Just the opposite; we've been throttling it back—and have been for years."

I blinked. "So all of these storms, all this unnatural phenomena—"

"Are man-made, yes." Teresa spread the fingers on both hands. "All over the world, climate change has been progressing rapidly for decades. The World Storm I was talking about? It already exists. We do our best to keep it in check, but we're fighting a losing battle."

"So the Unktehila's plan—"

"Was to get rid of the dampening systems we've put in place. Kill the Thunderbirds, and the world will be racked with unspeakable storms. Civilization will almost certainly fall."

"But—but we all have to live in the same world! They'll be doing this to themselves, too!"

Teresa gave me a small, sad smile. "Unktehila consider themselves to be apex predators. They're sure of their ability to survive. The last time something like this happened—the last time our species went to war—they hid in the depths of the sea. No doubt they think they can do so again. And with the Thunderbirds gone, they can slither out of the water any time they want and go back to preying on humanity."

"This is—this is ridiculous," I said. "Nobody wins in that scenario. And I don't believe it for a second."

Teresa shrugged. "I understand your reluctance to face these facts—"

"What does either side gain from you letting things spiral out of control?"

"It will force their hand," said Teresa grimly. "This is a runaway train, and they want the brakes to fail. Striking at us now will give them an inevitable victory, one they won't want reversed. They'll attack to ensure that."

"So you're deliberately making yourself targets by doing exactly what they want? What if they just let you wreck the world? *What if that was their plan all along?*"

"They are manipulative cowards at heart, it's true. But we have information you do not, and letting the World Storm grow in strength will give us more—it will reveal the Unktehila to us."

She paused. "Ever since the first war, the Unktehila have sworn they will bring us down at the height of our power. It is the story they teach their young and have done so for hundreds of years."

"Stories, huh?" I shook my head. "Well, you know what? I've heard a few stories of my own about the Unktehila, and they don't exactly match up with yours. According to my source, human beings were just as much to blame for the first war as either the Unktehila or the Thunderbirds. And the more I hear, the more I think this is a case of neither side being willing to back down. You like to paint the Unktehila as beings of utter evil, but Maxine Danger was a friend of yours. You can't believe everything you know about her is a lie."

Teresa stared at me, her jaw set. "And what if it is? Her life is based on deception. I can't deny the evidence of my own eyes."

"Neither can I. And I believe Maxine when she told me she wanted to prevent this war, not cause it. I think that's why Lockley Hades was here—to prevent her from doing just that."

Teresa's scowl deepened. "And what if the reverse is true? That Lockley Hades was a traitor to his own kind who was here to betray them?"

"Then he would have found a way to leave his list to someone in case he was killed, wouldn't he? And so far, I haven't been able to find anything like that. He wasn't even wearing clothing when he died."

"I don't know what the answer to that is. If this list even exists, it seems lost forever. And Maxine Danger is long gone."

I didn't believe that, but I couldn't prove it. And I needed proof—I couldn't make Teresa see that she was wrong about the Unktehila, not unless I could undo generations of mistrust. Grandfather Serpent's tales had given me a different view of the shape-changers, one Teresa just couldn't see. Almost like she was wearing blinders, or—

And suddenly, I realized I knew where Maxine Danger was.

"Okay," I said calmly. "Give me twenty minutes. Can you do that?"

Teresa eyed me skeptically. "What could you possibly accomplish in twenty minutes?"

"Just trust me. What have you got to lose?"

Teresa considered this. "All right. Twenty minutes won't make any difference. What's been set in motion has its own momentum, now."

"But if I come back in twenty minutes with hard evidence, you could still stop it?"

She studied me for a moment then said, "Yes. I could call an emergency meeting in Thunderspace, where time moves differently. The process could be halted. But what do you hope to accomplish in such a short span of time?"

I got to my feet. "I'll tell you in twenty minutes."

Ben jumped up as well. "Foxtrot?"

"Just trust me, Ben."

"I do. I just wanted to say—good luck." He gave me a quick peck on the lips; I smiled encouragingly at him and then raced out of the room.

I grabbed a long trench coat out of the closet in the foyer and then looked around for my cat. *Tango!* I hissed mentally. *Front door, kitty. I need you.*

She sauntered in a few seconds later, saw that I was putting rain gear on, and said, *<Nope. I am not going out there. Wet ugliness is falling from the sky.>*

I bent down and scooped her up. *<Hey!>*

"You can stay nice and dry inside my coat, okay?" I belted the jacket loosely, tucked Tango inside, then grabbed an umbrella for good measure.

Outside, the rain was still coming down heavily. I snapped the umbrella open and made my way across the grounds to the edge of the menagerie, where Oswald's pen was. He wasn't outside, of course; ostriches are from warm, sunny places, and he wasn't partial to great sheets of rain pummeling the ground.

I unlatched the door to the pen and stepped inside. I made my way to his enclosure, a shed with a large hole for Oswald and a regular door for his keepers.

Inside, there was a trough for feed and a pile of straw and soft grass for a bed. Oswald nestled on one edge and cocked his head at me when I entered.

"Hello, Oswald," I said. "Kitty, can you translate for me?"

Tango, though clearly still annoyed, made the necessary hissing noises.

"You're feeling kind of confused, aren't you?" I said. "Events over the past few days have been unusual, to say the least."

I paused, waited for Tango to translate, and then went on, "But everything's okay now. Because I figured it out. Maxine, you can release your hold on Oswald, now."

Oswald gave me the same blank, wide-eyed look that was his usual expression.

And then, the far end of the nest stirred—and a second ostrich stood, shedding the grass and straw it had been buried under.

"You're both probably a little confused," I said carefully. "From what I understand, the longer you take on a form, the more like it you become. If you stay in close proximity, you can absorb knowledge and memories, too. Which means that while you've been hiding out here, you've slowly been becoming more ostrich-like."

I eyed both ostriches warily as Tango continued to translate. An adult ostrich, in many ways, is as close to a present-day dinosaur as you're likely to get; those muscular legs can kick you right through a wall, and the talons they usually used to scratch in the dirt can easily be repurposed as tools of disembowelment.

"I'm talking to you in both Ostrich and English because I'm not sure which one makes more sense to you right now. What I do know is that you've been mentally controlling Oswald to keep him calm, and the added weight of that has taken its toll. That's why he seemed so muddled when I talked to him earlier, wasn't it? Or was it you I was talking to?"

The second ostrich bobbed his head at me—and then began to change.

I've seen Ben shift into his Thunderbird form, so it's not like I was a complete newbie to this—but it was still an amazing sight to see. The head swelled and sprouted hair; the neck shrank; the body and legs transformed. In a few seconds, a naked Maxine Danger stood there, bits of grass and straw still clinging to her skin.

She hugged herself, shivering, but didn't say anything. The look in her eyes was still a little vacant.

"Tango, I'm going to have to put you down," I said softly. I undid the belt of the coat then lowered her softly to the ground. She wasn't happy about it and told me so with an indignant meow that needed no translation. I shrugged out of the trench coat and offered it to Maxine, who stared at it, cocked her head to one side, and then reached out and took it with one hand. I picked Tango back up—being that close to Oswald's talons was making both of us nervous.

Maxine put on the coat. Then she made a face, and spat. "Gah. I can still taste birdseed."

"The list, Maxine. I need the list, or the war you've been trying to stop is about to start."

She put a hand to her head. "That's . . . tricky. Memorized it. And now my head's full of feathers . . ."

"Listen, Teresa Firstcharger's inside the house. You tell her that list, you can put a stop to this craziness."

"How . . . how did you figure out where I was?"

"I got a few tips about how Unktehila abilities work from a friend. It took me a while, but I got there in the end."

"So you did," said a voice from the doorway.

Teresa Firstcharger stood there, lightning crackling in her eyes.

"Uh-oh," said Maxine.

Chapter Twenty-Four

"I watched you from a window," said Teresa. "When I saw you run over here, I knew you'd tracked her down—"

Maxine bolted through Oswald's door. I bolted after her, Tango clinging to me for dear life.

The rain outside drenched me in seconds. Maxine had already made it out of the enclosure and was sprinting across the front lawn. I gave chase but had to stop after a few seconds to put Tango down—running with a freaked-out cat attached to your chest does not increase your speed.

Behind me, I heard a screech of rage, and the sudden FLOMPH! noise that a Thunderbird makes when it changes out of its human form. Birds don't generally do a lot flying in heavy weather, but the rules are different for supernatural beings.

Maxine was running for the graveyard.

A large form hurtled over my head as Teresa took flight. I ran, trying to catch up to Maxine, but slipped on the wet grass and went down hard. It only took me seconds to get back on my feet, but Maxine now had a lead I couldn't catch.

A brilliant bolt of lightning crashed to the ground at

Maxine's heels. She made it to the graveyard and through the gate in the hedge. Overhead, Teresa screeched again in fury.

Whiskey appeared out of nowhere, probably alerted by me mindcasting panic. He made it to the graveyard before Tango and I did, but we were there within seconds.

And when we arrived, it was to find Maxine had stopped running and fallen to her knees on the wet grass. She was gasping one word, over and over.

"Sanctuary. Sanctuary. Please, *sanctuary*."

With a mighty flapping of wings, Teresa landed just behind me then stepped forward. She changed back into her human aspect and said, "The list. Give it to me, *now*."

"Not unless I'm granted sanctuary. Foxtrot, please."

This was a new one on me. I mean, yes, I'm officially the Guardian of the Great Crossroads . . . but Eli never told me I had the power to grant anyone sanctuary.

Then again, he never told me I didn't, either.

"I grant you the sanctuary of the Great Crossroads," I said, trying to sound as official as possible. "And my boss will back me up on this." I hope.

The look Teresa gave me was several degrees beyond murderous. "Do you have any idea what you're doing?"

"Yeah, I do," I said. "I'm making sure nobody else gets killed on my watch. But Maxine, Teresa's right—we *need* that list."

"And I'll give it to you," she said. "But I need assurances. Assurances that you won't just slaughter all the names on that list."

"The names," Teresa said with a glare, "of the *assassins* on it, you mean? The names of the ones who intend to *slaughter* my people?"

"Let's just walk this back a second," I said. "First off—Maxine doesn't want anyone to die. She came here to give you that list because she's your *friend*, Teresa. She risked her own life to do so, and she's already paid for that with the death of her partner."

Teresa's look cooled a little. "I am sorry for Summer's death. But I'm not responsible for that."

"Oh, I know," said Maxine. "Lockley Hades was. He killed her and took her place just before we performed the trick. Then he shifted into a gorilla and planned to stab me in the middle of the performance."

"But he wound up dead instead," said Teresa. "You had no qualms about killing one of your own."

"Lockley Hades and I are nothing alike," snapped Maxine. "He was a talented illusionist, but his mimicry needed work. I saw through him—and did what I had to do."

"Which was transform into a bull ray inside the vault and stab him through the heart when he entered. Must have been tricky, using an aquatic form like that out of the water."

"I can hold my breath for four minutes," said Maxine. "Regardless of what form I take. Escape artists train, you know."

"So you killed him, planted the knife he was carrying to disguise your own attack, and then transformed into a form you knew well—Summer's. You thought you could hang around long enough to get the list to Teresa, but when Summer's body was discovered inside the trailer, you had to switch forms again. You'd been feeding Oswald earlier and decided to use him—you could keep an eye on the house from the pen and use your mental abilities to keep Oswald quiet and hide him inside his own shed. But that didn't work so well—you weren't prepared, and found Oswald's brain confusing your own. So you've been hiding out, only half aware, while we all looked for you and wondered where you'd gone."

"Enough of this," said Teresa. "The list."

Maxine got to her feet and met Teresa's gaze. "I've known you a long time," she said. "Our friendship isn't an illusion. I went through all of this because there was no way I was going to kill you—you do know that you're *my* target, right?"

Teresa said nothing, but her gaze was stony.

"I know how much your word means to you," continued Maxine. "Give me your word that my people won't be killed, and I'll tell you who they are."

"And what if I do? What are we supposed to do with this knowledge?"

"Start a conversation. Both sides lower their arms and just—just *talk*."

"And I'm expected to believe you will just give up your plans?"

"We already have. The plan depended on a coordinated, surprise attack—that was gone the moment you found out about it. This is closer to a surrender."

A little of the hardness left Teresa's expression. "I will take your proposition to the council. I can't promise anything—but I will argue on your behalf."

"You won't have to—you can take me with you. I'll personally deliver the list to the council."

Teresa gave her a slow nod. "Very well. You will accompany me to Thunderspace, where our power is supreme. Even if you had treachery planned, it would not succeed."

She held out her hand. Hesitantly, Maxine stepped forward and took it. Wind began to swirl around them in a vortex, faster and faster, capturing the rain in its slipstream to form a silvery, shimmering whirlwind. Behind this shining curtain, their forms grew fainter, until they disappeared completely.

Then the rain itself sputtered to a stop. I looked around and noticed that we seemed to have gathered a large group of animal spirits, all of whom were now dispersing now that that the action was over.

I looked down at Whiskey, who was already trying to shake himself dry, and an extremely wet, glaring cat, who seemed ready to swear off water completely.

"What's the verdict, guys? Did we just avert a war? Or is one about to start anyway?"

[We did our best,] Whiskey said solemnly. [I believe both of them are honorable beings. I suppose now we have to wait.]

I peered hopefully up at the sky. Was that the sun trying to peek out?

I could only hope.

"You wanted to see me?" I asked.

Shondra looked up from the paperwork she'd been studying and nodded. "Come on in, have a seat."

I did so. Shondra wore her usual attire, a black pantsuit with a white blouse, and sat behind two large monitors to either side of her desk. I knew those monitors were subdivided into smaller inset screens that showed her the views from the security cams on the estate's perimeter, and even when she was talking to someone in her office—like me—her attention was never far from them.

"Foxtrot," she said. "We should talk." Her tone was perfectly neutral, which meant nothing other than the fact that she was in superb control of whatever face she decided to show the world. Similar, in some ways, to certain supernatural beings who could exert the same control over their entire appearance; the difference between the two being that with Shondra, I always knew where I stood.

Shondra's office was the same size as mine, but it seemed larger because of her minimalist aesthetic; no sofa, no plants, no clutter on her desk. The chair I sat in was one of only three, and all of them were plain, black, and functional.

"I'm guessing this is about Maxine Danger?" I said. "I still have no idea how she slipped away." After a thorough search of the grounds over several days, even Shondra was forced to admit Maxine couldn't possibly still be present.

"No matter how good your border security is, a determined person can always find a way around it," Shondra said. "No, finding her now is a job for the police. But they're not going to, are they?"

I gave her a puzzled smile. "You think she's disappeared for good? Never to be seen again?"

"Maybe. What I know is that she vanishes things for a living, and I respect her professionalism. What do *you* think?"

The *you* was just pointed enough to be sharp, which meant I had to pick my next words carefully. "I think that any actions she took were in self-defense—and will continue to be so."

"Uh-huh." She raised an eyebrow at me. "You know, I put up with a lot of weird stuff around here, and now and then, I just have to shake my head and look the other way. So far, I've been able to do that. The bad guys always wind up where they belong in the end, no matter how long and twisty the road is that gets them there. But two murders is a lot to swallow, Foxtrot."

"Lockley Hades killed Summer," I said. "I can't prove that, but I know it to be true. Even if it contradicts the known facts."

She studied me then nodded. "I'm going to trust you on this. But even if you can't explain how the murders occurred, can you at least shed some light on how Ms. Danger got out of that damn vault?"

"Oh, that's the easy part," I said. I explained about the hidden scanners and the 3D, remotely printed ice key. "It's when we get to the magnetic parts of the key where it gets tricky. But how she did it was simple: she had a small magnet implanted in the tip of her finger. When she passed her finger over the key, she could feel the tug or the push from the key's magnets internally."

Shondra looked skeptical. "And how did you figure that out?"

Because she also has a brainstone embedded in her skull, and that made me think maybe she could have a different sort of implant somewhere else, was the reply that went through my head but not out my mouth. "Just doing research on the Internet. You know, poking around different sites and such."

"And how did she communicate this knowledge? She was locked up in the vault almost immediately afterward, wasn't she?"

"Oh, magicians and assistants commonly use codes to communicate secret information right in front of the audience. In this case, it was only a four-part binary message. Not hard to do." And the only reason the killer knew the code was because he'd been hanging around Summer long enough to pick it up in her thoughts—but I didn't mention that, either.

"So the assistant let Danger out—and then a body magically appeared in her place?"

I shrugged. "That part, you'd have to ask Maxine. If you can find her."

"You don't think that's likely, though."

"You know what I think? I think Maxine Danger might just disappear from public view forever. Although she did mention something to me the other day about having a protégé other than Summer. I wouldn't be too surprised if somebody else showed up on the public stage, doing very similar illusions."

Shondra nodded slowly. "Okay . . ."

It was Ben who brought me the news while I was huddled in the study with everyone else watching the TV; weather systems around the world had started to behave normally again, and though it takes a while for a hurricane—or a blizzard—to wind down, the commentators seemed cautiously optimistic.

"Hey," Ben said, pulling me aside. "Got a minute?"

"I sure as heck hope so," I said. "In fact, I'm hoping for a whole bunch of them, running consecutively into the future and uninterrupted by global catastrophes."

"Well, then, you're in luck . . ."

We walked out into the hall as we talked. Ben told me that Maxine had coughed up the list and the council had accepted the Unktehila's surrender. There was still going to be some tension, as many of the Unktehila assassins had disappeared into the woodwork as soon as they were revealed—but not one had attempted to kill anyone. And many of them, like Maxine, had elected to try to bridge the differences between the two species by sticking around. It seems she was far from the only one who'd grown attached to her intended target.

"Thank God," I said. "I'm not sure which one, but thanks all the same."

"I'm still a little confused, though," Ben said. "You mean Maxine was disguised as Oswald the whole time?"

"Let's see if I can run this down for you," I said, leading him down the hall to the ballroom. "It all starts with Lockley Hades—who was here right from the beginning."

"He was?"

"Yes—in the form of Esko Karvenin. He must have

disposed of the real Karvenin before arriving here and spent enough time around him beforehand to pick up his knowledge of 3D printers."

We entered the ballroom, which still had the stage set up, though all the broken glass from the shattered column had been cleared away. "Karvenin's plan was simple: kill Summer, take her place, then kill Maxine in mid-trick. He had a knife for the job, with the added muscle of a mountain gorilla behind it."

I stepped up on the stage then began to look around it carefully. "Karvenin hid in the trailer, ambushed and killed Summer, and hid her body in the secret refrigerated compartment. Refrigerated, by the way, so it could print a key made of ice." I pointed out the hidden cameras to him and explained what they were used for.

"But a key made of ice alone wouldn't be enough," Ben said. "What about the magnets?"

"Those were embedded in the ice at the same time the key was being made," I said. "What was important, though, was that they had to be in the correct sequence, or the key wouldn't work. And the only person who had that sequence was Hironobu Masuda."

"Who swears up and down he never divulged it."

"And he didn't." I explained how Maxine had used her implanted finger magnet to suss out the combination and then relay the information to her assistant. "To get by the metal detector, she faked us out with a phony finger, played for comedy. The metal detector was actually reacting to the magnet in her fingertip."

"Okay, so what happened to the key after the murder?"

"Simple. Maxine removed the magnets, stuck them together—there were only four of them, and they were already pill size and shape—swallowed them, then broke the key and discarded the shards among the glass on the floor, where it melted and disappeared. That first part, by the way, is more dangerous than it sounds—magnets can get trapped inside the bowel, causing injury and even death."

"And how did you figure all this out?"

"Research," I said. "I started thinking about all the weird junk ostriches have been known to eat, and that led me to wondering about what Maxine had eaten while she was an ostrich, and reminded me of the well-known fact that escape artists sometimes hide keys or picks in their mouths. Plus, Unktehila can hold three forms in their memory at any given point, and I knew two of Maxine's: a bull ray and Summer. I'm guessing the bull ray was supposed to be her assassin form and Summer was her deception form—which made me wonder what the third form was. Something capable of holding magnets in their stomach with minimal risk seemed likely."

Whiskey nosed his way through the door, followed by Tango, who had finally dried out to the point where she was no longer mindcasting murderous thoughts to anyone in her vicinity.

"Hey, guys," I said. "I was just filling Ben in on how the trick was done."

<Yes, very clever. Ben, I need you to promise that it will never rain here again, ever.>

Ben grinned. "Kind of a tall order, kitty. But I can promise you blue skies for at least the next few days."

<Hmmmph. That'll have to do.>

Whiskey sat, a doggy smile on his face, and said, [The trick, while interesting, was hardly the most vital part of this investigation. It's a shame we couldn't find an eyewitness to Maxine's transformation into an ostrich. We could have located her much sooner.]

"Yeah, well, we have Owduttf to thank for that," I said. "He intimidated any of the animals that saw anything into silence—then screwed himself by giving me information that almost made sense. He did in fact see Maxine transform into an ostrich—he just added the detail of her flying away. Must have thought changing that one bit of information would give him more leverage for demanding chicken."

[But all it did was convince you his entire story was a fabrication. Hard to trust someone that greedy, in any case.]

"It did get him three chickens, though."

"Is *that* where all my chickens have been going?" Ben said. "I was starting to wonder."

"Sorry about that," I said. "I would have offered him cold, hard cash, but Owduttf is all carnivore."

<*Hey, don't put down us carnivores.*>

"Wouldn't dream of it, kitty," I said, bending down to give her some skritches. She butted her head up against my hand and commenced purring.

[Ahem,] said Whiskey. I sighed, put out my other hand, and gave him some, too.

Ben leaned in next to me, his face on level with my own. "Double ahem," he said, and I grinned and kissed him.

The world was still a pretty crazy, messed-up place—but right at the moment, I was okay with it.

Very okay.